Criminally Insane

The Gecko Murders

The Sequel to the Child Taker

Detective Alec Ramsay Series

The Child Taker

Criminally Insane

Slow Burn

Frozen Betrayal

Desolate Sands

Concrete Evidence

Soft Target Series

Soft Target

Soft Target II 'Tank'

Soft Target III 'Jerusalem'

The Rage Within

Blister

The Child Taker

Unleashed

Hunting Angels Diaries

A child for the Devil

Black Angel

Blood Bath

The Book of Abominations

CRIMINALLY INSANE

Copyright © 2010 CONRAD JONES

All rights reserved.

ISBN: 1494386658
ISBN-13: 9781494386658

Prologue: *The Past*

Jack Howarth was waiting for his client to arrive. They were often late; it was part of the business he was in. It was a dangerous business, an evil business, but also a very lucrative one. Jack supplied people to order. Whatever his clients wanted, he could provide; men, women and children. The more specific the order was, the higher the price. Some clients were very specific; others just wanted random people. Today's client wanted a teenage girl. He had been vague about the type of girl he wanted, so finding one whose loved ones would not report her as missing and taking her off the streets had been easy enough. Working girls went missing all the time and Jack had used that to his advantage. Tonight's deal was not a rental agreement paid for by the hour or charged according to how much damage he would cause her, this deal was for keeps. Jack would take the money from his client and hand over the girl, job done. He had drugged her and snatched her from the backstreets of Manchester where she plied her trade. Now Jack had the unfortunate girl trussed up in the back of his campervan, covered with a quilt. From the outside, she looked like she was sleeping peacefully. Once the handover was complete, it would be the client's job to dispose of the girl when he was finished with her. Jack climbed into the back of the camper and checked that there were no gaps in the curtains. Sometimes they moved when he was driving. It was the umpteenth time he had checked them but he could not be too careful. He was always one mistake away from life in jail. The girl moaned softly and moved beneath the quilt. He pulled the edge back and looked at her face.

"I hope you slept well, darling," Jack smiled. He touched her cheek with a gloved hand. She opened her eyes and blinked. Jack peeled the tape from her mouth and placed his index finger to his lips. "Don't scream or I will hurt you," he whispered.

"Where am I?" She asked. She was confused and the chloroform made her feel sick. The camper was warm and cosy and a battery lantern cast an amber glow inside. "How did I get here?"

"I took you," Jack smiled again. "What is your name?"

"Sarah," she croaked. Her throat was dry and her tongue felt swollen and rough. "Could I have a drink of water please?"

"I don't see why not, as long as you behave." Jack said sternly. His face became serious and he raised his finger to his lips again. "No noise, understand?"

"Okay," Sarah whispered. Her senses were returning slowly. "My arms are hurting me." Cramps were creeping from her shoulder sockets down her arms and into her hands. She tried to move them but he had tied them together tightly. Her memory of the last few hours was hazy but she recalled someone clamping strong hands over her mouth and then a nauseous smell had filled her nose. Then there was nothing. "Why have you tied me up?"

"Keep still," Jack said. "I'll move you onto your side." There was a kitchen unit behind the driver's seat and Jack took a bottle of water from the camping fridge. He twisted the top off and placed it to her lips.

Sarah lifted her head and gulped from the bottle. The water trickled from the side of her mouth and ran down her neck. "Why am I here?" She asked.

"Don't worry about it. I have a job for you." Jack grinned and his face looked evil in the half-light. "You like selling your body for money, don't you?"

"No," she croaked. A bolt of fear shot down her spine and she could feel tears welling up in her eyes. "I don't like it. None of the girls do but I need to pay the rent. I hate what I do."

"Whatever," Jack whispered. "You sell your body for sex."

"I'm only doing it until I get on my feet."

"Poor Sarah," Jack whispered. "Don't kid yourself, darling. You're a slut."

"I wasn't always like this." Sarah spoke softly, trying to keep her captor calm. All the advice she had ever read told her to try to keep a potential rapist calm. She had to try to make him see her as a seventeen-year-old girl, not a piece of meat. "I ran away from home and I was desperate."

"Blah, blah, blah," Jack chuckled. "I've heard it all before, princess, but it all adds up to the same thing. You're nothing but a little whore."

"If you are going to rape me, I won't tell anyone, I promise," Sarah said bluntly. She had been on the streets for nearly two years, and rape was an occupational hazard. Some of the older girls had warned her about the psychos she would encounter on the job. They had told her not to resist if a punter turned violent. It had happened a few times. She learned that resisting only made it worse. Her number one objective was to get away from this man in one piece. It was better to let him do what he wanted and leave unharmed. "I can make you feel good. If you untie me, we can have some fun. Do what you want but please don't hurt me."

"Oh Sarah," Jack smiled. "As much as I would love to indulge myself, I'm afraid you belong to another man, or you will once he pays me."

"What do you mean?" Sarah tried to stay calm. There was something intrinsically bad about this man, very bad indeed. Cold shivers ran down her spine and her stomach contracted with fear. Sarah knew fear well. It was a fellow traveller through her life. Fear had always been her companion. She remembered the nights when her mother went to bingo and left her in the care of her stepfather. She dreaded hearing the front door closing and the sound of his footsteps coming up the stairs. When her bedroom door handle turned, a knot would appear in her stomach to the point where she could hardly breathe. She remembered the feeling of fear well, very well indeed. She felt fear when he came to her and she felt fear when he left her lying in his sticky fluids. The fear of her mother finding his stains in her bed was almost as bad as what he did to her. Sarah knew fear and she knew guilt and self-loathing. They were constants in her world. It was the fear of him hurting her night after night that had driven her from her home onto the streets. She was frightened now, terribly frightened. "What are you going to do?"

"Sell you, darling. I'm your new manager, sort of," Jack smiled again. He stuck the tape back over her mouth and smothered her nose with the chloroform soaked cloth. "You sell yourself for a few pounds here and there but you don't realise how valuable you are, darling. Sleep tight, pretty Sarah," he whispered in her ear as he held her down until the feeble struggle waned. Sarah drifted off into a dream in which she was at home after a normal night, a long shower and a bowl of tomato soup on her mind. They made her feel more human. Galaxy chocolate worked too. She loved the cookie crumble bar best. It did not take the sick feeling away but it was her little piece of sanity in an insane world.

Jack watched her eyes close and when the struggling stopped, he climbed back into the driver's seat. He opened the door and stepped out into the night. It was cold as he waited, and a light drizzle began to fall. The temperature was falling day by day now as autumn turned to winter and the dark nights closed in. Jack liked the winter months because the darkness hid a multitude of his sins, not that he saw them as sins, business was business. Headlights swept the night sky and illuminated the trees on the edge of the car park. The branches were losing their leaves and there was a thick covering of dead foliage on the ground. Jack watched from the cover of the trees, waiting until he was sure that it was his client in the car. It might be a courting couple looking for some privacy for their lovemaking or it might be a random police patrol car looking for drug dealers, who frequented this isolated spot. There was a long approach road from the main arterial route to this park. It gave him plenty of time to make sure the vehicle was the one he was waiting for. He could not be too careful.

Jack had arranged the deal on the internet. His client had said that he would be driving a dark blue Nissan pickup with a lid fitted on the back. Vans and campers were better for this kind of work but a closed pickup truck would suffice. The girl could be bundled into it within seconds, and then she would no longer be Jack's problem. The Nissan pulled in and the driver dipped the lights three times as agreed, so far, so good. Jack had to be careful. He was a hunted man. Police forces all over the continent, Europe and Africa wanted him removed from society and his trade extinguished. As the vehicle stopped, Jack walked to the passenger door and opened it. He climbed onto the running board to jump into the front seat.

"Nice night," he sneered. His teeth were blackened and crooked. He had thought about having them fixed so that children would not be as wary of him but he had not gotten around to it yet. Anyway, he quite liked the look of disgust on their faces when he smiled. Dentists wanted too many personal details before they would accept a new patient these days, and changing his identity so often meant that he had to change his documentation constantly. Jack could not stay in one place too long. If they caught him, they would lock him up for the remainder of his life. He had had a few close shaves with the law, and he did not need any more. The last time the police had caught him, they had cuffed him to a hospital bed whilst his injuries were treated. Jack had had to slice off his own thumb with a scalpel to slip the handcuffs. Since then, he had been extra careful, never staying in one place for too long, constantly changing his identity. The client looked nervous, holding the steering wheel tightly. Jack blew into his hands to warm them as he spoke. When it was cold, the scar tissue where his thumb had once been, ached with pain. "She's sleeping like a baby, nice and compliant, if you know what I mean."

"How old is she?" The client asked without looking at him or letting go of the wheel. He stared around the empty car park searching the shadows for danger. Jack could tell this was his client's first time and he loved his discomfort.

"She told me she was at least sixteen, Your Honour," Jack joked. "She's as old as you want her to be. What does it matter?"

"You must have an idea," the client said curiously. He could feel his nerve endings tingling at the thought of what he was about to do. On the way to the meeting, he had stopped the truck twice. Part of him was excited. Part of him was terrified. "I wouldn't feel right if she was too young."

"You've bought a girl to keep. How right can that be?" Jack laughed at the client's confused morals. "What do you want, adoption papers?"

"Of course not, but I don't want anyone to think I'm a paedophile."

"I don't give a fuck what you are. You asked for a teenager," Jack shrugged. "That's what I have. Do you want her or do you want to discuss the deeper moral issues of kidnap and rape and its effect on modern society for a while?"

"There's no need to be arsey, I'm nervous, that's all." The client's face darkened. He was angry and embarrassed by Jack's bluntness. He coughed and asked, "Can I see her?"

"Afraid not," Jack whispered. "You asked for a teenage girl who would not be missed, and that is what I have. Once the payment is complete, you can look at her all you want. She's all yours."

"Where is she from?" He didn't know why he wanted to know, but he did.

"What?" Jack frowned.

"I just wondered where she was from." The client felt silly for asking the question. The seller was making him nervous. There was something creepy about him.

"She has her wallet, mobile phone and driving license in her handbag." Jack smiled.

"Has she?" The client's eyebrows rose in surprise.

"Of course," Jack smiled again, "and she has her pyjamas in her overnight bag."

"Are you taking the piss?" The client realised that what Jack was saying was ludicrous. "There's no need to take the piss. I'm not stupid."

"Then don't ask stupid questions," Jack stopped smiling and glared at him. His eyes were dark and piercing and the client broke his stare and looked away. "Let's cut to the chase, shall we?"

"What do you mean?"

"Let me see the money."

The client twisted in his seat and reached for a holdall. As he came closer, Jack could smell alcohol on his breath, whisky and beer. He placed the holdall between them and unzipped it. There were bundles of twenty-pound notes in the bag. The price for the girl was five grand but there was much more than that in the bag; much, much more. The client looked at Jack for a reaction, and Jack saw that there was a glaze on his eyes. His client was drunk and stoned. The man was a fool. He was driving under the influence to pick up a random kidnapped girl with a bag full of money. If the police pulled him over, he would have some explaining to do. Jack was annoyed and he wanted to get away from the client. Drunken people make mistakes and Jack had to be careful.

"You're pissed," Jack hissed. It was no wonder the client was asking stupid questions. "I warned you, no drink or drugs before the handover."

"Look, if she's good, there's plenty more where this came from," the client nodded and smiled. He had had to drink to calm his nerves. "I've had a big payoff from the army. I've got money and I want a regular supply."

"From the army?" Jack asked. The sight of the bundles of notes made him stop in his tracks for a moment. His mind was ticking.

"Yes, they booted me out but I got a good payout," the client said, trying to make a joke of it.

"Very good," Jack leaned toward him and sneered again. He didn't think he was going to do the deal as arranged anymore. He thought about the drugged prostitute in his camper and he looked at the bagful of banknotes again. That amount of money would last a long time, and he could keep the girl for himself for a few days until she bored him. He felt his pulse racing as he thought about hurting her. This was a great opportunity, and he was never one to miss an opportunity. His hand slipped into his pocket and closed around the handle of a carpet knife. "I think we can conclude our business without any further chitchat, don't you?"

"Yes, that's fine," his client stammered. He tried a smile but it didn't hide his nervousness.

"Shit!" Jack hissed, nodding his head towards the entrance road and pointing his spindly finger. "Police car," he lied.

The client turned to look where he was pointing and Jack moved quickly, pushing his client's head back against the seat. The blade flashed in the darkness and a crescent-shaped rent appeared in his client's throat. The man twitched and thrashed his arms around, trying to stem the jet of blood, but Jack held his head tightly until the gurgling sound subsided and the thick coppery smell of blood filled the air.

Chapter One

DS Alec Ramsay

Detective Superintendent Alec Ramsay was about to put his coat on and go home when there was a knock on the door. The handsome face of DI Will Naylor appeared along with a waft of Armani aftershave. Will was dressed in a sharp black suit with a crisp white shirt underneath. His silk tie had cost more than Alec's entire suit. Alec rarely had his top button fastened at the office but he buttoned his collar and neatened his tie whenever he was dealing with his junior detectives. They were like chalk and cheese as far as their dress sense went, but when it came down to solving crimes, they thought along the same lines and made a good team. Will was a rough diamond but Alec was shaping him into a fine detective. He covered for him when he made mistakes and allowed him the space he needed to mature into the role of lead detective. It had been a battle to have him promoted to DI, as Will wasn't always the most politically correct officer on the force. Despite his indiscretions, Alec could see the long-term potential in him, and he had stuck his neck out to help him progress.

"You're still here then, Guv?" Will said smiling. His teeth were straight and white. Some people took his smart appearance as a sign of weakness, but they were wrong. Will was scared of no one, and his detective skills were as sharp as his dress sense. Several of the city's crime lords had threatened his life over the years but he had never wavered or asked for a transfer. His attitude was, "what will be will be."

"No, this is a hologram. I left ten minutes ago, you plonker, what's up?"

"We've just had a call from Uniform. They've found a woman's body in a factory unit near the river."

"When was this?" Alec asked. His forehead creased with deep furrows. His skin had never been perfect but age had made it pitted and wrinkled as if he had spent decades under the desert sun. He hadn't spent much time in the sun at all; it was genetic. Alec looked ten years older than his true age.

"They found her four hours ago and uniform informed vice immediately." Will could see that his boss wasn't impressed with his pitch so far. "I've got a feeling they're going to bat it over to us."

"It has been a long week for MIT, and I'm due a few days leave." Alec Ramsay always had deep lines etched into his forehead and around his eyes but they looked deeper today. His piercing blue eyes were made dull by a lack of sleep over the previous days and his greying blond hair was tussled. "Are you sure this one is coming our way?"

"I think so, I know you're off home, Guv, but this is a nasty one by all accounts. I think it will drop in our lap so I thought you'd want to know." Will could see that Alec was tired and stressed. "Do you want me to take a look at the scene and call you when I'm done?"

"I don't know if it's sensible to let you go alone," Alec joked. He sighed and looked at his watch. "Gail was expecting me home two hours ago, her mother has come to stay for a few days, those usually turn into a week which stresses Gail to a breaking point, and I get it in the neck."

"I'm surprised the old bird is still clucking, Guv."

"Oh yes, going strong," Alec shook his head. "She's a little abrasive at the best of times, the rest of the time she's an obnoxious old crow, but what can you do? What have we got so far?"

He decided to listen to what Will had to tell him before making a call home. It would be either the 'I'm going to be late' call or the 'I won't be home tonight, luv' call. Neither ever went down well.

"The body was found four hours ago in an unused unit off Jamaica Street."

"Jamaica Street," Alec whistled as he breathed out. "If I had a pound for every time I hear that road mentioned in a crime report, I would have retired by now."

"I know, Guv, but this one stands out." Will held his hand up to signal there was more. Jamaica Street was one of Liverpool's most notorious red light districts. Finding a dead female there was a common occurrence but apparently, the brutality of this death was out of the ordinary. "She was strung upside down and tortured to death, Guv."

CRIMINALLY INSANE

"Is she known to vice?" Alec stood and put his coat on. There was no doubt they would have to inspect the crime scene but Will was capable of doing that alone. "I'm wondering if it will fall to them."

There was a fine balancing act going on in his mind between his home life and his work commitments. Things at home were strained. His team had spent the last four weeks working on a double murder. Uniformed police had found two men, brothers from a notorious local crime family, in the toilets of a large supermarket. Their rivals had shot them through the back of the head, execution style. The murders had kicked off a spate of retaliatory attacks between the city's gangsters, putting pressure on his team to find the killer quickly in order to put an end to the violence. Explosive devices had been used, and the Counter Terrorist Unit had been all over it. Alec had cancelled all leave until they arrested the suspect and charged him with both murders. He had led his team from the front, which meant he hadn't been home much for a month.

"They can't identify her yet, Guv." Will shrugged. "She'd been there a while by all accounts but Dr. Libby is sure there is more to it than just a random murder."

"If she is known to vice, it might be best to let them see what the score is before we go jumping in with both feet," Alec sighed. If she were a known prostitute then the vice detectives would look at the case first. If they did know the victim and it turned out to be a sexual crime it would be down to them to look into it before it came to MIT. "I think we should take a look anyway." Alec sighed. "I can drive along the dock road, inspect the crime scene and then take the coast road home."

"It sounds complicated, Guv." Will frowned. "I can't get a straight answer from anyone at the scene, that's why I thought you would want to see it."

"They're all complicated, Will." Alec looked out of the window across the river. It was a grey day and it looked cold outside. "What is the doctor saying so far?"

"Vice are saying it's too early to tell who she is yet, but Graham Libby says it was a prolonged attack possibly carried out by more than one attacker."

"There must be a reason why he thinks that, what's he said?"

"All he said was there are multiple blood pools at the scene," Will shrugged. "He thinks that there was at least one other victim at the scene, possibly more, although there's only one body." Will's mobile beeped and he took it from his pocket. "Text message from Bruce at vice, there is definitely more than one victim according to forensics. I'll handle it if you like, Guv, I just thought you should know that Doctor Libby has gone down there."

Graham Libby was the head of Liverpool's crime laboratory. "If he goes to a crime scene in person, then it is a bad one, and the old Ramsay mental alarm bells have started ringing." Alec sighed. "Jesus Christ, more than one victim. This sounds like a messy one," Alec sighed again. He stood up and looked out of the window toward the Anglican cathedral dominating the hill above the Jamaica Street area of the riverbank. It was about half a mile away from the city centre. "I remember in my youth Lime Street station was the red light district in the city. Somewhere between then and now, prostitution has moved across the city to the cathedral area. Why, I'm not sure."

"We were probably put under pressure to move the girls out of the city centre so that we could pretend it doesn't exist." Will laughed. "Doesn't matter what we do, it will always be there, Guv."

"There have probably been more murders in that part of the city than in Whitechapel by now." Alec mused.

"I think Jack the Ripper might be a little old to be making a comeback. Didn't you work on that one, Guv?" Will teased.

"Hilarious, Inspector," Alec laughed.

Will teased his boss whenever he referred to criminals of the past, despite admiring his knowledge of them. "Even the Yorkshire Ripper is too old for me."

"Well, if 'Take That' can come back, who knows?" Alec turned to face his D.I. "So, if there is only one body, what makes them think we have more than one victim?"

"He said there are several blood pools in the unit," Will shrugged. "You know what the doc is like, Guv. He doesn't give anything away until he's ready to."

"Yes, he is what you'd call eccentric," Alec laughed. It was the most polite word he could think of to describe the doctor. "A pain in the arse is more realistic," he mumbled, but he had to admit Dr Libby was sharp and his forensic team was thorough.

"I could think of a few better words to describe him than that, Guv." Will raised an eyebrow and smiled. He had issues with the doctor, but they were personal ones.

"I think you should keep your private opinions to yourself, Inspector," he smiled as he reached for the phone. "I'll be five minutes, I need to call home." He rolled his eyes skyward in anticipation of the ear-bashing he was about to receive from his wife. He was glad that he didn't have to go straight home, if he was honest. The mother-in-law grated on his nerves.

"Good luck with that, Guv." Will was smiling as he closed the door behind him. There was a spring in his step as he headed toward the briefing room. A new homicide always made his adrenalin flow.

Chapter Two

Connections Nightclub

Jinx lit a menthol cigarette and inhaled deeply on it. The smoking ban did not extend to this gathering. The minty smoke burned its way into his lungs and the nicotine cocktail of toxins was absorbed into his bloodstream, soothing his nerves. He inhaled again as the fourth card was placed next to the flop, and it took all his skill and experience to contain his excitement. It was the seven of spades. There was a seven dealt on the flop, and he was holding a pair of pocket sevens in his hand, giving him four of a kind. It would take a miracle to beat him now, and there was over thirty grand on the table already. He didn't want to give any signs to the other players that he had an unbeatable hand.

"Check," Jinx said. He was bluffing. That was where the skill in the game lay, hooking them and then reeling them in for the kill.

"Bollocks, I'm folding." One of the men tossed his cards into the middle.

"Me too, I'm out." The other players folded their cards, leaving Jinx and Leon Tanner in the hand. They looked at each other through the cigarette smoke.

"Raise a grand," Leon growled. He flicked a black chip into the pot. "It's on you to bet, Jinx," Leon said tapping his hand nervously on the green felt of the poker table. He was fat and his upper body wobbled as he moved his arm. Beads of sweat glistened on his black skin. Heavy gold rings covered his fingers and a thick bracelet hung from his wrist. He eyed Jinx with caution, trying to read his mind without looking too uncertain about his own cards. He had an okay hand, but nothing great. He hated folding to Jinx. He hated Jinx, full stop. The feeling was mutual. They were on a collision course and everyone knew it.

"I know whose bet it is, Leon, I'm thinking," Jinx bluffed. He wanted him to think that he was unsure about his cards. Leon had a good hand, Jinx could tell by the sweat on his forehead but there was no way he could beat four of a kind. It didn't matter what Leon had,

Jinx was unbeatable for this hand. He played with a stack of poker chips and they clicked annoyingly. The longer he delayed the call, the more confused Leon would be about how strong his hand was. The atmosphere in the club was tense and charged with testosterone. Cigarette smoke curled upwards and swirling tendrils clung to the yellowed ceiling tiles. There was an acrid smell to the room at the back of the nightclub that hosted the monthly card school. It was an invitation only game where each of the eight players needed a stake of twenty thousand pounds in cash. There were no markers or cheques allowed, strictly sterling only. There was no trust between the poker players because they were all gangsters of one type or another. Armed robbers, fraudsters, drug dealers and people traffickers sat at the table. They did not like each other but they were certainly of use to one another. The underworld is like any other business community, it is not what you know, it is whom you know that counts. The poker players at this table were responsible for ninety-nine percent of all the crime in the city.

"I'll call your grand. No raise," Jinx bluffed again. He wanted Leon to think he had nothing in his hand, and then he was going to trap him. Jinx Cotton was the youngest man there but he had earned his place amongst them because he was a ruthless moneylender and debt collector. Over recent years, he had recovered thousands of pounds for the men playing poker and carved himself a fearsome reputation in the process. Jinx only lent money to people that had money and could pay it back. He never lent to the poor people in the community he lived in. Most of his business came from drug dealers who were looking for a large amount of cash for a short period, while they conducted a deal. Jinx would extend a loan to them at an extortionate interest rate, and if the deal went wrong or there was a delay in repayment, the dark side of him would take control. Jinx was a God-like character on the streets of Toxteth, one of Liverpool's most infamous areas. The youth of the community idolised him while the adults involved in crime feared and respected him. Jinx was a modern day Robin Hood, making fortunes from his rich clients but often handing out cash to the less fortunate members of the black community. Although he did business with them, he hated drugs and drug dealers, pimps and prostitution. Leon Tanner was both a pimp and a dealer leeching off the very community Jinx tried to protect.

"Re-raise. All in," Leon wiped sweat from his brow and grinned as he pushed all his remaining chips onto the table. Gold teeth glinted in the light that hung above the table. He thought he had Jinx beaten with the pair of aces he had in his hand. With the sevens that were on the table he had a high two pairs but there was the chance Jinx had another seven in his hand. That was why Leon was sweating. When Jinx hadn't raised, it had signalled to Leon that he wasn't confident enough to bet on his cards to win, but that was the bluff.

"Call," Jinx pounced and closed the trap. "How much have you got left?"

"Fuck you, Jinx, you're bluffing," Leon growled angrily. His jowls wobbled as he shook his head in dismay. He was already regretting making such an impulsive bet. Once a player's twenty thousand pound stake was gone, they were out. There were no re-buys back into the game and no second chances.

"We'll see if I'm bluffing, how much have you got?"

"Sixteen thousand," Leon felt sick to the core. It was obvious that Jinx had another seven in his hand, or was it? He could be bluffing but it was too late anyway, as the bet was all in and he couldn't change it. Jinx had called him.

"I've got that covered," Jinx counted the equivalent number of chips out and turned his cards over. "I have four sevens; you're drawing dead, Leon."

There was still a card to be played but it didn't matter now; Leon couldn't win. Jinx stood up and stared Leon in the eyes as he cleared his chips away from him. Leon was a bad man. He was the biggest pimp in the city and he moved more crystal meth in a week than most importers handled in a year. He was over twenty stone in weight, most of it nestled around his waist, but he was no fighter. His enforcers did his fighting for him but there were no minders allowed in the room once the poker game started. That was one of the rules of the game. Jinx however was a fighter. He was over six feet four inches and weighed about the same as Leon, but hard-earned muscle mass packed his frame. He looked like a heavyweight champion in his prime. If Leon wanted to make something of it, there was only one winner.

"Four of a kind, Jinx?" Leon sat back and relaxed. His many chins folded into his neck. "Your turn to be lucky this time, next time it'll be a different story, boy." Leon pronounced the last word of his sentence to reinforce its derogatory meaning.

There was silence at the table while Jinx counted his chips. He hated Leon because he turned beautiful teenage girls into pox ridden meth addicts and then forced them into prostitution to meet their drug bills. Jinx had his eye on Leon's empire, and he intended to knock the fat man out of business sometime in the near future. Others would try to move in and abuse the young and the weak, but he could deal with them when they came. He wanted Leon and his henchmen out of Toxteth, the sooner the better.

"What did you say?" Jinx stopped counting and looked up at Leon. There was darkness in his eyes that terrified the debtors he dealt with. Leon knew he didn't stand a chance in a fistfight with Jinx, but the young pup was snapping at his heels, and he intended to slap him down permanently very soon. Jinx was on his hit list. The silence in the room was tangible as the two men glared at each other. Calling Jinx a boy was not a bright idea. "I asked you what you said, Leon." Jinx repeated slowly. He pushed Leon, trying to provoke a response.

"I said, next time it will be a different story." Leon stood up as he spoke. He couldn't lose face to this youngster but he had dropped the word 'boy' this time. Their business was all about respect and reputation. "You were lucky, that's all."

"Sit down, Leon," Dava said. David Lorimar was a wiry-built man in his fifties. He was an ex-paratrooper, and mercenary. He had seen action in Kosovo, Bosnia and had fought for the highest bidder during several African conflicts. Dava made his living by selling reactivated weapons and making people disappear. Some of Jinx's clients thought that killing him would be an easier option than repaying their debt to him. When that happened, Jinx would employ David Lorimar to square things up. Dava was a professional. He was a quiet man, but nobody messed with him. "You were beaten fair and square, let's not have a scene." He said quietly but with an edge in his voice. Some of the players shifted uncomfortably in their seats. The situation could flare up at any moment.

"Like I said, he was lucky this time," Leon never took his eyes off Jinx for a second. There was no point in kicking off. He would definitely lose a fight with Jinx and lose all respect from his peers in the process.

"Next time you see a pair on the table, it means that your two pairs isn't worth shit, Leon," Jinx changed his glare into a big wide smile and laughed. He was a clever man, and he knew that by being magnanimous about it, the others would see Leon's reaction as churlish. He turned it into a joke. The men around the table realised that he was winding Leon up and burst into laughter. There was a sense of relief around the table but Leon looked confused. Jinx stuck out a spade-sized hand for Leon to shake but there was no friendship in his eyes. "Come on, Leon, sixteen grand on two pairs? Are you snorting your own drugs?"

Leon grinned and then began laughing with the others. His eyes darted around the table looking at their faces searching for any sign that they were ridiculing him. There was a fine line between them having a laugh, and them laughing at him. He decided that it would be wise to accept the handshake for now. He wanted to shoot Jinx in the face. Jinx would need a favour one day, and it would cost him twice what he had won tonight when the time came. The fact that Jinx was black cut no ice with Leon; his card was marked for the future. The laughter reached full volume. No one heard the beer cellar door creaking open as two masked men crept in carrying Uzis.

Chapter Three

Jamaica Street

DS Alec Ramsay pulled on the handbrake and switched off the engine. His silver BMW smelt of leather polishes and air freshener. It had been valet cleaned the week before at a carwash staffed by Eastern Europeans. They had done a good job, and he had been impressed until one of them had offered him cocaine. He had tipped off the Drug Squad, and they had watched the place for three days before swooping in on a raid. The police had arrested four of the staff and interviewed the owners for employing illegal immigrants. The owners had closed the business the day after. It was a shame because it had been the cheapest carwash in the area. He would have to find another one. Such was the price of drugs, but they were everywhere he looked nowadays. The city was swamped with the stuff fuelling a rising crime rate and leaving a swathe of destruction in its wake. Statistics showed that eight in ten homicides were attributed to drugs and the drug trade.

There were two police cars and a mortuary van parked side by side outside a single storey industrial unit. It was a grey prefabricated building with a corrugated iron roof, sloping at a gradient towards the river. The concrete render was decayed and crumbling, exposing the breezeblock beneath. Green patches of mould and damp snaked up the exterior of the unit and weeds had forced their way through the tarmac forecourt. The river was five hundred yards away down the hill. An assortment of similar factory buildings lined the road leading to the water. There was a faded sign hanging loose above the metal shuttering, but years of exposure to the elements had rendered it unreadable. The huge Anglican Cathedral standing further up the hill dominated the skyline, a gothic sandstone titan surrounded by residential properties. Alec looked at the clock. He had promised Gail that he would be home within the hour. She hadn't sounded happy but then she rarely did lately. It was his doing. His work was always his priority. Alec checked the time again and sighed as he opened the door and stepped out into the cold sea breeze. The wind was blowing off the Irish Sea and it cut through his clothing with ease. He shoved his hands deep into his pockets and jogged across the road to the unit.

A uniformed officer lifted the crime scene tape as he approached. He had a white safety mask over his nose and mouth to keep out the cloying smell of death drifting over from the building. There was no sign of the press yet, but it wouldn't be long before they turned up.

"The smell's that bad, eh, George?" Alec said as he ducked under the tape. He made a point of calling the uniformed police by their first names whenever possible.

"Worse, Sir." The constable sounded muffled. "She's been in there a while."

"Were you the first officer on the scene?" Alec wrinkled his nose.

"Yes, Sir," he pointed to his patrol car. "I was eating my breakfast around the corner when the call came in."

"Well, I hope you finished it," Alec smiled.

"I did, Sir, but it came straight back up when I saw her," the officer nodded toward the factory unit. "Don't worry; I threw it up out here."

Alec patted his arm as he walked by him and stooped beneath the roller shutters. The investigating officers had left it open at waist height to allow the crime scene officers easy access. The smell of rotting flesh became much stronger as he straightened up on the other side of the shutters. Engine oil stained the concrete floor and holes pitted the walls where screws and fixings had once lived. A few strong thistles poked through the cracks in the floor, a reminder that Mother Nature is constantly trying to reclaim what we have taken from her. Will Naylor waved from the back of the unit. He stood with the SOCO, the scene-of-crime officers, and Dr Graham Libby. Behind them hung the remains of the poor soul that had brought them to this isolated place. From this distance, it barely resembled a human being. She reminded Alec of the smoked hams he had loved when he had holidayed in Spain. Thinking about the holiday reminded him that he had to go home to his wife.

As Alec approached, the men turned from their work to greet him. They were dressed in white paper suits and blue plastic overshoes. Will gave him a mask to help cope with the putrid stench coming from the corpse. Alec placed it over his nose without speaking but the sickening smell clung inside his nostrils, and he knew it would stick to him for days, no matter how many times he showered. Alec often told friends that there was something about the smell of rotting human flesh that made it linger, usually at the dinner table, on the odd occasion when he and Gail entertained 'her' friends. She called them 'their' friends, but Alec hardly knew them at all.

"Alec," Graham said in greeting, while the superintendent inspector climbed into his suit. He was always short and to the point. "This is a bloody mess, excuse the pun."

"Doc," Alec took in the scene as he spoke. "What do we know?"

"The corpse is hung upside down from an anchor ring, fixed to a metal rafter," the doctor began. The rafters were open and supported the corrugated roof. They had been painted pale green once, but now rust blistered the metal and orange was the predominant colour. A heavy black chain dangled from the ring, a hook its end which threaded through the ropes binding her ankles together. Oil and carbon crusted the chain.

"It is an engine block tackle," Graham nodded to the ring and chain. "I think it was here already, back from when this place was a vehicle radiator specialist."

"What do we know about her?" Alec circled the hanging corpse. The ropes around her ankles cut deep into the swollen mushy flesh. The body was black and blue with contusions, the head swollen beyond recognition. Rats had eaten away some of her flesh and gnawed, yellowed bones were exposed in places. Congealed blood caked her long auburn hair. There was a pool of various bodily fluids beneath her where her body had begun to decompose.

"The body is that of a female aged between twenty and thirty five at a guess." The doctor pointed to her mouth. "I am guessing her age from the condition of her teeth. I think the cause of death was shock and haemorrhaging caused by these wounds here at the wrist."

There were deep cuts on the back and chest and shallower wounds around the nipples and thighs. The wounds were blackened with age and maggots wiggled in them, feeding on the flesh. The left hand was missing and the doctor pointed to the stump.

"The hand was removed with a saw of some description and, unfortunately for her, it was removed prior to death. The killer applied a tourniquet to stem the blood loss. I can't be sure, but I would say the tourniquet failed. I think the blood loss from this injury was probably the final straw."

CRIMINALLY INSANE

"Any sign of the hand?" Will asked. If it was available and decomposition wasn't too advanced, there was a chance that they could print it while the SOCO worked. Will was making an effort to keep things between himself and the doctor professional, but there was a look of distain on the scientist's face whenever he asked him a question.

"No, it's not here," the doctor shook his head, dismissing the question without looking at Will. "If it is, we haven't found it yet."

"Could we be looking for a trophy hunter?" Will thought aloud. The scene had all the markings of a serial murder from television forensic shows. He had read several textbooks on profiling and he relished the opportunity to use the knowledge he had gleaned from them.

"I'm not sure we should be thinking trophy hunter just yet, Inspector," the doctor said. He looked at Will and shook his head as if his theory was ridiculous. "The chances are the rats have had it."

Dr. Libby wasn't a fan of Will Naylor, nor was he a lover of profiling. He preferred to follow the evidence as it appeared to him, rather than painting a picture of a suspect and trying to make the pieces fit that profile. Investigating officers had made too many mistakes in the past by bringing profilers into their case.

"Is there any evidence of sexual assault?" Alec circled the corpse again.

"I think so, but again, until I get her on the table, I can't be sure. None of the knife injuries were inflicted to her female organs, so for now I'm thinking that this was either punishment, or maybe just for fun."

"Nice," Will said. This wasn't the first woman to be tortured to death by a deranged killer. He had seen a few in his years on the force. "How long has she been here, Doc?"

"It's difficult to say because it's cold in here, which could have slowed down the decaying process. The fact that the killer left the body to hang means the air has circulated around the flesh, causing it to dry out. Her body has gone through several stages of putrefaction. Hypostasis or lividity begins about four hours after death; in this instance, it is all in the head and torso because the red corpuscles have sunk to the lowest part of her body. The body is stained and starting to distend so it's at least a week, but definitely no more than two weeks, even with the temperature taken into account."

"How can you be sure?" Will frowned. He asked as many questions as he could, which annoyed some people, but the doctor loved to show off his forensic skills. They didn't get on, but the doctor was good at his job.

"There are maggots in these wounds here. They are third stage bluebottle larvae and they become flies within twelve days." Dr. Libby grinned. "These little beauties are still wriggling."

Alec nodded in agreement. He was piecing the evidence together in his mind. The scene consisted of far more than just a mutilated corpse left hanging in a disused building. Something terrible had happened in this unit, and it had happened to more than one victim. The evidence was all around them.

"What are you thinking, Guv?" Will asked.

"There is a significant amount of blood underneath her, but there are other pools over there and they look older," Alec looked to Graham for his thoughts.

"I agree, Alec." The doctor nodded his head, his watery eyes looking towards the victim. "There's no way this woman had enough blood to create several pools of this size. Until I get the results I'm assuming there were other victims at some time in the past."

"What makes you think there was more than one attacker?" Alec asked.

"Look here." The doctor walked behind the hanging body. "There are two sets of footprints in the blood and when we measured them, they turned out to be different sizes."

"What happened here?" Alec frowned and the creases in his face deepened. He looked more like the celebrity chef he shared his name with every day.

"What about the chairs?" Will asked.

There were two wooden chairs placed near to the freshest blood pool. Blood stained the arms and the seat pads were wet and smelt like a latrine.

"I've taken swabs from the seats and we'll test them, but my nose tells me they are stained with urine and faeces." The doctor looked over his glasses.

"Someone was either tied up there for a long time, or they were so scared they wet themselves?" Alec grimaced. "There are footprints here probably belonging to a victim, because they were not wearing shoes."

"There are none next to the other chair," Alec pointed out.

"No, and that is the most concerning thing about the whole scene," the doctor's face darkened.

"Why?" Will asked. "What are you thinking?"

"I think we have a conundrum. I'll know when the DNA comes back. It could be hers, but something tells me it isn't." The doctor smiled, but it was a sad smile.

"Come on, Doc, spill the beans," Alec prompted him to carry on. The doctor only smiled when he was being clever.

"Look here." He pointed to a dark patch at the front of the seat pad. There was another dark patch on the floor underneath. "This smells of urine. From the position on the seat pad and the staining on the floor, I think a man secreted it. The female urethra is much further back in relation to this stain."

Alec raised his eyebrows as he thought about it. The doctor was right. The staining was at the front. The stains indicated that the chair had had a man tied to it. "Okay, I'll buy that." Alec moved closer to the second chair. "What about this one, what is bothering you, Doc?"

"There are no footprints in the blood here but the seat pad is still stained with secretions."

"So what?" Will asked.

The doctor raised his eyebrows and frowned again. "Someone was tied to this chair but their feet did not reach the floor."

Alec felt a cold shiver touch his spine and his stomach tightened. "Even a small adult would touch the floor with their feet."

"Exactly," the doctor nodded slowly.

"A child?" Will felt stupid for not seeing it earlier.

"Well done, Inspector." Dr. Libby said. "You got there in the end. Look here."

They walked away from the hanging corpse and the doctor knelt down near a cone-shaped marker. "There are tyre tracks everywhere, as you would expect, but these are fresher."

"The killer brought a vehicle in here?" Alec followed the marks towards the shutters with his eyes.

"We think so," the doctor nodded. "Now look here."

Alec and Will looked at each other in shock. They were processing the evidence, trying to make sense of what they were seeing. "That means they were taken away from here alive?" Alec said.

"Maybe," the doctor was hesitant. There were footprints near to the tyre tracks. Small footprints, smeared in blood. "They were probably carried from the chair and then put down on the floor here while the attacker opened the vehicle door."

"How long will it take for the preliminary results?" Alec asked. He had seen enough for now. They had a missing child and a dead woman to identify, and a vicious killer to catch.

"The bloods will be back tomorrow and the DNA within a few days if we work flat out."

"Will, have we got a list of missing persons yet?" Alec turned to walk away. The stench of decay followed him. "Why haven't we heard about a missing child?"

"Smithy is collating all missing person reports we can access," Will followed Alec. "It should be on your desk already, Guv."

"Okay, cancel all leave and call the team together. I want a full briefing when the blood reports come in." Alec knew he would have to go straight back to the office. His mother-in-law and his wife would have to lunch without him. It would cause tensions at home, but he had a job to do. He walked out of the unit and thought about calling home, but he decided that he could do it later. He took a deep breath of fresh air through the mask. Alec took off his mask when he stepped outside and breathed the sea air deeply into his lungs. It couldn't erase the fetid stench of putrid flesh. The sea breeze cut through his clothing and chilled him to the bone.

Chapter Four

Connections Nightclub

When the masked men appeared, the laughter around the poker table stopped. One of them covered the poker players with his weapon while his accomplice threaded a thick steel chain through the door handles leading into the club. He fumbled with the links as he padlocked them closed. He slammed the bolts home at the top and bottom of the door to ensure no one could disturb them. There were at least a dozen minders on the other side of the doors, waiting for their bosses while they played their game. They would be drinking free cocktails and eyeing up the young women that filled the dance floor. The last thing on their mind was their employer's welfare. There were no weapons allowed in the poker room; tempers could fray during the game, especially as the alcohol went down.

"Do you have any idea who we are?" Leon growled. He twisted his mouth into a scowl. The men at the table looked at each other for a silent signal from someone. A sign to make a move and rush the gunmen, but they were covered with automatic weapons. One wrong move and eight of the city's most prolific criminals would be twitching in their own blood on the carpet. For now, the best option was to wait to see what the masked men wanted.

"We know who you are, Leon." The taller of the gunmen spoke first. He walked behind Leon, ramming the muzzle of the machinegun into the folds of fat on the back of his neck. "You're a fat pimp with a penchant for teenage boys, but I bet your friends here don't know about that, do they, eh, Leon?"

All eyes turned to look at Leon. Despite the circumstances, this was a very surprising snippet of information. There were several eyebrows raised and the odd smirk around the table. Leon snarled and shrugged his shoulders as if he didn't know what the gunman was talking about. Sweat trickled down his chubby cheeks. He did have a thing for teenage boys, but he had thought it was a closely guarded secret. Someone from his outfit was blabbing.

"So you know who we are. Why don't you tell us why you're pointing Uzis at us, and then we can go back to our poker game?" Leon tried to recover some self-esteem.

"I think you lost all your chips, didn't you? Two pairs is a crap hand, Leon." The men at the table laughed nervously. "What do we want? That is easy. We want the stake money in the floor safe under the poker table. Oh, and we'll have the five kilos of cocaine stashed under the ice machine." He waved the Uzi and herded the poker players out of their seats. "Move over there."

"You must be crazy men," Jinx raised his hands as he spoke and a crooked grin crossed his face. He towered above the masked men but there was nothing to gain by becoming a dead hero for now. Jinx eyed the gangsters in the room, looking for any sign of recognition in their eyes.

"This is an inside job." Gus Rickman hissed. The gunmen knew where they held the stake money while the game was in progress. "Only people that have played with us before could know that."

"Shut up," the gunmen snapped.

"As for the five kilos of cocaine under the ice-machine, only Jessie and his men could possibly know that there are a shitload of drugs on the premises, eh, Jessie?"

"Who else could know?" Jinx certainly didn't know it was there until now.

"Shut your mouth, Jinx," the tall gunman waved his weapon. The skin under the mask was white around the eyes and there was a tinge of an accent in his voice, but Jinx couldn't place it. He wasn't black or foreign.

"If you know who I am, then you know I will find you," Jinx smiled again and walked away from the group at the table. "That's what I do, find people who take money."

Dozens of his customers had gone into hiding when it was time for them to repay their loans, but Jinx would always find them. He used cutting-edge technology to track people. He put tracers onto customer's vehicles or mobile phones before he handed over any cash loans. If they went into hiding, they had no idea that they had been bugged until Jinx knocked on their door.

"All of you kneel down facing the wall. Put your hands behind your head and shut up." The gunman ordered.

The gangsters moved slowly to the wall and followed the gunman's instructions. Jinx knelt down reluctantly. The nightclub manager knelt down next to Jinx. He was a big Welshman called Joseph James, or Jessie by his associates. He had a reputation for carrying a Smith and Wesson six-shooter like a cowboy, hence the nickname. Jessie moved in criminal circles and most of the faces in town used the nightclub as a drinking den. The club's clientele consisted of the more dishonest members from all sections of the population. Jessie was well known and well liked, but everyone knew he was a puppet for a Turkish mob that had moved into the city five years prior. Five kilos of cocaine was way out of Jessie's league. He was hiding it for the Turks. Jinx looked at his face trying to get a reaction. Jessie shrugged at Jinx, shaking nervously.

"Don't look at me like that, Jinx," Jessie whispered. "I've got fuck all to do with this." He was at a loss. Jessie knew the fingers of suspicion would point at him and the Turks would be looking for blood if the gunmen took their drugs. They would spill his blood first as a lesson to everyone. The Turks were brutal bosses and they didn't tolerate failure.

Jinx could see the fear in his eyes and he ruled Jessie out as the culprit for now, but he knew one of the men in the room was involved. They had to be. No one else would have the affront to pull a gig like this. It was an inside job. There was no doubt about it. The poker table slid easily to one side and the chips clattered as they spilled onto the floor when the gunmen moved it. Jinx had won forty-six grand in the last hand against Leon, and two muppets were about to waltz away with the lot. He didn't care about the drugs, they were for someone else to worry about, but he was sick about his winnings being taken from him at gunpoint. There would be hell to pay when he found out who was responsible.

"What's the safe code, Jessie?" One of the gunmen asked. He sounded calm and collected.

"Thirty-two, twenty-six," Jessie closed his eyes tightly as he lied. He was giving them the wrong code because the safe was alarmed. If they entered the wrong code, the bells would ring. Jessie hoped the alarms would alert the small army of armed heavies that were drinking in the club, and they would come to their rescue and annihilate the gunmen. It was a calculated risk.

"You are lying to me. I know the code is forty-six, thirty-two, Jessie," the masked man corrected him. It was a trick question to see if Jessie would tell the truth. He walked behind the big Welshman and took a pair of pruning shears from his pocket. He held the Uzi in his left hand and used his right hand to place the shears over Jessie's ear.

"What the fuck are you doing?" Jessie hissed. The shears snapped closed and snipped the top of his ear off. Jessie hadn't been expecting the pain; he fell forward, screaming. Blood flowed through his fingers and down his wrist from the savaged appendage. A kick in the ribs knocked the wind from his lungs and silenced him. The music in the club drowned out any sound from the poker room. The gangsters looked at each other helplessly.

"You are dead men," Leon growled.

"Spend the money wisely and leave the country," Dava advised them. "Trust me, I will find you."

"Take the money and fuck off!" Jinx growled. He was the closest to Jessie. The gunman grabbed the injured man and pulled him upright. Jessie's eyes looked into his, pleading, but there was nothing Jinx could do for now. "You're dead men, so spend the money quickly."

"Shut up, Jinx, or I'll put a bullet through your brain. I can think of a few of your customers that would have a party if you croaked it, eh?" He shoved the muzzle of the Uzi into Jinx's back. "Jessie lied to me, so I've had to teach him that there is a consequence to that. The next lie will cost him another ear, then his nose, then his fingers, and so on."

"I have the stake money from the safe. There is one-hundred and sixty thousand here." The second masked man said as he stuffed a bundle of fifties into his bag. Jinx clocked his accent as local. He was from Liverpool, which meant he would be easy to find. Someone had sold them the Uzis. There were a handful of arms dealers in the city who could obtain automatic weapons. Several of them were in the room already. That would narrow his search down.

"Good, now, Jessie, I need the code for the lockbox beneath the ice machine, please." The masked man said calmly. He was as cool as could be.

"If I give you that number, I'm as good as dead anyway." Jessie sucked in a deep breath and steadied himself as he answered. "Do what you have to do."

The gunman stepped forward again and placed the shears over Jessie's remaining ear.

"Last chance, Jessie."

"Fuck you," Jessie whispered and closed his eyes.

The shears sliced through the gristle as if it were cheese. They snapped together as the blades folded and Jessie tried to cry out, but a gloved hand stifled the scream.

"The code, Jessie, or it's your nose next."

"Tell him the code, Jessie!" Leon shouted from a few yards away. He had seen enough. "It's not your gear anyway, and we'll square it with the Turks. Just tell the bastards the code!"

"Leon's right, Jessie," Jinx nodded. "Tell them the code, and we'll square it with the Turks. We'll tell them the gear was stolen."

"They'll kill me, Jinx." A tear ran down Jessie's face. He was in pain, but he wasn't going to let them see him as a jabbering wreck. He tried hard not to cry but he was in agony.

"Jessie, listen to me. Tell them the code and we will square it with the Turks. I promise you." Jinx spoke slowly and calmly. He looked Jessie in the eyes to convince him it was the only thing to do. The sooner the gunmen got what they had come for, the better. He wanted them gone.

"It's the same code as the safe," Jessie hissed through clenched teeth. Under different circumstances, it would have been embarrassing to admit that he used the same code, but right now, he didn't care. His memory wasn't great so he used the same four digits for everything; the safes, his credit card and pin-number, even the lock on his bike.

"Got it," the second gunman shouted from behind the ice machine. He stuffed the packages of white powder into a sports bag and moved to cover the kneeling gangsters as they backed away toward the cellar door.

"Goodnight, gents. You men peddle filth in my city, and so you can look at this as compensation for the shit you cause. We will remove your stocks and money, and take the wealth you make from selling this shit. It's been emotional but also a pleasure doing business with you. The cellar door is booby trapped, by the way, so I wouldn't try to follow us if I were you. Oh, and by the way, I will be seeing you again!"

The door slammed shut after the gunmen and the gangsters moved as one unit. They ran to the door and began banging at it. They unbolted the locks, yanking on the chains as they shouted for their minders to come and help. The doors began to vibrate violently as heavy blows rained down on them from the other side. There was a three-inch gap between the doors now, only the chains held fast. The wood splintered, but the guards couldn't gain entry.

"Move away from the doors!" A voice bellowed. The gangsters stood to the side. Three shots rang out and the handles holding the chain blew off. Huge ragged holes appeared where the twelve-gauge shotgun shells ripped through the doors and a small army of heavies stormed into the room.

"What's happened?"

"There are two men leaving through the back of the club with our fucking money!" Leon shouted. "Get out there and stop them!"

"Which way did they go?" Another minder pulled a Glock-17 and waved it around, looking for a target.

"Through the cellar," Leon shouted over the chaos. There were men running back and forth asking questions and waiting for hurried instructions. Voices were raised and bedlam broke out as several accusations were made about who was responsible for the robbery.

Jinx watched as two minders ran towards the cellar door. Leon was waddling behind them as fast as he could, trying to keep up. Real time turned to slow motion as he watched them. He remembered what the gunmen had said as they had left. The cellar door was booby-trapped. Was it? The operation had been slick and well planned, so he had no reason to think they were lying. In his mind, he believed them, but his brain wasn't reacting to the information. Three men walked by dragging Jessie, pressing bar towels to his severed ears to stem the blood. Jinx wanted to shout a warning to Leon and his minders, but they could not have heard him over the bedlam. He covered his ears and ran for the doors as the minders reached for the cellar door handle, glancing back just as they twisted the handle and yanked the door open.

There was a blinding flash as a concussion grenade exploded, blowing Leon and his men backwards off their feet. As the blast knocked Jinx unconscious, he saw four sevens in his mind and darkness closed in.

Chapter Five

The Gecko

An hour later, the Gecko watched while his accomplice counted the stake money that they had stolen for the third time. Gecko knew there was something very wrong with the man, but by the time he had realised it, he had already been involved with him. He was obsessive-compulsive, always washing his hands and wiping surfaces with a tissue to remove dust. They had eaten together in restaurants, where he constantly wiped his cutlery with his napkin. He was beginning to annoy Gecko immensely. He was becoming a liability. Some of the things he had done in the last few weeks were unfathomable and very evil. When they had first met, Gecko had found him amusing and they had had a mutual enemy, but as time went by, it had turned out that he was a lunatic. He was obviously a clever man, but there was a distinct lack of common sense to his partner's actions, which Gecko found hard to stomach. Idiots irritated him, but greedy idiots were worse still and careless idiots worse again. It was becoming obvious that his partner was schizophrenic. Gecko was having serious doubts about the man's past and his present. His future didn't worry him too much since he did not intend to be a part of it.

"That was easier than I thought it would be," his accomplice bubbled with excitement as he counted the stacks of fifty-pound notes again. He licked his gloved fingers before recounting another bundle. "Easy money, easy money, easy money," he chuckled to himself as he counted it again. He stopped suddenly and looked at Gecko. It was as if something had suddenly occurred to him. "What will we do with the drugs this time?"

"You don't have to worry about that." Gecko frowned at him. He could hear laughter from the streets below. The rain was pelting on the window and it sounded like tiny bony fingers scraping to get in. Maybe it was the ghosts of those he had hurt in the past, letting him know that they were there, watching. They were there waiting for him to suffer as they had before they had died screaming.

"What do you mean?" His accomplice stopped counting. His eyes darted from the money to the drugs as if he couldn't make up his mind which to touch first.

"You get half the cash. That was the original deal, and it stays that way." Gecko lit a cigarette and puffed on it. He watched his accomplice closely. His eyes had a glaze to them when he became excited. Gecko had seen it many times before. It was a look mad men had. Evil men had it too but he knew that evil men were not necessarily mad.

"Yes, I know it was the deal originally, but we didn't know about the cocaine then. If it weren't for me, we wouldn't have known about the drugs at all. I deserve half at least." His partner eyed him angrily. "We agreed to split the money, but five kilos of cocaine is worth more than I can earn in years. It seems fair to split everything down the middle."

"The drugs are going into the rubbish." Gecko inhaled smoke and tried to keep calm.

"I risked everything to get that information," his accomplice was talking at a million miles an hour, "it was my handiwork that gleaned the information about the drugs and the poker game."

"I saw your handiwork, as you call it," Gecko looked out of the window again. "You've lost the plot, Patrick."

Patrick wanted the drugs. They were worth enough money to melt away again and reinvent himself somewhere else for a while.

"You've lost the plot!" Patrick mimicked. Gecko was boring him with his suicidal crusade. All he wanted was some fun, his own special kind of fun. At first, he had thought Gecko was like him, but he wasn't. "I thought we were partners in this?"

"No. I offered you half of any cash we recovered, nothing more. The drugs are not in the deal." Gecko had stored some previously captured narcotics in a lockup, but it had been broken into the week before. He had his suspicions as to where the drugs had gone. Things were coming to a head. "I am doing this to take the shit off the streets and put the scumbags out of business. What is the point in letting you re-circulate them?"

"There will always be drug dealers to kill as long as people want to get high. Fuck them, let them have it." His partner shook his head. He couldn't comprehend why Gecko wouldn't want the revenue from the drugs. It would be compensation for his loved ones. Gecko had lost people dear to him. The money could take the sting out of that. "Look what happened to the stuff you left in your lockup. You left them lying around and someone nicked them."

"I think you took the drugs from the lockup." Gecko stared him in the eye, looked for a reaction. "I think you broke in and stole them."

"Fuck you!"

"Who else would know they were there?"

"Anyone could have broken into it," his partner retorted. His eyes widened as he manufactured an answer. "It was probably a couple of kids looking for tools to rob."

The Gecko stood up and looked out of the window. "I have seen men lying a million times. Some men lie to protect others and some men lie to protect themselves, either way, I can spot them a mile away."

His skill had been making liars tell the truth and identifying it when it came, and he had been the best there was at the time. Sometimes their faces came to him in the night. Especially the ones that had told the truth; no matter how much pain they had suffered, they had stuck to the same story. They were the ones he felt guilt about, not the liars. They could rot in hell, but the innocent ones haunted him. Of course, it was difficult to tell at first. Most liars were convincing until the pain became too much, then they broke, and everyone had a breaking point. Gecko hadn't been responsible for who the government took to interrogate. He had been responsible for extracting the truth from them. Many times, they had taken the wrong people. Too many times; and they were the ghosts that haunted him, them and the voices of his family.

The streets below the hotel window were crammed with drunken revellers staggering from one bar to the next, and the base lines of a dozen tunes mingled into one never ending beat. Three teenage girls ran across the cobbled street, looking for cover from the pounding rain. They huddled beneath one coat as they ran. One of them caught her heel in the cobblestones and she tumbled, grazing her knees as she fell. Gecko could hear her cursing and her friends screeching with laughter as they took shelter in a doorway. They giggled, pointing towards the fire and the commotion at the top of the street.

They were three hundred yards from Connections nightclub, overlooking Concert Square. In recent years, the big brand bars and hotels had moved into that quarter of the city and transformed it from a maze of dirty backstreets to a booming social hub. Smoke still billowed above the roofline of the buildings as the firefighters tried desperately to quell the flames. Something inside Gecko yearned to go back in time and live his youth again. Maybe life would be different if he had chosen another path. The truth was he couldn't go back. No one could.

"Take your half of the money now and go. We need to stick to the plan. I'll contact you when I'm ready to move again." Gecko sighed. He inhaled smoke from the cigarette again and watched it curl against the glass as he blew it out. His partner was a liar. He had told him he was ex-army but over time Gecko had realised it was a lie. There were too many inconsistencies in his stories. Gecko had spent the majority of his working life in the armed forces, and he knew that his partner had not, despite his tales.

"Look, I don't expect a full cut, but it's only fair to give me some of it. I have friends who can shift this stuff with no problems and no questions asked. They don't sell to school kids, they sell it to suits." Patrick was pushing his luck. He had stolen a stash of taxed drugs from their lockup. Gecko had been stupid leaving them there to rot, in his opinion. His crusade against organised crime was a folly. He would wind up dead in the boot of a car. Drugs were currency, and Patrick wanted his share.

"I offered you half the cash, full stop. The drugs are nonnegotiable," Gecko said.

"Yes, but that was before we found out about this cocaine, come on!" His partner pleaded. "Let me take this and we can burn everything else we find!"

"There will be more work, plenty of it. Don't be greedy," Gecko lied. The time had come to sever the partnership. They wouldn't be working together again.

"We worked well together. We're a good team," Patrick said.

"The thing is we're not a team, are we?"

"What do you mean?"

"Well, you took the drugs from the lockup and you've been entertaining yourself again, haven't you?" Gecko accused him. "You're putting the whole plan in jeopardy."

"I don't know what you mean." His partner looked guilty.

Gecko stubbed out the cigarette and walked to the wardrobe. The hotel lodge room still smelled of new paint and polish. He took out a carrier bag and dropped it on the bed. There was a vacant look in his eyes as he tipped the contents onto the quilt. Gecko wasn't squeamish but his partner had gone too far. He looked at his associate and waited for his reaction.

"What is that?" The man's eyes were flickering with recognition. His brain was working overtime trying to find an answer. A lie that could cover up what he had done. "I haven't seen that before."

"That tells me you're a liar. Take your half of the money and leave now. I have things to do." Gecko emptied the contents of the haversack onto the bed. He picked up a canvas roll and untied the cord, which bound it before spreading it out on the bed. There was an assortment of medical cutting equipment sheathed in the roll. The steel handles glinted in the artificial light. Congealed blood stained the cutting edges. "These are yours, I think. I found them at a unit on Jamaica Street."

"Yes, they're mine. You've been following me, that's sneaky."

His accomplice reached over and grabbed the cutting tools off the bed. He rolled them up as if they were fragile and put them inside his coat lovingly. He looked embarrassed and it was obvious that he didn't want to talk about the instruments. He quickly changed the subject. "Okay, half the money and one kilo?" His accomplice stuffed half the money into his sports bag and grabbed a kilo package of cocaine. "One kilo, that's fair."

"Fine, take this too. I think it belongs to you." Gecko tossed a freezer bag over to his irritating accomplice, who caught it and smiled as he looked at the contents through the clear plastic. Then his expression changed into one of shock and horror.

"What is this, some kind of sick joke?"

The rotting hand inside had a gold sovereign on the index finger. The wrist bone was exposed and yellowed and the flesh was beginning to liquefy inside.

"Open it."

"No way, why did you go there?" Patrick knew it was real but he didn't want to admit it to himself. His hobby was his business and no one else's. He enjoyed his games but he wasn't comfortable with people knowing what he liked to do. His mind wasn't too warped to realise society loathed monsters like him.

"I said open it." Gecko pulled a Glock. It had a dull black suppressor attached to the barrel, making it look more lethal than normal.

"Okay, okay. I'll open it. Keep all the cocaine, I don't want it." Patrick opened the zip seal and the stench hit him like a sledgehammer. He tossed the offending bag away onto the bed and the hand spilled out. "You're sick. I can't believe you kept that. Why did you bring that? You should not have followed me there. What the hell is this all about?"

"It's about you crossing the line. It is about you shattering the boundaries every time I ask you to do something. It is about trust and greed. You have to push everything to the limit, don't you? You have to go too far every time. There was no need to go that far." Gecko pointed to the rotting hand.

He hit Patrick hard with the butt of the gun and his accomplice fell to his knees. Another heavy blow silenced him. Putting a bullet into his brain crossed Gecko's mind but he refrained when he heard voices in the corridor outside. He needed time to think about what had happened. Leaving a corpse in a city centre hotel was not a bright idea, and there was no way he could dispose of the body before someone discovered it. His accomplice had been self-indulgent to say the least, leaving a trail of evidence for the police to follow when they eventually found the woman. He had thought about cleaning up the factory unit but there was nothing there, which could lead them to him, so he had left it. It was time to go on alone. He wished he had done things on his own from the start but it wasn't something he could change. What was done was done, his past was his past, and he couldn't alter it. He could shape the future though, and that was what he had to concentrate on. After a little rearranging of the hotel room, Gecko stepped onto the busy streets and blended into the crowd with the cash and the drugs safely tucked into his bag. He would deal with his accomplice later. Their partnership was over. There was one more task to complete, and then he would get rid of him for good.

Chapter Six

Connections Nightclub

When Jinx opened his eyes, there were bells ringing in his head. He was cold and wet and water was pouring from the ceiling. There was smoke everywhere and women were screaming in the nightclub. He saw his fellow poker-playing gangsters picking themselves up from the floor. There were flames flickering up from the cellar and the doorframe was well alight. The fire was taking a hold and spreading quickly. Strong hands grabbed him and pulled his substantial frame upward.

"Come on, Jinx. It's time to get out of here." The gravelly voice belonged to a monster called Gus. Gus Rickman was one of the top villains in the country and if anything happened in Liverpool then Gus knew about it before it happened. If he didn't, there was trouble. Gus had been a competitive body builder in his younger days and although he had stopped competing, he was bigger than ever. He was shaven headed with a grey goatee beard and tattoos covering his arms. He was responsible for one of the biggest bullion robberies ever carried out, and the police didn't even have him on their list of suspects. They had him linked to a few security van robberies a decade ago, but they never had enough evidence to charge him with anything. Jinx liked him because he was straight. There was no bullshit with Gus, what you see was what you got. Treat him with respect and he'd help you any way he could, but cross him at your peril.

"Get the fire extinguishers!" Someone shouted.

"No!" Gus shouted over the noise. "Get everyone out of here and let it burn."

Confused faces looked at Gus. The fire was growing but they could extinguish it if they acted quickly. Jinx read his mind. Gus was right. Five kilos of cocaine belonging to the Turkish mob were missing. A decent size fire could hide a multitude of sins, and they had promised Jessie they would cover him. Letting the back of the club burn would just about do it. The fire brigade would save the rest of the building, maybe.

"Move now!" Gus growled. People limped and carried others toward the main part of the club. Leon and his minders were struggling to stand up. They had taken the brunt of the blast when the grenade exploded. It was lucky for them the gunmen had used a concussion grenade, not a fragmentation grenade. It was designed to incapacitate people, not kill them with shrapnel. Gus and Jinx ran to Leon and his colleagues. They dragged them up and bundled them towards the nightclub. Gus stopped near the poker table and grabbed a bottle of scotch from a drinks trolley. He took a huge gulp and then hurled the bottle toward the fire. It shattered and the flames roared as the liquid ignited.

"Let's go!" Gus shouted. "Make sure everyone loses their guns quickly when we get outside. There will be police everywhere in a minute."

"Who do you think pulled this off?" Jinx asked as they stumbled through the smoky nightclub.

"I don't know." Gus looked sideways at Jinx, suspicion in his eyes. "I can have a good guess, though."

"It has to be an inside job, right?"

"There's no doubt about it."

As they made their way through the club, bouncers were herding the stragglers towards the fire exits. A young woman in a tight leather dress was so drunk that she couldn't walk unassisted; the bouncers carried her between two of them. Her condition was nothing to do with the blast. Vodka was to blame. The disco lights were still spinning and red lasers pierced the smoke. Half-empty glasses littered the tables and several handbags lay abandoned by their owners. The music was blasting as they crashed through the front doors of the club and Leon stumbled onto the pavement. He landed with a thump face down on the rain soaked pavement. His nose was bleeding and his face looked puffy and swollen as Jinx and the others picked him up.

"Who did this, Jinx?" Leon scowled. He wiped blood from his nose with the back of his hand.

"You're the drug dealer, you tell me," Jinx snapped. He was angry beyond words.

"What's that supposed to mean?" Leon spat blood on the floor.

"I don't know yet," Jinx replied. "But we'll find out, Leon. We will find out for sure, believe me."

"Make sure no one is carrying!" Gus shouted to the crowd of heavies that surrounded them. Several men ran toward the car park opposite to hide their weapons. Sirens approached; two police cars screeched to a halt and the first fire fighters were on the scene within minutes. They dismounted from the tenders and began to clear the crowds while their colleagues began feeding hosepipes into the club. One of Gus' men approached. He looked like a bigger version of Gus, but his goatee was black and he had fewer lines around his eyes.

"There was nothing around the back, Gus."

"Any sign of a vehicle?"

"Nothing and the back door is locked from the inside."

"How do you know that?"

"There are no keyholes, Gus, just a steel plate. It's shut tight."

"Where's Jessie?" Jinx asked.

"He's in that ambulance," the minder said.

Gus and Jinx ran to the ambulance where two paramedics were trying to stop the bleeding while a uniformed officer asked the Welshman questions.

"How did you get these injuries?" The constable asked. The police officer was in his early twenties at most. He had spiked his dark hair and there were tattoos on his forearms. He looked out of his depth in the mayhem that surrounded him.

"Fuck off," Jessie replied, shaking as the paramedics tried to stem the flow of blood, but it wasn't the pain that was affecting him. The theft of his employers' drugs had stunned him. They would come to him first for answers and he didn't have any. The last thing he needed now was a snotty nosed copper straight out of college asking him stupid questions.

"There were reports of gunshots," the young officer carried on unperturbed. "Can you tell me what happened?"

"I don't know if you've noticed, Sherlock, but my ears have been damaged," Jessie pointed to the side of his head where the ambulance men were working.

"Damaged?" One of the paramedics said. "They've been cut off!"

"Shut up! Nobody asked you a question," Jessie turned angrily on him. If the bleeding hadn't been so severe he would have walked away, but he was losing a lot of blood.

"So how did you receive those injuries?" The officer tried again. He took a white notebook from his pocket and opened it in anticipation of recording Jessie's replies.

"Write this in your notebook, Sherlock, fuck off!" Jessie's face was purple and his hands were shaking.

"I don't think he wants to make a statement, Officer," Gus growled as he looked into the ambulance. Jessie laughed but his laugh changed to a wince when a paramedic pressed too hard. The young police officer looked on bemused.

"Jessie, is there any other way out of the cellar apart from the back door?" Gus asked.

"Why?" Jessie was confused.

"Just answer the question."

"No, the door to the alleyway is the only exit."

"Can it be opened from the outside?"

"No, it has a steel plate welded over it and it's bolted from the inside. It hasn't been opened for years. Why are you asking?"

"We need to take him to hospital right now", one of the paramedics said as he grabbed the back doors and pulled them together, "he's losing a lot of blood."

"I'll travel with him if you don't mind," the officer said unsurely.

"It's up to you, mate, but we need to go now."

"I don't want him in here asking me stupid questions," Jessie whined. "I'm not going to say anything, Sherlock, so why don't you just fuck off?"

The ambulance men laughed. It was just another Saturday night in the city to them. The police officer decided he was getting nowhere and bailed out of the back. Jessie was shouting questions at Gus as the doors slammed closed and silenced him. The siren wailed and the blue lights flashed as the van drove away from the burning nightclub, slowly weaving through the crowd that had gathered.

"They must be in the cellar." Gus turned to Jinx. Jinx was looking around and scanning the crowd. There were familiar faces everywhere. They all looked shocked.

"No way." Jinx shook his head. "They were smart, Gus. There's no way they left themselves trapped in the cellar with no escape route."

"There's only one way to find out, but the club is full of police."

"I'm telling you they're not down there, Gus. They're long gone."

"Well, how did they get out?"

"The same way they went in. Grab some of your men and let's go and take a look ourselves." Jinx walked toward the rear of the club. Gus didn't like being told what to do, but he called his men together and looked for the remaining card players and their heavies. The emergency services had put Leon into an ambulance, which left David Lorimar and the remaining three poker players plus their minders. The police watched closely as they gathered and whispered to each other in a huddle. To a bystander, it looked like there were angry words being exchanged before the group moved away to the back of the club. As they slipped down the service alley at the rear, the rain began to bucket down. The alleyway was dark and lined with huge red wheelie bins that were overflowing with cardboard and waste from the retail outlets that bordered the nightclub. A single yellow streetlight poured out a dull glow, hardly penetrating the darkness.

"What are we supposed to be doing here, Gus?" Big Mick asked gruffly. Mick was one of the poker players, a grizzly bear of a man, thickset and bearded. He exported ninety percent of the stolen prestige cars taken from the North West. Most of them were destined for Eastern Europe, and the trade link gave him access to heroin smuggled from Afghanistan through Russia. He didn't have time to chase around after a couple of chancers who had stolen his twenty grand stake money. It was nothing to him.

"The cellar door is locked from the inside, which means they are still in there," Gus replied and pointed toward the back of the club.

"So what, Gus, I don't care. I've got better things to do." Mick wanted to be away from the scene before the police began sniffing around. "We'll find out who did this before long, and we can deal with them then."

"Mick, did you hear what he said?" Jinx came out of the shadows. "He said we peddle filth in his city, and he was going to take your produce and your money. Now it sounded to me like he means to do this again. If we don't stick together and make this bastard disappear, then they could hit anyone of us at anytime."

Mick stopped and thought about it for a second. "Fair enough, Jinx, what do you suggest?" Mick was shrewd and he shrugged his huge shoulders. "Shall we knock on the back door and ask for our money back?"

"It was an inside job, Mick. One of us set it up," Gus said.

"Maybe one of you did, but I think you're forgetting that whoever stole the money had an Uzi in his hand, and right now all I'm carrying is twenty Lamberts and my lighter. I'm as pissed off as you are, but there's nothing we can do about it."

"He's right," Jinx added. "I think we should start asking questions tomorrow, and we can rule Jessie out of the sting."

There was a murmur of agreement amongst the men. There were also suspicious glances. Old rivalries simmered beneath the surface.

"What about you, Jinx?" Bodger spoke. His real name was Barry Hodge, but no one used it. He was a major fraudster and scammer. He manufactured software in the Far East that could capture credit card and bank account data and sold it all over the world. He had made over two million dollars selling the latest computer gaming consoles to American internet customers; of course the goods had never materialised. "Where are your boys tonight?"

Jinx had arrived on his own for the poker game. He always did. No one needed to ask why he didn't have a minder; it was obvious. Unless someone was going to shoot him, he could look after himself, but the insinuation that he was involved was there.

"I don't need my boys all the time, Bodger, but you do."

One of Bodger's men stepped forward. "Watch your mouth!"

"Or what, sweet cheeks?" Jinx didn't move but his grin turned into a sneer. "Do you fancy a shot at the title?"

"Don't mind if I do, it's about time someone shut you up, you prick!"

Instinctively the men cleared a space between the antagonists. Tensions were running high after the robbery and the explosion.

"Knock him out, Billy," Bodger goaded his man. Billy was an ex-boxer. Moreover, his nose said he wasn't the best defensive fighter in the world; it was flattened to his face. He had been a handy man in his youth but never good enough to make a career in the ring. Billy came from a family of fighters and villains, and he resented the rise to power of some members of the black community. He had been a racist from an early age and didn't care who knew it.

Billy Williams raised his hands to his chin in an orthodox boxing stance. He looked light on his feet for a big man. Jinx didn't change his expression as the boxer circled him. Billy lunged forward with a hard left jab but he was slow at getting his arm back out of danger. Jinx grabbed the extended limb and twisted it violently to the left, forcing Billy down onto one knee. In one fluid movement, he hit the back of Billy's elbow joint with his forearm. His entire weight was behind the strike and Billy's arm snapped like a twig, bending in the completely wrong direction. Billy screamed and fell on his back in a puddle, blubbering like a girl. Bodger looked to his other minder, who looked scared and picked up his screaming colleague. He didn't want to take Jinx on. The pouring rain was running down his face in rivulets.

"Anyone else?" Jinx looked around the crowd. There were no takers for now. Some fancied their chances one to one, but not in front of this particular crowd; losing here would damage their standing and Jinx was a formidable opponent.

"Evening, Gentlemen," a voice from behind them stopped everyone. "Well, we have quite a gathering here."

Looking around, the gangsters were faced with Chief Carlton. He was the head of the division's uniformed police force and more than familiar with the rogues in the alleyway. There were eight uniformed police officers with him and more arriving every second. Big Mick decided it was time to go and moved away from the group.

"Not so fast, Michael," Carlton said sternly. "We'll need to speak to all of you before you go anywhere. What happened to him?" The police officer nodded toward Billy. He was whining in agony.

"I didn't see anything, and you can't hold me," Mick snarled. The last thing he needed was a lengthy interview with Merseyside's finest. "He fell."

"I think you know better than that, Michael. You can answer some questions here, or we can do it at the station. It's up to you. Did anybody see anything?"

"Like Mick said, Billy fell," Gus added.

"Okay, he fell. Put him in an ambulance," Carlton nodded to one of his officers. He stepped forward and helped Billy onto the main street where the emergency services were working flat out, ferrying the shocked and injured to casualty. There was thick black smoke billowing from the entrance to the club and an army of firefighters was battling the flames inside the building. "Witnesses are telling us they heard gunshots and an explosion of some kind," Carlton said. Would you care to enlighten me what went on here?"

The gangsters remained silent. There was no point in making a smart reply; Chief Carlton was nobody's fool. They had all had prior dealings with him. He knew who ran the city's underworld, but knowing who was in charge was not enough to lock them up behind bars.

"Okay. My constables will take your details and a brief statement. If I need to talk to you, I'll be in touch. I don't suppose any of you are carrying firearms?"

The group of villains stayed tight-lipped again. The weapons had been stored in vehicles when they had come out of the club. They stared stony-faced at the police chief.

"Fine, let's get them processed, Constable." Chief Carlton walked by them and further into the alleyway. He was curious as to why they were there. "What were you doing here?" He mumbled to himself as he looked around.

Jinx watched him while waiting his turn to speak to the uniformed officers. The police officer stopped near the backdoor and pulled on the steel plate. It was solid. There was a skip next to it, overflowing with empty boxes and bin bags. He shoved it out of the way with his shoulder. Some of the bottles rolled off the top and smashed onto the floor. Behind it was an arched basement window set into the wall. There were rusted bars set into the brickwork. Chief Carlton knelt down and studied them. The bolts, which should have secured the metal frame, were missing. He poked his index finger into one of them and frowned. Jinx smiled as Carlton tugged at the bars and they came away in his hands. He looked around at Jinx as he pushed against the grimy window they protected and it creaked open. "Is this what you were looking for?" The police officer raised his eyebrows as he spoke.

Jinx looked away. That was how they had gained access to the club and escaped unnoticed. Someone had known where the stake money was. They had known how to get into the cellar, and the hiding place for five kilos of uncut cocaine. Jinx wanted his money back and he wanted Leon put out of business. The arrival of the mysterious masked men could prove to be useful if he played his cards right. On the other hand, the Turks would be looking to recover their cocaine and slaughter whoever had had the nerve to steal from them in the first place. Bodger would have a score to settle with him too for wasting his minder. Whatever happened over the next few days and weeks, someone was going to die. Jinx was adamant that it wouldn't be him.

Chapter Seven

MIT

Alec Ramsay waited for the team to gather in the briefing room. There was an air of excitement and anticipation as they arrived and took their seats. Photographs of the crime scene were flashing across a bank of screens on one wall and the detectives chatted and made comments to each other as each picture appeared. Alec took off his suit jacket, rolled up the sleeves of his crumpled white shirt and loosened his tie before standing up at the front of the room to the left of the screens.

"Good afternoon. I'm sorry if you have been called in from your leave, but as you can see from the crime scene photos, we have a nasty one to deal with." There were murmured responses from the gathering, and then a hush descended over them as they listened to their superintendent. Some of them had been at home less than twelve hours before Alec had summoned them back to work. "At eight o'clock this morning a letting agent working for a company called Ashfords opened up this factory unit on Jamaica Street."

The screens showed pictures of the building and the surrounding streets. Most of the officers were familiar with the waterside area as a notorious red light district. It bordered both the river and the city centre and to its north was the Toxteth area.

"He made an emergency call at one minute past eight when he discovered the body of a woman hanging from the rafters." Alec turned toward the screen as pictures of the tortured female flashed across them. The brutality of the scene they were looking at reflected on the faces of the detectives. It didn't matter how many times they had seen death, this scene hit them hard.

"We have a list of missing persons going back six months who fit the profile of the victim. She is female, long auburn hair, mid twenties to thirties and as you can see, the killer strung her up and tortured her to death. We don't know if she was a working girl or not, and for now it doesn't matter because we have evidence that there was a child at the scene. We may be looking for a mother and child whose family has not reported them as missing, or they may not be related. We need to know who she was."

Will handed out lists of the missing persons. "The list is compiled of women who match the age of the victim, but we don't know if any of them have children." Alec spoke to the team as the lists were distributed. The detectives scanned the names and images as they listened.

"Some of the women are known prostitutes and others are not. It doesn't matter at this stage, they are all someone's daughter, mother or sister, and they will be treated with the same respect. Are we clear?"

"Guv,"

"Vice have spoken with many of the girls who they know work in that area," Alec continued. "None of them are aware of any friends missing. We are waiting for preliminary results to come in. I want to be in the position to match them to our missing persons list as soon as we have them. Smithy your team has the top half of the list to work on. Work down to M, please."

"Yes, Guv." Smithy was a well-built detective with thinning red hair and a beer-belly that hung over his belt. He looked slovenly but he was a key member of the Major Investigation Team. His commitment to the job had cost him three marriages and left him with limited access to his kids and grandkids. He played prop forward for the police rugby team and drank heavily after every game, which had compounded the tensions at home. Life as a bachelor suited him for now. "What about rounding up the usual suspects, Guv?"

"Uniform are picking up all known sex offenders on our patch," Alec pointed to Chief Carlton. His uniformed officers usually did the groundwork and sifting on major cases. They flagged up anyone without a concrete alibi and brought them in for further questioning. "We can get on with identifying our victim for now and find out whose footprints they are."

The picture changed to the small bloody footprints from the unit. "Will, your team takes the bottom half of the list."

"Yes, Guv." Will snapped his fingers and his team began sorting through their part of the list of names. The teams moved and studied their lists. They chatted quietly as they studied the information. Some of the women on the list were similar in appearance, but photographs could be misleading and people often changed their hairstyle. They couldn't make assumptions at this point.

"We need as much detail as we can get our hands on before the initial forensics are completed. I want dental records, bank details, credit card transactions and, where possible, samples we can match to the DNA results. Find out the names of friends and relatives and the places they frequented. Tread carefully. I don't want their families rattled by our investigation. I want to know who the child is without alerting the killer that we've found the body. We don't want to spook him yet, in case the child is still alive." Alec was worried that clumsy police work might upset the families of the missing and alert the press. He had never had children, but he could empathise with the parents of missing children and he had witnessed the mistakes made by fellow detectives who had worked on some of the high profile child abductions and murders in Liverpool over the last few decades. He needed to avoid a press circus at all costs.

"Guv. I have another question." Smithy put his hand up.

"What is it, Smithy?" Alec smiled. He told his team repeatedly that the only stupid questions were the ones you wished that you had asked earlier.

"Will mentioned that we may be dealing with more than one victim, Guv." The detectives in the room nodded. "Apart from the child, I mean."

"We may be." Alec paused. Speculating at this point could hamper the already complicated investigation. "There are several blood pools at the scene and we don't believe they could possibly be from the same victim, but until we get forensics back, we should concentrate our efforts on her." Alec nodded to the screens. The woman's distorted features stared out of the screens for all to see.

"We need to work through these lists thoroughly because if we do have multiple victims, then they will be on those lists, no mistake. I do not want the press to know anything about the missing persons list or the child until we're ready to tell them. Are we all clear about this?" There had been leaks in the past, usually spreading from careless conversation at home or at the pub. The job of a murder detective was a tough one; they often played hard during a case to unwind and take their minds off their work for a few hours. When alcohol numbed their senses, it also numbed their brains. Sometimes people overheard details of investigations and leaked them to the press. "I do not want this case discussed over the pool table down at the pub, clear?"

"Guv."

This investigation possibly involved more than one victim, and the press would go to town when it became public knowledge. High profile cases attracted society's nutcases and just dealing with the number of crank calls that a newspaper feature could generate became a fulltime job for at least one detective. They needed every detective employed in the investigation.

"Crack on, find that kid."

"Yes, Guv." They replied in unison.

"Kisha," Alec turned to a slim black detective who was sitting in Will Naylor's team.

"Guv?" She replied as she looked up from her list. She was marking some notes in the margin of her list. Kisha was keen and her superiors had already noticed her potential.

"I want you to gather the names of everyone who has rented that unit for the last ten years, and everyone who has worked at Ashfords and had access to their keys," Alec said. He knew that Kisha would find it a mundane task, but he needed a detective with focus to sift through the pages of irrelevant information and come up with the leads the investigation would require if they were to find the killer. She was a good detective and that was why he had picked her for the task. He knew that she wouldn't see it that way now, but one day she would.

"Guv," Kisha sighed and looked disappointed. A task like that could throw up dozens of names and an equal number of dead ends. Anyone could have had a set of keys cut. She felt as if she was being sidetracked from the main team and her heart sank. It was like being left on the subs bench during the cup final.

"I also want a list of employees who worked in that factory unit and a list of service companies that have completed works on the building since it has been empty. Stevie, you take that, please. Work with Kisha and cross-check the information." Alec didn't rate Stevie. He was a probationary officer and his detective review date was close, but Alec couldn't see him cutting it. He knew that Kisha would keep him on track and double-check his side of the investigation. He had paired them up for a good reason.

"Yes, Guv," Stevie smiled and looked across at Kisha. She was gorgeous and Stevie had a thing for her, despite the fact she knocked him back at the Christmas party. Kisha didn't return his gaze and she certainly didn't share his enthusiasm for the task they were to work on together. She had no interest in Stevie, or any other men, for that matter. Kisha hid her sexuality from her colleagues. She was female and black. Prejudice was frowned on in the modern police force, but it was still there, lurking in every department, and she knew it. Kisha was ambitious and she wanted to progress as far as she could on the merits of her abilities as a detective. In a meritocratic world that might have been possible, but she lived in the real world and knew that being a black lesbian would stifle her progression. Working on a list of names going back years was bad enough, but working with Stevie compounded the issue. She despised him and had no respect for his abilities as a member of MIT.

"Get moving, everyone. I want this information collated as soon as we can, please." Alec clapped his hands together and the detectives began organising their investigations. Within minutes, they had assigned a list of names and the telephones lines were buzzing. Alec watched them delegate tasks and begin their search with a sense of pride, but there was a nagging doubt in his mind. There was more to this crime than one murder. The other blood pools were a mystery. The child's footprints were of huge concern, but they had to start with the woman who had been tortured to death before they could piece together what had happened in that unit. The evidence didn't add up at the moment and waiting for the forensic results to be processed was time wasted, but that was all he could do. Wait.

He pulled out his Blackberry and scrolled through his contacts for his wife's number. She was annoyed that her mother was visiting and Alec couldn't take his days off. They had planned to go to Chester to shop and to have some lunch on the banks of the river, but now she would have to suffer her mother alone. Their twenty years together had been happy enough and they got on well, but their marriage was plagued with Alec's absence. They had become brother and sister rather than man and wife. She mothered him, constantly feeding him Quorn instead of meat in an attempt to give him a healthy diet. He thought of the last lamb chop that he had tasted and he craved meat as he dialled her number.

"Hello," Gail sounded stressed.

"Hi, it's me." Alec always said that and it irritated his wife immensely, which he couldn't understand.

"I know it's you, Alec. I have your number programmed into my phone and your name comes up on the screen when you call. Your phone does the same thing, too." She sounded angry.

"Yes, sorry. Are you okay?" Alec stuttered. His mind went blank when he had to call home to make excuses. He could never find the words to tell her how he felt. When he said sorry, it didn't sound like it was enough.

"I'm fine."

"You don't sound fine."

"Is there a reason for the call, Alec?"

"I was just saying hello."

"Hello, Alec."

"You sound pissed off."

"Don't swear, Alec. It doesn't suit you."

"Sorry."

"When are you taking a day off?"

"I'm not sure. This is a nasty one, darling. We don't know what we're dealing with yet, but there is a child involved." The line stayed silent but he could hear her breathing. He felt sick with guilt whenever this happened. "I'll try and get half a day when we have the forensic results back."

The phone clicked and she hung up.

"That went well, Alec. Well done." He said aloud as he walked into his office. He had at least one murder to investigate and then he had promised that he would take some holidays and take Gail away. They needed some time alone together. He couldn't remember the last holiday abroad they had had. Then he did, and it made him cringe. They had gone to Gambia for a fortnight and Gail had hated the place as soon as she had landed there. The poverty was overpowering and they hadn't been able to walk up the street in their resort without being accosted by a mob of limbless beggars. Alec had gotten a call from headquarters two days into the holiday when the bodies of two men had been discovered in an abandoned car near the city centre. They had cut the holiday short since Alec had had to fly home and Gail had refused to stay in Gambia alone. She hadn't spoken to him for a week afterwards. Maybe they could go somewhere nearer to home this time, he thought.

Chapter Eight

Leon Tanner

Leon pushed open the front door of a shop called, 'Crazy Computers'. Situated next to a Chinese chippy and a sunbed salon, it stood on a bend in the road opposite a carwash. The road led to the docklands at the mouth of the Mersey. Most of the small butchers, bakers and post offices were long gone. The supermarket chains had slowly strangled their profit margins until it was impossible to continue trading. There were a few new businesses trying to establish themselves; Polish food stores and Turkish barbers were dotted about every half a mile or so.

Leon looked at the frontage from inside. The glass was thick with grease and there was a display of keyboards in the window covered in a thick layer of dust. The shop had never sold a single computer in the five years it had been there. It was a front for the brothel above it. A staircase led up to the first floor. The hundreds of punters who trudged up them every week in search of sex had left the beige carpet soiled with their footprints. Leon had a soft spot for the building. Although it was a rundown dilapidated whorehouse, it was the first one that he had opened and it represented the start of his business enterprises. The first woman he had pimped out was his younger sister. She was slow and had had a string of boyfriends before she was sixteen. Leon had thought that if she was going to be a slut, then she might as well make him some money at the same time.

He had pimped her out to his friends and their associates. Heroin had been her best friend and as long as he had kept her stoned, she had gone along with it. She was a looker and word had soon spread that she was on sale. It hadn't been long before he had taken on another local girl who had been struggling against a heroin addiction and needed the money urgently. Leon had decided that he could supply her with both, and so his empire had started to grow. Within twelve months, he had paid cash for five lockups across the city and he had peddled sex and heroin from both. He had been making a lot of money when his ambitions had focused on the growing crack cocaine market. His customers had been moving away from the brown and using crack instead. It hadn't mattered to Leon what they took, he had decided to supply it.

He had found it difficult to find a regular reliable supplier of the drug. It had been hitting the streets in dribs and drabs and the price had yo-yoed. Two of the city's notorious crime families had been at war over the supply of crack and their armed struggle had been driving their dealers underground, which had disrupted supply to the users on the streets. Leon had seen a gap in the market and decided to exploit it. He had gotten wind of a large shipment coming into the city and hijacked it, taking the drugs and the money and eliminated some of the key enforcers in the process. Four wanted criminals had been executed gangland style with a bullet through the back of the head, and a tip off to the press had allowed the photographers the chance to get to the scene before the police had had a chance to cover the bodies. The murders had been splashed all over the newspapers and television, but no one had been claiming responsibility. The warring families had blamed each other for the hit and escalated their battle with a string of murders that had virtually wiped out the top layer of both cartels. The importers had refused to do business with either family anymore, which had deepened the rift further. Leon had watched from the sidelines as they had annihilated each other and used the proceeds of the hit to establish himself as the number one importer and supplier of the drug. The rest was history.

It had all begun here, at the Crazy Computer shop, and he grinned as he stepped in the door. At the top of the stairs, a middle-aged blonde-haired woman who looked like she had applied her foundation with a trowel greeted him. Mascara caked her false eyelashes and her pencilled eyebrows gave her a surprised appearance. The days when men had paid her for sex were long gone. Now she took the money from the punters and organised washing the sheets and towels. She was one of Leon's first working girls and he trusted her to a degree.

"Hi, Leon."

"How much have you got?" Leon pushed her aside and walked into a small waiting room area. Two nervous punters avoided making eye contact with him or each other. Leon scowled at them. He loathed the men that used his brothels. They were weak and so were the girls he employed to service them. He used their weakness to make money. It was the right of the strong to exploit the weak.

"Just over five thousand." She followed him like a shadow but kept at an arm's length from him. Leon was volatile and she had often felt the weight of his hand across her face. "It's been a quiet week, Leon."

She went to a cupboard under a bookshelf that was crammed with porn magazines and removed a carrier bag full of cash. Leon snatched it from her and stuffed the money into his inside pocket. Five thousand wasn't a bad week's takings, considering he had another thirty premises like this one. He grunted and walked down the stairs before unlocking the adjoining door to the mock computer shop. It smelled of must and damp. The wallpaper was peeling off one wall and black mould climbed the others. At the back of the shop was a door fitted with a metal grill. The top and bottom were fitted with padlocks. Leon took a bunch of keys from his black leather overcoat and unlocked them. The grill squealed as he swung it open and he pushed against the wooden door behind it.

"Alright, Leon." A voice came from behind him.

"It's freezing out there." A second voice called chirpily.

"Pissing down again." The first voice added.

The two men stepped into the computer shop and rubbed their hands together. They were both black and heavily built. Jackson was in his forties and had his hair braided to his scalp. Dean was younger and had shaved his hair off to the skin. He carried a sports bag in his right hand and his left hand was in his pocket, next to his Luger.

"I don't need a weather report, Dean. Have you got the cash?" Leon growled. He was usually pleased to see them but rarely showed it. Talking down to them had become habit, his way of remaining in control.

"Take a chill pill, Leon." Dean looked hurt and offended. "The money is in the bag." He tossed the sports bag to his boss and Leon caught it awkwardly with his right hand.

"How much is in here?" Leon unzipped it with his left hand and poked around inside. There were bundles of fifties tied up with elastic bands.

"Just over a hundred big ones." Jackson whistled to emphasise the amount.

"Good. What about the gun?" Leon grunted and walked into the storeroom.

"It's in the bag." Dean pointed to the sports bag. "What are you going to do with that thing anyway? It should be at the bottom of the Mersey, Leon. It's dirty."

"I'm not going to do anything with it, Dean." Leon grinned. "You are."

CRIMINALLY INSANE

Dean looked at Jackson and shook his head. He didn't like the tone of Leon's voice. There was definitely trouble heading their way. Dean rubbed his shaven scalp and waited for the punch line. He was Leon's enforcer and Jackson was his partner. Together they collected Leon's monies, protecting his interests with their own lives. Leon paid well and it was easier than working. Not that he could get a job. Dean had hated school and could barely read and write. He had left high school at fifteen and signed on the social at sixteen. A decade of petty crime had followed before Leon had taken him onboard as muscle. Dean was a tough man with a reputation as a fighter and it hadn't been long before he had moved up the ranks. He was loyal and trustworthy and Leon had recognised those strengths in him. Leon had dragged Dean into the business faster than he had been able to think and when Leon had given him his first hit, he had realised just how deep in he was. His wife and kids were his life and they wanted for nothing, but he dreaded the possibility that one day they may find out what he did to earn his money. Worse still, one of Leon's enemies may hurt them to get to him. His wife was a practicing Christian with deep beliefs. She took their children to Sunday school every week and if she ever found out what Dean did for a living, it was going to kill her. Dean wanted out, but it wasn't a job where he could give a month's notice. He had squirreled thousands of pounds away and planned to disappear with his family, far away from Leon and the people who would come looking for him. The right time hadn't come yet, though. The last thing he wanted was more blood on his hands before he ran.

"What's happening, Leon?" Jackson stuffed a stick of gum into his mouth and chewed it with his mouth wide open.

"Jinx, that's what's happening." Leon scowled. "I want the man wasted."

"What?" Dean frowned and shook his head. "Jinx is okay, Leon. We go back a long way."

Dean was from the same area of the city as Jinx. They had never been friends, but they knew of each other and there was a level of respect between them. Jinx was a popular character with many friends. He had given Dean's sister the deposit for a flat when her ex-boyfriend had put her in the hospital before burning all her clothes in the front garden. Jinx had found out about her plight and found her somewhere to live the same day. He had chucked her a thousand pounds to buy a new wardrobe and the basic furniture she needed. Jinx did that kind of thing. He helped people out and was popular. If he were harmed, there would be plenty of dangerous people looking for revenge. Dean didn't want any part of messing with Jinx. Although he didn't really know him, Dean liked the man.

"I want him dead, Dean, and then this gun goes into the boot of Bodger's car. We kill two birds with one stone. Jinx is dead and that arsehole Bodger is in clink. We move in and take over their business interests." Barry Hodge had rented a lockup from Leon two months earlier. He used it as the base to operate an internet fraud, worth tens of thousands selling pirated computer games. When the fraud squad had investigated, they had searched the entire building and discovered the massage parlour above it. The vice squad had been down on Leon like a ton of bricks. Bodger had known it would cause Leon hassle but he didn't really care. Leon wanted to show Bodger the consequences of disrespecting him were dire. If he could take Jinx out in the process, then it was happy days.

"Brilliant, Leon. You might as well broadcast it on the television that we killed him. If we move in it'll be obvious who was responsible," Dean ranted. "We don't want Jinx's friends on our case."

"Dean is right, Leon. We don't want to mess with him," Jackson added. "They are dangerous people."

"What the fucking hell are we?" Leon shouted. "The boy scouts?"

"It's madness, Leon. It will start a war we can't win. Everyone will turn on us." Dean felt a knot of tension in his guts. He needed to be away from this business before Leon got them all killed. They had soldiers they could call on, but they were mercenaries, loyal to the highest bidder. Leon hadn't endeared himself to anyone over the years. If he started a war, they would be on their own.

"No one will know it was us, you clown." Leon puffed up his chest and his fat chin wobbled. "We take Jinx out of the game and then plant the weapon on Bodger. Then we spread rumours around that he was responsible for robbing the poker game and that's why Bodger shot him."

"Bodger is an internet scammer, Leon. No one will believe he shot Jinx!" Dean shouted back.

"They will when we tell the Turks that they were in it together and they stole their cocaine," Leon grinned. "We'll tell them that Jinx set up the heist and then stitched Bodger up by keeping all the cash for himself."

"Now I know you've lost the plot, Leon." Dean rubbed his head again in frustration. "If you get the Turks involved there'll be a bloodbath."

"Good. We can watch it from the sidelines and mop up what's left when they've finished." Leon took out the gun from the sports bag. A Hessian cloth covered it. They had used the weapon the month before when a crystal meth dealer and his partner had failed to pay their debt to Leon. They had taken them to a remote part of Delamere Forest, where they had forced the dealer to dig his own grave before burying him alive while his partner watched helplessly. Then they had made him dig a second grave while he begged for his life and promised to pay the debt immediately. They had agreed to let him live if he paid up, but he had tried to make a run for it and Jackson had shot him in the back as he ran through the trees. The injured dealer had made it to the road before he died and Leon's men hadn't been able to find him in the dark. The police had recovered a bullet and the ballistics were on file, which made the weapon dirty. If they killed Jinx, it could link them to two murders.

"This is madness, Leon." Dean felt crushed by the pressure. Leon was behaving erratically lately. He had been paranoid before the nightclub robbery, but now he was on edge all the time. His cocaine habit was becoming ridiculous and it was beginning to warp his mind. Jinx was becoming the focus of his aggression. He wasn't thinking of the backlash his murder would cause. "You are forgetting another thing, Leon."

"What's that?" Leon took a silver box from his pocket and flipped the lid. It was designed to hold rolling tobacco but he had filled it with cocaine. He dug his fat thumbnail into the powder and snorted it. His eyelids flickered as the powder dissolved into his bloodstream. "What am I missing?"

"Who did rob the poker game?" Dean's eyebrows lifted, his forehead creasing. Speculation was rife on the streets. The city's underworld was in uproar about the heist. Accusations were flying about and several suspected culprits had been beaten to a pulp as the gangsters looked for retribution. So far, no one had confessed. Word was out that two men were sitting on five kilos of cocaine and eventually, they would try to offload it. Every dealer in the city was waiting for an approach. "If we finger Jinx for the heist and then the real robbers are found, we could be in deep shit, Leon."

"They're in the wind, Deano, gone." Leon licked the remaining powder from his thumb as he spoke. "There is twenty grand in it for you, plus a cut of whatever we take over when the dust settles." Leon knew everyone had a price. Jackson would shoot his mother for twenty grand but Dean was different. "Twenty grand, Deano, you could a lot with that."

Jackson whistled again. He patted Dean on the shoulder and laughed. He liked Jinx and the way he helped the community he lived in, but he didn't like him enough to warrant missing that kind of payday. Jackson was approaching his fifties faster than he wanted to and that kind of money would secure his future. If Leon gave them a cut of any other business he picked up then he could live with killing Jinx, but the look on Dean's face told him that his colleague wasn't so sure. Dean was going soft lately, talking about his family. He had big plans for their future; plans that didn't involve shooting rival gangsters or burying people alive in the forest. If Dean didn't want in on the deal, he would do it himself.

"Come on, Deano." He slapped him on the back again. "Twenty grand, you don't like Jinx that much, do you?"

"It's what comes afterwards that worries me. Killing Jinx won't be the end of it, Jackson. You won't live long enough to spend the money, you fool, none of us will."

"I'll take my chances for that kind of money."

"People will think Bodger did it, or the Turks. They'll believe whatever rumours we put out there," Leon grinned. "We have a meth shipment arriving tomorrow night at the docks. We'll put our business in order and then we'll take out Jinx. The money for the meth is all here. Pick it up tomorrow before you get the drugs."

Dean agreed with a grunt. Jackson smiled and thought about his bonus. The drug pickup was not complicated. They had the security guards on the docks in their pocket. Dean could concentrate on that for now and worry about the Jinx problem later. He wasn't sure what he was going to do, but he knew that he didn't want to be around when all hell broke loose. Leon placed the bag of money into a safe at the back of the storeroom and the door clunked as it closed. The storeroom smelled musty and damp. Apart from the safe, it was empty. There were no computers or keyboards for sale here, just the women upstairs. The men secured the metal grills over the door and padlocked them into place. As they left the Crazy Computer shop, the Gecko watched them from a parked car across the road in a side street. He had listened to their conversation via a scanner and picked up some very interesting information. They were planning to make a hit on the moneylender Jinx Cotton. That was a problem, because Gecko wanted Jinx around. His enquiries had taught him that Jinx didn't like the drug dealers in the city any more than he did. He could be useful for taking out Leon's network of brothels and drug dealers. Gecko needed the safe combination to steal Leon's money, but now he knew when it would be open, and he knew where they were collecting a large shipment of meth. Tomorrow would be a busy day.

Chapter Nine

Hotel Clean

Maria was checking rooms on the third floor. Time was ticking away and the team of cleaners that she supervised were the worst she had ever worked with. The majority of them couldn't speak English, especially when she was reprimanding them. Their level of understanding dropped dramatically sometimes when it suited them.

"Yasser, have you finished your block yet?" She shouted down the corridor. A bedroom door slammed and then there was silence. "Yes Maria, of course I have finished my block, would you like me to help the others finish theirs?" She answered herself as no one else was there.

The corridors were dark. Too dark to see properly on a gloomy day when the daylight coming into the hotel was limited. The owners had built the hotel inside a converted cotton warehouse and the walls were exposed red bricks. Huge iron girders supported the floors above. The public areas had stripped wooden floors. The architects had kept the vaulted ceilings as a feature. It added character to the building, but the lighting was poor. "Shannon!" She shouted down the next corridor. "Shannon!"

"What?" A bedroom door opened and the voice made Maria jump with fright. "Do you have to shout?" Shannon laughed.

"It's the only way to be heard in this bloody place," Maria smiled. Shannon was a great help. She was quick and her standards were good. Checking her rooms took nothing more than a cursory glance.

"How are we doing for time?" Shannon asked. The hotel would want the rooms handed back to them ready for new guests.

"We are nowhere near done." Maria wiped her brow. Her back felt clammy and sweaty. "I feel like I'm coming down with something," she moaned.

"I'll help you check the rooms." Shannon felt her forehead. "You do feel hot though, Maria."

"I feel like shit," Maria tutted. "Menopause, I hope. At least I'll have an excuse to be a grumpy bitch."

They both laughed. "I'll take the floors above, you check this one and we can meet on the first, okay?" Shannon suggested.

"Thank you," Maria clasped her hands together. "Now where is that lazy bastard, Yasser?" She shouted, "Yasser!"

"In here, Maria," his voice came from further down the corridor. The fire doors muffled the sound. "Man in here is fucking sleeping, lazy prick head." Yasser held a cloth in one hand and a spray bottle in the other. "I've been knocking all the morning!"

"Keep your voice down," Maria hissed. She suppressed a laugh. "The word is dickhead, Yasser."

"Me know, dickhead," Yasser frowned. His English was coming on slowly.

"Which room?" She asked.

"This one." Yasser pointed to the door rather than try to say the number. Numbers were still hard. "Lazy prick head," he muttered as he opened the door to the room opposite to check if he had cleaned it. He had.

Maria checked her watch. It was way after checkout time. She knocked loudly on the door. "Housekeeping!" She shouted as a warning. There was no sound from inside the room.

"Open the door!" Yasser was annoyed. "Lazy dickhead!" He smiled as he pronounced the words correctly.

"You have to knock, Yasser," she said, knocking again. "I've lost count of the number of people I've disturbed shagging or masturbating over the years."

"I'll knock." Yasser tried. "Housekeeping!"

"One time, I walked into a room to find the occupant handcuffed and gagged." She raised her eyebrows and laughed at the memory.

"Oh, lady was playing the game?" Yasser asked with a straight face.

"It's *on the game*, Yasser. On the game," she explained. "Anyway, someone had left the poor bloke face down on the bed dressed in stockings and a leather miniskirt. The fire brigade had to cut him free."

"Him, it was a man?" Yasser looked confused.

"Yes, you get all sorts in this job." She had some stories to tell. "Housekeeping!" She shouted as she opened the door. She stepped inside and froze when she saw the blood on the carpet. The smell of rotting flesh hit her like a hammer.

Chapter Ten

MIT

Alec listened to Chief Carlton, trying to make sense of the previous twenty-four hours. "It's an impossible task to put the jigsaw together when the jigsaw keeps on growing."

"We cannot be certain if we have all the pieces, let alone begin putting them together." Will leaned back in his chair and chewed his nails as he listened to the uniformed officer.

"Nothing makes sense." Alec added.

Early that morning, there had been an unexpected incident in the city centre, which seemed to be connected to Alec's investigation.

"What time was the hand found?" Alec reached for his pen. It was a silver Parker that his wife had bought for his birthday and looking at it reminded him that he hadn't been home for two days. Every time he called her, the conversation was terse and she ended the call in a huff. It was easier not to call for now.

"A chamber maid used her pass key to open the room at eleven thirty this morning. The guests are supposed to checkout before eleven so they knocked on the door and then used the pass key when they got no reply," the chief explained. "She found the hand and called in when she realised it wasn't a prank. She is in a bit of a state, poor woman. Our first officers arrived at eleven forty-five. Graham Libby thinks it belongs to your victim at Jamaica Street."

"What do you think?" Alec frowned.

"It isn't every day that a severed human hand is found in a hotel room."

"I am confused as to why it was left behind by the killers." Will chewed his nails. "The murder was weird enough before, but this adds to the strangeness of the case."

"There is something missing," Alec frowned.

"It's connected to your murder investigation. There's no doubt in my mind, although it is odd." The chief loosened his tunic at the collar.

"They made no effort to hide it?" Alec frowned again.

"No. It was lying on the bed in clear view."

"Did they leave anything else behind?" Alec was curious to see if they had planned to return to the room before the maid discovered the hand.

"Nothing, except some blood spatter on the carpet," the chief replied. "The room was booked under a false name and paid for in advance, with cash. Forensics are collecting evidence and dusting the place for prints now but they think that the blood is fresh."

"What has Graham Libby said about it?" Will asked. The forensic investigator would be in possession of the hand already.

"Closer inspection revealed the severed hand is in a decomposed state, matching the timescale of your victim. It cannot be a coincidence."

"So it is from our victim." Alec frowned and looked at Will. There seemed to be little doubt about it. "Something happened to make the killer leave it there."

"Well, it's a left hand. He says the state of decay means that it could be from a body in that condition, and it looks like they removed it with a saw," the chief shrugged. "The only useful thing we have for you is that there was a gold ring on the index finger."

"We know what type of ring it was, a sovereign, right?" Will sat forward. "We haven't seen it though. Do we have a picture yet?"

"Yes, here," the chief handed them a picture. "I've sent the photos to your computers. Smithy called to let me know they had them."

"Thanks, Chief. That might help to narrow down our missing persons." Alec had already spoken to Smithy about the discovery, and the team had been informed. Will made a call while they chatted and informed his officers about the sovereign ring. It was a personal effect and it would help identify the victim. They had found nothing else so far.

"Whoever left it in the room was in a hurry, and they're connected to your murder investigation." The chief didn't envy Alec's position. "The CCTV discs are on the way to you."

"Let's hope there's something useful on them," Will said.

"Is there anything regarding the victim?" The chief asked.

"Nothing." Alec frowned. "We have to hope that the child is still alive."

"It doesn't help that we don't know who we're looking for," Will added.

"Until we identify the woman, we're shooting in the dark," Alec agreed.

"Have you thought about going public yet?" The Chief looked troubled. "An appeal could yield something to work with."

"We're searching for a needle in a haystack as it is." Alec shook his head to disagree. "An appeal would throw up so many distractions that we'd be looking for a needle in a mountain of needles."

"I agree with the super, Chief," Will said. "Until forensics comes back, we should keep the investigation under wraps. If the kid is alive, then we could spook the killers into disposing of them."

"You are guessing that those footprints belong to a living child, not another victim?" The Chief's face darkened.

"We have to," Alec said vehemently. "We know two people were tied to those chairs and we know there was a child in there. We also know that the kid left the footprints getting into a vehicle, not getting out of one. We have to assume the child is alive until we have evidence to prove otherwise."

"It will be hard to keep this from the press, Alec," the chief commented. "The entire staff at the hotel will know about that hand by now."

"We've kept the murder concealed from the press but it won't stay that way for long," Alec agreed. "We cannot make an appeal based on what we know now, it's a shambles."

"What the hell is going on?" Will shook his head as he ended his call to Smithy.

"We might have found a link to our killers but I can't see what it is yet," Alec said.

"Maybe it is a breakthrough, but we aren't out of the starting blocks until we get the forensics back," Will sighed. The case was a mystery.

"God knows why they would leave a severed hand in a hotel room, something happened there," Alec repeated and sighed. "I believe you have a conundrum of your own, Chief. What happened at the nightclub downtown?"

"It's a mess, Alec." The Chief looked tired and the weight of his investigations seemed to be grinding him down. "We have reports of an explosion and gunshots. One witness said he saw one of the bouncers firing a shotgun at the doors leading into the back of the club before the explosion happened. Then there was a fire and that's about all we have, except the owner lost the top of his ears somewhere along the way and none of the CCTV tapes have shown anything from that room."

"Is the manager Jessie James?" Alec was familiar with his name from previous investigations into the club.

"That's him," the chief confirmed. "The hospital said his ears were cut off with scissors or something similar but he's saying nothing. He alleges that he's having trouble remembering."

"I bet he's not hearing well either," Will said sourly, but it got a smile from his superiors. "Jessie and his cronies play poker in that back room sometimes, don't they?"

"Yes." The chief nodded. "There were more villains there that night than on Crime Watch. We found them searching the alleyway behind the club for something but none of them will elaborate about what happened to the place or Jessie's ears."

"What about the CCTV tapes?" Will asked. "Don't they show *anything*?"

"Not the ones from the back room of the club. They've mysteriously disappeared, I'm afraid," the Chief replied with a shake of the head.

"It sounds like you've done all you can with that one then," Alec said. He couldn't connect it to their investigation.

"Gangsters with missing ears points to a row over drugs or money in my mind."

"I agree," Will said. "Jessie must have pissed off the wrong person and if he won't report it, then there is no crime to investigate."

"Leave them to it," Alec added. "It's been pretty quiet since we nailed the Nelson brothers' killer, but it doesn't take much to rock the boat again."

"What do you know about what happened inside the club before the fire?" Will asked.

"Nothing yet, there's a wall of silence around it." The chief shook his head. "We had a few eyewitness statements taken outside the club but when we re-interviewed them, their memories were blank."

"It sounds like a few phone calls have been made," Alec smiled.

"It does, unfortunately."

The three officers went quiet for a moment. It seemed that both cases were dead in the water until the scientists finished their tests. "If you want to get off for a few hours, I'll let you know when the results come in, Guv," Will said. He was aware that his boss should be at home. The forensic team would be finished soon and it looked like the severed hand was from their victim. The pace of the investigation would accelerate when the results came in. If he was going to go home, he needed to go now.

"Well, I'm going to take you up on that offer and go home to face the music." Alec looked at his watch. It would be hours before any forensics came in and his teams were out looking at the missing persons who matched the age of their victim. He had time to build some bridges at home.

"Is Gail still cracking the whip, Alec?" The chief laughed.

"Don't they always," Alec tried to make light of his domestic situation, but he knew he was in the doghouse. He stood up and walked to the door. "Call me as soon as anything comes in."

"Good luck, Guv," Will laughed and waved. He turned to the chief. "See you later, Sir. I'm going to go to the hotel lodge and take a look around the room if you don't mind."

"Not at all," the chief replied and jokingly saluted. "I am more than happy to leave our mystery hand with you!"

Alec took the stairs down to the car park. He couldn't be doing with making small talk in the elevator. The signal in the car park was poor so he dialled Gail's number on his way down the stairs, but it rang once and then clicked to answer phone. She had 'busy buttoned' his call again. Gail knew it annoyed him when she did that. Alec was stuck between his workload and his responsibilities as a husband. He didn't have a job where things could wait. Evidence disappeared if it wasn't gathered immediately, and criminals disappeared faster still. Over the years, Gail had always been supportive, but recently she had become distant and cold. Alec wished he had a time machine or a stunt double, but deep inside he knew his marriage was in crisis. The sad thing was that his investigation took priority. They always did.

Chapter Eleven

Louise Parker

Paula James turned off the engine and checked her appearance in the mirror. She tied her blonde hair up in a tight bun and clipped it to the back of her head with a black crocodile clip.

"I need to get my roots done on my next day off," she moaned as she touched the widening dark parting on the top of her head.

"Book me in, will you, Paula?" Her partner laughed. "When did you last go?"

"I made detective two years ago and I haven't been to the hairdressers since," she pulled a face in the mirror. "I've done it with Tesco home kits since!" They laughed.

"It's so hard to find the time."

"This is a life style, not a career, but it is what I want to do." When her friends were out enjoying themselves, Paula was usually busy chasing bad guys. Some of them had stopped ringing her altogether. She had had to sacrifice a lot to be a detective. Her relationships rarely lasted more than a few weeks, as she couldn't commit enough of her time to keep her boyfriends interested.

"Nice house," Sharon Gould commented. Sharon held the same rank as Paula. "Let's get this over with."

"What did the Governor say about the ring?" Paula wanted to clarify the latest information they had.

"There was a small gold sovereign on the index finger."

"Well that should help us to narrow it down." Paula opened the door and climbed out of the silver Ford Focus. Sharon followed her and they met at the boot of the car. The driveway was white gravel; it crunched beneath their shoes as they approached the house. It was a red brick building with a slate roof and a three-car garage attached to the left hand side. A weeping willow tree to the left of the front lawn caught their eye. The leaves were gone and the bare branches looked naked without them. "She doesn't have any kids, though?"

"There are none in the missing person's report."

"Who filed it?"

"Her father."

"I like the waterfall," Paula pointed to a feature on their right. Water trickled down a stone gulley into an ornamental pond. As they approached, the water glistened with bright reds and gold. "Look at the size of the Kio-carp."

"They're monsters," Sharon laughed. "I wonder why nobody eats them," she mused.

"You wouldn't get them on your plate."

"I could try. I love fish."

They walked toward the house and Paula guessed it had at least five bedrooms, maybe six. The front door opened before they reached it, and a small man with thinning grey hair greeted them. He was immaculately dressed in a pale grey suit with a silver tie.

"Detective James?" He stepped out of the front door and closed the gap between them. "Is it about Lou? Is there any news?"

Paula held out her right hand. "I'm Detective James, Mr Parker. We spoke on the telephone earlier."

He shook her hand and she noticed his grip was weak and his palm was clammy. The whites of his eyes were red and he looked tired. There were liver spots on his hands and face. Paula put him at about sixty-five.

"It's nice to meet you," he said in a well-educated voice.

"I'm Detective Gould," Sharon introduced herself.

"Hello." He shook her hand. "Is there any news about Lou?"

"Could we talk inside, Mr Parker," Paula smiled and tried to make him relax.

"Yes, sorry. I am forgetting my manners. Please come in." He stepped aside and allowed them to enter his home. They walked into a wide hallway, tiled with polished white marble. A pine staircase led to the upper floor. A large picture window allowed the daylight to flood in. "Come in here, please." He opened a white panelled door and guided them into a long through room, which had double patio doors at one end and a bay window at the other. Well-manicured lawns surrounded the building. Paula wondered how long it would take to cut them. "Please sit down, would you like some tea?"

Paula sat on a black leather armchair, her body sinking into the thick padding. There was a picture of a pretty girl on the coffee table next to her, sitting on a grey pony with an older woman holding the reins. Paula thought the woman looked like the girl's mother.

"Is this your daughter, Mr Parker?" Paula asked. She picked up the heavy silver frame, which contained the photograph. The girl looked like the one in the missing person's picture they had in their file, but younger.

"Yes." He took the picture from her and looked at it. His mind seemed to drift as he stared at it, tears forming in his eyes. "Yes, that's my Lou with her mother. She was only eighteen then. I took it at the stable where she keeps her pony, Yoyo. A silly name for a horse, but she insisted. He is still alive, you know. She rarely visits him nowadays, but he's still there in good health, costs me a fortune in livery bills!" He tried to sound cheery but his eyes said something different. "That's her mother, Gill. She died of breast cancer six years ago. It broke Lou's heart and she was never the same girl after that." This time a tear broke free from his eye and trickled down his cheek. He quickly wiped it away. "Is there any news about Lou?"

"I'm sorry about your wife. We don't have anything new to tell you, Mr Parker, but we need to ask you some questions and look around her room. It could help us find her," Paula lied.

"Look around her room, what for?" Mr Parker looked perturbed.

"We don't know, Mr Parker, but sometimes we find things that may have been overlooked and they lead us to where the missing persons are." Sharon smiled and tried to calm him. "Did Lou have any children of her own?"

"No, why?"

"Just routine, Mr Parker."

"I see, well if you think it might help."

"When did Lou go missing?" Paula checked her details as she spoke.

"Eleven days ago today. She took a shower, got changed and left without saying a word."

"Had you argued, Mr Parker?" Paula asked.

"Yes, constantly since her mother died." Tears filled his eyes again and his voice broke as he explained. "She went off the rails, I'm afraid. Drink and drugs, cocaine, you know how it works; I'm sure, being detectives."

"What did you argue about?"

"Money, as usual." He tutted and rolled his eyes. "I'm a wealthy man, Detective James, and Lou tries to spend my money faster than I can earn it."

"Paula, please call me Paula."

"Paula it is, then, and you are?" He turned to Sharon.

"Sharon."

"Paula and Sharon. I'm Robert, but everyone calls me Bob." He tried to smile again but the pain was still in his eyes.

"You were telling us about the argument, Bob."

"Yes, I was." He walked to the patio doors and looked out at the grass, his hands clasped behind his back. "When Gill died I set up a trust fund for Lou, in case anything happened to me. Everything would go to Lou, of course, but you know how long these things can take, and I didn't want her to struggle while they managed the estate. Lou couldn't cope with her mother's death, she became angry and bitter. She was out partying all the time, drinking herself into all kinds of trouble. Then along came the cocaine and the men. God knows how many different men I've seen creeping out of here in the morning, some days there were more than one."

He turned to face them and he wiped his eyes. There was a painful silence before he continued.

"It was terrible watching my baby girl losing her dignity and self respect. I tried to help her. We went to grief counselling at first, which didn't help her at all. She just became more depressed. The more depressed she became, the more she drank. I sent her to rehab three times in the last two years, but she slipped back into the gutter every time."

"I'm sorry about Lou, Bob. It must have been very difficult for you. What made you report her as missing? Could she have stayed out partying with her friends?" Paula hoped Lou was drunk somewhere, high as a kite on cocaine, but alive. She did not want her to be the woman who had been butchered in Jamaica Street. Robert Parker seemed to be a nice man. Finding out that someone had strung his daughter from the rafters of a derelict building and tortured her to death would break his heart.

"No. You see, she always came home. I never chastised her for bringing men home because it was better than not knowing where she was. It was the lesser evil for me."

"I see. You said you argued about money before she left," Paula prompted him.

"Yes. I found out that she was taking money from her trust fund. She had spent thousands of pounds. I give her a generous allowance every month but she has squandered it on drink and cocaine. Gill would be spinning in her grave if she could see what her precious daughter has become." His voice cracked again and he took a crisp white handkerchief from his trouser pocket and wiped his eyes.

Paula swallowed hard. If he had known why they were visiting him, he wouldn't have said that. His daughter had possibly become the victim in a horrific murder investigation.

"Do you have any recent pictures of Lou?" Paula asked. They wouldn't help in identifying the body, but they might help them to find witnesses who had seen the victim before she was murdered.

"Yes. I'll dig some out for you. I'm sure there are some on a disc we took at Christmas. We managed to spend a few hours together on Christmas day, before she rushed off to a party, of course." He headed for the door, which led into the kitchen. "Would you like some tea while I'm in here?" He called. Paula heard drawers opening as he rummaged for his camera.

"Tea would be good, please, Bob," Paula answered.

"What do you think?" Sharon whispered.

"It doesn't look good given she always came home after a night out. Eleven days is a long time to be out partying." Paula had a bad feeling about it. She stood up and followed Bob into the kitchen. It was a modern design fitted with new appliances that looked unused. "Did Lou have any close friends we could speak to?"

Bob took his camera from a drawer and turned it on. He scrolled through the pictures while he thought about Paula's question.

"Not really. All her close friends from university moved away and the others stopped talking to her when she began behaving badly. Here is a picture of her taken at Christmas." He showed Paula the screen. Louise was a pretty woman with long auburn hair. The same colour as the victim.

"She's a pretty girl." Paula chose her words carefully, making sure she didn't use the past tense. "What about boyfriends?"

"There were many, I'm afraid. Before she left she was seeing a foreign chap, Turkish, I think."

"Do you know his name?"

"Should I be worried, Detective James?" His eyes looked into her, searching for the answer, and the softness in his voice was gone.

"We're just trying to find her, Bob," Paula lied again. She wasn't sure if he could sense there was something wrong, but she couldn't let him know anything about the victim unless they were sure it was her. "Did you know his name?"

"Salim. She called him Sally when she spoke to him on the telephone. I always got the feeling he was supplying her with cocaine. She asked if he was bringing Charlie to the party one night. I didn't think anything of it until I realised she was taking drugs. Then I realised who Charlie was. I felt like a fool, of course. I found some in her handbag once when she left it in the living room."

"Do you mind if I look into her bedroom, Bob?" Sharon was listening to the exchange from the doorway.

"I don't see why not if you think it will help to find her. It's the second bedroom on the left. I haven't touched anything. She was very particular about me going into her room, especially when I'd challenged her about the cocaine in her handbag. She called me a snoop and insisted that I keep out of there."

Sharon went to check the bedroom while Bob made three cups of tea. He looked lost.

"What can you tell me about Salim? She wouldn't be the first woman swept off her feet by a handsome foreigner. Lou might be sat on a beach somewhere sipping cocktails," Paula smiled, but she didn't believe Lou was on a beach. She believed that her mutilated body was lying in the morgue. Bob passed her a mug of tea.

"Maybe she is. That is what I'm hoping, Detective James." His tone changed and he stopped calling Paula by her first name. Maybe he could sense something wasn't right.

"Paula, please."

"Sorry, Paula. I have the feeling that there is more to your enquiry than you are telling me."

"We need to check that we haven't missed anything that will help us to find her. What do you know about Salim?"

"Not much. I never talked to him. He couldn't look me in the eye when we he left in the mornings."

"How did he leave, Bob?"

"Sorry. I don't understand."

"How did he leave the house, taxi, or did he drive?"

"Oh, I see what you mean. He drove a white Porsche of some description. They all look the same to me."

"We'll need to show you some pictures of the different models to see if you can identify what it was. It's important."

"I'm not sure you'll need to do that. He had a private registration plate, SAL 1. I told all this to the investigating officers who took all her details at the time I reported her missing. Why didn't they follow it up?"

"Maybe they hit a dead end, Bob, but we'll double check anyway." Paula sipped her tea and avoided eye contact with him. He was becoming suspicious; she could see it in his eyes. She wasn't sure the investigating officers would have taken Lou's disappearance seriously, as she was drinking, taking drugs and sleeping around. If the preliminary investigations had hit a brick wall, then they would have assumed Lou was partying somewhere.

"Why are you here, Detective?" Bob asked her in a crisp voice. He was regaining control of his faculties. The grief was subsiding momentarily. "You have found someone, haven't you?"

"Bob we have to be sure that we haven't missed anything that will help us in finding Lou. That is why we're here." Paula wanted to ask him about the jewellery, specifically if Lou had worn a sovereign ring. It would be too obvious now. He would realise they were trying to identify a body.

"Paula, could you come here a minute, please," Sharon called down the stairs.

"Excuse me a minute, Bob. She may have found something of use to us." Paula smiled, but it was not returned. Bob sipped his tea and looked out of the window. A feeling of dread was creeping into his guts. Burying his wife had been the hardest thing he had ever done. He wasn't sure he could bury his daughter too.

Paula climbed the pine staircase and headed for the second door on the left. The door was open and Sharon was standing near the bedside cabinet. The bedroom was untidy. There were clothes scattered on the floor. There was an odour of stale cigarettes mixed with perfume.

"What is it?" Paula asked. "He's getting suspicious."

"I think we'd better call the Guv." Sharon pointed to a photograph on the cabinet. It was a picture of Louise in a nightclub somewhere with three friends. She was wearing a black dress and holding a cocktail in her hand. On the index finger of her left hand was a small gold sovereign.

Chapter Twelve

The Oguzhan Cartel

Jessie woke with a start. His skin was damp with sweat, his heart racing. It was three in the afternoon and he was trying to catch up on some sleep. The pain caused by his ears kept him awake despite swallowing boxes of ibuprofen. The hospital had given him some strong painkillers when they discharged him, but they had been gone within days. Every time he moved his head, the pain was unbearable. When he did fall asleep, his dreams became nightmares. The robbery at the poker game haunted him and so did the conversation he had had with his bosses, the Oguzhan family.

The Oguzhan cartel was a branch of the Turkish mafia from Istanbul. The Turkish mafia dominated the world's heroin trade; for nearly four decades, they had processed the raw opiates from the Middle East in clandestine labs. They trafficked eighty percent of the heroin and cocaine that reached Western Europe and the United States. Jessie didn't know much about the top members of the cartel. The 'Babas', or godfathers, were a mysterious and deadly group with connections to the police, the military and the governments of their region. At a historic conclave in Sophia, Bulgaria, the Babas had carved up Europe between them, and the Oguzhan cartel had moved into the United Kingdom. Jessie was trying to clear his head when his mobile rang. He rifled through his pockets looking for the device. The caller was Gus Rickman. He was a handy guy to have on your side and a dangerous enemy too.

"Hi, Gus," Jessie answered. Talking hurt him. Every time he moved his jaw, spikes of lightning flashed in his brain.

"Alright, Jessie?" Gus' gravely tones came through the speaker. "How are you?"

"I'm okay, thanks, considering," Jessie replied bravely. He had never felt worse in his entire life. He was sore and scared.

"Have you heard from Salim?" Gus asked. Word on the street was spreading and the city's jungle drums were beating. No one could believe that mavericks had hit the poker game. It was suicide. Gus wanted to know who had taken his money, but he was also concerned about how the Turks would react to losing their drugs.

"No, nothing," Jessie answered between clenched teeth so that he didn't have to move his jaw.

"What about the Oguzhan family?"

"I had a long conversation on the telephone with one of them," Jessie explained. "I don't know who he was but he was right up his own arse."

"Salim's family were the first of that bunch to come here, Jessie." Gus sounded serious. "There are thousands of the slippery bastards here now, but his side of the family are the real power mongers."

"I thought they were all loosely connected," Jessie said, "but I didn't realise he was that important." Jessie swallowed hard. If Gus was trying to help or cheer him up, then he was failing miserably.

"He is the main Baba's grandson," Gus explained. He had done his homework. "During the nineties, they were the biggest firm down south, unrivalled in London, but in recent times, there's war with the Kurdish and Albanian mobs."

"They're all fucking lunatics, right, Gus?" Jessie tried to laugh but it hurt too much.

"Dangerous lunatics, Jessie," Gus warned him. "The Green Lane area of London has been a blood bath for the last decade. Most of the killings are attributed to the Oguzhan clan."

"Great," Jessie moaned. His head was banging. "How the fuck did I get involved with this lot?" The Turks had gradually moved north, buying nightclubs to front their drug businesses. Jessie had been struggling financially and they had made him an offer he couldn't refuse, paying way over the real estate value of the club to get a foothold in the city. The deal had seemed perfect at first, especially when they offered Jessie the opportunity to remain the manager and co-owner of the business.

"How involved are you, Jessie?" Gus growled.

"What do you mean?" Jessie gasped. "In the robbery?"

"You tell me," Gus replied calmly. "Were you involved?"

"No. I fucking was not, Gus." Jessie stood up and his head felt like it might explode. "They cut my ears off!"

"Maybe that wasn't part of the deal."

"What?" Jessie sat down again.

"Maybe they did that to make it look real," Gus said. "I wonder if you and Salim set it all up."

"No way, Gus," Jessie cried. "I get on with Salim, but I don't get involved in their shit."

"Okay, Jessie," Gus said. "You tell me how involved you are with the Turks and then we can take it from there."

"Look, I was on my arse, Gus," Jessie sighed. He could sense the underlying venom in Gus' voice. It wasn't just the Turks he needed to worry about. "Salim called me out of the blue and offered me stupid money for the club and he offered me a job running the shithole!"

"Okay, I'm listening."

"I soon realised the deal was flawed, when he asked me to hide a shitload of heroin and cocaine." Jessie's throat was dry as a bone. He needed a drink. "I flipped at first but he said that if I didn't do it, I would be shot dead and so would Rose. He said it as if he was asking me the time. Cool, as you like."

"Sounds like a good incentive to help out," Gus said sarcastically.

"I just kept my mouth shut and did as I was told," Jessie explained. "They paid me good money and I'm retiring in a few years. It was easier to keep my head down."

"What did they say on the telephone?" Gus seemed calmer.

"Well, I explained that the fire had caused substantial damage to the nightclub, but the insurance companies would pay to rebuild it eventually, and they were not too bothered about it." Jessie paused. "Then I had to tell them about the robbery and the drugs. He was livid about losing five kilos of cocaine and I was terrified that they'd kill me. I thought that the fire might conceal the robbery but it didn't. The contents of the safe, some passports and other documents were untouched by the fire and the drugs were gone."

"What did they say?" Gus asked. "What exactly did they say, Jessie?"

"He asked if I had heard from Salim Oguzhan. I told him that he had disappeared and wasn't answering his mobile. He didn't say much about Salim."

"Salim is an important member of the cartel." Gus reinforced what he had said earlier. "I can't understand why you didn't get more of a reaction."

"I don't know. I asked the family for the chance to explain what had happened at the poker game and they told me to expect a visit soon."

"What did he mean by a visit?" Gus asked.

"I don't know, Gus," Jessie sighed. He sat back on the bed and pulled the quilt over him. It was cool and there was a breeze coming from downstairs. "He just said to expect a visit from the family to explain to them what happened." Jessie wasn't sure what a visit entailed and he was anxious.

"You need to be careful what you say, Jessie," Gus said after a few seconds silence.

"What do you mean?"

"I mean that the biggest drug dealers in the country have had their stash nicked and their grandson is missing," Gus sighed. "They will be looking for someone to blame, and if they look in the wrong place, then you could have more than your ears to worry about, understand, Jessie?"

"Yes, I think so," Jessie replied quietly.

"Keep me informed, Jessie." He heard the line go dead. It was obvious that Gus Rickman was distancing himself from the situation. Jessie wondered whom he could turn to if he needed help. He threw back the quilt and swung his legs over the edge of the bed. A bolt of pain scythed through his brain as he sat up and he groaned. He waited for the pain to subside before standing up. Jessie caught a glimpse of his reflection in the mirror. A thick bandage swathed his head; the gauze dressings over his ears looked comical. There were dark stains on the dressings where blood had seeped through the stitches.

"Bloody idiot," he grumbled at his reflection. "You should have given him the combination the first time he asked." He wrestled a pair of black trousers on and then grabbed a cardigan off the end of the bed. Jessie hated cardigans, but he couldn't pull anything over his head. It was too painful. He shouted downstairs as he dressed. "Put the kettle on, Rose."

Rose and he had married twenty-five years earlier in South Wales. They had met at a rugby game between Pontypool and Cardiff and married a year later. Jessie had been a keen rugby player back then, and he had been handsome despite his broken nose and cauliflower ears. Rose had fallen for him immediately. Now he didn't have all of his ears. The man he saw in the mirror looked old and tired. They had worked in the license trade all through their marriage, running various pubs before they had moved into the nightclub business. Things had been good at first, but the breweries had begun to push landlords' margins to the limit, and combined with the smoking ban it had been the death knell for thousands of pubs and clubs. Jessie was a scallywag. He wasn't a villain or a gangster, but he liked to mingle in their company. There was always the odd deal floating around when he mixed with people like that, and that was what had kept them afloat for years until he had sold the club to the Turks. Now he wished he hadn't, but it was too late for hindsight.

"Rose, put the kettle on, darling!" He shouted again. She didn't answer. Jessie thought she might have nipped out to the shops while he was sleeping. As long as she didn't buy any more handbags, he thought. She had hundreds of handbags, half of which she never used once they were taken out of the box. "Rose, are you there, darling?" There was still a touch of the valleys in his voice.

A breeze blew up the stairs as he walked down them, keeping sudden movements to a minimum. "Rose." He stopped halfway down. Something was moving in the living room, but the door was closed and he could not see inside. "Rose?" There was nothing but silence. He felt a breeze again and a shiver ran through him. "Rose." Silence answered him.

Jessie wasn't sure if it was his imagination running away with him, but he felt as if something was wrong. He set off and walked down the stairs slowly. When he cleared the landing, he leaned over the banister and peered into the kitchen. Another bolt of pain shot through his head. "Shit!" He moaned, pressing his hands to his ears until the pain subsided. "Rose, are you there, darling?" The kitchen was empty. The backdoor was open, but everything was where it should be. The kettle was switched on and reaching boiling point, and there were two cups placed next to the appliance waiting to be filled up with hot water. The fridge door was ajar. That was unusual. Rose often scolded him for leaving the fridge door open while he put milk in their tea. "Rose!" He called her name again. Silence. He reached the bottom of the stairs and put his hand on the balustrade as he turned toward the kitchen. The kettle was boiling, steam gushing out of the spout. It clicked loudly as it switched off. Jessie felt like something very bad was about to happen. He didn't know why, but he felt that something was wrong. Maybe she had nipped out to the bin or something. "Rose."

There was a thud in the living room. Jessie stopped next to the door and listened. He reached down and touched the brass handle. It felt cold. His heart was pounding and he held his breath as he twisted the handle, but he didn't push the door open. Jessie changed his mind, let go of the handle and walked into the kitchen instead, instinctively closing the fridge door as he went by. The backyard was empty, she wasn't out there. He opened the cupboard under the sink and picked up a claw hammer before returning to the living room door. He hid his revolver at the club. He never brought it home. Rose didn't like guns. Jessie took a deep breath and swallowed as he twisted the handle and pushed the door open. The room was long and wide and the door was set in the middle. He quickly looked left and right, but the room was empty. Today's newspaper was folded neatly on the beige armchair where he had left it earlier. Rose's pink slippers were side by side on the floor in front of the settee. A clock on the wall ticked loudly just as it had for years. Everything was normal.

The living room door slammed into him with enough force to knock him off his feet. Jessie cracked his head on the doorframe as he fell and the searing pain from his ears made him feel like his head would burst. He dropped the hammer and fell to his knees as the door slammed into his head again. A blinding flash of pain exploded in his brain like a giant camera had gone off in his mind. The door swung again, trapping his head between it and the frame. He cried out and tried to stand but a blow to the back of his head forced him back down again. As darkness flooded his mind, he felt strong hands dragging him across the carpet, the rough fibres burning the skin on his back. His head bounced off the floor, the pain in his ears unbearable. Jessie's mind shut down. The pain was more than his brain could stand.

Chapter Thirteen

MIT

Alec was halfway through a chicken salad that his wife had prepared for him when his Blackberry began to vibrate. He turned the ringtone off while they ate. The atmosphere was frosty and Gail had not spoken more than a few words to him since he had arrived. His mother-in-law was lecturing him on the subject of work-life balance. Apparently, he neglected her daughter and prioritised his job. She was right, but Alec didn't need to hear it from her. To top it all, the chicken salad was not chicken. It was chicken substitute, which tasted nothing like chicken. Alec decided to eat it and say nothing. Things were bad enough as they were without insulting the salad. He could call at the sandwich shop on his way back to the station. It was open all day long.

"Are you listening to me?" Marjorie tapped a wrinkled finger on the table. She was pushing eighty-five and gave no impression that she was about to slow down yet. Alec ignored her. He glanced at her neck and decided she looked more like a turkey every day.

"Excuse me. I need to take this call." Alec picked up his plate and walked into the kitchen. It was the opportunity he needed to escape Marjorie's droning voice, plus he wanted to scrape the salad into the bin.

"Can't it wait until we've finished eating?" Gail called after him.

"Sorry, but it's important." He looked at the screen. It was Will Naylor.

"It's always important, Alec. It's always more important than me." He heard her parting shot across the bows and it stung. He grimaced as he answered the phone.

"Hi, Will. What's up?"

"We've had some forensic results back."

"Good, about time. What have we learned?" Alec opened the lid of the pedal bin and scraped the remainder of his lunch into it. He rearranged the garbage to hide the evidence from his wife.

"The forensic boys found a dozen different prints in the hotel room. We've run them against our files and one of them belongs to a local man with a record, Patrick Lloyd."

"The name rings a bell."

"He's a small time crook; we know him from the Bluebell estate. Uniform lifted him two years back over the murder of a drug dealer on his estate, Jacky Benjamin. They couldn't make it stick."

"I remember it. Benjamin was badly beaten and tortured before he died, right?"

"That's right. They tortured him with a steam iron. The perpetrator cleaned down the house after the murder. Forensics found nothing they could use. They didn't find any money or drugs in the house and it was written off as a local gang feud. Uniform arrested Lloyd weeks later when a witness identified him as a man he had seen walking away from the house in the early hours of the morning, but the witness disappeared before Lloyd could be charged."

"He walked away from it, didn't he?"

"That's the one, Guv."

"We need to know where he is and who he's been working with since then."

"We're on it," Will replied. "He's not at the same address anymore, we've checked. The team are looking through every database available. If he's still around, we'll find him."

"Have you pulled his file from the Benjamin case?"

"Yes, Guv," Will replied. "I am looking at it now."

"What do we know about him?"

"He's ex-army, discharged five years ago for an alleged assault on his superior officer. He appealed and got a large compensation pay off. We only have a summary of his army record here. Since then he has been in the frame for a few grievous charges, a common assault, and he was questioned about the murder of Benjamin, but nothing has stuck. He has never been charged with anything."

"Any sexual assaults on his file?"

"Not here, Guv, but we're checking back through other forces too. His army record was clean apart from the incident he was discharged for, but it is only a summary."

"It's a big step from a few minor assaults to torturing a woman to death, Will."

"I agree, but his superior officer was a woman. It maybe something or it may be nothing. According to the autopsy report, the dealer, Benjamin, was systematically beaten to death over a period of hours. If he was responsible for killing him, then it's not beyond belief that he could be involved in our murder. I'm having his army records sent over to us."

"We'll see what the MOD has on him, but until we've identified the victim we're stuffed."

"Good news there. We've indentified the girl, Guv."

"Is it a positive?"

"Yes, there's no doubt about it."

"Why didn't you say?" Alec wanted coffee.

"I was getting around to it, Guv." Will laughed at his boss's impatience. "The results all dropped in at the same time. We may have another suspect to look at too," Will added.

"Okay, sorry, let's hear it." Alec switched the kettle on and grabbed a coffee mug. He needed to get back to the station but he would have to wait until he had heard all the results. He could work through them in his mind on the way.

"The victim is Louise Parker. She was twenty-eight years of age, a graduate from Chester University. She lived at home with her father, Robert Parker. He's a retired property developer. He reported his daughter missing eleven days ago when she failed to come home after a night out."

"Has he been informed?" Alec opened the cupboard and reached for the coffee. His wife bought decaffeinated coffee as part of their healthy eating regime but Alec threw the granules into the bin each time and replaced them with the real thing. She would never notice the difference. He twisted the lid and spooned two heaped spoonfuls of the real granules into the cup.

"Paula and Sharon are bringing him in, Guv. He's insisting that he wants to see the body."

"What have they told him?"

"They've told him everything we know."

"Make sure they look after him. There is no way he can see his daughter in that state. Carry on."

"Louise Parker didn't have any children, but Mr Parker told us his daughter had come off the rails. She was drinking heavily and taking cocaine, but she always returned home at night. When she didn't return, he reported her missing. Paula and Sharon followed up on the missing persons and visited the Parker residence. They found a picture of her, Guv. She had long auburn hair and a sovereign ring. Bloods and DNA tests are in. The victim is Louise Parker."

"That's good work, Will." He poured the water into his mug and added semi skimmed milk. He wanted to add two spoonfuls of sugar but that was unhealthy, apparently. He had asked his wife to buy sweeteners but she had informed him they were carcinogenic. Alec carried a tube of them in his jacket pocket covertly and he sneaked two tablets into his brew. "What else do we know?"

"Louise had a boyfriend, Salim Oguzhan." Alec was familiar with the Oguzhan family. The MIT had investigated them many times over the years. They were a powerful outfit with their fingers in drugs, arms and prostitution. Their power base was London, but they were expanding into every major city. The police linked them to a number of murders and disappearances over the previous few years but there wasn't enough evidence to press charges. Witnesses had a habit of vanishing.

"Bloody hell," Alec gasped. He slurped some of the coffee while he digested the news. "Salim Oguzhan. Now that is interesting. He owns Connections nightclub, right?"

"Exactly. His name is on the deeds and he employs Jessie as the licensee."

"We know he isn't at the top of the Oguzhan family though, he was financed to buy that building."

"That's what I said, Guv. He's the grandson of the main man in London, Zamir Oguzhan. We're trying to track Salim down, but it looks like he hasn't been seen for a couple of weeks. He disappeared around the same time Louise Parker was murdered."

"Where does he live?"

"He has a house in Woolton, on Gatacre Brow."

"Nice." Alec slurped his coffee again. The properties in that area were worth millions.

"He's married with three children, Guv, but his family live in Turkey," Will added.

"We need to talk to him, rapid," Alec said.

"We have a uniformed unit there in case he turns up."

"Have you applied for a warrant to search his house?"

"Smithy is at the courts now. We should have it within the hour."

"Good. I need you to call Chief Carlton."

"Why, Guv?" Will asked. "What are you thinking?"

"Ask him if he's had any contact with Salim since the fire at the club and see what his investigation turned up on him."

"Do you think there's a connection with Connections?" Will joked.

"Funny, I can't see how but the chief may have had some communication with him. He might know where he is."

"It could all be a coincidence," Will mused, but he didn't think it was a coincidence and he could sense that Alec didn't either.

"Something happened at the club before the fire." Alec swallowed some more coffee. "I want to know what it was."

"Okay, Guv." Will agreed. They needed to know what had happened before the fire had started.

"How long was the victim involved with Salim?"

"Mr Parker wasn't sure, but he estimated it was about three months. He gave us Salim's private registration plate. That's how we traced him."

"Is there any sign of his motor?" Alec asked.

"No, Guv. There's no sign of him or the Porsche. We're trying to get hold of the manager of the club, Jessie James, but he's not answering his telephone. A uniformed unit called at his address, but there was nobody home. We'll keep trying."

"I don't like where this investigation is taking us, Will." Alec slurped on the hot coffee. He leaned against the cupboards and reached for the biscuit tin. He pulled the lid off with his free hand. Empty. She must have cleaned the tin out and left it empty. No more chocolate Hobnobs? This health kick was going too far.

"Do you think Salim was involved in her murder?"

"I can't rule anything out. There's a reason why he's disappeared and we need to know what that is."

"If it was a domestic that got out of hand or a crime of passion, fair enough, but the level of violence rules against that."

"True, but he vanished about the same time as the murder was committed, so where is he?"

"Why would Salim Oguzhan do that to his girlfriend? The guy is loaded and could take his pick from a string of bimbos; I can't see the motive." Will knew they were missing something.

"Who said he did kill her?" Alec sighed. "The fire at the club wasn't on my radar until now, Will, but now it has to be."

"I agree, Guv, but what have we really got so far?"

"Salim Oguzhan owned the club. He employed Jessie as his manager and license holder. There were reports of gunshots and an explosion before the fire spread, and Jessie was minus the tops of his ears. Combine that with the disappearance of Salim and the discovery of his girlfriend, who was murdered, and we have a big fat nothing." Alec paused and thought for a second. "The only thread between the two is Salim and torture. Whoever cut off Jessie's ears wanted something. Either it was a punishment, or someone interrogated him. The Parker girl was tortured to death and the bloodstains in the factory unit indicated that others were tortured. There is a link but I can't see it yet. We need to know what happened in that nightclub, Will."

"The chief said no one at the poker game would talk. They refused to say anything." Will said.

"What about Jessie?"

"He made a no comment statement with a solicitor present."

"So there was no crime reported?"

"No, Guv."

"Pull them all in, Will. I want everyone from that night brought in and interviewed." Alec swallowed another mouthful of the hot liquid. "This is no longer about a fire or an assault. I'm convinced it is linked to our murder investigation. Bring them in, run thorough checks on their motors, tax, insurance, and the works. Get uniform to crawl all over them and put them under pressure until they realise it will be easier to tell us what happened at the club than to remain silent."

"Okay. You're the boss, but I can't see the chief being happy if we run all over his investigation."

"Tough. They are not investigating it anymore, Will. A room full of villains playing poker, gunshots, a fire and the manager gets his ears sliced off. If no one makes a statement then it's just another chorus of gangster's paradise, right?"

"Maybe that's all there is to it, Guv," Will said cautiously. The young detective was ambitious and he didn't want to rock the boat. He had damaged his reputation as a first class detective by making indiscretions in his personal life. He was a player, but he'd played with the wrong women and wrecked several marriages. Will couldn't afford to rock the boat with the senior hierarchy. Alec Ramsay would not be around to babysit his career forever.

"Maybe, but I want to know what happened that night. Call it a hunch if you like, but I believe it's connected. I don't know how, but I think it is. I think Salim Oguzhan is the key. When you bring them in, I want our detectives to hold the interviews. You and I will take Jessie." Alec poured the dregs of his coffee into the sink. "I am on my way in."

He ended the call and looked out of the window. Calderstones Park spread out before him. There were wide grassy spaces and a huge boating lake. It had been raining for the last week but the sun was out for a while and people made the most of the warmth. There were families sat on the grass eating picnics and couples walking hand in hand on the winding paths, which dissected the park.

"What have you done with your lunch?" His wife came into the kitchen and her voice disturbed his thoughts.

"Sorry, I was miles away then." He managed a smile but his mind was on the case.

"Did you throw it in the bin?"

"I finished it, Gail."

"Liar."

"Sorry, but I wasn't that hungry and I have to get back to the station." Alec leaned to grab her hand but she pulled away.

"I'm leaving, Alec." She opened the dishwasher and slammed her plate into it noisily. "I'll go to mum's for a while."

Alec frowned and sighed. He felt like he'd been punched in the guts. "Look, I'm sorry about this, but it is a big case and I have to be there. We found a young woman tortured to death and the evidence at the scene suggests there are more victims somewhere."

She looked thoughtful. She didn't look mad or angry. She didn't look sad either. "There will always be another young woman murdered, Alec. There will always be another big case. I don't blame you. I just can't spend my life alone anymore."

"We'll talk later. I have to brief the team on the forensic results. As soon as the briefing is over I'll come straight home and we can talk, yes?" He kissed her forehead and touched her cheek with the back of his hand. Her eyes seemed glazed and there was a faraway look to them. She was already gone. She had been gone for a long time.

Chapter Fourteen

Jessie James

When Jessie opened his eyes, he was in his armchair. His hands and feet were tied with thick black duct tape and he couldn't move. A slim built man in his fifties was sitting across the room from him on the settee. He was wearing faded blue jeans and white trainers. His skin was dark and wrinkled by the sun and his stubble greyed by age.

"Where is Rose?" Jessie croaked. Blood tricked down his neck from his left ear. The beating had burst the stitches. "What have you done to her?"

"She's with friends of mine. They're looking after her." The man said. His voice was thick and his accent guttural. Jessie knew he was from the Oguzhan family.

"Don't hurt her. She has nothing to do with this, you bastard!" Tears filled Jessie's eyes. This was his worst nightmare come true. He loved Rose, but he was helpless. Anger and frustration boiled inside him.

"You lost something that was valuable to us. Now we have something that is precious to you. When you return our property, we will return your wife to you. Does that seem fair to you?"

"I didn't lose your drugs. They were stolen."

"They were in your care. You lost them."

"I don't know who took them. How can I return them? I don't know who took them."

"I suggest you find out." The man pointed a nicotine-stained finger at him.

"How can I?" Jessie tried to move, but the Turk had fastened him tightly. Pins and needles were creeping from his feet up his legs.

"It was an inside job?"

"It must be. They knew the code to the safe."

"Who knew the code?" The Turk stood up and took out a cigarette. He put the packet back into the pocket of his grey leather bomber jacket. It looked too big for him and the sleeves covered his hands so that only his fingers showed.

"Me and Sally, that's it." A trickle of blood ran over his collarbone and tickled his skin. "No one knew about the safe beneath the ice machine except us."

"Have you heard from Salim?" The Turk sucked on the filter and swallowed the smoke.

"No. Not for nearly two weeks."

"When did you last talk to him?"

"The week before last." Jessie tried to remember the exact day, but couldn't. He drank with his customers most nights and the mornings were usually a haze.

"What did you speak about?" The Turk narrowed his eyes.

"I don't know, work stuff," Jessie moaned. He was in pain and panicking about Rose. He knew the Turks would kill her without thinking about it. It was their way.

"What stuff, Jessie?" He pushed. "It is very important to your wife that we recover our property."

"Don't hurt her!" Jessie shouted and saliva sprayed from his lips as they quivered. If he could free his hands, he would throttle the Turk to death. Jessie was losing it and he raised his voice again. "Work stuff, for God's sake. Beer orders, cellar stocks, how many fucking peanuts we had left, does it matter?"

"Yes, it matters." The Turk paused for a moment. "Was Salim alone?"

"When?"

"When you last spoke to him."

"Yes, but...." Jessie paused. "He was in a rush. He said he had someone waiting in the car."

"Who?"

"I don't know, his girlfriend maybe. Does any of that matter?"

"Obviously not to you, maybe that's why you gave away our property?" The Turk leaned closer and his eyes were dark and cold.

"Drugs!" Jessie shouted. "Stop saying property like you're businessmen working hard for a living. Someone walked into your nightclub and stole your fucking drugs. They cut my ears off to get into your safe where Salim kept them."

The Turk stayed quiet for a moment. Jessie was becoming irrational because of the pain. "Only you and Salim knew that the safe was under the ice machine?" He lowered his voice to try to calm the Welshman down.

"Yes. The robbers didn't know the code to that one. That's why they cut my ears off," Jessie stressed. "I refused to tell them the code and they cut off my fucking ear. When I refused again they cut off the other one."

"But you told them the code in the end, yes?"

"What else could I do?" Jessie shouted and tears rolled down his face. "They were cutting my ears off! I tried, I really did."

"Maybe you did. Maybe you could have tried harder." The Turk blew smoke from his nostrils and turned away from Jessie. "Nobody else in that room could have known about the drugs?"

"No. Not unless Sally told them." Jessie was saying what he had thought all along. Salim was missing and the drugs were gone. It couldn't be a coincidence. He must have told someone the drugs were there. Jessie was many things, but disloyal or stupid were not amongst them. He had hated Salim keeping smack in the club, but he would never have told anyone they were there, not even Rose. Especially not Rose.

"Are you insinuating that Salim betrayed his family for five kilos of cocaine?" The Turk turned quickly and leaned over Jessie. He sneered in his face. "He's a wealthy man, why would he steal from his family?"

"How else could they have known about the safe?" Jessie said sheepishly. He didn't want to upset the Turk anymore than he had already. He wanted Rose back safe and then they were out of this game for good. Things were getting out of hand and they were getting too old.

"How else could they have known, Jessie? That is why I'm here, to find out. You do not understand how we work. Salim is a grandchild of our Baba. They would die for each other before they would betray each other's trust."

"I know all that shit, but no one else knew about the drugs, I swear they didn't."

"Did you know Salim has a wife and children?" The Turk smiled for the first time, but there was no warmth in it.

"Yes, I've seen pictures of them." Jessie nodded and bolts of pain shot through his brain. His painkillers were wearing off.

"They live in Turkey most of the time, you know?"

"I know."

"Did you know that they were here visiting?" The Turk raised his eyebrows.

"No, he didn't mention it."

"His grandfather brought them over in an attempt to stop Salim fucking around so much," the Turk shook his head in disgust. "His generation has no respect for family values."

"I didn't know they were here."

"If Salim betrayed us, then his family would be slaughtered in front of him and buried in the sand." The Turk smiled again and shrugged. That was just the way it was.

"He must have told the men that robbed the club," Jessie sighed. He had no other explanation.

"He would not risk his family. If he was in on the robbery, then why didn't he give them the safe code and let them take the drugs when the club was empty?" The Turk relaxed and pulled on his cigarette again.

"I don't know. That bit doesn't make sense. They knew the combination for the floor safe where the stake money was."

"Which only contained the poker money, right?"

"Right." Jessie nodded.

"Then it is obvious." The Turk walked to the window.

"Not to me it isn't." Jessie shook his head and then wished he hadn't. Pain flashed through his head. "I don't get it."

"You said the men knew the safe code already?"

"Yes. They asked me for it and I refused. I gave them the wrong code to make them set the alarms off, but they knew it was a trick and they cut my ear off."

"Because they knew the real code?"

"Yes." Jessie was confused.

"We will assume Salim gave them that code for now. Men that cut ears off can be very persuasive. There is only one way they got that information from Salim." He looked at Jessie and stroked the bristles on his chin. "He's missing."

"You think they tortured him?" Jessie felt sick. What did they do to him to make him talk? "Oh Jesus, I didn't think of that."

"What happened next?"

"Then they asked me for the other code and I refused. They cut my other ear off."

"Then what?"

"Then I was bleeding on the floor and the others said they would square things with you if I gave them the code."

"Who said that?" The Turk raised his eyebrows.

"Why?" Jessie hesitated. He hadn't mentioned that Leon and Jinx said they would speak to the Turks. Now he wasn't sure if should have said anything at all.

"Who said they would square things with us if you gave them the code?"

"I can't remember who said it. I was hurt and bleeding," Jessie lied, and the Turk could sense that he was protecting someone.

"You know some of my friends like British women very much. I'm sure they would like your wife if I introduced them to her." He didn't smile but he looked amused as realisation hit Jessie. "She's hardly in a position to say no, is she?"

"You bastard!" Jessie struggled against his binds. "If you lay one finger on her, I'll kill you!"

"Will you?" The Turk stubbed the cigarette out on the fireplace leaving an ugly black smudge on the lacquered wood. "I doubt it. Who told you that they would square it with us if you gave them the drugs?"

Jessie closed his eyes and sighed. He had no choice. "Leon Tanner and Jinx Cotton, but they didn't mean anything by it. They meant that they would tell you the drugs were stolen, and I gave them the code because they tortured me."

"They said that they would square things with us, if you gave them our drugs, yes?"

"Yes, but–"

"But nothing, Jessie. I want to know who robbed the club. I want to know where Salim and his family are, and someone from that room knows the answers. Your friends persuaded you to give up our drugs. Now they owe you for that."

"They are not my friends. Look, they're not going to give me that kind of money. They meant they would tell you what happened, that's all!" Jessie whined. He wished he hadn't said anything.

"You have forty-eight hours to return our property or come up with the equivalent amount of cash, plus the information that I require. If you don't, I'll give your wife to the men to play with before they bury you both in concrete. Do you understand me?"

Jessie nodded his head slowly and stared into space as the Turk cut him free. A tear ran from his eye and mingled with the blood from his ear.

"Salim and his children are very valuable to my employer, very valuable indeed, understand?" The Turk squeezed his cheeks together painfully. "Forty-eight hours, Jessie."

Chapter Fifteen

The Gecko: *The Past*

The Gecko had had a career as a military intelligence officer. He was a recognized expert in the fields of human intelligence, strategic interrogation, special operations, and special survival training for the military. He had been one of the most effective and prolific interrogators in the Department of Defence. He had served as an interrogator and senior advisor to a special operations task force during the operations Just Cause, Desert Shield, Desert Storm, and Iraqi Freedom. He had begun as a normal family man with a career in the military, but that had soon changed. He had become an intelligence expert with a family somewhere at home that he didn't see. His work had taken him all over the world, and over time, it had eroded his morals and numbed his emotions. When he returned home on leave, he was cold and distracted. He had nothing in common with his wife or his teenage son anymore and he spent his time at home working on his laptop or locked in his study whispering down the telephone in Arabic. He had travelled on more than twenty extraordinary rendition flights to over a dozen countries. During the 'war on terror', normal extradition had been useless and more extreme methods had been needed to extract information from terrorist sympathisers. Enemy suspects had been kidnapped, stripped, given an enema and drugged. Intelligence officers had then bundled them onto an unscheduled flight to a country where torture was an acceptable means of extracting information, and then they had been questioned. The Gecko had been classed as an advisor.

At first, Gecko had advised the foreign interrogators. He would compile the questions for them to ask, and make an educated decision as to whether the answers given were the truth. Information gleaned under torture was often inaccurate. As time went by, he had become more involved in the interrogation process, developing new torture techniques and discarding the ones, which did not work. Eventually the subjects had become nothing more than experiments to him. Their pain and fear had no impact on him. Their screams and pleas for mercy were part of the job. They were no longer humans, and deep inside, neither was he. There were doors in his brain, which had closed and never opened again.

When he left the military, he found it difficult to adjust to civilian life. Some of his victims haunted his dreams. Foreign regimes still paid him thousands of pounds for advice on interrogation and training, but he couldn't remember the person he was outside of the military. The man who had married his wife and fathered a baby boy was gone forever. He couldn't find any paternal instincts inside himself and his relationship with his wife had gone. She had begun drinking heavily while he was serving abroad and her dependency deepened when he left the service. Wine at first, but then whisky and vodka replaced Merlot and Shiraz. When she drank, she argued with him. She ridiculed him about his prowess in the bedroom. They rarely had sex and when they did, it was quick and mechanical, which left her frustrated and unsatisfied. She felt as if she had wasted her life while he had lived his in the army. Her youth was gone and she resented his career. Now he was retired, but he still wasn't interested in his family. All those years waiting for him to come home had been fruitless. Her resentment turned to anger and hatred. As her drinking worsened, her mental health deteriorated and she turned to drugs. Prescription drugs at first. She swallowed Valium, Prozac and an assortment of painkillers. When her doctor refused to increase her dosage, she found a street dealer who was happy to supply her with whatever she wanted. Her dealer could get his hands on anything she wanted as long as she had the money. The problem was she ran out of money. She began to steal her husband's cash cards, but he noticed that money was going missing and he put a stop to it. He cancelled her credit cards and did all the shopping himself in an effort to wean her off the drink and drugs. She sold her jewellery and pawned anything of value to buy her drugs, but eventually she ran out of options. One day after begging her supplier for valium, he offered her alternative methods of payment, and she began having sex with him and some of his clients in exchange for drugs. It wasn't long before she was chasing the dragon to blot out the memories of the men who had used her body. The more vile memories she had, the more heroin she needed. The combination of booze and drugs made her aggressive and violent at home. Her anger turned towards her husband and their son, Nate.

Nate was sixteen when his father left the forces, and he was looking forward to spending more time with his dad. Nate was a keen sportsman and a good footballer. He played for a local youth team in a Sunday league. His ambition was to score the winner with his dad watching on the touchline, but it was not an ambition he would achieve. When he left the intelligence services, his father showed no interest in his son and he seldom spoke to him. Nate felt his father was a stranger to him and his mother. He could see his mother was going downhill. She looked high as a kite most of the time and Nate started to notice bruises on her arms and legs. He suspected his father was hitting her, but he could not have been further from the truth. The bruises were from the men that abused her body in payment for her drugs. Nate decided to ask his mother if she had been beaten; this was the first time his mother ever slapped him, and he was shocked. His parents were not perfect but they had never hit him.

He had no idea why she had hit him and the next day when he asked her about it she blushed and apologised. She said she couldn't remember it. Three hours later, she was paralytic and she launched a dinner plate at him, which missed his head by inches. When his father heard the smash, he came out of his study to investigate the noise. He looked at his wife and studied her with a blank expression on his face.

"What's wrong with her?" Nate asked his father. "She's behaving really strangely."

"She's taking opiates," his father replied. He had seen the signs of drug abuse for years. Her pupils were tiny black dots and she could hardly speak sometimes. Many of his interrogation subjects were drugged with opiates to make them talk. He could recognise it a mile away.

"What do you mean, Dad?" Nate asked.

"Your mother is using heroin, Nate."

"I don't believe you." Nate shook his head in disbelief.

"I'll deal with her," Gecko said in a strange monotone voice. Nate couldn't tell what his father did next, but it looked like he applied a type of wristlock. He led his wife upstairs with the same blank stare in his eyes, and although she struggled, she couldn't resist the lock. Nate never saw her alive again.

Chapter Sixteen

Jinx Cotton

Jinx dropped the bar onto the stand and sat up. That had been his last set of bench press for the day and his vest was soaked with sweat. He tensed his muscles in the mirror and they knotted beneath his black skin. He was in good shape. Jinx had opened the gym two years earlier for the unemployed kids on the estate to use. There were some paying customers, but the majority of members were non-profit clients. The gym was a real hardcore bodybuilders' paradise. It was more like a scrap yard than a gymnasium. A dog-eared piece of A4 paper was pinned to the wall above the full-length mirror. It warned the clientele that spitting on the floor 'would not be tolerated'. It was early in the morning and there was only one other member training. Jinx grabbed a towelling jacket and pulled it over his huge shoulders. The gym was on the first floor of a converted warehouse. Jinx could hear a single set of footsteps coming up the staircase. He was surprised when Jessie turned the corner at the top of the stairs.

"Jinx," he said. He offered his hand. Jessie looked tired and worried.

"Alright, Jessie, I didn't know you were into weightlifting." Jinx squeezed his hand and smiled. "How's the ears?" He wiped sweat from his brow with a white towel. It was a stupid question, but Jinx didn't really know what to say.

"Don't ask. I need to talk to you, Jinx." Jessie lowered his voice despite the fact there was no one in earshot. "I'm in trouble."

Jinx nodded his head slowly. He wasn't sure what Jessie wanted from him, but he liked him enough to give him a listen. That couldn't hurt. "Come into the office." Jinx led the way down a narrow corridor, which smelled of sweat and tiger balm. He opened the door with a Yale key. He pushed the door open and allowed Jessie in first. Jinx had manners. He was a tough man with a dark side, but he believed that manners and respect were priceless.

"Sit down. Do you want a drink?" Jinx asked. He opened a glass-fronted fridge and took out a tin of protein drink. He ripped of the ring-pull and took a mouthful.

"No thanks. I'm okay." Jessie twisted uncomfortably in his seat. He had dark shadows beneath his eyes and the whites were bloodshot.

"How can I help?" Jinx sat opposite him and smiled again. Jessie looked nervous and frightened. The dark circles beneath his eyes made him look like he had been crying. Jinx looked at the clock on the wall and made a mental note of the time. He had a busy day ahead. There was no time to waste.

"The Turks have kidnapped Rose." Jessie leaned forward and put his elbows on his knees. His hands cradled his head. "They've taken her and I have forty-eight hours to return their drugs or they will kill us both."

"Who told you this?"

"I don't know his name, but he's one of their family. He's way above Sally."

"Have you spoken to Sally?" Jinx knew they had a decent working relationship. They got on together.

"He's disappeared," Jessie shrugged. "I can't track him down and he isn't answering his phone."

"Sounds to me like he was in on the robbery." Jinx emptied his protein drink and tossed the tin into the bin with a clatter. He had people making enquiries into who could possibly have carried out the robbery, but no one was coming back with answers.

"I'm not so sure, Jinx," Jessie shook his head. "They didn't have the code for the safe under the ice machine. If Salim was in on it, why didn't he let them take it when the club was empty?"

"That could have been a blag, Jessie," Jinx smiled. "Sally is a clever man. If they had had the code, then it had to be you or Sally that told them."

"I agree, but he's too clever to cross his family for a few kilos of gear. That kind of money is nothing to him."

"Okay, he wasn't involved if you say so." Jinx was confused, but he couldn't be bothered arguing about it. "What do you want from me?"

"You said you would help me with the Turks. They have taken my wife and I need help, Jinx."

"Whoa, there!" Jinx held his hands up. "I said we would square it with the Turks. I said we would back up your story and confirm that it was a robbery. That's all."

"They have my wife, Jinx!"

"I'm sorry about that, Jessie, but what do you think I can do to help?"

"Could you lend me the money to cover the cost of the drugs?"

"You can't pay that kind of money back, Jessie."

"Please help me."

"I can't, Jessie."

"They'll kill her," Jessie whined.

"I can't help you."

"Speak to them for me."

"I can do that." Jinx shrugged. He didn't mind talking to them and explaining what had happened at the poker game, but that was all he was prepared to do. "Tell them to call me."

Jessie was about to speak, but a mobile phone began ringing. They both had the same ringtone and they reached for their devices. Jinx looked at his screen. The number was unrecognised. He stabbed the green button and put the phone to his ear.

"This is Jinx," he said. He looked at Jessie as he spoke. The call was a welcome respite from the conversation he was having. It would give him time to think. The Turks were in a league of their own. They had more soldiers than any other outfit he could think of, and they were all prepared to die for their family interests. They had a reputation unrivalled by any other crime family. If you crossed them, then you died, and so did your family, simple. Everyone knew the score. Jinx was a tough man, but he was just one man. He didn't want to get involved in their business.

"Listen to me. I will not repeat this," the voice on the telephone said.

"Who is this?" Jinx growled. He looked at the phone as if it had offended him.

"Shut up and listen. There is a hit out on you."

"Go on." Jinx stopped frowning. He could hear his heart beating in his chest.

"Leon Tanner has put a hit on you. He is paying forty thousand pounds, twenty to Jackson Walker and twenty to Dean Hines. Leon has a shipment of crack landing at Liverpool docks tomorrow, which gives you, time to react. They are planning to take you out in the next few days." The Gecko hung up. He had a few more calls to make to muddy the waters of the underworld. If he could turn all the sharks against each other, then a feeding frenzy would ensue. The more gangsters died, the happier he would be.

The line went dead. Jinx looked at the screen. He pressed recall and dialed the last number. It was dead. It had probably been a prepaid SIM.

"Look, I know you're busy, Jinx, but I don't have much time. I need your help."

Jinx stood up and opened the office door. "I'm sorry, Jessie, something urgent has come up. If I were you, I would talk to the police. It's the only chance you have."

"Please, Jinx, I have only forty-eight hours."

"I don't think I've got that long. Sorry, Jessie, but I need you to leave now."

Jessie nodded his head, resigned to the fact he was on his own. He couldn't expect anyone to take on the Turks on his behalf. It would be suicide.

"Go to the police, Jessie." Jinx shook his hand. "Tell them everything, it's the only chance you have. Nobody else can help you." Jinx closed the office door. He felt sorry for Jessie, but the call he had received changed everything. His own safety was his priority. He wasn't surprised. He had been on a collision course with Leon for years. Leon despised the people Jinx tried to help. Leon abused the teenagers Jinx tried to protect. The city wasn't big enough for them both, and it was obvious Leon felt the same way. Jinx knew both the men who were coming for him. Jackson was a maverick, but Deano was a family man. Jinx had no choice but to take all three of them out. Dean's kids would be orphaned, but he couldn't risk leaving their father alive. He would make a few calls, cash in some favours and hit them before they hit him.

Chapter Seventeen

The Gecko: *The Past*

CRIMINALLY INSANE

The day after his mother had hit him, Nate went to school as normal. His mother was crashed out in bed and he didn't see her before he left. The revelation that his mother was taking hard drugs had shocked him deeply. He was horrified. His father's reaction was equally shocking. After taking his mother upstairs, his father hadn't said a word to him and Nate had been so shocked that he didn't know how to ask him about his mother's drug taking. His father had seemed ice cold and unapproachable.

Nate walked to school as normal that morning. A double lesson of mathematics before lunchtime was more of a drag than usual. He couldn't concentrate. All he could think about was his mother. How could his mother have developed a heroin habit, for God's sake? She watched Jeremy Kyle and Big Brother and wore Levis jeans and other yesterday brands. It was too much to take in one go. The bell was a welcome break and he met up with some friends on the way to buy his dinner. He knew some of the lads at school had dabbled with drugs. He chatted to them about the effects of heroin. One of his close friends told him the signs, explaining how to tell that someone was using and what to look for. When he asked him why he wanted to know, Nate clammed up and blushed.

"You're not thinking of trying that crap, are you?" His friend Carl Lewis asked him. They were walking toward the chip shop to buy their dinner. Chips, mushy peas and gravy today, Nate thought. He hadn't eaten the night before as his mother had been smashed out her skull on smack. How embarrassing could a parent be? Talking to his friend was helping, but he didn't want to tell him the real reason why he was asking about drugs.

"No," Nate replied. He kicked a stone and it clattered down the road before rattling off a lamppost. "I'm just curious, that's all."

"E is okay and I've done a bit of weed, but smack is for dickheads, Nate." His mate sounded like a man of the world. His parents had sheltered Nate. He was quiet and didn't have many friends. Listening to his friend made him feel stupid, as if he had missed out. The other kids seemed to know all about drugs and girls and Nate knew nothing about either.

"You've tried E, wow," Nate said impressed. Carl was one of the cool set in his year. He always had the newest trainers and the trendiest clothes. Nate liked him, but he made himself scarce when Carl's other friends were around. They teased Nate about his boring haircut and dated fashion. His mother always bought him branded gear just as everyone else had stopped wearing it. She had a knack of buying un-cool trainers.

"Yes, of course I have," Carl laughed. "You should come out with us sometime and drop one, great fun, you'll be buzzing off your tits, mate."

"Yes, I might," Nate laughed too and doubted that he ever would. "Where do you get them from?"

"Got a mate who does a bit of dealing, know what I mean?" Carl tapped his nose with his index finger.

"I see," Nate nodded. He didn't have a clue, but he pretended he did.

"Hey, Carl," a voice interrupted them.

"Hey, Grebby," Carl shouted and threw his hand high into the air. His friend jumped up and slapped it with his own. "This is my friend, Nate."

"Alright, Nate," Grebby put his hand up to be slapped and Nate obliged. He felt embarrassed but welcome at the same time.

"Hi," Nate replied meekly.

"Where are you going?" Grebby asked his friend.

"Chippy," Carl laughed. "Starvin Marvin am I," he said imitating Yoda from the Star Wars films.

"Nice one, I'll join you," Grebby slapped him on the back.

Grebby looked like a bit of a hippy. His hair was long and greasy and he was definitely not a fashion victim. Nate thought he was in the year group above them.

"I was just telling Nate here about E," Carl chuckled and tapped his nose again.

"I wouldn't know anything about that," Grebby laughed and tapped his own substantial conk. Nate noticed he had blackheads all over his nose and chin and his skin looked greasy.

"He was asking about smack before, weren't you, mate," Carl patted Nate on the back.

Grebby looked at Nate and then looked away quickly. Nate got the feeling he was not comfortable with the subject.

"Yes, I was just asking, that's all," Nate looked at his shoes as he walked. He was worried about his mother and the look in Grebby's eyes when they had mentioned heroin made him more concerned.

"It's best to stay away from that shit," Grebby said seriously. "It gets a grip on people and fucks them up, Nate."

"I need to shoot home for a minute," Nate blurted. He felt sick inside. "Catch you later, I've forgotten something important." He turned on his heels and ran toward his house. It was a half mile away down a cul-de-sac and he never broke his stride once. The roads were quiet when he reached his street and he chose to run on the road instead of the pavement. He was hot and sweating when he turned the last corner and his breath was coming in deep gulps. Blood pumped loudly through his brain and the air he sucked into his lungs felt scorched. He had a stitch when he reached his road. As he cleared the corner house, he saw an ambulance parked on his driveway.

Nate stopped in his tracks. He was breathing heavily as a police car screamed past him with its siren blaring. His father stood on the driveway with his head in his hands. Nate sprinted as fast as he could toward the house.

"Dad, what's happened?" He shouted as he approached. The police officers were climbing out of their car as he reached the driveway.

"Why aren't you at school?" His father looked shocked to see him. He positioned himself between Nate and the front door.

"What's happened?" Nate was panicking. Somehow, he knew it was his mother. "Where's Mum?"

"Nate, she's not good, Son," his father replied.

Nate was running at full pelt and he used his sporting prowess to sidestep his dad with ease.

"Nate!" He shouted as his son bounded through the front door and cleared the first three stairs, heading for the upstairs. Nate took the stairs two at a time and then stopped suddenly.

There was a paramedic kneeling next to his mother's body on the bathroom floor. She had a needle hanging from her arm and there was dried vomit down her chest and around her mouth and nostrils. Her skin was grey and blue veins stood out around her eyelids.

The next few hours were a blur as the police and ambulance crew inspected his mother's dead body.

The inquest declared it was death by misadventure, heroin overdose. There were no other needle marks on her body, but there were opiates in her hair and fingernails, which indicated she had been using for months.

Nate couldn't help but think his father had something to do with his mother's death, but their relationship was so estranged he couldn't talk to him about college, let alone his concerns. He felt isolated and alone. He loved his mother. She was the only real parent he'd had. His memories of his father were waving goodnight at the study door on the few occasions he came home.

The funeral was a blur. A handful of family showed up, then disappeared as quickly as they had arrived. His college friends rallied around and tried to console him with an ecstasy tablet and tequila shots. Nate collapsed in his friend's bedroom. After two weeks in high dependency care his kidneys failed, and the Gecko organised his second funeral in a month.

Chapter Eighteen

Nate Bradley: *The Past*

The death of his wife and son hit him hard. Harder than he thought it would, when he considered how estranged they had been to him. He hunted through the house and gathered as many photographs as he could find. There were a few faded pictures of him with his son, but nothing recent. The years he had spent apart from them suddenly seemed like a wasteland in his mind. He had wasted so much of their precious time together working. His work had torn other men from their families and none of them had ever returned. He had returned, and done nothing with his opportunity to be with his family. He had wasted the chance he had had. Guilt began to tear at his soul. Guilt for the pain he had caused others began to eat into him, but he justified it. It was because he had been at war. His work extracting information had saved thousands of lives in the long run and made sure that most of their troops had gone home to their families. At least that was what he had told himself then. Now he wasn't sure if he had saved any lives at all. He had taken plenty of them, and perhaps his loss was retribution from divine forces that he didn't understand.

In his mind, his family suddenly became the most important thing in his life, and they were dead. They were dead. Dead. The scumbag who had given his son the ecstasy tablet had murdered him. The dealer who had supplied his wife with heroin had murdered her. The supplier who had shipped the filth into the country had murdered them both. Nate decided he would use his skills to discover who had murdered his family. He would find the suppliers, take their drugs and money and stop them killing anyone again. All of a sudden, he had a new focus in life. He wanted revenge for his family.

The next day after making some calls, he went looking for Nate's friends. He needed to find whoever had given his son the ecstasy tablet that had killed him. That would be the beginning, and he could work his way up from there. The first boy he spoke to was reluctant to say anything, but when Nate threatened to speak to his parents, he gave up the name, Carl Lewis. Another one of his son's friends gave up the same boy's name. Carl had provided Nate and his friends with drugs at the wake. Carl Lewis had provided his son with the ecstasy tablet that had killed him. Carl Lewis had murdered his son.

The Gecko went home and prepared a few things for the next part of the mission. He would need to ask Carl where he had bought the drugs. Carl was young, so frightening him into talking should not be too much trouble. It was what he did. That was who he was, the Gecko. When he found Carl Lewis, he was walking along a pavement next to a playing field. He slowed his car down and pulled close to the curb. Carl saw him and put his head down. He felt responsible for his friend's death and meeting his father was a nightmare coming true. What was he going to say?

"Carl," Gecko called through the window. He stopped the vehicle and opened the passenger door. "I need to talk to you."

Carl was red faced and he looked scared. He carried on walking for a few steps before turning around. It was a huge mistake to make. He climbed into the car and turned to speak to Nate's father.

"Hello, Mr. Bradley," Carl said nervously. Carl wanted to say sorry. He wanted to cry and tell him how sorry he was that Nate had died. He wanted to tell him that he had not slept properly since Nate had been admitted to the hospital and that he had been physically sick when he was told that Nate had died, but he did not get the chance. As he sat down, Mr Bradley, the Gecko, chopped him in the throat with the edge of his hand. Carl gagged, stunned by the blow. Gecko used a chloroform soaked rag to knock him out and then he tied him up, taped his mouth and bundled him into the back of the car.

Chapter Nineteen

Jackson Walker

Jackson didn't believe that Dean was going to go through with the hit on Jinx. He wasn't answering his mobile and Jackson had left four messages already that morning. Dean had the gun they had used before, so he decided to use a different one and claim all the hit money for himself. Leon didn't care who pulled the trigger, as long as it was pulled. All he had to do was clarify that he would get the entire forty grand if he killed Jinx. Jackson picked up a steel coloured Smith and Wesson and wiped it clean with a soft yellow duster. He clicked out the cylinder and pushed six bullets into it. He cleaned the trigger guard to remove any partial prints and then wrapped the gun in the duster. Jinx wouldn't know what had hit him. He was often alone, especially when he walked to the gym he owned. It was all part of his workout. Jackson chuckled to himself. Walking to the gym was going to be very bad for his health this time. Jackson would have to be very careful that there were no witnesses. If anyone realised he was responsible for murdering Jinx, he wouldn't see the week out. That was the only downside to the hit. Jackson didn't care that Jinx helped people in the community that he lived in. He was wasting his time and his money as far as Jackson was concerned. The losers, drug addicts and prostitutes who lived in his community were beyond help. Jackson wanted the money and all he had to do was pull the trigger.

He put the gun onto a glass coffee table, next to a half-drunk can of cider. He picked up the can and drained the contents in one gulp. The cider was warm and flat.

"That's shit, man," he complained to himself. "Get yourself a fresh one, Jackson. This time tomorrow you can fill the fridge with that shit." He chuckled as he thought about his payday. Forty grand would make a huge difference to his life. New duds, new motor, a few foxy ladies. It was all within his grasp. He stood and crossed a beige carpet to the kitchenette. His bedsit was tiny and the kitchen was crammed into one corner of the living room. The sink was piled high with pots that needed washing. He opened the fridge and grabbed the last can of cider from an empty shelf. The shelf above held an open tin of baked beans and a discoloured pork sausage. Jackson wasn't broke, he was lazy. Food came ready prepared in his world. He opened the ring-pull and gulped the bubbly cider down as he pressed the play button on his stereo. Bob Marley began to sing 'Exodus' backed by the Wailers.

Jackson walked to the window and looked out over the city. He lived on the edge of Toxteth near the river. The giant Anglican cathedral filled his view. The river flowed into the Irish Sea behind it. There was a paperboy delivering to the flats across the road. Jackson recognised him as the son of a friend. He should be in school today, and Jackson made a mental note to tell his father the next time he saw him. The mountain bike he was riding looked expensive. It was way out of his father's league, probably stolen. Jackson sipped his cider and contemplated life. One member of the community would die today, and he would profit from his death. A large shipment of crystal meth would land tonight, and with it would come misery and desperation for the community's addicts. Jackson would profit from that too. Jinx tried to help this community and Jackson was going to murder him. Jackson didn't think it was right somehow, but that was life on the streets.

Bob Marley was singing about the movement of 'Jah people', when the front door splintered in half. Jackson turned to see the door disintegrate beneath repeated blows from a sledgehammer.

Chapter Twenty

Carl Lewis: *The Past*

Gecko drove north on the M6 for an hour until he reached the Carnforth turnoff. The roads were narrow and lined with hawthorn hedges obscuring the view of oncoming traffic. He slowed the vehicle down using low gears until he reached the track that led to the quarry. When he stopped, Carl had come around. The boy was so frightened he had soiled his jeans. The rear seats were pulled down so that Gecko could speak to him despite him being in the boot. He leaned over and removed the gaffer tape from his mouth.

"Did you give ecstasy to Nate?" He asked in a calm voice.

"I don't know who gave it to him, Mr Bradley," Carl lied. Tears ran down his cheeks and he was shivering.

"Your friends told me that you gave Nate the tablet." Gecko took a carpet blade from the glove box and showed it to the whimpering boy. "Don't lie to me please."

"I didn't mean to kill him, Mr. Bradley, please don't hurt me."

"So you did give Nate the ecstasy tablet?"

"Yes, but I've had them loads of times, honest," Carl cried. "I've never had any problems with them, Mr. Bradley. It was just an accident."

"Just an accident?" Gecko raised his eyebrows as he repeated the word. *Accident.*

"You know what I mean, Mr. Bradley. Please don't tell the police or my mum." Carl thought this was all about finding out where the rogue tablet had come from. His parents had questioned him repeatedly about Nate's death and Carl had sworn blind that he had never taken drugs. The police had questioned everyone who had been at the funeral, but none of his friends had grassed. Carl was crippled with guilt about his friend's death, and he knew what it would do to his parents if they were to find out that he had supplied Nate with the tablet that had killed him. They were active members of the school fundraising board. Their friends included many of his friend's parents and their families. The news of Nate's death had shattered the community. Parents and teachers had rallied around trying to react to the issue of drugs. Sniffer dogs had been brought into the school the week after the funeral and letters had been sent to every parent, explaining that the school was adopting a zero tolerance policy to drugs. Nate was terrified that his parents would find out about his part in Nate's death and that he would be expelled from school.

"Please don't tell anyone, Mr. Bradley," Carl sobbed. "I am so sorry about Nate, he was my friend."

"I asked the police where Nate got the tablet from and they spoke to you didn't they?" Gecko said.

"Yes," Nate replied. He blinked and tears rolled down his face.

"What did you tell them, Carl?" Gecko shrugged.

"What do you mean?"

"When the police questioned you, what did you tell them?" Gecko repeated.

"I was scared," Carl cried. "I didn't know what to say to them."

"So what did you tell them?"

"I was scared, Mr. Bradley."

"Answer the question," Gecko raised his voice slightly. He was used to interrogation subjects stalling a question when they didn't want to reveal the answer because they knew it would incriminate them.

"I told them I didn't know where he got the tablet."

"Okay, Carl," Gecko lowered his voice again. "You gave my son the tablet that killed him."

"Yes, I'm sorry, I really am," Carl started blubbering.

"Shut up and listen to me." Gecko slapped him hard across the face. The boy was shocked into silence. "You gave Nate the tablet which killed him and then you lied to the police about where the tablet had come from?"

"Yes," Carl whimpered.

"So because you lied to the police, someone else could be burying their child this week, or next week?"

"I was scared of getting into trouble, Mr. Bradley." Carl drew breath sharply. "I just didn't think properly."

"You say you are sorry about killing Nate, yet you have done nothing about it, Carl. I don't think you are sorry at all."

"I am sorry, honestly," Carl tried to stop his voice breaking. He wanted to sound sincere.

"Okay, where did you get the tablets from?" Gecko asked and smiled as he spoke.

"What?" Carl seemed confused.

CRIMINALLY INSANE

"Where did you buy the drugs from, Carl?"

"I can't tell you that, Mr. Bradley. I can't grass. No one will talk to me again." Carl was scared of the people Grebby bought his drugs from. They were older and he knew Grebby's mother was involved somewhere in the mix. One of the boys at college had been given a good hiding for telling his father where he had bought the cannabis found in his room. The kid had looked like he had been in a car crash when he had come back to school. Carl was genuinely sorry about Nate, but he didn't want to wind up in the hospital. Mr. Bradley was trying to frighten him and it was working, but he was more frightened of the dealers. At least, that was what he thought.

"No one will talk to Nate again, ever." Gecko opened the door and climbed out. He walked around to the boot and opened it. "Where did you buy the drugs, Carl?"

Gecko wanted to know where he had bought the ecstasy tablet that had killed his son. Carl was mumbling and stuttering but he would not give up his supplier immediately. Nate picked him out of the boot and carried him over his shoulder into the woods.

"Please, Mr. Bradley, where are you taking me?" Carl blubbered. "There are kids at the school who bought more drugs in a week than I did in a month, honestly."

"Shut up, Carl." Gecko trudged through the undergrowth scratching their arms and legs on the low branches that clawed at them. "I want the name of your dealer."

"They are older than me, they'll kill me, and no one will talk to me," Carl repeated his excuses. He had no idea how much danger he was in. "If I tell you, everyone will know that I grassed."

The night closed around them as they entered the woods. Carl felt his breath being forced out of him with every step. Mr. Bradley's shoulder bone was pressing into his diaphragm and he couldn't catch his breath. He couldn't think properly and he desperately tried to come up with the words that would end his torment. His eyes adjusted to the darkness slowly but there was nothing to see. There were no houses nearby and no passing traffic. The chances of help coming were zero. It was just him, Mr Bradley and the darkness. He had no idea what Mr. Bradley had in mind. Where could he possibly be taking him and why? Was he going to hurt him? His mind raced through the different possibilities, but still he couldn't come up with an answer. Mr. Bradley was upset, obviously. His wife had died and then his son had died a few weeks later. He was bound to be upset but what was he doing?

"Mr. Bradley, where are you taking me?" Carl gasped and tried to catch his breath. There was no reply from his captor, just the sound of twigs breaking beneath his boots as he walked. The canopy of branches thinned out and they entered a clearing in the trees. There were large blocks of sandstone spotted around the clearing. They looked like dark blobs with darker patches on them where they were covered in moss. Gecko weaved between them until they reached the edge of the quarry. He had scuba-dived there a few times when he was in the army. It was deep, too deep to reach the bottom without technical diving equipment and much too deep for visibility at the bottom. The water looked black as oil and it rarely reached double figures on the Celsius scale. Carl looked past the sandstone blocks into the water below, blinking his eyes to focus on the blackness. The water looked like a mirror of black glass reflecting the darkness around it.

"Mr. Bradley, what are you going to do?" Carl was suddenly very frightened. Why would Mr. Bradley risk going to jail for kidnap and assault? How did he think he could get away with this?

"I want to know where you bought the drugs that killed my son." He dumped the boy on the damp woodland floor knocking the wind out of him. Carl groaned and turned on his side in a foetal position and gasped for air. "Who did you buy the drugs from?"

"I'm going to call the police when I get home, Mr. Bradley," Carl sobbed. "You can't do this to me."

Gecko sighed and knelt down next the boy. He ripped a strip of tape off and covered his mouth with it to keep him quiet while returned to the car for a length of chain. He took his time coming back to give Carl a chance to think about his question. Carl was tied up and terrified and seconds felt like hours under those conditions. Nate Bradley senior was an expert at forcing other human beings to feel terrified. Allowing the subject plenty of time for their imagination to run wild was sometimes enough to loosen their tongues. The thought of being hurt or killed was often more frightening than the actual physical act.

Carl lay on his back and tried to slow his breathing down. He had to gather himself and make Mr. Bradley see sense. Nate had been unlucky and Carl was sorry he had died, sorry, but it had not been his fault. He looked around and the sandstone blocks seemed to loom up at him from the night. He counted them silently in his mind. There were six blocks in a line. They stood like mute sentinels at the edge of the quarry. To his left were the edge and a sheer drop into the icy water. Something flickered in the night sky above him. It darted left and right and then disappeared into the trees. Then another small shape followed its erratic flight path. Carl watched and listened. The bats continued to come and go from the woods while he waited to see what Mr. Bradley had in mind. He heard breaking twigs and rustling leaves and he held his breath as his captor emerged from the darkness.

Gecko walked to the edge of the quarry and looked over the still water. He peered into the inky depths for what seemed like ages before turning back to Carl. He dropped the chain on the ground with a clunk and stood over the boy.

"Where did you get the drugs, Carl?" Gecko kneeled down next to him and looked into his eyes. "Are you going to tell me?"

Carl shook his head and sobs wracked his body. Snot ran from his nose, over the tape and down his chin. Gecko took the carpet blade and sliced the boy's shirt off. Carl tried to scream and his eyes bulged from his head as the blade cut the material with ease.

"Who did you buy the drugs off?" Gecko put his fingers under the waistband of the boy's trousers and pulled them away from his body. He sliced the material from the belt to the knee on the left leg and then repeated the process on the right. Carl was frantic as he was stripped naked. His face was flushed and he was hysterical. It had dawned on him that Nate's father was not quite right in the head. His concern to protect his dealer was withering. Mr. Bradley was bang out of order and Carl was adamant that he was going to tell his parents and the police even if it meant his part in Nate's death was revealed. This was weird. Carl wondered if Mr. Bradley was a paedophile. 'What's he going to do, bugger me in the woods?' Carl thought.

"Last chance, Carl." Gecko removed the tape. "If you scream, I will slit your throat. Do you understand?"

Carl stopped wriggling immediately. He held his breath, frozen with fear. No threats had been made yet, but when one came, it was a bombshell. "Do you understand?"

"Yes," Carl gasped and then despite the threat, he tried to scream.

Gecko fastened the tape back over his mouth, picked up the length of chain and lifted the boy as he slid it beneath him. Carl began to panic. The boy wriggled, kicked and screamed as he wrapped the chain around his body and secured it with wire. The metal links were rough and ice cold. They grazed his skin and as the wire was pulled tight, he could feel it cutting into his limbs. Carl's eyes were wide and pleading when Gecko placed another length of wire around his body. He pushed the boy closer to the edge so that he could see the black water thirty-feet below him. He took the tape off his mouth and tears rolled down the boy's face. They had no impact on Nate. He was numb to the fear and pain of those he interrogated. He had a job to do and he was the best. This boy had murdered his son and he was the judge and jury.

"You killed my son, Carl," Nate said calmly. "I want to know who your dealer is. If you tell me, I will forgive you for his death."

Fear had completely overtaken his sense of loyalty and being beaten up by Grebby's suppliers now appeared to be the better option for Carl. "A guy in the year above us called Grebby," Carl gasped. "His name is Paul Grebe but everyone calls him Grebby."

"Okay, and who does he get his drugs from?" Gecko carried on threading the wire through the chain as he spoke.

"I think it's a guy on the estate called Benny something, but I'm not sure. I really do not know. I just buy a bit of weed and a few pills sometimes. Please don't hurt me," Carl was about to say he was sorry when Nate stuck the tape back over his mouth. Carl began to writhe and kick out his legs but the chain held him tightly. He didn't understand what was going on. He had told Mr. Bradley what he wanted to know but he wasn't letting him go.

"I forgive you for killing Nate, take my forgiveness with you into the darkness," Gecko said coolly as he grabbed the boy and edged him toward the drop. Carl had murdered his son. His sentence was death. The boy wriggled like a racing snake as he fell thirty-feet into the black water filling the quarry. His mother's face flashed through his mind as he hurtled toward the water. She was crying. He knew he wouldn't see her again in this world. Carl hit the water face first and it felt like he had slammed into a brick wall. The impact stunned him, the coldness forced him to breathe through his nose, and the water flooded into his lungs. He disappeared into the depths in seconds. Gecko had dealt with the direct supplier of the tablet, which had killed his son, and acquired the name of the next target. The first part of the mission was completed.

Chapter Twenty-One

Alec/Jessie

Alec felt the wind in his hair as he walked from a sandwich shop called 'The Filling Station'. It was clean and the food was always fresh. He had invested in a chicken, bacon and mayo sub with jalapeno chilies and extra chili sauce. His stomach was rumbling; he wasn't sure if it was hunger or stress causing the gurgling. The Parker murder was as complicated as a case could be, but it was the thought of his wife packing her bags, which left him feeling sick inside. He knew the next forty-eight hours would be crucial to cracking the case and the opportunities to eat would be few, and far between. The spicy sub would supply him with some sustenance to keep him going. Once the case was under control, he would go and talk to Gail and sort things out. He needed to push her up his list of priorities. She was correct though. There would be another Louise Parker, another big case. There always was another case. Maybe she was better off away from him where she could have the life she deserved with a man who could give her the attention she deserved. Maybe not. He was debating the why and wherefore of his marriage when his Blackberry buzzed. The screen displayed Will's number calling.

"Hi, Will, what's up?" It was twenty minutes since they had spoken.

"I've had a very interesting telephone conversation, Guv!"

Alec unlocked the driver's door and climbed into the seat. He placed the sub on the passenger seat and closed the door. "Oh, really, who with?"

"Jessie James. He wants to speak to you."

"Well, we need to speak to him, did you tell him to come into the station?"

"He won't come in, Guv. He wants to meet you alone," Will explained. "Jessie sounded frightened and stressed on the phone. He will be at the Mersey View at three o'clock this afternoon. I said that I would let you know."

"Did he give you anything on the telephone?" Alec asked as he worked out the route to the Mersey View in his mind. If he took the coast road over the Runcorn Bridge, he would be there fifteen minutes before three, as long as the traffic was clear. The Mersey View was a hotel perched on the top of Frodsham hill, a huge sandstone outcrop that had been a cliff at the edge of the sea centuries ago, before the sea level had dropped. It offered a view over the River Mersey at its widest point and the mountains of Snowdon beyond. Alec remembered that the road to the hotel was steep and winding. He had been there many times with his wife when they were courting. A twinge of guilt pricked him as he thought of the last time he had taken her anywhere for dinner. He couldn't remember when it had been. It was no wonder she was leaving him.

"Not really, Guv, but he sounded frightened," Will said.

"Interesting. Have we rounded up the others from the poker game?" Alec asked.

"Most of them are on their way in. There's no sign of Leon Tanner or Jinx Cotton, but we're tracking them down."

"Call him back and tell him that if he isn't prepared to come in, then I am too busy to meet with him." Alec didn't want to meet a known lag on the back of one phone call. Nine times out of ten when a villain asked for a covert meeting, they were trying to get a deal. Alec didn't make deals with criminals.

"I thought you would say that, Guv," Will laughed. "I told him to come in if he wanted to talk to you, but then he threw in a sweetener."

"How sweet?" Alec chuckled. This was getting interesting.

"He said he has the CCTV tapes from the club on the night of the fire," Will explained.

"Okay. Good, I'll drive over there, might be worth an hour of my valuable time. I'll call you when I've finished with Mr James." Alec tucked the phone under his chin and started the engine. "Hopefully he will shine some light on what happened that night."

"Okay, Guv. I'll oversee the interviews here as they come in. Talk to you later." Will hung up. Alec put the mobile on the passenger seat next to the sandwich and pulled into the traffic. He mulled over the questions he needed to ask Jessie and decided he would wait to see what he wanted. It was unusual for a man like Jessie to come to the police voluntarily. He was in trouble. Someone had cut the tops of his ears off. That kind of thing had a habit of influencing people. Jessie was on the periphery of a dangerous world where the animals all had teeth. If you lived there, sooner or later one of them would bite you.

The traffic was light and moving freely as he drove toward the View. It was a sunny afternoon and the breeze was moving the branches on the trees. Alec reflected on the Parker murder and tried to connect it to the nightclub. The link was Salim Oguzhan. It had to be. Louise Parker had been seeing him and the killer had butchered her. Salim was missing and somebody had robbed and torched his nightclub. Could it all be a string of coincidences? Alec didn't think so. As he turned onto the car park, he looked at the scattering of vehicles. None of them looked familiar or suspect. Jessie was sitting in the driver's seat of a silver Ford Focus. His head was bandaged, making him look ridiculous. Alec parked next to him. The big Welshman looked washed out. He had dark circles beneath his eyes and the whites were bloodshot. Jessie got out of the Ford and moved gingerly toward the BMW. It was obvious his injuries were restricting his movement. He looked much older than the last time Alec had seen him. He had a disc in his right hand.

"Detective," Jessie said as he ducked into the passenger seat. The car rocked as he wriggled his big frame into the car. "Sorry for the cloak and dagger shit, but if anyone knew I was talking to you I would already be dead. Could we just drive around, please?"

"Fine, but let's get one thing straight," Alec turned to him as he spoke and looked him in the eyes. Jessie looked terrified. "Whatever you say to me is on the record, Jessie. Is that understood?"

"Whatever, Detective," Jessie shrugged. "Things can't get any worse."

"Okay." Alec reversed the car and headed toward the exit. "What's on your mind?"

"I'm not sure where to start." Jessie bit his lip and looked out of the side window. His eyes looked watery. "I am in deep shit, Superintendent, and I don't know what to do."

"Start at the beginning, Jessie."

"You know who I work for, don't you?"

"The Oguzhan family."

"Correct, and you will be aware of their reputation?" Jessie felt stupid, but he wasn't sure how to explain his predicament without sounding like a grass. Talking to the police was taboo, but he had no other options.

"Yes, Jessie," Alec shook his head and sighed. "Every police officer in the country knows the family name. What is the problem?"

"They have Rose." A tear ran from Jessie's left eye and he wiped it away quickly. "They're going to kill her."

"Rose is your wife?"

"Yes, sorry, I thought you knew her."

"I think I met her at the club once when we were looking for you." Alec looked for a reaction. He laughed, trying to lighten the tension. Jessie looked like he was at breaking point. "I think you were a witness to a serious assault if I remember correctly, but you couldn't recall the incident when we spoke to you."

"You are going back a few years, Superintendent," Jessie nodded his head and smiled. "You never did let that one drop."

"I can't let anything drop, Jessie, or there would be bad guys running riot."

"I think they still do run riot, no matter what you do." Jessie stopped smiling as he thought about the men who were holding his wife captive.

"Sometimes I think we are fighting a losing battle, but we will never stop fighting it, Jessie. We can't."

"Don't you ever get sick of dealing with murderers and scum?"

"Yes," Alec nodded. "I do, but I never get sick of locking them up." Alec was a tenacious detective and his reputation was in the underworld was fierce. The bad guys did not want Alec Ramsay on their case. "Do you remember the Shah family?"

"Yes, I remember them." Jessie looked at Alec. There were similarities between them and his employers.

"Ten years ago, they were as big as the Oguzhan family are now," Alec guided the car through the narrow lanes as he spoke. "Now they are all either dead or serving life."

"You have a good memory."

"All part of the job," Alec laughed. "Why would the Oguzhan family want to kill your wife?" Alec looked across at the Welshman. He was obviously skirting around the reasons why the Oguzhan cartel had his wife. It could be any number of things. They were a nasty bunch with a reputation for brutality, but they tended to look after their employees, too. Something had made them turn on Jessie and his wife.

"It's complicated." Jessie didn't want to incriminate himself, but he had to tell Alec everything for Rose's sake. Her life depended on it. He was past caring about what happened to him.

"I am assuming you need my help to find your wife alive?" Alec asked.

"Yes, that's why I'm here." Jessie hung his head on his chest. He looked like a broken man. "I've brought the CCTV footage from that night as a peace offering."

"Okay, that's a start, but you realise that this is evidence and there will be no deals cut with you?"

"Yes. I want Rose back unharmed and I want out of that shithole club for good." Jessie didn't have a clue what they would do if they walked away from the nightclub. It had been their life for over a decade. He didn't know anything but running pubs and clubs. The future would be uncertain, but as long as he had Rose, then they could move on together. "I can't do it anymore."

"I don't think you were ever really cut out for the gangster lifestyle, Jessie." Alec looked at him. He dealt with hardcore criminals every day and Jessie didn't fit the bill. He was a big man with a reputation, but Alec saw a gentleman beneath the hard exterior.

"No, I don't suppose I ever was, really." Jessie looked the police officer in the eyes and tried to smile. "Jessie James, host to the gangsters and criminal elite. It's a fucking joke."

"I guess we all have to make a living, Jessie, some people choose to become plumbers and others chose a different path." Alec looked at him again. "Is it true about you?"

"Is what true?" Jessie frowned, confused.

"Why they call you Jessie James."

Jessie laughed and a tear ran down his face. "Now that is a classic."

"How so?" Alec smiled.

"There was a local hard nut in the club one night." Jessie took a packet of Lamberts from his pocket. "Can I smoke?"

"Go ahead. Just open the window a little." Alec opened his window a few inches too.

"Thanks." Jessie lit the cigarette and inhaled the soothing smoke. "He was a lunatic called Eugene Wells. Have you heard of him?"

"Yes," Alec laughed. "They fished him out of the Mersey about six years back, right?"

"Right, you do have a good memory."

"I locked him up in the nineties. He did a five stretch for armed robbery."

"Yes, I remember him going down." Jessie flicked the Lambert out of the window and exhaled the smoke. "Well, he kicked off in the club one night and the doormen moved in." Jessie laughed as he recalled the night. "He dropped three of them without blinking and the others were too scared to go near him."

"I remember he took a few officers down when they arrested him. He was a handful alright."

"Well, we had a standoff and I was pissed off with him. I put a gun to his head and asked him to leave. He went without another word and never came back."

"Smith and Wesson revolver?" Alec laughed.

"Yes, a very good replica!" Jessie laughed again. "I've never owned a real gun in my life, but the story spread quickly and it didn't do my reputation any harm. All of a sudden, I was Jessie James." They both laughed at the story.

"What would you have done if he had called your bluff?"

"Who knows?" Jessie stopped laughing. "I am no tough guy, Superintendent."

Alec nodded. "Do you think the Oguzhan family is serious about killing Rose?"

"Yes, I do."

"Then you need to tell me everything, Jessie. Otherwise we cannot help."

"It started at the club the other night," Jessie began. He took a deep breath and sighed.

"On the night of the fire?"

"Yes. There was a robbery."

"At the club?"

"At the poker game," Jessie corrected him.

"I am intrigued." Alec laughed at the thought of the city's villains being robbed. "What happened?"

"The game was ticking along nicely when there was a bit of friction over a hand," Jessie recounted.

"Between who?"

"Jinx Cotton and Leon Tanner. They always have an attitude with each other. They hate each other with a vengeance, but that night, Leon pushed all in and Jinx suckered him with four of a kind. Leon was pissed off and got nasty."

"How much did he lose?" Alec asked. In his mind, he could see Leon scowling as he lost his money. The man was always scowling. Alec couldn't stand the man. He was connected to crystal meth dealing and prostitution, but so far, he had avoided prosecution.

"Twenty grand in total."

Alec whistled. That was a lot of money in anyone's world, even to a drug dealer like Leon Tanner. "I can see why he would be pissed off."

"That's the price of the ticket to sit down at the game," Jessie explained. "I won twice my yearly salary last year playing in that game. It's usually a good-natured game; sometimes there is a bit of banter, but nothing too heavy."

"What happened then?" Alec didn't see the connection between Leon losing and a robbery. He frowned and his forehead creased with the deep lines that lived there.

"Two men came through the cellar door while we were distracted by the argument. They had Uzi's." Jessie paused for effect.

"Uzis?" There were automatic weapons on the streets, but it was still a shock when they were used in robberies. Alec swallowed hard. "Go on," he prompted. He concentrated on the road while he listened to Jessie talking. He seemed to be relaxing a little.

"They chained up the doors to the club and herded us against the wall. Then they asked me for the combination to the safe where the poker kitty was kept."

"What do you mean?" Alec frowned again. "You didn't play with cash?"

"No. We put all the money into a safe beneath the table while the game went on. We play with chips."

"Okay," Alec said. "That makes sense." Obviously eight people playing poker at twenty thousand pounds per person was a lot of money to have sat on a card table. It was illegal to play for cash outside a casino. Playing with chips was fine; two good reasons to hide the money. "Where was the safe?"

"It was set into the floor, under the table. They asked me for the combination and I gave them the wrong number."

"Why?" Alec asked. He couldn't take anything for granted. It could have been to delay the thieves, but there could be a different reason.

"The safe was alarmed. I wanted them to trip the alarm and alert the minders in the club," Jessie explained. He touched his bandage as the memories came back to him.

"Go on."

"They knew the combination was wrong and the bastard cut the top of my ear off."

"Did they try to open the safe with that code?" Alec asked for clarification. If they already had the real combination then the possible scenarios were myriad.

"No. They knew it was the wrong code. They opened it with the correct code and took the money."

"Then what?"

Jessie swallowed hard and looked out of the window. "It's nice up here, isn't it? Peaceful."

"What happened, Jessie?" Alec asked sternly.

"There was another safe." Jessie knew he had to tell all. "It was under the ice machine."

"Okay, so what?" Alec prompted.

"They didn't have the code to that but they knew it was there."

"Who else knew it was there?" Alec knew the answer before he heard it.

"Myself and Salim Oguzhan were the only ones that knew, unless he told his family."

"So they asked you for the combination?"

"Yes." Jessie shivered.

"Then what?"

"They cut off my other ear."

"What was in the safe?"

"Five kilos of cocaine." Jessie felt like a weight had been removed from his shoulders.

"Is that why the Oguzhan family has taken Rose?"

"Yes, they have given me forty-eight hours to find the drugs or replace them with cash." Jessie shrugged again. "I haven't got a clue who robbed the club, and I don't have that kind of money."

"Where is Salim Oguzhan?" Alec began to backtrack on the missing pieces.

"I haven't heard from him for weeks," Jessie replied. "Neither has his family. They asked me where he was, but they told me that his wife and kids were visiting from Turkey."

"When did they get here?" Alec frowned

"I don't know, he never mentioned that they were here."

"Do you think he's in on this?" Alec asked. Salim was missing and his girlfriend was dead. He could have carried out the murder and then stolen enough money to disappear, but it didn't sit right with Alec.

"I don't think so. He knew the combination to the safe and we always got on okay. I don't think he would hurt me unnecessarily, and he liked Rose."

"Do you know his girlfriend, Louise Parker?" Alec asked.

"Sally had lots of girlfriends. He always had a woman on his arm." Jessie couldn't place the name.

"She was pretty with long auburn hair. Think, Jessie, it's important."

"I know who you mean now. He usually went for blond women; she stood out with her hair. Yes, I know her. She came to the club a few times, usually off her box on Charlie. I never really spoke to her though. She seemed a bit well to do, if you know what I mean."

"When did you last see her with Salim?"

"The last time I saw Salim she was with him." Jessie frowned as he thought about it. "They had been drinking with a weird looking guy who I hadn't seen in the club before and then she collapsed. Salim was pissed too and their friend had to help Salim and carry her out of the club, but that wasn't the first time."

"I need you to come into the station and make a statement about the robbery and the last time you saw Salim. Then you need to report your wife's kidnap. Once that is done, we can start looking for her. Are we clear?" Alec stopped the car at the side of the road and looked into Jessie's eyes. The Welshman nodded silently and slumped in the seat. He was resigned to his fate. If he made a formal complaint against the Turkish cartel, he would spend the rest of his life in hiding. Things would never be the same again.

Chapter Twenty-Two

Paul Grebe: *The Past*

CRIMINALLY INSANE

The tablet that had killed Nate had come from an older boy at college and within seconds of returning to the car, using his laptop, Gecko knew his full name and address. When he returned home, it didn't take long to find the dealer, Grebby. Facebook is a useful tool for finding people and finding out about them, pictures included. Paul Grebe was a geeky looking kid with long greasy hair and blackheads. Gecko was surprised because he looked like a nerd, someone whom bullies would target at school. He watched him from his car as he sold two bags of weed to a group of teenagers wearing school uniforms. He focused the binoculars on the group and checked his watch. Grebby met the boys in the same spot at the same time every day. They shook hands and Grebby walked across the playing fields toward the car park where Gecko was waiting. The kid took this route home every day after school, meeting up with some of his young customers on the way. The car park was quiet and the other vehicles were empty. Gecko decided to move now rather than wait. There was no one around to witness him talking to Paul Grebe, and if it remained that way, he could take him as easily as he had taken Carl Lewis. The boy was on his mobile as he walked by the car. He didn't notice Nate Bradley's father as he got out of his vehicle.

"Excuse me, have you got a light?"

"What, oh yes, here." Grebby turned when he heard the voice, reaching into his pocket for his clipper.

"Thanks, Grebby," Gecko said, lighting his cigarette.

The teenage boy looked confused. "Do I know you?"

"You knew my son." Gecko looked around the car park to check there were no witnesses about.

"Who is your son?" Grebby shrugged nonchalantly. He hadn't noticed that the man had used the past tense. *You knew my son.*

"Here he is right now." Nate pointed to the playing fields and the young dealer looked over his shoulder. Gecko chopped him hard in the larynx and as his knees buckled, he scooped him up and bundled him into the boot. He was tied up and gagged in seconds and the journey north to the quarry began again. It was dark when they arrived and Gecko had to put the teenager over his shoulder to carry him through the woods, using a flashlight to light the way. Paul Grebe hadn't struggled as much as he thought he would, until he dumped him down on the damp moss at the edge of the quarry. He was scared of the dark and scared of the man who had abducted him. His eyes bulged from his face.

"Do you know who I am?" Gecko asked, shining the torch into Grebby's eyes. The teenager shook his head vigorously from side to side. "I am Nate Bradley senior," he said slowly as he removed the duct tape from the dealer's mouth.

"Nate Bradley?" Grebby was confused and frightened. The name registered in his brain and alarm bells began to ring. His friend, Carl, had introduced him to a geeky kid called Nate, and he remembered walking with him to the chip shop when the kid had freaked out and run off. The next thing he knew was the kid's mother had croaked and her death was a big mystery. Carl had bought some pills from him to liven up the night out after the wake, and then all hell had broken loose when the Bradley kid had ended up in intensive care. Grebby couldn't see why Carl had made such a drama out of the kid's death. Shit happened.

"Yes, you recognise the name?"

"Yes, you're Nate's father." Grebby tried to swallow but his throat was like sandpaper. Whatever this man wanted, he wasn't messing about. "Is this about Nate dying, man?"

"Correct," Nate Bradley senior smiled. "You sold the ecstasy tablet which killed my son to Carl Lewis."

"No way, Mr. Bradley!" Grebby looked shocked and shook his head. "I don't touch any of that shit," he lied. He could sense that the man meant business. He didn't know where he was but he knew he was too far away from help to scream. There was something missing from the man's eyes. He looked focused, almost robotic. There was no emotion in them, no anger, no hatred, just ice-cold focus.

"Carl Lewis was right here where you are yesterday. To be fair to him, when I asked him who he bought the drugs from, he didn't give the game away straight away. He lied too."

"What do you mean?" Grebby stuttered. "What did he tell you? He's lying."

"Do you know what I did for a living, Grebby, in the army, that is?"

"No, I didn't know you were in the army, why would I?" Grebby was sharp and he tried to sound convincing. "I hardly know Carl Lewis and I only met Nate once. I heard about him dying and I was gutted, Carl will tell you that."

"I was an interrogator." Nate ignored his rambling and shined the torch into his eyes. "Sifting lies from the truth is my profession, and you are lying to me."

"Look, man." Grebby tried to sound calm although inside he was far from it. He was a clever lad and academically he was doing well at college. His situation was precarious, but he didn't believe that Mr. Bradley was going to hurt him. Rational people didn't kidnap teenagers and took them to the woods to kill them. He wanted to know about the drugs, and that wasn't the end of the world. Grebby's mother had been dealing weed for as long as he could remember. That's how he had gotten into it. She made a good living out of supplying her friends and as Grebby had grown older, he had decided he could, too. She had been banging a dealer off the estate for years and Grebby had gotten to know him reasonably well. They had smoked weed together and soon, Grebby had been selling for him at school. When he got back home, he was going to call in some favours and have Mr. Bradley sorted out. Okay, he had lost his son, but this was going too far. "This is over the top, Mr. Bradley. I don't know anything about any drugs."

Nate stood up and turned around. He disappeared into the trees and Grebby watched as the torchlight faded into the dark. He looked around, but the torchlight had been shined into his eyes and they wouldn't adjust to the darkness. There was nothing but black and darker black to be seen. He hated the dark. It had always scared him. He thought about trying to wriggle away to hide, but getting lost in the woods or falling into the quarry weren't options he wanted to chance. As he debated his options, Mr. Bradley appeared from nowhere and the beam blinded him. He hadn't heard him approach despite the silence around him. Gecko kneeled down next to the young dealer and placed his college bag next to him.

"Who do you get your drugs from?"

"I don't get them from anyone," Grebby replied quietly. He was scared, but his mind was processing his position and trying to think of a way out of it.

Nate Bradley roughly turned the boy over and he pushed his face into the rotting leaves carpeting the floor. The dealer wriggled and kicked as he fought for air but Nate was too strong. He could feel strong hands searching through his pockets. The game was up. He was carrying drugs and money.

"A quick search of your pockets and schoolbag turned up a roll of twenty-pound notes, a bag of ecstasy tablets and a block of cannabis resin," Nate said calmly. "All of which are pretty consistent with being a lowlife drug pusher." He released the pressure on the dealer's neck and allowed him to breathe.

"Okay, okay," the boy gasped. "Look, I deal a bit for my mum's boyfriend. He is a complete arsehole and he beats the shit out of me and my mum if we don't sell his gear."

Nate grabbed a handful of greasy hair and dragged the dealer toward the edge of the quarry. Grebby squealed like a girl and twisted his body but he couldn't break free. "Please! He makes me sell it, honestly he does!"

Nate placed the chloroform soaked rag over his nose and mouth to shut him up while he prepared to talk to him. It was obvious that Grebby was not taking any responsibility for his part in his son's death. Not yet anyway, but he would before he died.

When the geek awoke, he was strapped to a concrete block at the edge of the quarry. His feet were over the edge. Nate asked him, "Who sold you the drugs?"

"I feel sick," Grebby moaned. He looked around and realised his feet were dangling over the cliff. Fear gripped him and he turned his face to look at his captor. "What do you want to know? I'll tell you whatever you want to know."

"Who sold you the drugs?" Nate grabbed his face between his forefinger and thumb and shined the torch into his eyes. Tears spilled over and ran down the boy's face. "You refused to talk at first, which means that you are not sorry about my son's death, nor are you worried about killing another teenager with the same batch of tablets." Nate pushed the block closer to the edge; the dealer's legs dangled.

"Stop, please!" Grebby cried. "What did Carl tell you?"

"That doesn't matter to you. Who sold you the drugs?" "His name is Jacky Benjamin. I know his address on the Bluebell housing estate," Grebby babbled. "Check my mobile, his numbers are in there."

Nate picked up the mobile and scrolled to the contacts file. He entered it and searched for the name. "What is it stored under?"

"Benny and Jacky, he has two phones that he deals from."

Nate checked the numbers were there. "What is his address?"

"Sixty five Huyton Lane, it's the corner house opposite the Bluebell pub."

"Who does he live with?" Nate asked.

"No one, he lives alone, but there are always people coming and going. He has a lot of friends, you know what I mean?"

"Does he keep weapons in the house?" Nate wanted to know as much information as he could about his next target.

"How the fuck would I know?" Grebby shouted. He was terrified and he wanted out of here right now. He had parted with the information and now he wanted to go home.

"Have you been to his house?" Nate stayed calm.

"Yes, a few times, to hang out."

"To take drugs you mean?"

"We smoked a bit of weed, that's all, now let me go." Grebby struggled to get his words out.

"Did you see any guns?"

"No, let me go."

"Dogs?"

"What?" Grebby asked incredulously.

"Does he have any dogs?"

"Yes, he has three. Now let me fucking go!" Grebby rocked his body but only succeeded in cracking the back of his head on the block.

"What type of dogs are they?" Nate pressed on.

"Bull Terriers, now please let me go. I promise not to go to the police if you let me go now," Grebby replied angrily.

With the information gathered, Nate decided to explain briefly why he was going to kill the boy. "You killed my son, Grebby, and you have shown no remorse for doing that, so tell me why I should let you go?"

"I didn't kill him. How could I know which tablet Nate would take or how it would affect him? How could I know? He took the tablet on his own back, no one forced him."

"No they didn't, but if you hadn't sold them to Carl, then Nate would be alive."

Gecko decided he had enough information from the young dealer to progress to the next level. He heaved on the concrete and pushed it toward the edge. Grebby was hysterical as Nate pushed the block over the edge and the boy plummeted into the freezing cold depths of the quarry. His body settled just yards away from his younger friend Carl. Mission number two was accomplished. It was time to move up the chain.

When he arrived home that night, he charged up his wife's mobile phone and pressed in the numbers he had acquired. Both numbers were stored in the memory, one under Benny, the second under Benjy. Jacky Benjamin was responsible for murdering his son and his wife. Nate planned to take Benjamin out of circulation, but a reconnaissance of his home revealed that it was like a fortress. The dealer protected his doors and windows with bars. There were cameras fitted to the front and back and he could hear at least two dogs barking. It would not be simple to break in, and when Benjamin left his house, several youngsters dressed in black shellsuits escorted him. There was a pub across the road called the Bluebell where Gecko could sit and watch the house through the window. It was there that he met Patrick Lloyd.

Chapter Twenty-Three

Jackson

Jackson Walker was rooted to the spot as his front door shattered into splinters. His brain was telling him to sprint across the room to pick up the gun he had cleaned minutes ago, but his muscles refused to respond to the messages. A man dressed as a construction worker stepped through the splintered frame and walked calmly towards him. He had a yellow hardhat and a navy blue jumpsuit on. Around his waist was a utility belt with an assortment of tools attached. A grey respirator covered his face. David Lorimar, Dava as his associates knew him, often used this disguise to enter buildings without attracting anyone's attention but that of the most observant members of the public. He aimed a silenced Glock at Jackson's chest area and waved the weapon, indicating he should get down onto the floor. A similarly dressed man was covering the doorway with a black plastic membrane. A yellow warning triangle stood on guard in the hallway, telling any nosey neighbours that chemical vermin control was underway.

"Get your hands up, Jackson," Dava said calmly. "Make a sound and you are dead, understand?"

"What the fuck is this all about?" Jackson asked. He knew it was a hit, but he didn't know for sure who wanted him dead. It could be any of a dozen people that he had crossed recently, or a hundred others he could have thought of if he had had the time to go back further into his past. Not that it mattered, he was living his last few minutes on this planet, unless he could escape. "Who is paying you?" Jackson knelt down and raised his hands above his head.

"Shut up or you will die slowly," Dava hissed.

"So this is a hit, right?" Jackson smiled nervously. The hit man had not squeezed the trigger yet, which meant either he didn't want to make a mess and leave evidence or he didn't want to carry a body out of the building. If they tried to take him out alive at gunpoint, he had a chance to escape or call for help. His mind was screaming at him to do something or say something, but he was still in shock.

"Well done there, you should have been on Mastermind."

CRIMINALLY INSANE

"At least let me know who is having me wiped!" Jackson smiled again although his guts were churning. He was supposed to be executing a man today, but the tables were turned. There was a sick feeling of panic in his stomach. A dreadful feeling of complete hopelessness seeped through him. There was nothing he could do. He remembered Delamere Forest, where he had watched a man digging his own grave and begging for his life. Tears and snot had mingled on the dealer's face as he dug his resting place in the dark damp soil. It had been Leon's idea to bury him alive while his associate had watched in horror, but it had been Jackson who had kicked him into the hole screaming. It had been Jackson who had stood on his chest and covered the poor man in soil. He remembered stamping on the rotting forest floor as he had compacted it around the man until the muffled screams stopped and the undulating soil became still. Somewhere the dead man's soul would be pointing at him and smiling. What goes around comes around. 'This is karma,' he thought. Jackson swallowed hard and waited for his fate.

"Let's just say someone is hitting you before you hit them, shall we?" David Lorimar looked toward his associate. "Put your hands in front of you."

He waited for his colleague to cut another length of plastic membrane. He placed it on the floor while Dava fastened plasticuffs around Jackson's wrists. Jackson was shaking with fear as a thin plastic noose slipped out of the utility belt and his attacker tried to slip it over his head. He realised why he had not shot him already. The hit man was opting for a quieter method of execution. Jackson knew he was about to be garroted and he threw himself backwards across the floor. His hands were tied but his legs were free and he ran desperately for his life. There was nowhere to run. The doorway was blocked. Jackson stumbled toward the window and he hurled himself headlong at the glass. David Lorimar kicked out as he ran and he caught his ankle, knocking it violently from under his fleeing target. Jackson crashed into the window frame full force and the skin on his skull split like an egg. Blood poured from the wound and blinding white lights shot through his brain. Before he could recover and bolt again, he felt the plastic zip tie sliding over his head and tightening around his throat. It was a murder weapon frequently used by David Lorimar. There was no sound except a thick guttural gurgling sound as the noose tightened and crushed Jackson's larynx. He felt the blood vessels in his brain swelling before they burst. His eyes protruded and looked like they would pop out and his tongue lolled out of his mouth. As the darkness closed in, the third vertebrae in his spine snapped.

David Lorimar felt Jackson's body go limp and he let it fall onto the plastic sheet. They moved silently and with a practiced purpose about them. They wrapped Jackson Walker in his own carpet and carried him out of the flat into a battered old Renault Traffic van. No one saw the hit men enter and no one saw them leave. Two hours later, they forced his dismembered body through a mincemeat processer and mixed him with a new batch of pigswill. Jackson Walker was nothing more than a memory, just another gangster who had disappeared in the dangerous quicksand of the underworld.

Chapter Twenty-Four

Patrick Lloyd: *The Past*

Patrick Lloyd was in the Bluebell, leaning against the bar reading the sport pages when Nate caught his eye. Patrick watched him closely. He could tell that Nate was watching the property opposite. He lived locally and knew that a well-known drug dealer occupied it. He was curious why this stranger was interested in the property. Patrick figured that he must be a police officer, and he was wary of police officers, although it was obvious that this man was not looking for anyone else except the occupant of the property across the road. After an hour, he approached Nate and began a conversation.

"Tell me to get lost if you like, but are you police?" He whispered with a cheeky smile on his face.

"Get lost." Nate didn't look at him.

"Don't be like that. I'm being nosey, I know, but why are you watching Benjamin's gaff?"

"I don't know what you're talking about." Nate looked at him this time. The fact that the man knew the dealer's name worried him. He needed to know if the guy was curious or a friend of the drug dealer. He was annoyed that he had made it so obvious he was watching the house. His hatred of the man who owned it was dulling his senses. He needed to keep sharp if he was to revenge his family's death.

"Are you drugs squad? I hope you are, that bastard needs stringing up by the bollocks, mate." Lloyd spoke with a thick scouse accent, but there was something false about it. "If I had my way, I would put a bullet in the back of his skull."

"Do you know him, then?"

"Nah, I know of him. He's a drug dealing scumbag. It pisses me off that everyone knows what he does, yet the police do nothing about it. The kids on the estate are knocking on the door from dawn until dusk. Are you drugs squad, then?"

"No."

"Rival dealer?"

"Definitely not."

"Customer?"

Nate laughed. This man was persistent; he had to say that. He was a strange looking character, but there was something amusing about him. "Let's say I have a similar opinion to you."

Lloyd held out his skinny hand. "Patrick Lloyd."

Nate ignored the gesture and continued to look out of the window. He didn't want to shake the man's hand. He was too pushy and there was something strange about him. There was something about his eyes. They were bright and darted everywhere. Gecko had seen that look in people who were being hunted. "What do you do, Patrick?" He asked without looking at him.

Patrick was skinny and lean. He wore his hair cropped short. He looked like he could have been a squaddie once. He took a mouthful of dark bitter and smiled. His teeth looked false. "You know, a bit of this and a bit of that. I'm ex-army, Cheshire Regiment."

"I thought so," Nate nodded. "Me too, intelligence."

"Desk jockey, eh?"

"No. I didn't have a desk." Nate looked him straight in the eyes for the first time. It was then that the dealer's front door opened. Nate looked inside the house while the entourage filed out.

"Benjamin is the lad in the Parka. The others are his lowlife mates. The things you see when you haven't got your gun, eh?" Patrick winked.

"That is very true," Nate laughed. "I wouldn't advise shooting a drug dealer in broad daylight anyway."

"Do you think anybody from around here would give a shit?" Patrick shook his head as he spoke. "No one would remember seeing anything that happened on this estate. Do you want a pint, mate?"

Nate looked at his glass. It was empty. It was a long time since he met someone who made him laugh. "Why not, I'll have a lager, please."

"Nice one, I'll be two minutes," Patrick smiled and walked to the bar. Nate looked around the pub, taking it in for the first time. He had been so focused on the Benjamin property that he hadn't noticed his surroundings. The pub was clean and modern in design. The floors were polished pinewood and the brass rails on the bar sparkled. There were four bandits spaced out, one on each wall. All four machines were being pumped full of dole money; the players were all similarly dressed in tracksuits with the trousers tucked into their socks and training shoes. Patrick chatted with a fat barmaid as she poured two new pints. He eyed her up and down with a little too much interest. She flicked her hair and laughed, flirting with him. The drug dealer and his cronies had disappeared into the maze of alleyways that dissected the estate. "So, are you police or what?" Patrick returned with a big grin on his face.

"No. I'm an advisor nowadays, a consultant of sorts."

"I can get you into that house." Patrick stopped smiling and winked again.

"Why would I want to go inside the house?" Nate frowned and looked away. He suddenly felt uncomfortable. It was as if Patrick could read what he was thinking.

"I don't know. That is your business. But if you did want to, I can get you into that house." He took a long sip of his beer and licked the froth from his top lip.

"He has cameras all over the place." Nate looked out of the window again.

"Let's just say I'm an advisor like you, a consultant expert on breaking and entering peoples' houses," Patrick laughed. "The cameras are no problem. He has an old system that uses wires. Wires can be cut."

"What about the dogs?" Nate knew all the answers already, but he wanted to test Patrick.

"Poison."

"Here, you two," one of the tracksuits had approached the table that they were sitting at. "Do you want any weed?" The youth wore his hair shaved and he had stars tattooed beneath his left ear. His accent was local and he looked over his shoulder nervously as he spoke.

"Fuck off," Patrick Lloyd said politely.

"What did you say, you blurt?" The youth snarled. He was trying to sound tough, but he couldn't carry it off.

"You heard me," Patrick stood up. "Fuck off."

The youth looked him in the eye, trying to decide what to do next. Patrick smiled, but there was no humour in it. It looked more like a grimace. The dealer muttered under his breath and walked away. As he did, he raised his middle finger and waved it in Patrick's face. Patrick was fast. He grabbed the extended digit and twisted it hard against the knuckle. The dealer went down onto his knees in seconds.

"Ah!" He cried. The pub went silent, everyone looking toward the scuffle. Patrick twisted the finger harder and the youth went over onto his back. "Fuck off! Get off me!"

"I told you to fuck off, now do it!" Patrick was still smiling as he helped the dealer up onto his feet. The other tracksuits in the pub were looking on with interest. Some were laughing at the youth and enjoying his embarrassment while others were snarling. Gecko thought it was time to leave.

"Finish your pint. We'll talk at my place." Nate swallowed his beer and stood up. He met the glares with his own stern eyes. They were outnumbered, but the youngsters were wary. Patrick followed suit and emptied his glass. As they left, a beer glass shattered above the door and their legitimate birth rights were questioned, but no one followed them.

"I could have done without that," Nate said.

"What's the problem?" Patrick laughed.

"I was trying to be discreet."

"Well, you weren't," Patrick laughed again. "It could not have been more obvious that you were watching Benjamin's gaff. You were behind a desk too long, soldier."

Nate laughed too. He was right. Patrick Lloyd was sharp and he could be useful. They climbed into his car and made the short journey in silence. Both men knew they were about to plan a serious crime. A burglary at best, but murder was more probable. Nate lived in a large detached house in a secluded cul-de-sac. Most of the driveways were empty, their owners at work. There were a few obligatory four by four vehicles parked up waiting for the school run, but the road was quiet. As the Gecko parked up, a dark Audi pulled in behind him.

"Rozzers," Patrick said, looking in the wing mirror. "They've been behind us since we turned into your road. I can spot them a mile away."

"Shit!" Nate whispered. He had left the drugs and money he had taken took from Grebby under the back seat.

"What do they want?" Patrick raised an eyebrow.

"I'm not sure. I lost my son not long ago. It's probably something to do with that." Nate opened the door and climbed out. He closed the door before Patrick could say anything. Two overweight detectives approached him, wearing crumpled trousers and scruffy overcoats. The pride of the police force they were not. "How can I help you?" He asked as they came closer.

"Do you know Carl Lewis?" The detective asked without making any small talk.

"He was a friend of my son."

"Have you seen him at all?" The police officer eyed him suspiciously. He shoved his hands deep into his pockets. His shoes were scuffed and dirty.

"No, not since Nate's funeral."

"One of his friends told us you were asking questions about him," the second officer added.

"I did ask questions about him, because you didn't." Nate answered icily. "I wanted to know who gave my son the ecstasy tablet that killed him."

"Did you see Carl Lewis?"

"No. I asked who brought the tablets to the wake. That's it."

"So you found out who gave the tablet to your son, and then you did nothing about it?" The detective pushed.

"I did do something about it."

"What did you do?"

"I reported it to you!" Nate jabbed his finger towards the detectives accusingly. His face contorted into an angry snarl. "I reported it to you and you did nothing!"

The detectives looked at one another and blushed. They shuffled uncomfortably on the pavement. "There was no offence committed. Your son took the tablet. Nobody forced him."

"Fuck you!" Nate snarled. "He had just buried his mother."

"Where were you last Wednesday?" The detective pushed on regardless.

"Why?" Nate shrugged. He needed to buy some time.

"Answer the question."

"We were fishing on the Wirral," Patrick Lloyd spoke. He appeared from behind Nate. "We went to New Brighton last Wednesday."

The detectives looked deflated. "Were you there all day?"

"We got there about seven and didn't leave until midnight. We landed shitloads of mackerel, didn't we?" Patrick turned to Nate. "What's this all about, anyway?" He grinned.

"Carl Lewis is missing." The detective answered.

"I'd be looking at his friends and his dealer," Nate said. "He was selling ecstasy to teenagers at college. It's a dangerous game to play."

"Thanks for your time." The detective mumbled and walked back to their car. Nate and Patrick Lloyd watched them drive away. It was the beginning of a murderous partnership.

CRIMINALLY INSANE

Chapter Twenty-Five

The Gecko: *The Past*

Nate Bradley wanted to get into Jacky Benjamin's home and interrogate him. He needed to know who supplied him with drugs. His investigations so far had told him that not only had he supplied the tablet, which had killed his son, he had also supplied his wife with a cocktail of drugs. Patrick Lloyd had a score to settle with Jacky Benjamin, too. He had ordered a plaything from him and then pulled out at the last minute. Jacky Benjamin had wanted a Chinese woman for a night. Simple enough to arrange, but he had called it off and made Patrick look foolish with his contacts. To make matters worse, Benjamin had spread rumours that it had been Patrick who had reneged on the deal. He lived or died by his reputation, and he couldn't allow that to happen. When Patrick had contacted Benjamin about the rumours, the dealer had threatened to have him killed and thrown in the Mersey. Patrick wasn't having that from a man half his age. He wanted payback, and luckily for him, so did Nate Bradley. Patrick had an affinity with him. They were both killers. Bad people magnetise with one another. What he didn't understand was the fact that Nate killed for a purpose, whereas Patrick killed for pleasure. They were planning to break into Benjamin's house, take his money and drugs and execute him. Patrick wanted to redistribute the drugs for profit, but Nate would not hear of it. He had lost his wife and son because of drugs, and he wanted them taken out of circulation. There was quite a stash building up in his lockup again. He wasn't sure what he wanted to do with them, but he didn't want Patrick to sell them. As they planned the hit, Patrick had other ideas.

They sat a distance away from the dealer's house and watched. After a week of reconnaissance, they knew his movements and decided to hit him the following night. They drove to the Bluebell estate and waited for the shellsuits to leave. It was two o'clock in the morning when the bedroom light went off, and then they climbed out of Patrick's van. Benjamin must have gone to bed for the night. They pulled balaclavas on and grabbed their tools. Patrick was fascinated by Nate. There was coolness about him that he admired. It was obvious that he was a professional. He didn't know how far he would go or what he was trying to achieve exactly, but he would find out tonight.

"Did you kill him?" Patrick asked unexpectedly.

"Who?" Nate answered.

"Carl Lewis, the kid that disappeared." Patrick smiled beneath the balaclava. He knew the answer but he wanted to know how deep their trust went.

"Yes, he killed my son," was the simple answer.

"What about Benjamin?" Patrick pushed.

"He killed him too. Let's get on with it." Nate closed the door and walked toward the back of the house.

"What about whoever supplied Benjamin? When does it end?" Patrick beamed as he spoke.

"We'll find out who supplied him tonight." Nate mumbled. He wasn't sure when it would be over. He didn't care.

As they approached the house, Nate kept low and moved fast. It was basic training in the forces. Keep low, move fast and watch your corners. Soldiers never forgot it, because it was what kept them alive in urban warfare. The dogs were already dead. Patrick had poisoned them three days earlier. Benjamin was devastated, thinking it had been retaliation by someone with a grudge. Patrick used pliers to cut through the camera wires and disable the alarm box. He drilled through the window frame and threaded a wire around the window latch. They were inside the house in seconds.

The living room was a mess, beer cans and fast food cartons littered the floor. There was a teenage boy asleep on the settee, snoring peacefully. Nate moved quickly and pulled him off the settee by his feet. Patrick was on him, gagging him with a strip of towel. They fastened zip ties around his wrists and ankles and then dragged him into the corner.

"Make a sound and you are dead," Patrick hissed. The teenager nodded. As Nate moved out of earshot, Patrick whispered in the boy's ear. "You're dead anyway, but we'll have some fun first, kiddo." The teenager's eyes widened in fear and tears formed. Patrick liked it when they cried.

"Where does he keep the drugs and the money?" Patrick asked. It was a long shot, but worth a try. The juvenile shook his head. He was scared, but he didn't want to grass. Patrick slapped him hard across the face, splitting his lip. They moved upstairs as one unit, listening for any sign that their presence was known. It was silent. Patrick opened the front bedroom door and they moved toward the slumbering lump in the double bed. There was a baseball bat leaning against the wall next to a bedside table. The table was packed with dirty coffee mugs in various stages of deterioration. There was a smell of mould mixed with sweaty feet pervading the room. Patrick picked up the baseball bat and before Nate could protest, he smashed it into the drug dealer's knees.

"What the fuck!" Benjamin bellowed. He sat up and tried to scramble for the drawer of the bedside cabinet. There was a gun there, but he couldn't reach it. They were too quick. He was bound and gagged in minutes. They carried him down the stairs between them and fastened him to a wooden chair with bungee cords. His teenage friend looked on with fear in his eyes, especially when Patrick plugged in the Morphy-Richards steam iron he had found in the kitchen. Nate was sharpening a carving knife in front of Jacky's face. His eyes widened in terror as he started to cut his bedclothes off with the blade. He looked at the iron steaming and realised what was going to happen. As Nate cut the elastic in his boxer shorts and ripped them off, Jacky Benjamin panicked and started choking on the gag. He was trying to say something.

"Take the gag off," Nate said.

"I think he's nervous, do you?" Patrick laughed.

"Most people hate ironing." Nate bent down and looked into the dealer's eyes. "Especially naked it can be dangerous. You wouldn't want to burn the crown jewels, would you?"

"What do you want?" Benjamin gasped as the gag was removed. "Who are you?"

"We want your money and your drugs, Jacky." Patrick picked up the iron and held it close to his face. He pressed the steam button and the iron hissed as it released boiling vapour from the ports in the heat plate. It was close enough to act as a warning.

"I don't keep anything here," Benjamin lied.

Nate was about to speak when Patrick pressed the iron against the dealer's face. He held it there and pressed the steam button again. Jacky Benjamin screamed. Nate rammed the gag back into his mouth, worried the screaming could be heard from outside. He glared at Patrick, but didn't say anything. There had been no need to burn Jacky yet. The psychological threat was enough. It was becoming clear that Patrick was impulsive and impulse lead to mistakes. Nate Bradley didn't like mistakes.

"I'll ask you again. Where are your drugs and your money?" Patrick asked. He sniffed the burnt skin that was stuck to the iron and laughed. There was a perfect imprint of the heat plate burnt into Benjamin's cheek. He was trembling with shock and tears streamed from his eyes. Patrick pulled the gag out of his mouth.

The drug dealer gritted his teeth and swallowed hard before answering. "Fuck off!"

Patrick was about to burn him a second time, when Nate stopped him. "Wait." He held up his hand. "Do you want this crazy bastard to burn your face off for the sake of your money? He will carry on all night, can you?"

"There's a couple of grand in the drawer next to the bed," Benjamin said. "Take it and piss off."

"Oh, I think you are insulting our intelligence, Jacky boy," Nate laughed. "A clever boy like you keeps more than a few grand around. One last time, then I'll leave him to it. Where are the money and the drugs?"

Jacky Benjamin looked at the iron and winced at the sight of his blackened skin melted to it. He thought for long seconds about his answer. "Look, whoever is paying you, I'll double it."

"No one is paying us," Nate said flatly.

"Are you Leon's muppets?" Benjamin asked, looking from one to the other. "Is he pissed off with me? Is someone else after my area or what?"

"Last chance, where is it?" Nate asked calmly. Patrick pressed the steam button once again.

"Fuck off!" Jacky Benjamin threw his weight backward in an attempt to escape the bungees. The chair toppled and he landed on his back. He thrashed about, desperately trying to escape. Patrick forced the dealer's knees apart and pushed the steam iron into his groin. Benjamin let out a bloodcurdling scream as his testicles sizzled on the metal. "Okay! Stop," he gurgled. His breathing was shallow and his eyes looked as if they may pop out of his head. Despite his pleas, Patrick held the iron there, fascinated by the pain his captive was feeling. "Stoooooop!" Jacky wailed.

"Stop it." Nate pulled Patrick's arm.

"What is your problem?" Patrick turned on him. "This scumbag killed your son." The smell of scorched flesh filled the air. Nate saw something in Patrick's eyes. Pure hatred. He had seen a thousand interrogators at work. Some of them enjoyed their subject's pain more than others, but Patrick had something else. He was just plain evil.

"He is no good to me unconscious just now," Nate said calmly. He was cool as a cucumber. They looked at each other and there was tension between them, but Nate had to take control of the situation. Patrick had to realise who was in charge here. "We need him to talk."

"Yes, I suppose so," Patrick laughed again. "I bet that hurt, lad." He mocked Benjamin cruelly.

"It's in the washing machine," Benjamin gasped. "Take the panel off the front. My stash is in there."

Nate nodded to Patrick, who reluctantly put the iron down and went into the kitchen to check out the washing machine. The younger boy he had tied up earlier was sobbing as he watched things unfold. He patted the terrified teenager on the head as he stepped over him. "Don't worry, you're next," he laughed. The teenager started crying and a dark stain spread across the crotch of his jeans. Watching them burning his boss was too much. He decided that drug dealing was not the glamorous career he had thought it might be. Patrick grabbed a screwdriver from a drawer and forced the front panel. It clattered on the floor.

"What did he mean?" Benjamin sobbed.

"What?" Nate replied.

"What did he mean, I killed your son?" He was sobbing and his face was twisted with pain.

"He died after taking one of your ecstasy tablets," Nate answered calmly.

"What?" Benjamin tried to turn around to see Nate properly. "When? How do you know he bought it from me?"

"He bought it from a kid called Carl Lewis."

"Is he the kid that's gone missing?" His eyes widened as he spoke. "The police have been all over me about him and his mate, Grebby. They're both missing. You must be Nate Bradley's father."

"Bingo," Nate nodded.

"Is that what this about?" Benjamin whined.

"Pretty much."

"I'm sorry about your son. What's your name?"

"Nate," he said quietly.

"Well, Nate, I am sorry about your son. I am really sorry about your son," the dealer sounded genuine. "I have never wanted to hurt any of the youngsters."

"Hurt them? You killed Nate." Nate Bradley senior was still calm. His voice was clear and crisp. "You killed Nate but you haven't stopped selling the same shit that poisoned him, have you?"

"It was an accident, Nate. It was a one in a million accident," the dealer cried.

"One too many from where I am stood," Nate answered.

Patrick walked back into the room with a sports bag full of money and drugs. He was laughing and rooting through the contents like a child in a sweet shop.

"Look what we have here. We have Charlie, weed, speed, ecstasy and smack, plus about a hundred grand. We've hit the jackpot," he laughed.

"Take it all. Take it all and I give you my word that I won't come after you. Call it compensation," Benjamin was talking quickly. Patrick's reappearance had made him panic again. He knew the identity of his attacker and so did the teenager. That was not good. If they left him alive, there was the chance of him looking for revenge or his drugs and money back. He could go to the police, although that would be unlikely; how did you complain that somebody had stolen your drugs? The chances of them leaving him alive were slim. "Take it. I am genuinely sorry about your son."

"Shut up, scumbag." Patrick stamped on his chest.

"Who supplies you?" Nate asked calmly.

"What?" Benjamin looked incredulous.

"Who supplies you with drugs?"

"What does it matter?" Benjamin whined. He didn't think he was going to walk away from this one. Patrick picked up the iron and pressed the steam button. Benjamin began to sob uncontrollably. He shook his head. "I buy them from Leon Tanner. He gets them from a Turk called Sally. His name is Salim. He owns Connections in town."

"Where does he get them?" Nate asked. "Who is at the top of the tree?"

"I know him," Patrick interrupted. "He's one of the Turkish mafia. They're the biggest importers in the country. They're right at the top of the pile."

"Fair enough," Nate nodded. "Then I'm done here."

"Okay, boss. You take the stash and I'll finish things off here. I'll catch up with you tomorrow," Patrick said. He handed Nate the bag and guided him toward the backdoor. "There is no need for both of us to hang around. You put the gear safe and I'll tidy up here."

"Please don't leave me here with him," Benjamin said.

"You didn't care who you hurt. Why should I?" Nate replied. He wasn't sure why Patrick was so eager to stay, but he didn't care.

"Your missus liked her smack, didn't she?" Jacky laughed like a wild man. He realised he was going to finish the night dead or dying. The guy with the iron was a lunatic. He could see that in his eyes. There was a little comfort in hitting back the only way he could. "Hey, I said your missus liked her smack."

"What?" Nate stopped at the door and turned back.

"Yes, when you said the name, Bradley. I knew that was your missus," Jacky sneered. "She was alright for her age, when she wasn't smashed of her head, that is."

"She was my wife and Nate's mother," Nate spoke quietly. "You destroyed her for cash."

"Cash?" Benjamin laughed wildly. He knew he was dead anyway. "She ran out of money a long time ago."

"What do you mean?" Nate asked. He had heard the ranting of dying men many times before. They rarely told the truth.

"Did you know she was taking it up the arse for her smack?" Benjamin grinned. "She fucking loved it. There was nothing that she wouldn't do for a hit."

Patrick Lloyd brought the iron down onto the dealers face. His scream was stifled as his lips sizzled. His body twitched as Patrick pressed the steam button and a cloud of boiling vapour engulfed the dealer's head.

"We need to discuss your manners," Patrick smiled as the dealer desperately tried to escape the pain. Nate Bradley took the bag and unlocked the steel plate, opening the door and stepping out into the night without saying another word. Nothing needed to be said. Patrick seemed to enjoy hurting people, buzzing off their fear. Nate never did. It was purely a means to an end. As he reached the van, he heard Benjamin's muffled screams. They meant nothing to him.

Patrick Lloyd took his time killing Jacky Benjamin. Most of the man's skin was burned with the iron before he shattered every major bone in his body with the baseball bat. It felt good, and making the teenager watch was exciting. When he was done, he fetched his camper and returned for the boy. He took him to an empty factory unit near the river, Jamaica Street, and had hours of fun with him. It took the teenager days to finally die, and it entertained Patrick so much, he didn't pick up his share of the tax until three days later. Working with the Gecko was fun, but his extracurricular activities were mind-blowing. He hadn't enjoyed himself so much in years.

Twenty-Six

Kisha Arobe

Kisha sat at her desk and sighed as she looked at the notes her fellow officer, Stevie Nelson, had left next to the computer. They looked like a five year old had scrawled on a piece of A4. He had circled some of the names in balloons; ticks and crosses were marked randomly in the margins. There was no sense to his workings. She picked her own notes and tried to compare them to his. Her handwriting was beautiful; she formed the letters perfectly. Kisha was proud of her work, and her reports looked more like a dissertation than a brief update.

"How is it going, Kisha?" Will asked, disturbing her thoughts.

"Slow," she answered, forcing a smile. She didn't want to drop Stevie in the mire, but it was obvious that he hadn't finished entering the information they had gathered into the database before leaving the station. "We seem to be going around in circles entering all the key holders."

"How come?" Will leaned over the back of the chair but maintained a comfortable distance between them. "How much info have you got?"

"Over three hundred names to crosscheck against flags in the investigation." She pushed her chair back and frowned. "We've gathered a list consisting of anyone who had access to the building's keys. We've included the owners, partners, shift managers, painters, joiners, roofers, bailiffs, the current estate agents and their service contractors!"

"It's a lot to filter through," Will laughed. The crime scene on Jamaica Street was a rented industrial unit, which had changed hands numerous times over the past decade.

"Tell me about it, she sighed. Stevie had done nothing but hamper her work, but she didn't want to tell Will that. "We've established that it has stood empty for the last four years, which has done little to narrow down the search."

"Keep plugging away," Will said. "Let me know if you need any help."

"Thanks, Will."

"Where is Stevie, by the way?" Will stopped as he walked away.

"I think he's running late," Kisha lied. Will nodded and frowned. He walked across the office without making any comment about her partner's absence.

Kisha had no idea where Stevie was, but she didn't feel it was her place to say that. She picked up the top page of information and scanned it to see where they were up to.

"Do you want a brew, Kisha?" Smithy walked past and patted her on the shoulder on his way to the kitchen. Normally the touch of a man made her skin crawl, but Smithy was different because she knew he had no sexual interest in her. She looked up to him. The Superintendent had paired them as a team on several cases. As a new detective, he had given her a mentor to guide her. Smithy had taken her under his wing and they had gotten on well. They went for a drink after work some days and Kisha felt comfortable with him. He treated her as a fellow officer and had no sexual interest in her. If he did, he kept it a secret.

"Yes, please, Smithy," she said. She smiled as he walked by although she didn't feel much like smiling. She wanted to be at the cutting edge of the investigation, not tied to a computer.

"How are you finding working with Stevie Nelson?" Smithy lowered his voice. He didn't like the man. Kisha was his pet newcomer and as her mentor, they had become close friends.

"He is grinding me down." She looked tired out.

"Is he behaving himself?" Smithy asked. "I know you said he came on to you at Christmas."

"Don't get me started." She looked around to see if anyone was listening. "He is constantly making sexual innuendoes and brushing against me when there's no need to."

"Do you want me to have a word with him?"

"I can fight my own battles, but thanks," she chuckled. "He's a sexist pig."

"He is," Smithy agreed with a smile.

"It has crossed my mind to make a formal complaint already, but we're only a few days into the task."

"If it's pissing you off, then you should."

"No, Smithy. I can't do that." She put her head in her hands for a moment. "You know how things work. It's hard enough for a female to fit in with you macho-men!" She laughed. "I can't leave a trail of harassment complaints behind me on the way to becoming chief!" She took a deep breath and smiled again. There would be plenty of Stevie Nelsons along the way.

"Chief constable?" Smithy laughed. "Just remember who your friends are when you reach the top, missus!"

"What's your name again?"

"Very funny," Smithy smiled. "Seriously though, maybe I should have a little word in his shell," Smithy clenched his fist and laughed. "A clip around the ear is all it takes."

"No, you fool," she smiled. She knew he meant it, but that wasn't the answer.

"You look really down," he said seriously.

"Things aren't great at the moment." She tilted her head to one side.

"Do you want to talk?"

"Maybe later, but thanks," she smiled again, but there was sadness in her eyes. Her partner was an idiot and on top of all that, things at home were on a downhill slide. Her partner of three months was having a crisis. She had left her husband and two children to live with Kisha, but now she wasn't sure if she was gay or not. How could she not know? They had argued about it day in and day out for weeks, but Kisha could not understand her uncertainty. She said she wasn't gay, she must be bi-sexual, some days she fancied Chinese food and other days she fancied Indian food. That comment had hurt Kisha deeply. How could her partner compare their love to takeaways? The situation was making life difficult, and she wasn't sleeping properly. Kisha was tired and working with a pig like Stevie was not helping matters one bit.

"How is the list of key holders coming?" Smithy's voice disturbed her thoughts. She could hear cups clinking in the sink as he rinsed them out. "Are you getting anywhere?"

"Slowly, needle in a haystack is crossing my mind," Kisha shook her head and she tried to fathom what system her partner was using to enter the information. Stevie was a stubborn man and he always knew better. Kisha tried to explain her dilemma to Smithy. "I've been entering the names of key holders in date order, as it seems more likely that recent key holders should be the priority, but Stevie disagrees and he is insisting on entering information in alphabetical order. We're going around in circles."

"The system is tetchy at best, so if you're entering the same names twice, it will cause it to crash," Smithy said.

"It did yesterday, and we had a heated exchange," Kisha moaned. "I don't want to fall out with the man, but in the end I went out and interviewed some of the recent key holders on my way home and left Stevie to it."

"You two need to sort it out before the governor finds out," Smithy said quietly. "He won't be pleased if you're getting nowhere."

"I know. Stevie must have had the same idea and given up inputting names. He has probably gone to interview some of the key holders." At least that was what she thought.

"Call him and see where he is. Then catch up with him. Neither of you should be working on your own, you know that, Kisha," Smithy warned.

"I know," she said. "Thanks, Smithy. I'll do that."

"Do you want a chocolate biscuit with your brew?" Smithy sang the words. He always seemed to be happy no matter what was going on around him.

"No, thank you," Kisha replied waving her finger. "I have to watch my weight." She laughed. She didn't have to watch her weight at all. She was one of those lucky people who could eat whatever they liked without putting on the pounds.

"I have been watching mine for years, but it just keeps going up," Smithy chuckled. "One won't hurt."

"That's the start of a slippery slope, Smithy." Kisha smiled at him. "One leads to two and suddenly the packet is empty."

"What do you mean?" Smithy frowned. "You cannot possibly leave any biscuits in the packet, Kisha. They go stale."

"Spoken like a true chocoholic in denial," she laughed. The problems at home were gone for a second. Smithy had the ability to make people laugh.

"My body is a temple, young lady. The problem is I worship the Buddha."

"The Buddha is cool, Smithy," she laughed. "Fat but cool."

"So I am fat now, am I?" He frowned in mock disgust.

"No. The Buddha is fat."

"Do you want a biscuit or what?"

"Yes, Smithy," she grimaced and nodded her head. "I am afraid I do."

"Just one, though."

"Just one," she agreed.

Kisha hit the return button on the keyboard to look at the last entry that her partner had made. Smithy clumsily put down a cup of weak brown liquid, and it splashed coffee onto her disorganised pile of names. Entries were in neither date nor alphabetical order. She couldn't work in such a random fashion. She needed to work to a system. Stevie was holding her back. She couldn't read his handwriting because it was so bad, which caused arguments when they were entering names into the database.

"Oops!" Smithy chuckled as he walked away. He had a biscuit between his teeth and a cup in each hand. "Sorry, Kisha."

"Thanks for nothing, Smithy!" Kisha laughed. She reached into the bottomless pit of her handbag for a wet wipe. They were essential kit, and she never ran out. She dabbed at the spill and wiped coffee from the papers. One of the cleaners walked towards the desk to empty her wastepaper bin. They started work at stupid o'clock in the morning.

"Hi, Sue," Kisha pushed her chair back. "Have you seen Stevie this morning?"

"You mean Slimy Steve?" Sue replied with a wicked giggle.

"Sue! You can't call him that," Kisha whispered.

"Bollocks," Sue giggled. "That's what all the girls call him. Slimy bastard he is. Anyway, he was in earlier."

Listening to the banter, Smithy stopped and frowned. "Maybe he's gone to see some of the people on your list. My advice is to ring him, Kisha. Then meet him somewhere."

"Yes, I think I will." She raised her eyebrows and smiled. Smithy got the message; she didn't want to expand on the issue between her and her colleague in front of the cleaners. He pointed a finger to his lips and nodded.

"Say no more!" He said.

"Smithy!" Will shouted from across the office. He was pulling on his jacket in a hurry. "We have the warrant to enter Salim Oguzhan's house."

"Fucking hell," Smithy put his brew down. "I've just made a brew." He laughed and grabbed his coat. "Kisha, my dear, we'll see you later."

"Yes, see you later." She felt her heart sink as she watched the team heading for the lifts. The rest of the team would be out there on the case while she sifted through a pile of crap. She took a mouthful of coffee and searched through the pile. Kisha sorted the five most recent key holders from the pile and then checked their addresses against the electoral role. Three of the names were still living at the listed address, and she decided to go and do some legwork. It would take her out of the stifling office for a few hours, and she needed some fresh air. If Stevie was out there knocking on doors and expecting her to sit there and input data like a secretary, then he had another think coming. She dialled his mobile number. It rang twice and then jumped to voice mail.

"Bastard has just busy buttoned me!" She whispered to herself. She grabbed her car keys, her handbag and the list with the three names on it. If he wanted to play silly buggers, then so could she. She decided to make a few enquiries on her own while she calmed down. The first name on the list was Patrick Floyd.

Chapter Twenty-Seven

Dean Hines

Dean Hines looked at his mobile phone and sighed. He had nine missed calls in total, shared between Leon and Jackson. They were stressing because he hadn't answered their first calls. He looked up at the morning sky, tears rolling down his cheeks. There was a sick feeling in his stomach. It was the worst feeling he could ever have imagined. He felt like the situation was ripping his heart from his chest. His children were in a crisis, close to death. The night before, when he had arrived home, his wife, Denise, had been tired and in a mood. The kids – Kaylee, aged three, and Dean junior, aged five – were under the weather. They had been grumpy and unresponsive all day, but now they were feverish and floppy. When Dean had touched their hands, they had been cold despite the fever. When a rash had developed and spread quickly, he had placed a glass over the rash, but it hadn't faded. Meningitis had struck his sister's baby two years ago, and by the time they had diagnosed it, it had been too late. He was not about to allow the same thing to happen to his kids. Denise and his children were his life, the reason he lived and breathed. Dean had telephoned an ambulance and they had been in the hospital all night. The children had deteriorated in the ambulance and their condition had not improved since. Dean had turned his phone off the first time it had rung, and he hadn't looked at it since.

Dean knew why Leon was calling. He was expecting a huge shipment of crystal meth to arrive and Dean was supposed to collect the cash from the 'Crazy Computer' store and pick it up. Jackson would be calling about the hit on Jinx. He wanted the blood money. Dean didn't want anything to do with the hit. His kids were in a critical condition in the intensive care unit. Denise was hysterical one minute, and zombielike the next. His in-laws were doing their best to support them and offer encouraging words, but right now Dean was numb. He could never have imagined the fear he felt for his children right now. The pain inside him was unbearable, and he was helpless. He couldn't do anything to make them well or to stop their suffering. They were in the hands of the doctors and nurses who were flocking around them. From the expressions on their faces and the whispered concerns, Dean could tell the prognosis wasn't good at all. Their fingers and toes were turning black, which they told him was a sign of septicaemia. When the doctors mentioned amputation, Dean was physically sick. He ran to the gents' toilet and vomited until there was nothing left inside him, and then he staggered outside in a daze to get some fresh air.

He was not sure why he turned on his phone. Looking at it was a habit, he guessed. As he looked at the missed calls, it rang again. Leon's name was flashing on the screen. Dean looked at it as it flashed, debating whether to answer it. He had to explain his predicament to his boss, or he would assume the worst. Leon had looked after him for years and despite the recent issues, he was grateful to him.

"Hi, Leon," Dean gasped into the telephone.

"Where the fucking hell have you been?" Leon ranted. He liked to rant. "I've been calling you all morning."

"I'm at the hospital, Leon," Dean shouted to stop the tirade. "The kids were rushed in with meningitis. They're in a bad way, Leon."

"How long are you going to be?" Leon moaned. He jabbed a podgy finger against the dashboard of his Bentley. He was calling on hands free from London. He made sure he was out of town when a shipment came in. The plan was to stay out of town while the drugs were sold on and Jinx was shot. He didn't need any cock-ups.

"What do you mean, how long are they going to be?" Dean was incredulous. He felt like his heart was being ripped out. His children were close to death and he needed to be with them. He lost his cool and shouted into the phone. "My kids could die, Leon. They haven't got measles. They could die!"

"Listen, Deano," Leon growled. "I'm in London. You're not answering your telephone, neither is that twat Jackson, and I'm not fucking psychic!"

"Jackson has been calling me, but my phone has been off."

"Like I said, I am not fucking psychic," Leon calmed his voice a little. "Look, I'm sorry about your kids. I'll get Monkey and Gareth to make the pickup, but if I can't get hold of Jackson, then I need you to get the cash from the shop safe."

"Fucking hell," Dean whined. He scuffed his white Adidas training shoe against the hospital wall. "I really do not need this shit right now, Leon."

"Just remember that it's this shit that has been feeding your kids since they were born." Leon sounded like he had gravel in his throat. "I will keep trying Jackson. You ring him too just in case there's a reason why he isn't answering the phone with me, but if we cannot reach him, you have the only set of keys. I'm in London, Dean, and empty-head Jackson is nowhere to be found. I need you to get that money out of the safe." There was no compromise in his voice. Dean had little choice but to do as Leon asked. The drug money was under lock and key, and the importers would not wait around.

"What time do they need the money?" Dean looked at his watch. He needed to get back to the ward.

"Twelve noon at the latest," Leon replied. He grinned at his reflection in the mirror. This was a big deal. It would net him millions and it was low risk. "Drop the money off at the McDonalds on Queen's Drive. I'll arrange for Monkey to meet you there. Pass the money over and fuck off back to your kids, okay?"

"Okay, but keep trying Jackson, yes?" Dean kicked the wall again in frustration. "If I haven't heard from him by eleven, I'll leave here."

"Sorted," Leon grunted.

"Yes, sorted," Dean replied sulkily.

"I hope your kids are okay, Dean," Leon said.

"Thanks," Dean said as the line went dead. He pulled up Jackson's number and pressed dial, but it clicked straight to voicemail. Something told him that Jackson wasn't going to show.

Chapter Twenty-Eight

MIT

Alec left Jessie to be interviewed and processed by his officers. It had taken most of the evening to debrief Jessie and he had taken them over the story of the nightclub multiple times before Alec had been positive that he hadn't missed anything. It was late when they finished, and he grabbed a few hours of sleep on a saggy settee in his office. He was tempted to go home, but he didn't see the point. The house was empty. Gail had left him. He felt his stomach tighten when he thought about her. The drive home would come soon enough and he would face that when the time came. The Parker murder was his priority for now. He would catch up with the hunt for Rose James once the formalities were completed. Jessie would have to go into the witness protection program for the remainder of his life, but Alec hoped that he could return his wife to him first. Then he would have to convince his own wife to return, too. That could prove to be the more difficult task, even though she was at liberty to go where she liked.

The robbery at the nightclub puzzled him. It was a conundrum indeed. There was a link between what had happened at the nightclub and Salim Oguzhan. There was also a link between Salim Oguzhan and the Louise Parker murder, but he couldn't see it yet. Will Naylor and his team were about to enter the Oguzhan residence. Alec decided to wait for his call before following him. If the house was deserted, it could be a waste of his time.

Chapter Twenty-Nine

Oguzhan Residence

"Nice house," Smithy said as he climbed out of the car. "Upside down, but nice." The house had a long sloping roof and white rendered walls. The living room was on the first floor, and full-length picture windows offered a panoramic view of the landscaped gardens. The daylight was fading and shadows were creeping up the walls. The occupants had drawn the thick drapes closed. "Are we just going straight in?"

"That's the plan," Will replied. He pulled on a black stab vest and tossed a large one to Smithy. "Does this fit?" He laughed.

"Fuck off, with respect," Smithy laughed and pulled his body armour on.

"Let's go and see if Salim is in, shall we?"

The detectives walked across a neat lawn to the front door where an armed unit was waiting. The lead officer was holding a red battering ram over his shoulder, ready to smash the front door open. Will held the warrant in his right hand, but he had a feeling that no one would ask to see it.

"Let's get in there, please." Will waved to the lead officer. As he spoke, he noticed a movement from one of the bedroom windows to the left. "Hold on!" He shouted.

"What is it, Will?" Smithy asked, following the inspector's gaze. "Did you see something?"

"That curtain moved," Will pointed. "The black one."

"That will be one of the bedrooms."

"Okay," Will said to the armed officers. "Take the bedrooms first, please, we'll move upstairs when they're cleared."

"Will!" Smithy shouted. He had walked toward the window. There was a narrow flowerbed between the lawn and the house. Winter pansies smiled up at him in a uniform pattern.

"What is it, Smithy?"

He was staring at the curtain. It seemed to be moving slightly, as if a breeze was causing it to ripple slightly. At first, he thought someone might be looking through it or the owner might have left a window open, but then he realised that the curtain itself was moving. "That's not a curtain." Smithy banged on the glass. A clear space appeared in the curtain, then it covered the glass again. He banged again. "They are flies, Will."

Chapter Thirty

Jinx

Jinx checked his scanner program to confirm the whereabouts of Dean Hines and Leon Tanner. Leon's Bentley was clearly on the way to London, which made sense if Leon had put out a hit on him. The first thing he would do was leave the city. Jackson was the priority to Jinx. He was a mercenary and he was dangerous. Jinx had acquired the services of David Lorimar to neutralise the threat against his life. If all had gone according to plan, Jackson and Dean should be dead already. Dean's tracker had been stationary outside the Royal Liverpool hospital all night. Jackson didn't drive, so Jinx couldn't tag his vehicle. Maybe Dean had been shot, or maybe Jackson had been shot. He had not heard from Dava since the contract had been placed, that was just the way it worked. There would be no contact between them until the he had completed the job. Telephone records were evidence, which could connect them to the murders at a later date. Silence was essential.

Jinx wanted to know what the state of play was. He searched for the contact details on the internet and decided to phone the hospital. He clipped a prepaid sim card into his phone and rang the general enquiries number.

"Hello, Royal Liverpool, how can I help you?" The switchboard answered.

"Hello, I'm trying to find out how my brother is. I think he was admitted last night," Jinx lied.

"What's your brother's name?"

"Dean Hines."

"Hold the line; I'll transfer you to the children's ward."

Jinx took a breath. The children's ward? His brain tried to compute the information. Dean Hines was in a children's ward. Why?

"Hello, ICU," a female voice answered abruptly.

"Hello," Jinx was struggling to think straight. "I am enquiring how Dean Hines is."

"Are you a relative?" The voice answered impatiently.

"I'm his brother." Then it clicked in his brain. Dean's son was called, after his father. His kid was in hospital. Dean's car had been there all night.

"I see; I'm afraid that the children are very poorly. I can't say any more than that."

"Children?" Jinx asked as the line went dead. He took the back from the phone and swapped his sim card into it, scrolling through his contacts list. One of his business associates was related to the Hines family through marriage. He pulled up his number and pressed the dial button.

"Alright, Jinx," a broad scouse accent answered. "How's it going, kidda?"

"Hiya, Jason," Jinx replied. "Listen, I've heard Deano's kids are in hospital. Have you heard anything?" He stood up and paced the room as he spoke. There was a hit out on him; he couldn't afford to let his guard down, but this changed things.

"Yes. They're in a bad way, lad." The scouse drawl sounded like he had phlegm in his mouth. "Meningitis. I've heard they might not make it. Who told you?" Jason asked curiously.

"Just one of the lads at the gym mentioned it to me. Thanks for that," Jinx said.

"No problem, mate," Jason said. "That was bad news about the Nelson brothers, eh?"

"Yes, bad news," Jinx was distracted. "Listen, I've got to dash, mate, thanks again," he cut the call short. Jinx looked out of the window of his riverside apartment. It was located in one of the many new developments along the River Mersey. It was in walking distance to the city centre, but far enough away to use as a retreat. He liked the river and the tranquil feeling it gave him as he watched it flowing slowly by. Jinx didn't have kids, but he knew how precious they were. He wanted them, someday, with the right woman, just not yet. Jinx had a lot to think about, but he had to do it quickly. David Lorimar did not waste time, and he had the contract to kill Dean Hines.

CRIMINALLY INSANE

Chapter Thirty-One

Oguzhan Residence

After three hits of the big key, the armed unit moved into the Oguzhan residence. Will and Smithy waited until they heard the first calls of 'Clear!' before following. They could hear the armed unit pounding up the stairs and slamming doors open. If there was anyone home, then they were in for a rude awakening.

"Will!" A muffled call came from the corridor to the left. "You need to see this!"

Will walked into a wide kitchen diner. It was a modern design, lots of white units and chrome fittings. There was a dining table in the centre and something had upended two of the chairs on to the floor. A large church candle was lying on the black tiled floor, and Will decided that it had been the centrepiece of the table, obviously knocked across the kitchen during a struggle. He looked around. Then the smell reached him. It was the unmistakable stench of death. There were bluebottles on the ceiling and walls. A small squadron of them flew past him towards the open door. Will used a gloved hand to open a door to his left. It was dark inside and much cooler than the kitchen.

"It's the garage." Will turned the light on. "No white Porsche in here."

"I didn't think there would be, to be honest," Smithy said, wrinkling his nose at the smell.

"In here, Will!" A muffled voice called from the hallway, which led from the kitchen.

"This isn't good." Smithy said. He pulled a scarf from inside his vest and put it over his nose but it did nothing to stop the rotting smell from invading his nostrils. "I'll call SOCO and the coroner. I don't have to look any further to know this is a murder scene."

"You'd better call the governor too," Will nodded. His face was stern as he walked through the kitchen. There was blood smeared across the floor tiles where the kitchen met the hallway. Smithy followed as he called for the science teams to attend.

As they moved down the hallway, one of the armed officers ran past them with his hand over his mouth. They heard him retching as he reached the kitchen door. Two corridors led away from the kitchen and a carpeted staircase gave access to the upper floor. They could hear the armed unit stomping about as they conducted their search. Will walked toward the hallway and spotted bloody handprints on the magnolia painted walls. The bloodstains smeared the paint as if someone had clawed at it. Finger marks covered both sides of the hall. Whoever was bleeding had not wanted to go down the corridor to the bedroom. They had put up a fight on the way. The first bedroom door was on the left, an armed officer blocking the way. He stood staring at the scene, transfixed.

"Excuse me," Will touched his elbow. "Let the dog see the rabbit." He smiled despite the nervous tension he felt inside. Keeping calm and emotionally unattached from the scene was important at a murder scene. Any sympathy for the victims had to be shelved while they worked on the evidence before them. Personal feelings didn't matter here.

"Sorry, Will, but I've never seen anything...!" The man couldn't finish his sentence. "How could anyone do that?"

"I don't know," Will said as he moved into the bedroom. "Check upstairs with the others."

"Fuck me!" Smithy whispered under his breath as he followed Will. The dull buzz of bluebottles came from behind the curtains. One of them landed lazily on his face and he spat it away with a shudder. The room was small with a single bed and a wardrobe in it. An Everton team photograph was pinned to the left hand wall and the Undertaker and some of his wrestling pals were scowling on a poster to the right. A sticky piece of flesh was hanging on the poster, making it look like the wrestler had a piece of raw meat in his mouth. Blood splashes traced across the walls and ceilings in arcing patterns and the bedding was soaked with it. A crack ran across the wardrobe door; the middle had caved in on itself as if something heavy had fallen against it. On the floor was a black handled hatchet. Congealed blood coated the stainless-steel shaft and blade. A piece of skull was stuck to it. Long black hair clung to the fragment of rotting scalp.

"We don't have to look far for the murder weapon," Smithy said. Sometimes, sarcasm was his shield against the horrors of the job.

"Jesus wept," Will said. The body on the floor hardly resembled a human being. The face was nothing but blackened mush and the limbs were so badly hacked that there was no shape to them. The victim's clothes were scattered across the bed as if the killer had removed them during a violent struggle. Maggots crawled beneath the flesh, making the remnants of the face undulate. "Whoever this is, it's not Salim Oguzhan."

"Looks female to me, Will," Smithy said through the material of his scarf. The body was naked; the killer had hacked at the chest and torso so badly that the sex of the victim wasn't obvious. "Female, definitely," he added looking at the genital area.

"Is there any ID in the clothing?" Will pointed to the clothes.

"I can't see anything without moving them." Smithy kneeled down and poked the clothing gently with a pencil. "Better wait until Dr. Libby and his team get here."

"Inspector," a voice came from the doorway.

"Yes," Will found it hard to look away from the corpse. "What is it?"

"Two more bodies upstairs, Will." The armed officer was shaking visibly. "Both children."

Chapter Thirty-Two

MIT

Following a phone call, Alec joined Will at the Oguzhan home. The crime scene was like a clip from a zombie movie. There were now three more victims to add to their list.

"I am fucking stunned," Will said as they left the house. Crime scene officers had to study the building before they could remove the bodies. "Just when I thought I had seen it all."

"That's natural, Will," Alec said. "The guy is an animal. We need to shrug off what we've just seen and try to catch whoever is responsible."

"We don't know any more now than we did before we went in there, Guv." Will leaned against the wall and took in a deep breath of fresh air. "I wish I smoked, I could just go for a cig right now."

"I wish I smoked, too," Alec smiled thinly. "I could pinch one of yours."

"Fucking hell, Guv." Will shook his head and wiped a tear from his eye. "How scared must those poor kids have been?"

"They would have been terrified, Will, but we can't help them now. We can only do all we can to catch the bastard who did that to them."

"Where do we start piecing that together?" Will scoffed. "We have searched Salim's house and found nothing that can help us."

"We know he isn't in there," Alec nodded to the house. "We know that his car isn't in there and we know that whoever killed Louise Parker was here. This is the work of the psycho that strung her up, no doubt about it."

"His girlfriend, his wife and his two children have been slaughtered," Will snapped. "Either he killed them or he's dead too."

"We know he had three children, and there are two children's bodies in there," Alec thought aloud. "My guess is the third child was in the unit at Jamaica Street, and so was Salim."

"It didn't look as if he has gone into hiding, there are too many personal things left behind."

"You're working on the theory that our killer has the mentality of a well balanced mind, Will." Alec moved away from the house. "Whoever did that was in a rage beyond human comprehension."

"His bank accounts remain untouched." Will counted the points he was making on his fingers as he spoke. "His mobile phone records show that no calls or texts have been sent, although there are dozens of messages stored on his voice mail. His car is missing and we know that one of his children is unaccounted for. In my mind, all that means he is dead."

"You're probably right, Will." Alec could see that his inspector was tired. He looked drained and shattered by what he had seen. "Look, I need you sharp for the morning, Will. Go home for a few hours and get some sleep. I'll see you back at the station first thing."

"Thanks, Guv," Will sighed, "can't see me getting much sleep."

"We can't do anything tonight." Alec patted him on the back. "Have a shower, something to eat. Get some rest."

"Are you going to do the same, Guv?" Will laughed. He knew the answer to that.

"The mother-in-law is still at my place," Alec lied. "I'll get my head down at the station for a few hours."

Will nodded and turned to walk away. Alec headed for his car and ran over things in his mind when suddenly he heard Will beside him again. He obviously needed to talk.

"You know the chances of Salim Oguzhan being alive are next to zero, Guv," he said.

"Maybe," Alec shrugged. "He may have lost his mind, killed his wife and kids and then turned his attention to Louise Parker, robbed his own nightclub and gone on the run with the drugs and the money."

"Bollocks," Will laughed. "You don't believe that."

"No, I don't, but I'm thinking out loud." It was pushing the boundary of his imagination to believe that it could be true. It was rare that a fugitive went on the run leaving thousands of pounds in the bank. Usually they stashed their monies before they left their lives behind them. His bank accounts hadn't been touched for weeks.

"He may have taken the money from the poker game and the five kilos of heroin and done a runner?" Will said dryly.

"It is possible," Alec replied, but he had a gut feeling that it wasn't the case. "The Oguzhan family are killers, but this is in a different league. They're gangsters and they kill other gangsters. We're looking for a totally different type of killer."

"We're looking for a lunatic, Guv," Will shrugged.

"We are indeed, but I know one thing for certain," Alec turned to Will. "Our killer has killed before, without a doubt, and he doesn't care about getting caught, either."

"I agree," Will nodded. "He has lost the plot and that's what worries me. Look what the crazy bastard did to that family."

"We'll catch him, Will, but we need to find out what has happened to Salim Oguzhan." Alec knew Salim Oguzhan was the key, but they couldn't find him, and they were convinced that he was either the killer or another victim. "Go home, Will. I'll see you in a few hours."

Chapter Thirty-Three

MIT

Alec sat in his car at the Oguzhan home and closed his eyes for five minutes. His exhausted mind shut down and he fell into a troubled sleep. He was in bed with Gail, cosy and warm, until the alarm disturbed their sleep.

"Turn it off," Alec grumbled to his sleeping wife, but she wasn't there. He woke with a stiff neck and a cramp in his leg. The car was cold and he shivered as he looked around for his phone. There was a message alert on his Blackberry. He took the phone from his pocket and pressed *Retrieve*. He noticed that his trousers looked creased and scruffy.

"That's what you get for sleeping in your car or on the settee in the office," he heard Gail's voice in his imagination. "Why didn't you come home and sleep in your own bed?" She continued in his mind. As his wife's imaginary voice pecked his head, he read the message on his phone. It was an urgent message telling him to contact Graham Libby at the forensic labs. He decided to go straight there instead of calling the doctor. Alec turned the radio off and travelled to the station in silence. The roads were quiet. He went through the drive-thru of a twenty-four hour McDonalds for a sausage muffin and a strong black coffee. He left the hash brown because they gave him heartburn. Alec screwed up the wrappers and stuffed them into the brown paper carryout bag he'd received his breakfast in, and then tossed it into the backseat foot well with a half a dozen others.

When he arrived at the station, he took the lift to the forensic labs, rubbing his fingers across his wrinkled forehead and his tired eyes as the doors closed. The lift juddered to a halt a few seconds later and as he stepped out of the elevator, he could feel a buzz of excitement in the air.

"Superintendent," Libby greeted him enthusiastically. "Just the man I am looking for. We have had a productive night while you have been slumbering."

"Slumbering?" Alec said grumpily.

"I saw you in your car, sleeping on the job, but don't worry; your secret is safe with me."

"Doc, I don't know how to thank you," Alec responded sarcastically. "You have the look of a man who knows something that I don't."

"Absolutely correct, Detective Ramsay," the doctor said solemnly. "Dreadful business at the Oguzhan house, Alec, the bodies are on their way here now. It is one of the worst that I have seen." He took off his glasses while he thought about it. "I am right. I have seen the worst murder scene in my career tonight. Any sign of the other child?"

"No, not yet," Alec shook his head. "At least we have some idea who the child at Jamaica Street is."

"The missing child is a boy?"

"Yes," Alec frowned. "He had two sons, one ten and one six. We're guessing from the size of the body in the house that the six year old is missing. That would fit, right?"

"Fit with the size of the footprints at Jamaica Street?" The doctor asked. "Yes, probably, do you know if the boy was at the house at the time of the murders?"

"There are three sets of kids' clothes, so we think he was, but we can't be sure."

"Let's hope we find him alive and well. My preliminary findings are in your e-mail." The doctor took his glasses from the pocket of his lab coat and wiped the lenses on his tie. "You look tired."

"Thanks, I'm fine," Alec forced a smile. He was tired and numb. Gail was on his mind. Maybe he should have thought about her this much before she left. How many times must she have thought about leaving? How many times had he ignored the warning signs?

"I have some very interesting results from some of the samples we collected at Jamaica Street, Superintendent," the doctor explained as he pushed his glasses onto his nose. Every result was interesting to him, especially when he was the only one who knew the results. "I know we will have a lot to work on from the Oguzhan house, but let's take one result at a time, shall we?"

"It's about time we had some results, Dr Libby," Alec returned the mock formality. "Pray spill the beans." He could feel the tension in his stomach, like butterflies taking off inside him. Perhaps some of the pieces of the puzzle would be revealed at last. He needed the images of the Oguzhan family pushed to the back of his mind. He needed a break in the case, just one piece of evidence that would make the rest of it fit together and lead them to the killer.

"Ah, not so fast, Superintendent." The doctor wagged his finger in Alec's face. "Will is on his way up. He said he would be two minutes. We may as well make it a 'ménage a three', as people who didn't pass their French exams may say."

"I sent him home to get some rest," Alec smiled politely, but he felt like poking the forensic doctor in the eye with his pen. They had a close working relationship, which was fine, but the doctor wasn't the type of person Alec would have socialised with. Not that Alec socialised often, but if he did, it wouldn't be with Dr Libby. His sense of humour was almost juvenile at times, especially when he had discovered vital evidence in a case. He revelled in knowing. Alec heard the lift arrive and he hoped it would be Will to step out. It was. He had changed his clothes and shaved. He looked fresh and smart in a silver grey suit and pale blue tie. The lab technician he was chatting to was getting his best Hollywood smile, and from the gleam in her eyes, she loved every second of it. They stepped out of the lift and continued their chitchat.

"When you are ready, Detective," the doctor's tone turned sour. The jesting was over. Noticing his tone, everyone within earshot stopped talking.

"Calm down," Alec said beneath his breath. "Don't make a big scene in front of everyone. We're all tired, Doc."

"I am not tired, Superintendent," Libby hissed. "Your DI was the cause of one of my best technicians leaving her post."

"She was a grown woman, Doctor." Alec was curt and to the point. He didn't have time for this. "Granted, their affair was less than discreet and her husband found out, but it was her own doing, nobody twisted her arm."

"That's rubbish!" Graham Libby would never forgive Will for his unprofessionalism. "He crossed the line at work."

"Fine." Alec looked at the scientists watching their conversation. "Bring it up when you're asked to contribute to his annual review. Not here in the middle of the lab while your team have front row seats."

The doctor looked up at his staff. He coughed embarrassed and lowered his voice. "Well, he makes my blood boil, and seeing him flirting with another employee is like rubbing salt in the wounds." The doctor turned and walked toward his desk. He couldn't warm to the detective at all.

"Morning, Guv, you look tired." Will was blushing. He realised why the doctor was angry with him. The affair was public knowledge across the force and throughout the support departments, and Will had tried hard to curb his philandering ways. He did try to be subtle if he was chatting a female colleague up, but he wasn't good at subtle. "Is the doctor taking the moral high ground again?" Will whispered, trying to make light of the situation.

"He may be, but then again you could be taking the piss," Alec replied quietly. He kept his face straight. This wasn't the time or the place to be taking sides. He slapped Will between the shoulder blades a little too hard, and they followed the doctor.

"Right you are, Guv." Will stopped smiling and put his professional face on. He wished he could repair the damage he had done to his reputation, but mud stuck.

Dr Libby picked up a brown envelope from his desk as they approached, removing a still and an autopsy report. He cleared his throat and talked directly to Alec, ignoring his colleague. Will was still in the doghouse.

"Louise Parker's injuries were so bad; we couldn't determine the cause of death at first." The doctor waved a finger. "Then we checked the x-rays of her body and we found this."

He placed an x-ray over an illuminator and pointed to the neck area of the spine. "If you look here, you can see that the neck was snapped cleanly, probably caused by a single quick twist of the head."

"That's not something your average Joe could do," Alec said. He studied the break. "This is something that someone with a military background or a serious martial arts exponent could execute."

"I agree," the doctor nodded. "It is impossible to get such a clean break unless done by an expert."

"In contrast to the other murders, this was kind," Alec said. "It put her out of her misery."

"Absolutely," the doctor agreed enthusiastically. Spittle escaped his lips as he spoke. "It is totally out of context with her other injuries. The other injuries were inflicted to cause her as much pain as possible, but this break was meant to kill her quickly."

"That's strange," Alec said. "Maybe the killer had finished with her?"

"I don't think so, Alec." The doctor was adamant. "The two mindsets are poles apart. One intended to cause terrible pain over a prolonged period. The other meant to end the torment."

"Maybe," Will agreed. "That doesn't help us much."

"Finding the cause of death in a murder investigation is critical, Detective." The doctor looked irritated.

"Not on its own, Doctor," Will came back at him. "What else have you got?"

"Could you two please remember why we're here," Alec spoke quietly. "Get on with the brief." There was a look on his face, which dared them to challenge him.

Graham Libby was livid, and he took a deep breath before continuing. "We have matched the blood type samples from Jamaica Street to one of your suspects." He kept his opening pitch as vague as possible. It was all part of the fun of knowing. "We do not have all the results back yet, but these tests are conclusive."

"What have you got?" Alec repeated Will's question. He pushed his fingers through his tousled sandy hair, lifting it off his face. The doctor was becoming annoying, more annoying than usual.

"We tested blood, urine and excrement samples collected from the chair at the Parker scene." The doctor looked over his glasses as he spoke. "We tested them, and they matched with samples taken from the home of?" He paused for the officers to guess.

"Who?" Will shrugged. He didn't want to wait or play the doctor's game.

"Get on with it," Alec smiled.

"Salim Oguzhan." The doctor handed over two sets of results, one for each of the detectives. "It is too early to match the DNA, but the blood type is a match to his children."

Alec and Will looked at each other for a moment, digesting the information. Alec knew Salim was either on the run or dead. Now dead seemed more likely.

"So Salim Oguzhan was strapped in that chair and tortured?" Will mused.

"I am guessing he was made to watch what happened to Louise Parker, too," Alec added. "This is our link to the nightclub, Will."

"What about the boy?" Will gasped.

"The man who killed the Oguzhan family wouldn't give two hoots about making the boy watch." The doctor looked over his glasses patronisingly.

"You think the robbers extracted the safe code from Salim?" Will asked. "Making him watch what he did to Louise Parker and having his son in the chair next to him?" It made sense, but the method seemed extreme. "Would they need to go to that extreme?"

"It depends, Will." Alec stroked the greying stubble on his chin.

"On what?"

"What they knew already," Alec replied.

"I don't get it."

"Let's say you're the killer, and you know that Salim Oguzhan is a gangster, but that's all you know."

"Okay, I'm with you."

"To go from nothing to extracting the whereabouts of a large amount of cash and drugs and a safe code would take some doing."

"So he could have gone all around the houses before he got anything useful."

"Exactly, plus he enjoys doing this," Alec added.

"So we think whoever robbed the nightclub did this?"

"I think they tied up Louise Parker, tied up Salim Oguzhan and his son and started asking questions. They ended up with a safe code and the location of the safes, and the whereabouts of five kilos of cocaine," Alec thought aloud.

"He never gave up the second safe code," Will grimaced.

"Obviously not," Alec agreed.

"We have to assume he's dead."

"Agreed."

"The killer could have taken them to Jamaica Street in the Porsche and driven the car inside," Will surmised. "There was plenty of room and the streets are quiet at night."

"Correct, and he would have had all the time in the world to extract the information he wanted," Alec added.

"He or they?" The doctor asked, removing his glasses. "Remember there were two sets of footprints in the Parker blood pool. We are still running tests on the older bloodstain, but I have my reservations, Alec."

"Let's hear them," Alec smiled thinly.

"The victims at the Oguzhan residence were subjected to a frenzied attack." The doctor shook his head as he spoke. He looked troubled. "The killer chased and attacked the woman and her children, but from the evidence at the scene, I would say that they were badly injured by the first attack and then killed sometime later. There are crawl marks near each body."

"Okay, I'm with you so far," Alec agreed.

"If I combine that with the detailed and torturous injuries to the Parker woman, then I believe that we are looking for a killer who works alone. He is indulgent, and indulgence is a solo affair. He enjoys things that he alone can stomach."

"Maybe he has a weaker accomplice. It has to be 'they'. There were two gunmen at the nightclub," Alec disagreed.

"The other gunman may not be aware of where the information came from or how it was obtained," Will guessed.

"You may be right," Alec said.

"If we find one of them, we'll get them both, won't we?" Will asked.

"We need to find Salim Oguzhan," Alec said. "We've been looking for Salim Oguzhan and his Porsche all over the country, but he was right under our noses the entire time."

"We've been looking in the wrong place so far," Will smiled.

"Where would you hide a body and a Porsche if you had killed the owner?" Alec smiled.

"Especially if you killed them a few hundred yards from the river," Will returned the smile. They were finally getting somewhere. "I'll call out the divers."

"You do that," Alec nodded. "Doctor, I need your team to go into that nightclub and search the beer cellar again when they have finished at the Oguzhan house."

"Alec! That is a waste of time!" The doctor protested. "Any evidence we find will be contaminated by now. By the fire, the smoke, by water, by an army of firemen, and god knows who else has been in there since."

"Humour me, Doc," Alec smiled. "We're looking for two very dangerous killers, but they're sloppy. Look at the evidence they've left for us. The Jamaica Street scene, the hotel and now three victims left to rot in their home. I'm certain there will be something in that nightclub if we look for it. When we find them, and we will, I want as much evidence to pin them down as we can muster."

Dr Libby frowned and removed his glasses. He chewed on the end of them thoughtfully as if he had a choice in the matter. "I will need more man-hours. We are already flat out on this case." He raised his eyebrows.

"Use whatever you need, Doc," Alec said. "I need the rest of these results yesterday."

"Don't you always, Detective?" Libby grunted.

"All in the pursuit of eradicating crime, my good Doctor," Alec touched his head and bowed.

"You sound like Batman," the doctor grumbled.

"That would make you Robin," Alec turned to Will and winked.

"I could think of several other names for him," Dr Libby said as he walked away from them.

"How long for the remaining results, Doc?" Will called after him. The forensic man turned and raised two fingers in a v-sign and waved them in the air offensively. "Two hours or so," he smiled sarcastically.

"I don't think he likes me," Will shook his head.

"You deduced that all by yourself?" Alec frowned. "You should become a detective, Detective."

Chapter Thirty-Four

Patrick: *The Past*

Nate Bradley was aware that Patrick wanted to capture Salim Oguzhan immediately, but he wanted to take more time to plan it properly. They had agreed to plan it together, but while Patrick was watching Salim in the planning stage, he saw Louise Parker and became obsessed. He had to have her. He had to hurt her. Patrick had violent urges sometimes, and they were becoming more frequent and more difficult to control. This time around, he was desperate to get to her. There was nothing in the world he wanted more. She was on his mind night and day. He wanted her, and he wanted her now. Interrogating Salim became secondary. Louise Parker was his focus, and nothing else mattered.

It was Friday night and Patrick knew that Salim and Louise would be at the club. They arrived at around ten o'clock. He waited in the alleyway outside of Connections nightclub until Salim arrived and parked his Porsche behind it. Louise Parker was with him, and as she climbed out of the car, her skirt rode up, exposing her tanned thighs. He groaned aloud in the dark and felt himself growing hard. Her thighs were lean and muscular and her skin looked silky smooth. Patrick couldn't wait any longer. He wanted her badly. She was beautiful and she was a slut. She would be his slut and she would do whatever he wanted. Patrick decided that he couldn't wait for Nate Bradley to finish off his 'pissing around' reconnaissance. He would take Salim and Louise and kill two birds with one stone. He could question Salim and have some fun with Louise, too. Patrick couldn't risk taking them at gunpoint. He would need to be more subtle than that, and he had the Porsche to think about, too. Patrick parked his car a few streets away and walked back to the club. Salim and Louise were talking to the bouncers outside and smoking cigarettes. She was laughing and tossing her hair back as she giggled. She was flirting with them, the slut. She had no idea how much he wanted her, but she would soon. No one had ever wanted her as much as he did, and he would show her things that no other man had ever shown her. He would show her pain and excitement beyond her wildest dreams, beyond her wildest fantasies or dark nightmares. She would know how it felt to *really* feel before she died.

Patrick waited for ten minutes after the couple had entered the nightclub. Then he approached the door and paid his entrance fee into the club. He watched the couple from a distance and waited until they had drunk half a dozen cocktails before standing near them. Louise was drunk and high on cocaine. Everyone was her friend when she was in that zone and she was hugging people left, right and centre, especially the men, the slut. Patrick spoke to Salim first.

"You must be Salim," Patrick stuck out his hand.

"Who's asking?" Salim stopped smiling and ignored the outstretched hand.

"Barry Mills," Patrick lied. "I worked with your uncle in the Smoke."

"Which uncle?" Salim was suspicious.

"Checo," Patrick said, keeping the hand outstretched. "We did a job together on Green Lane, if you know what I mean." Patrick laughed and looked around to see who was listening. "I had to disappear sharpish."

"Right!" Salim relaxed. "How is the old goat?" He still ignored Patrick's hand.

"He's okay, still ducking and diving."

"Is he still driving that old Rolls Royce?" Salim asked.

"Rolls Royce," Patrick looked thoughtful and Salim's eyes narrowed. "No, he's been driving an old Golf convertible for years. He won't part with the thing! When did he get a roller?" Nate Bradley had researched the Turks well. Maybe he wasn't such a waste of space after all.

"He has one parked in the garage," Salim shook his hand. The suspicion in his eyes was gone. "How long have you worked with Checo for?"

"Over two years now," Patrick answered. "He doesn't know I'm up here, no one does. It's better that way."

"Yes, better safe than sorry," Salim smiled. "Do you want a drink?"

"I'll have whatever you're having, thanks."

"Who's your new friend?" Louise Parker joined them. She looked wobbly on her feet and her speech was slurred.

"A friend of my uncle's from London, sorry, what was your name again?"

"Barry," Patrick held out his hand to Louise. "Barry Mills, my pleasure."

"Nice to meet you, Brian," Louise said without taking the handshake. She didn't like him. Patrick sensed her distaste. He didn't mind. She would grow to love him soon. She would do anything he asked to stop the pain. She would look into his eyes and beg him to stop the pain. They all did, eventually.

"Barry," Patrick corrected her.

"Barry," she frowned. She didn't like him at all. "Can you get me a drink please, Sally." She turned away and spoke to someone behind them. The snub would cost her dearly.

Patrick chatted to Salim when he returned with the drinks. Their research into Salim had armed him with enough names and places to sound credible. The Turk bought him another drink, and when Patrick returned the gesture, he laced their drinks with Rohypnol. Twenty minutes later, Salim was feeling unwell and Louise was passing out on her feet.

"The champagne's gone to my head, Sally," she mumbled her words. Salim was holding her up. "Can we go home?"

"I'll get us a cab," Salim slurred. His eyes looked glassy.

"Have you brought your motor?" Patrick asked.

"Yes," Salim struggled to focus. "It's round the back."

"Here, I'll take you home," Patrick held up his glass. "I've only had two and you won't be the first Oguzhan I've driven home from a club," he laughed. "I'll drop you off and then drive back here, shall I?"

"You sure you don't mind?" Salim was feeling the drug slowing him down.

"Not at all," Patrick smiled. "I can be back here in an hour and I'll leave your keys with the landlord, how's that?"

The couple left with Patrick. He had offered to drive the Porsche back to the Parker residence, pretending to be concerned that Salim was over the limit. Salim believed that Patrick had worked for his family and he agreed. He was in a drug-induced sleep within the first two miles of their journey. When Salim passed out, Patrick turned the Porsche around and headed for Salim's house. He knew that Louise lived with her father, and that wouldn't do at all. They arrived at the house in Woolton. Patrick took the keys from the car and opened the front door. The house lay in darkness. It was perfect for what he wanted to do. He wanted Louise.

Salim was a dead weight and dragging him into the house was a struggle, but he managed it. He went back for Louise. Salim was tied up on the floor. Patrick scoured the garage for tape, and that was where he found the hatchet. Patrick was sweating with anticipation. Louise Parker was lying on her back on the kitchen table. She looked beautiful. He pushed up her skirt and pulled her thong to one side, and then he unzipped his jeans. She was about to become his forever when Mrs Oguzhan and two sleepy children appeared in the kitchen doorway. Patrick Lloyd was demented with anger and a red mist descended.

When they came round, Louise was strapped to a workbench in Jamaica Street and Salim was tied to a chair nearby. Next to him was his six-year-old son. Patrick raped Louise while she was still half-unconscious, and Salim's cries for help and abusive threats about what his family would do to him turned him on more. His insane lust was satiated momentarily, and he turned his attention to extracting information from Salim. Salim was compliant because he didn't want Louise or his son hurt. Had he known what he was about to witness, he would have tried to overpower Patrick despite the bonds which held him. Had he known the pain he would endure himself before he died, he would have taken a bullet instead any day of the week.

Chapter Thirty-Five

The Gecko: *The Past*

Nate Bradley scribbled notes in a shorthand style he had learned in the intelligence service. It was unreadable to the average person. His notes referred to the people involved in his family's tragedy, the murder of his wife and son. He listed the people he considered lowlife drug dealers, and he aimed to kill them all. They would pay, and they would keep on paying until they locked him up or shot him. He didn't care who came first. The boy who had given his son ecstasy was dead, as was his supplier. Their dealer, Benjamin, was dead too. And this was where the Gecko made a crucial mistake. He allowed Patrick Lloyd into his trust.

Nate knew he was a special kind of person. His years working in extraordinary rendition had changed him inside. He had no sympathy for human emotions any longer. Killing to avenge his wife and son was simple. Taking the drugs and money from dealers and ruining their business was his mission, and it wouldn't be finished until they were all dead. Simple. Nate knew that his mindset was not that of your average male, but Patrick Lloyd was different again. He was mad, a psychopath. Patrick killed because he enjoyed hurting people.

He thrived on it. Nate knew that Patrick had tortured Benjamin to death for fun, not because he was a drug dealer. The difference between them was obvious to Nate. Nate was killing for a reason, whereas Patrick was a lunatic.

Patrick passed the information he was gleaning from Salim on to Nate, but he wouldn't disclose where he was holding him and he didn't mention that he had Louise Parker too. He said that it was safer if Nate didn't know. Nate knew there was an ulterior motive, and he followed Patrick one day. Patrick led him to Jamaica Street. Hours later Patrick left the unit and Nate broke in. What he found shocked him to the core. Louise Parker was close to death. She was barely alive, and her injuries were horrendous. Patrick had removed her hand with a saw and left it on a workbench. There was no sign of Salim Oguzhan, but there was blood around a chair, which Patrick had screwed to the floor. Louise opened her eyes for a split second and Nate knew what he had to do. He slipped his right hand around her head and grabbed her chin. Twisting his body at the waist, he snapped her neck and put her out of her misery where Patrick Lloyd couldn't hurt her again. Nate took Patrick's roll of medical tools, scalpels and bone saws, and he put Louise's hand into a bag. He would confront Patrick once they had completed the nightclub heist, and the hand would prevent him from talking bullshit. Nate knew his partner had made a huge mistake.

He had hoped the body would remain undiscovered until after the heist, but the police found the body before Patrick could move it. Nate could not believe Patrick had been so careless. His obsession with hurting people was clouding his judgment. Although they had discovered the body, the police were keeping quiet about the details of the murder until they were ready. It didn't matter how hard they suppressed it, the Parker murder would hit the press soon. Nate knew the police had found the body and he was amazed they had managed to keep it quiet so far. It would lead the police to Salim Oguzhan, and they would eventually connect it to the robbery at the nightclub. Patrick was a liability, a threat to his mission. He had to remove Patrick from the equation and then demolish Leon Tanner and the Oguzhan cartel. Nate Bradley packed up his gear and headed to the car. First stop was Patrick Lloyd's home.

Chapter Thirty-Six

Kisha

Kisha shivered as she drove through the derelict streets of Kensington. Once families had sought after the houses for their size and desirable location close to the city centre, but now developers had boarded up the majority, ready for demolition. It was a playground for local teenage graffiti artists and vandals. In the seventies and eighties greedy property owners had begun buying up the rundown houses and had turned them into bedsits. They rented the bedrooms to unemployed people and made fortunes from the social services. Tenants were easy to find, and Giro cheques never bounced. It was a recipe for disaster as communities of unemployed people turned into crime hotspots, red light districts and drug havens. After decades of decline, the city had put compulsory purchase orders on everything and a massive regeneration scheme had been planned.

That was before the recession had hit and the money had run out. Now the houses stood empty, stripped of electric wiring and copper water pipes by drug addicts who cashed in the metals for scrap. There were a small number of determined homeowners in the area, clinging on to their bricks and mortar. Some of them wouldn't move until the bulldozers came through the front wall.

Kisha listened to the Sat-Nav as she weaved her vehicle between shopping trolleys, burnt out cars and house-bricks. The voice announced that she had arrived at her destination, but as she looked around, she had the impression that the Sat-Nav was mistaken once again. On a day off the week before, the device had directed her along a public footpath, which she had followed until the track was so narrow the vehicle could go no further. She had had to reverse for nearly a mile before she had been able to turn her car around. Kisha sighed and shook her head in dismay. She brought the car to a halt and checked both sides of the street for any sign of habitation. The houses were boarded up and fire-damaged. The terrace on the left was scorched black around the windows and doors, and the roof had collapsed into one building. Kisha swore beneath her breath and drove on slowly. She couldn't see the numbers because the doors were covered in metal hoardings. She was about to give up when she spotted a house fifty yards down the street which looked lived in. The front of the house was dark red and the ancient paint was cracked and peeling. Faded curtains hung behind filthy nets and dirty windows, blocking the light and obscuring her view inside. The front door had broken glass panels, which the occupier had replaced with pieces of hardboard.

"What a little palace," Kisha muttered to herself as she pulled the car to a stop. "I really hope you're not in." There had been many times in her career when she had had to endure filth and clutter while interviewing a witness or suspect, but she never got used to it. Just the look of the house and the dereliction around it made her skin crawl. There were some places where the thought of accepting a cup of tea from the occupant made her feel physically sick. She checked her list and walked to the front door. Picking a panel carefully, she rapped the wood with her knuckles, hoping it wouldn't fall out. There was no reply. She looked through the letterbox and was surprised at how tidy it looked. A long hallway led to a fitted kitchen. Laminate wood covered the floors. It looked clean and freshly mopped. The smell of bleach and furniture polish reached her. Kisha knocked again and then peered into the front window, trying to penetrate the grime. As she covered her eyes with her hand to remove the glare from the glass, the front door opened.

"Can you see anything through them?" A man's voice made her jump. She blushed with embarrassment. "There hasn't been a window cleaner down this street for years, and I can't be bothered to do it myself. It's not as if the neighbours are going to talk about me, is it?" He smiled disarmingly. She noticed his teeth were false, repaired badly at some point in the past.

"Sorry, I didn't mean to be rude," Kisha stammered. She returned his smile despite her predicament. "I am looking for Patrick Floyd?"

"There is no Patrick Floyd here, sorry." He winked and smiled again. His eyes flicked over her body from head to toe, digesting her vital statistics in milliseconds. He liked what he saw. She was very sexy indeed. Kisha felt uncomfortable under his gaze and her distaste registered on her face. "Do you know where he moved to, or when he moved?" Kisha stopped smiling and showed him her warrant card. His face changed for a second, his eyes showing fear, but only for a moment. Then he smiled again.

"I am Patrick," he winked and shrugged.

"I haven't got time to mess around," Kisha frowned. "Are you Patrick Floyd?"

"No." He smiled wider than before.

"You said you were Patrick." She put her warrant card away and closed her bag. Her face looked like thunder. The guy was a letch, and he was mucking her around. One wrong move and she would be officially annoyed.

"I am Patrick." He shrugged. "But I am not Patrick Floyd."

Kisha looked at her list again. "What is your full name please, Sir?" She looked at him sternly. "You are wasting police time."

"Patrick Lloyd, Officer," he saluted and bowed dramatically.

"Lloyd?"

"Lloyd," he smiled.

"Not Floyd?" She blushed again.

"Nope, Lloyd, not Floyd." Patrick felt adrenalin rushing through his veins as she blushed. She looked vulnerable and weak. She looked easy to hurt. Hurting her would be fun. It was years since he had sliced black skin. Maybe it was about time he experienced it again. He had been to Africa many times in his life. He loved their skin, and he loved the way people could be taken without anybody noticing.

"Okay, Patrick Lloyd," she tried to recover her composure. Her partner's handwriting was dreadful. So bad he couldn't read it himself sometimes. He had entered Floyd into the computer instead of Lloyd, the wrong name but the correct address. "Have you ever worked for a company called Ashfords?"

He frowned and shook his head. "No, sorry. Who are they?"

"Estate agents in town," she answered. She saw a flicker of recognition in his eyes. "They have you down as a registered key holder."

"Me or Patrick Floyd?" He forced a laugh but it wasn't convincing. The bitch could tell he was lying. He had to hold himself together. It had never occurred to him that the police might connect him to that unit from a key holders list, which was years old. She was here looking for a key holder to a unit where a murder had been committed, but she was alone. They didn't have him down as a suspect yet, or there would be a dozen uniforms behind her.

Kisha raised her eyebrows in warning. "Have you ever been a key holder, Mr Lloyd?"

"Yes," he nodded and smiled convincingly. "It was the Ashfords thing that confused me."

"Explain it to me, please," she asked sarcastically. Patrick Lloyd was behaving like a man with something to hide.

"Look, I worked for a security company called First Security. I was a key holder a few times for them. Maybe one of the sites was for this Ashfords firm?"

"When was this?" She asked.

"Years ago," he shrugged. He didn't maintain eye contact. This was all circumstantial for now, but he knew he had left too much evidence behind. He had been greedy. Stealing the money and drugs from the Gecko had been a mistake, and keeping Louise in the unit for so long had been, too. They had found her, and now they would find her killer. Nate Bradley was pissed off with him, big time. He still had the lump on the back of his skull where he had knocked him out. It could have been worse. He could have slit his throat and left him there to bleed out. It was time to move on. His life as Patrick Lloyd was almost over. "I was sacked after two weeks, sticky fingers back in those days. I did a bit of time for it. Sorry, I was a little embarrassed," Patrick lied. He had done time, but not for stealing. Well, not stealing exactly.

"Can you remember which properties you held the keys for?" Kisha asked. He was on the key holder list, but if they were subcontracting the security out, then anyone could have used the keys. Patrick Lloyd was nervous, but his admitting to being sacked for theft could explain that. Ex-cons were always nervous around police officers. She decided to explore the issue without revealing anything about the crime she was investigating.

"Not really," he smiled. "They were in town mostly. Like I said, I was only with them for a few weeks."

"Did you inspect any industrial sites?" Kisha watched his eyes closely. He seemed to be thinking about the answer, but she didn't think he was lying.

"It was all industrial stuff we watched." He turned and walked toward the front door. "I'm a bit of a hoarder. I know I have the job description and all my contracts in a file along with the schedules I worked. Do you want me to get them?"

"Yes, please." Kisha was on red alert. Either Patrick Lloyd was genuine, or he was going to run out of the backdoor of the house. She had to decide which. His house was clean and well kept. The type of man that mopped his floors with bleach could easily be the type of man that kept paperwork organised in files for years. He seemed harmless enough.

"It won't take me a minute, if you want to wait there." He looked at her for permission to go into the house. "Or you can wait inside, if you think I'm going to do a runner." He smiled again. Patrick decided that if she stayed outside, he would be gone out of the backdoor. He always parked his van in the alleyway behind his house. He could be half a mile away before she would realise he wasn't coming back. If she followed him inside, he was going to hurt her so badly she would wish she had never been born. She would beg for her own death. He could hear her sobbing in the dark part of his mind, and her sobbing turned him on. Patrick hoped she was going to come inside.

Chapter Thirty-Seven

Salim Oguzhan

Alec watched a huge oil tanker drifting past on its way to the Irish Sea and the Atlantic beyond. The vessel dwarfed the other ships and ferries that were on the Mersey, going about their business. The smell of the sea was drifting in on the breeze, and seagulls called to each other as they soared above the water. There was the roar of an engine and a loud splashing sound as a winch began to pull a vehicle from the murky green waters. He waved to the driver to stop the engine while they got ready to inspect the submerged Porsche. The recovery team had parked a breakdown truck at the top of a slipway, ten miles upstream from the unit where they had found Louise Parker. The slipway was on an isolated part of the river used by a local rowing club to launch their skulls. Unfortunately, its isolated position had done nothing to keep the press away. A number of uniformed officers were holding back a crowd of reporters.

"That lot are going to wet their pants over this," Will said.

"How long have they been following the divers?" Alec asked.

"The first reporter turned up at the second dive site and a pack of photographers and news hounds soon joined her." Will shook his head. "You know what they're like. They live in each other's pockets. You never get just one. They followed the divers from one slipway to the next and waited for them to find something. I bet their twitter accounts are buzzing!"

"Bloody hell," Alec muttered. "There must be ten cameras up there."

"The arrival of the head of Liverpool's Major Investigation Team will have fuelled speculation that we have found something juicy to write about," Will laughed. "When you turned up the Blackberries went into meltdown."

Alec was furious. Despite his strict instructions, someone had tipped off the press. "I can't fucking believe it!" He hissed beneath his breath. "Enquiries from the press and television news desks have swamped the telephones this morning."

"It was bound to come out, Guv," Will said with a smirk.

"I didn't think it would come from one of our own, Will." Alec knew it had come from the team.

"Are you sure it has come from us?"

"I wasn't sure at first," Alec admitted, "but after a few quick calls to our press contacts, I found out that the Echo is about to reveal the details of the investigation in tonight's edition."

"How much have they got?" Will asked.

"My contact tells me they have the victim's name and they're in possession of the knowledge that there could be other victims linked to the case. The nationals will be all over it tomorrow."

"What about the Oguzhan family?"

"Not yet, but it won't take long."

"That information could only have come from within the team." Will spat into the water. He suddenly had a bad taste in his mouth. "I'll put a month's wages on who it is."

"That doesn't help, Will," Alec warned. "We've been wrong about leaks before."

"There's no way of dragging the Porsche out without that lot getting an eyeful." Will nodded toward the cameras.

It was the fifth access ramp the police divers had searched, and this time they had found a white Porsche lurking in the muddy river.

"Pull it out!" Alec waved to the recovery truck. The motor roared; the cable took the weight and began to pull. The rear of the vehicle came into view first, and Alec clocked the number plate, "Sal 1."

"That is the Porsche driven by Salim Oguzhan," Will said as the truck dragged the vehicle up the ramp.

Alec, Will and a SOCO approached it in silence, each one of them thinking their own thoughts about the fate of the vehicle's owner. Water poured through the door seals from inside the vehicle. It became obvious that there was nobody sitting inside the two-seater. It was possible Salim had dumped the vehicle himself, but unlikely. The likelihood was he was rotting in the boot of the Porsche.

"Hold her there for a minute," Alec shouted to the recovery team, which consisted of a group of divers and a breakdown truck. "I'll check the boot," the SOCO said. She walked towards the back of the vehicle and used a gloved hand to pop the boot.

"You're wasting your time there," Will laughed. "You couldn't fit your weekly shopping in the back. All the room is under the bonnet."

Will pulled rubber gloves on. They made a snapping noise as they hit his wrists. He opened the driver's door and peered inside. Water gushed out of the foot-wells. The bonnet popped up as he clicked the release. Alec reached the front bonnet and lifted it up in one smooth movement.

"Salim Oguzhan, I presume." Alec tried to hold his breath as the stench of putrid flesh reached his nose. He looked toward the snapping cameras and shook his head. "There is no sign of the boy. I think the spotlight is about to stop on us. How long before that lot connect this registration plate to Salim?"

"Tomorrow at a rough guess," Will grunted. He was no fan of the press. They had crucified him when news of his affair had broken. "Linking Louise Parker to Salim won't take them long either. What do you think?" Will asked the SOCO as she looked into the vehicle.

"Estimating how long he has been in the water is the post mortem interval, and it is difficult to judge." She shook her head. The body was badly decomposed. "The temperature of the water is the most important factor governing the decomposition changes that you can see." She took a pair of white plastic tweezers and pulled at the body.

"There are advanced signs of immersion and wrinkling of skin on the palms and soles. Loosening of the skin, hair and nails and the maceration of the hands and feet is equally well advanced and there is some complete detachment of the skin here, which indicates the decomposition is well into the second week. That's the best I can do for now."

"Thanks, Doc." Alec stood up; happy the body was indeed Salim Oguzhan's. He wanted to get away from the stench. "Who's breaking the story at the Echo?" Will asked.

"Get this onto the truck please. I want it in the forensic lab as soon as," Alec instructed the SOCO. "Make sure the body gets to Dr Libby, please."

"Yes, Guv." She barked orders to the uniformed men in the recovery truck. They worked at dragging the Porsche onto the back of the truck where they would hide it from view with tarpaulin. It was too late to hide the registration plate from the cameras, despite screens at the top of the ramp. Zoom lenses had captured it before it had come out of the water.

"She's a Rottweiler called Lara Bridge, one of the youngest editors to work there," Alec told Will. "Apparently she's destined for one of the redtops, an ambitious type."

"The worst journalists are ambitious!" Will laughed.

"Nothing wrong with being ambitious, but one of my team is talking to her, and I have a problem with that," Alec frowned. "I have tried to fathom out why anyone would disclose details of the murder investigation. I can't see why."

"The only answers I can come up with are money or sex," Will said. "Of course sex is always a motive to blab, but I wouldn't believe one of our officers would be so stupid as to trust a reporter in bed."

"Whatever their motives are, we need to silence the leak."

"I think we should speak to Lara Bridge and get it straight from the horse's mouth," Will said.

"I'll leave that to you," Alec said. "Tell her we want to go public with the disappearance of Amir Oguzhan. If she is going to blow the case open, then let's use the publicity to help us find him."

"Okay, Guv. I'll call her to meet up when we get back to the station."

"One more thing, Will," Alec added as an afterthought.

"What?" Will took his phone out of his pocket and was ready to dial the reporter to arrange a meeting.

"I want Salim Oguzhan's grandfather informed of his death, and I want to speak to him as soon as possible. No one else from the family, Will, I want to speak to his grandfather, okay?"

"No problem, Guv."

Thirty-Eight

Dean

"Denise, I'll be an hour, tops," Dean held his sobbing wife tightly. Her tears were making his t-shirt wet at the shoulder. "I have to open the safe and drop off some money, Babe. Jackson has gone walkabout and Leon is in London. No one else can open that safe."

"Your kids could be dead in an hour, Dean," her body shook, racked with sobs. She thumped his chest with a clenched fist. A nurse came into the room and eyed them coolly. She was used to seeing families falling apart and squabbling while their children teetered on the edge of life and death. Some families cemented their differences and pulled together, but the pressure pulled others apart. Any rifts in their relationships became chasms, and blame and guilt became bitter weapons.

"Your children are hanging on," the nurse said without looking at them. She was helping without appearing to interfere. "If there is something important you need to do, then do it now, and hurry."

"I will be an hour, no more, I promise," Dean lifted her chin with his hand and looked into her eyes.

"I cannot see what can be more important than your children." She pushed his hands away and walked across the room. Her mother hugged her shoulders and glared at Dean. She communicated her opinion successfully without saying a word.

"Look, its work." Dean sighed. "If anyone else could go, then I wouldn't think about leaving the kids, but I have no choice."

"What can possibly be that important, Dean?" Denise snapped. "Washing machines from China, mobile phones from Japan or pine scatter cushions from Timbuktu?" She put her head to one side and looked like a little girl. Mascara ran down her cheeks. "What can be so important that you would lie to me all the time, Dean?"

"What?" Dean raised his hands in despair. "What the hell are you talking about?" His guts clenched.

"Do you think I'm stupid, Dean?" She shook her head and wiped tears from her eyes. "Do you really think that I don't know what that fat bastard Leon does?"

"Now is not the time," Dean snapped. She was right. He had been a fool to believe that Denise would never find out what he did, a complete fool. She was not stupid. Her family and friends were from the areas Leon exploited. He was a name about town and everyone knew that Dean worked for him. "I'll be an hour at the most. We can talk when I get back."

Dean looked to his father-in-law for support, but Denise's father couldn't look him in the eye. He stared at the floor. It was obvious that the family thought it was outrageous to think of going to work when his children were in intensive care. Dean didn't have a choice. If Leon's men didn't turn up at the docks with the cash, then there would be no deal, and all professional trust, built up over years would be lost. It wouldn't take him long to open the safe and drop off the money. He didn't have to execute the deal. He shrugged and headed for the exit stairwell. There was no other option, and he would be as quick as possible. What could go wrong?

Chapter Thirty-Nine

Forensics

Alec had called the entire team together. Graham Libby had a batch of crucial results to communicate, and there was a buzz of anticipation around the MIT office. Everyone was present except Kisha, and Alec noticed her absence. The digital screen flickered into life and Alec clapped his hands to get the room's attention.

"Okay, we need to get started. You all know DS Eales, head of the Armed Response Unit. I've asked him to listen in, as we will be working together on the case from this afternoon," he began. "Stevie, where is Kisha?"

"She's out talking to key holders, Guv." Stevie looked at the screen where she had added a note beneath his data entry. "She has three people on her list. They're all on one of Ashford's' key holder lists." Stevie was annoyed that Kisha had gone out without him, but then again, he had done it first. She was a frosty bitch, no matter how hard he tried; she was not warming to his charms. She was probably a lesbian. He had heard the rumours, but he was convinced he could get inside her knickers. It was only a matter of time. He clocked the address she had gone to. It was a shithole near Anfield. Stevie was going to be nice to her and pretend to be interested in what she had to say when she came back. He decided to ask her out for a meal as a peace offering. A nice bottle of Chardonnay would go a long way towards getting her into bed.

"Why is she on her own?" Alec frowned. He was not one to reprimand officers in public, but the question was on everyone's lips. It was common knowledge that Kisha and Stevie were not getting on, but there was protocol to follow and procedures to stick to. Interviewing witnesses alone was not encouraged.

"We decided to split the list of key holders between us and save time, Guv." Stevie turned red as he lied. Smithy coughed behind a huge fist to communicate his disbelief. The big ginger detective was having none of it. Stevie had broken the rules by going out alone. Kisha had followed suit in protest at him leaving her to process data in the office. She was a good detective and deserved better than being chained to a desk. There were several sniggers around the room as Stevie wilted beneath their withering glances.

"Have you called her?" Alec raised an eyebrow. There would be a conversation about it later in private. Whatever was going on between Stevie and Kisha, he needed to nip it in the bud. Bringing personal feelings into the department was taboo. They couldn't tolerate it, especially during such a crucial investigation. He expected his team of detectives to be more professional than that.

"Yes, Guv, her phone is going straight to voicemail," Stevie lied again. He hadn't tried to call her at all. His eyes locked with Smithy's and Stevie looked away immediately.

"Let's get started." Alec clapped his hands together. He took a few paces to the left, a deep frown on his face as he selected his next words. "First off, someone from this team has been talking to a reporter from the Liverpool Echo called Lara Bridge."

The detectives in the room looked at each other in disgust. They shook their heads and whispered comments passed between them. The MIT was a close-knit group. Its members would not forgive betrayal easily.

"Tonight's edition is going to headline our investigation into the death of Louise Parker. We have a leak in this room." Alec scanned the faces in the room. His detectives looked stoic and returned his stare without flinching. All but one.

"We have had leaks before, and it always comes out who the leak is when this type of thing happens. It's usually the end of someone's career." Alec checked their faces again. No one flinched, except one person, the same person. "There will be no witch hunt while this investigation is ongoing, however the leak will be investigated once we have made the arrests." Alec looked annoyed, but there was important information to discuss. He would deal with the leak later and Kisha could catch up when she got back. Alec looked at the faces in the room. Everyone looked comfortable except Stevie. "Doc, when you're ready."

Graham Libby cleared his throat and tapped a button on his laptop. The screen on the wall showed a series of photographs taken from the hotel where they had found Louise Parker's hand. An enlarged fingerprint appeared next to the arrest photograph of a prisoner.

"As you are aware, we found several prints in this hotel room, as one would expect," he looked over his glasses as he spoke. "We identified one particular print which matched prints in your records, a Patrick Lloyd. Detectives questioned him during the investigation into the murder of a drug dealer some years ago, and they printed him at the time of his arrest. We analysed blood splatter found at the hotel and the DNA matches the samples taken from Lloyd. We know he was in the hotel room and we know he was bleeding, but we could not tie him to Louise Parker's hand at that point. The print could have been left there weeks before the hand was found."

The doctor removed his glasses and wiped them on his tie. "Please bear with me as there is plenty more to come." He smiled, enjoying the pregnant pause. "Next I want to discuss the results of the samples taken from Louise Parker."

The image on the screen changed, and pictures of her body began to flash across the screen. "We took samples of skin from beneath her finger nails, since she must have scratched her attacker," he paused. "There were several secretions taken from her hair. Apart from her blood, we found semen, urine and saliva, all from the same secretor. The DNA matches Patrick Lloyd."

There was a silent hush in the room. The killer had urinated, ejaculated and spat on his victim. The detectives were thinking silently as they listened.

"God only knows what the Parker women suffered before she finally died," the doctor added.

"At least we have a definite target to track down and catch," Smithy muttered.

Stevie looked at his computer screen again and swallowed hard. The name rebounded around his mind. It was just a coincidence. It had to be. The scientist's voice droned on in the background as a terrible reality hit him.

"The samples of blood and urine which were taken from the chair at the Parker scene match with the DNA samples which were taken from Salim Oguzhan's home. His body was recovered earlier today and initial inspection of his body show that he was tortured over a prolonged period. His eyelids were actually stapled open. The killer drove upholstery staples through the lids into the brow bone. The killer wanted him to watch whatever he did to the Parker girl. It is too early to establish the actual cause of death, but I am sure he was dead before he went into the water. His body was in the water too long for us to find any traces on him, but we found secretions around the chair, which the killer tied him to. They, too, match Patrick Lloyd."

Patrick Lloyd echoed around Stevie's brain. Patrick Floyd, Patrick Lloyd. Could he have made such a basic mistake? He searched through the file of paperwork on his desk, looking for his original notes. They were not in any order, as he and Kisha had disagreed on the best way to collate the evidence. Now he wished he had listened to her. It had to be a coincidence. As he rummaged through his papers, he realised others were watching him. He was making more noise than he thought. Sweat began to run down the back of his neck and his hands were shaking as he looked around. The Superintendent was looking right at him.

"Is there a problem, Stevie?"

"No, Guv," he lied. His face was purple and his heart was beating like a rock drummer on acid. He felt a bead of sweat trickle down his temple onto his cheek. He swallowed hard and folded his arms. He was in a huge dilemma. In an unsuccessful attempt to get a reporter called Lara Bridge into bed, he had teased her with the details of the investigation over a Chinese meal. She was young and pretty and had pretended to be keen on him. In fact, all she wanted was a source in the city's MIT, and a letch like Stevie was ideal. He was a sad, lonely man with a high opinion of himself. He thought women should be falling over to climb into bed with him. When they didn't, he put it down to the fact that they must be gay or frigid. She had played his game and let him grope her under the table for a while until he was hot and horny, then she had backed off. His touch had made her feel sick, but it had been a means to get her story. Whatever it took, it took. Stevie gave her more details and she rubbed his thigh for a bit, as she asked questions, keeping him on the hook.

When he had given her everything he knew, he had made some stuff up to keep her interested. He had thought he was taking her home for dessert, but when the bill had arrived, the bitch had laughed at him and grabbed her coat. She had gone without contributing to the price of the meal and left him high and dry. Stevie couldn't believe she had led him on so well. The silly bitch was about to blow the case open to the public, and he didn't have anything to show for his betrayal. She had promised she would keep it secret until they had a clear suspect, but she had lied. He had been so desperate to get her in his bed that he had disclosed information that only the MIT members knew. Now the Superintendent was looking for a mole. It wouldn't take him long to find out who it was. He could feel his career shattering into a thousand pieces. To make things worse, the name Patrick Lloyd was bouncing around his brain.

"Shall I continue, Superintendent?" The doctor frowned and sighed dramatically. The interruption was most unwelcome, as he was eager to disclose his team's findings. Alec smiled and nodded for him to continue. He wondered if the doctor would stop frowning if he kicked him up the arse. He doubted it, but at least he would have a reason to frown. "We have some very interesting results from the second blood pool at the Parker scene."

The detectives stopped looking at Stevie and the doctor had their full attention again. "The blood and DNA taken from the second pool, which in actual fact is the first pool because it is older, matched with samples taken from another murder scene." He paused and tapped the keyboard once more. Pictures of the battered body of the drug dealer appeared. "This was Jacky Benjamin, victim of a brutal and prolonged attack; as I said earlier, this was some years ago. There were two sets of secretions found at the scene, but only one body was recovered. We found urine and hair on the carpet, which did not match the murder victim. We did not know if there had been a second victim until now. Lloyd's DNA was found in the blood pool, too, semen, urine and saliva."

"Okay, people," Alec spoke. "We know Patrick Lloyd is responsible for a string of murders including Louise Parker, and we are sure he killed the Oguzhan family. We think he was one of the armed robbers that hit Connections nightclub, which means he has access to automatic weapons and an accomplice. Uniform had an address for him following the Benjamin investigation, but he has moved on. We need to find him and quickly. Will."

"Guv?"

"I want you to communicate with the Armed Response Unit, and I want an address for Lloyd today. Find him."

"Yes, Guv," Will nodded.

"Smithy," Alec said.

"Yes, Guv."

"I want you and your team to find out who was at the Benjamin murder scene. Who was taken from there to the unit? I want to know who else was tortured in that building."

"We're on it, Guv," the ginger officer replied. They would have to reinvestigate the Benjamin murder book and trace his associates, especially those who were now missing. In the drug world, people went missing all the time. It would not be an easy job, but missing persons' lists would reveal some possible candidates for them to work on.

"Guv," Stevie felt like vomiting as he spoke. He raised his voice so that he could be heard over the others in the room. As Alec delegated the tasks, the separate teams began to chatter.

"Yes, Stevie," Alec looked over to him. It was obvious that something was bothering him. Stevie looked guilty. Alec suspected he had had something to do with the leak, but his pallor was concerning. His face was ashen gray and he was sweating.

"The key holder that Kisha went to see, Guv," Stevie paused. His hands were shaking.

"What is it, Stevie?" Alec looked concerned. Will was about to speak to the DS in charge of the armed unit on call, but he waited to hear what Stevie was going to say. He looked grey and panicky.

"The key holder that Kisha went to see is called Patrick Floyd," Stevie swallowed again. He held up the piece of paper with the details on. The paper was shaking visibly as he held it up. The detectives in the room swapped worried glances.

"Patrick Floyd?" Alec frowned and the wrinkles in his face deepened. He did not want to see the obvious connection. Everyone in the room could see the similarity, but surely, they could not have made such a simple mistake?

"I entered it into the computer as Patrick Floyd, but my handwriting is shit, Guv. I wrote down Lloyd but entered Floyd."

"So the computer didn't flag up that Lloyd was already implicated in the case by the fingerprint?" Alec looked at Will to make sure his interpretation was correct. Will had been one of the first detectives to trial the software. It crosschecked names, dates, fingerprints and addresses. Will nodded his head silently. The name was similar but different. The addresses were different. The program relied on the data input being correct. It was at the mercy of human error.

"No, Guv," Stevie shook his head. He could feel every eye in the room on him. They looked at him accusingly. Kisha was a respected detective; Stevie wasn't liked at all. He printed off the Kensington address and walked up to his superintendent like a schoolboy waiting for the cane. "I've fucked up, Guv. Kisha has gone to this address to question Patrick Lloyd alone."

Will whispered to the DS from the Armed Response Unit, and the MIT sprang into action. One of their detectives was in dire trouble and alone with their main suspect.

"Wait, wait, wait!" Graham Libby shouted. The office became still. "There is more on the DNA, I am afraid," he looked over his glasses at Alec. "We have the Army's medical records for Patrick Lloyd and his blood type is not the same as our samples."

"What are you saying?"

"The blood types are different and cannot be from the same man we are looking for."

"How can that be? What do you mean, Doc?" Alec frowned, creasing his face deeply.

"Your Patrick Lloyd is not the same man that was discharged from the Army. He is the man who was arrested at the Benjamin murder, that is certain, but he is not that soldier."

"Someone has taken his identity?" Will asked.

"Yes and your 'someone' is a wanted man," the doctor said solemnly. "Our DNA searches have flagged up a name on the international database. Jack Howarth."

"Jack Howarth," Alec said. "That name will ring alarm bells all over the country."

"It should," the doctor took off his glasses again. "The newspapers called him 'The Child Taker'."

"Jesus, Will and I were involved with him years ago." Alec shook his head at the memories. "Why didn't his name come up in the Benjamin investigation?"

"He was never charged with the murder. There was no evidence against him, so the traces were never analysed until now."

"Howarth is wanted by everyman and his dog, and Kisha has gone to knock on his door." Alec stood up. They needed to move quickly.

"Alec." The doctor held up his hand. "His name is also being watched by the Counter Terrorist Unit. John Tankersley from the Terrorist Task Force is on the way to my lab as we speak. The DNA matches someone on his wanted list. By my reckoning, you have about a half an hour head start."

"What? They interfered the last time Jack Howarth was in our sights," Alec gasped. "I want this address surrounded and Kisha found before the spooks get here and take over our case."

Chapter Forty

David Lorimar

David Lorimar and his accomplice, Griff, took Jackson Walker's body to an associate's farm in the countryside. Carrying a body through the city during teatime traffic was a nervous time.

"How long is this going to take?" Griff asked distractedly.

"It's a twenty-minute drive from the city."

"Who is this guy?" Griff asked. He pointed his thumb to the back of the van, where a roll of carpet contained Jackson Walker. His identity didn't matter to Griff. This was business.

"Just a dead drug dealer," David Lorimar smiled.

"Did he cross someone?"

"He took on a hit, but the target got wind of it," Dava smiled again. "Quickest trigger wins, right?" His accomplice had worked with him in the Middle East when they had been mercenaries. He had asked too many questions back then, and he did now. "Enough said."

"Fair enough," Griff looked out of the passenger window and sulked. "I was just trying to make conversation."

"You sound edgy," Dava gritted his teeth and the sinews in his wiry neck protruded. It looked like there were sticks of bamboo beneath the surface of the skin. He kept his body lean and fit despite his advancing years. "Are you getting cold feet?"

"Bollocks," Griff snapped. "This is the boring bit. I just want to get to the pub. It's poker night tonight, and by the way, it's you that is being edgy. I just asked you a question."

"Sorry," Dava lamented. "I didn't mean to be abrupt. Old habits die hard. The least said the better, right?"

"No problems," Griff laughed. "Loose lips sink ships and all that old shit." Griff Collins was as fit as Dava, but ten years younger. He hated the military because of its hierarchy, and so his career in uniform had been a short one. His mercenary career had been much longer and more lucrative.

"Yes, something like that."

"Where are we taking him?" Griff asked.

Dava thought about not answering, but didn't really see the problem with telling him. He would see soon enough anyway.

"A farm out in Cheshire," Dava said. "I served with the guy in the Congo. He's solid."

"A farmer boy?"

"He bought the place ten years back and started breeding cattle and pigs," Dava shrugged and put on a posh accent. "Pigs says it all, he butchers his own animals and turns them into sausages, burgers and quality meats for the Cheshire set."

"So this guy is pig food?"

"Basically."

"Nice, I like your style."

Dava smiled and they made the rest of the journey in silence. They turned off the M62 at the Birchwood junction. A huge white telephone mast towered above the island, shaped like two angels kissing. The second exit was almost invisible to anyone who didn't know it was there. Bushes and trees hid the exit leading to a narrow farm track. Potholes pitted the track and gravel rattled off the underside of the van. The passengers bounced about, the headlights casting long shadows into the surrounding woodland. It was fifteen minutes until the track forked.

"Here it is." Dava turned the van off the track into a farmyard.

"Fucking hell, I hate dogs," Griff moaned as a pack of German Shepherds surrounded the van. They were yapping in a cacophony of barking. A security light switched on and flooded the yard with light. The halogen glare blinded them for a moment.

"There he is." Dava pointed to a large barn to the left of the farmhouse. It was a modern building, built from block and carbon panels. A big man in a flat tweed hat and black Wellington boots waved them toward a set of open barn doors. His Barbour jacket was open, showing a check shirt beneath. A long bank of fluorescent tubes hanging from the rafters lit the interior of the barn. They could see rows of walk-in freezers built into the side of the building. The low hum of condenser fans spinning. Dava steered the van cautiously through the pack of yapping dogs toward the open doors. He wound down the window as he approached the farmer.

"Alright, Luke, aren't you taking the farmer look a bit too seriously?"

"Alright, Dava, you're still as funny as a wasp up the arse." The farmer smiled. "How's it going?"

"Good, thanks, just one for now." Dava nodded to the back of the van.

"One?" The farmer shook his head and laughed. "I thought you were bringing three. Are you getting slow in your old age?"

"Something like that," Dava laughed.

"Who's this?" The man looked at Griff and stopped laughing.

"He's one of us," Dava said seriously. "We did a few gigs in the desert together."

"Okay, let's dispose of the problem, shall we?" The farmer waved the vehicle into the barn and closed the doors behind it. The sound of the dogs barking faded as they clanged shut. "Drive it over there."

"Will do," Dava saluted and pulled the van further into the building.

"This looks like a slaughterhouse." Griff looked around. There were stainless-steel chains hanging from an overhead track. Huge hooks dangled from the chains, waiting for the farmer to fix animal carcasses to them. "I like your style," he repeated.

"There will do." The farmer banged on the back of the van and Dava killed the engine. "Pop him on there."

"Let's get this done," Dava turned to Griff and climbed into the back of the van. Griff jumped out of the passenger door and walked around to the back doors. "Fucking hell, he's starting to stink already." The back of the van smelled of urine and excrement. The thick cloying smell of the corpse was beginning to evade the carpet roll. The sphincter muscles in the dead body had relaxed, and the stinking contents of the intestinal tract were beginning to leak out.

"Grab that end," the farmer grunted at Griff as the doors opened. Dava lifted the body from inside the van and they struggled to edge it to the tail of the vehicle.

"Yes, Sir," Griff replied sarcastically. He didn't like taking orders from anyone. "What do I call you anyway?"

"Sir is fine," the farmer replied abruptly.

"Okay, after three. One, two, three," Dava heaved the body toward the other two men and then jumped down onto the slaughterhouse floor. Deep gutters collecting the blood and waste ran through the concrete.

"Plonk him on here," the farmer said. He moved toward a stainless-steel slab, with a drain hole at one end. They lifted the carpet roll onto the metal table and un-wrapped the hapless gangster.

"Nice work," the farmer said, looking at the cable tie cutting deep into the victim's neck. The face and head had swollen to a hideous size, and the eyeballs looked like they would pop out at any moment.

"You never lose it, do you?" Dava laughed. Griff didn't laugh. He looked David Lorimar up and down. The farmer caught his expression and Griff looked away nervously.

"What's up with you?" The farmer asked.

"There's nothing wrong with me, mate," Griff grunted. "Is that it?" He asked Dava.

"Yes, that's it."

"I'll wait in the van." Griff turned and walked away.

"Thanks for that." Dava handed the farmer an envelope. There was no need to check the money inside. It would be an insult to count it. Trust was everything to men like them.

"How are things really, Dava?" The farmer shook his hand and looked him sternly in the eye. "Aren't you getting a bit old for this shit?"

"Maybe, Luke." Dava returned his look. They had shared some dangerous experiences in the Republic of Congo. "When we retired from the service, I thought I had enough money to keep me going." He shrugged his shoulders and looked down at the floor.

"I thought you had done okay out of it all?" Luke asked. "I saved enough money to start a legitimate business and live comfortably without getting involved in this nonsense."

"I fucked it all up," David Lorimar answered. "I squandered a lot on women and beer, as you do. The rest I invested into a diamond deal." He gave a wry smile.

"What? Don't tell me you did a deal in the Congo?"

"Yes, it's a bit embarrassing, really. I should have known better than to trust those evil bastards, but that's the way it goes."

"How could you fall for that old chestnut?"

"I know, I can't believe I did it now, but hindsight is a great thing, Luke." Dava stopped smiling. "Do you remember Squire?"

"Yes, he was a guide from the Congo regulars, wasn't he?"

"That's him." Dava nodded. "He set it all up. He assured us that the diamonds were coming from a government shipment they were going to hit in transit. They fucked it up, and he ended up dangling from a crane jib with his bollocks stuffed in his mouth."

"How much did you lose?"

"Two hundred big ones between the three of us," Dava chuckled sourly.

"So what are you going to do?" Luke looked concerned. "Have you thought about doing another tour?"

"It has crossed my mind, but my passport is marked. I went out to Afghanistan and turned back at Kabul airport. That cost me two grand to get fucked off!"

"Sounds like you're on your arse, mate."

"Well, I make a few bob selling reactivated gear to wannabe gangsters, and then there's always this line of work. Once this deal is done, I am out of it, Luke."

"Well, if you want to make a few quid, I'm looking at a stud farm near Delamere." Luke raised his eyebrows. "I'm looking for a partner to come in with me."

"Horses?"

"Horses and cattle, good money in it, Dava." Luke patted him on the back. "You could leave this shit behind you." He pointed to the dead man on the table.

"I'm in." Dava held out his hand again. There was genuine respect in their touch. "Thanks, Luke."

"How well do you know that guy?" Luke nodded to the van. Griff was looking at them through the passenger window. When they looked at him, he looked away.

"Well enough to know he won't blab if anything goes Pete Tong."

"Be careful, Dava." Luke lowered his voice. "I'm telling you now that he's a wrong one. Just watch your back."

"You worry too much. I can look after myself," Dava walked toward the van. "I'll be in touch."

"Move fast and stay low, Dava."

"Yes, you too, and watch your corners, Luke."

Luke watched the van reversing out of the barn. He had a bad feeling about his friend's associate. He picked up a large meat cleaver and got to work dismembering the body. It took less than fifteen minutes to remove the limbs and the head from the torso. The remains fitted into the funnel of an industrial grinder. He turned Jackson into mincemeat and fed him to his herd of pigs. The pigs were destined for the organically reared meat counter in a large supermarket, and there the DNA trail would end.

Chapter Fourty One

Jinx

Jinx made his mind up and decided to call off the hit on Dean Hines. His kids were critical in a high dependency ward, and that didn't sit right with him. The Leon problem wasn't going to go away, but he had to leave Dean out of it for now. He called David Lorimar again, but his telephone clicked straight to voicemail. Dean was at the hospital, and that was where David Lorimar would go. Jinx had to get there before it was too late. He picked up his car keys and grabbed his leather jacket. He was breaking all the rules calling his hit man at all, but he wanted Dean left alone. Jinx couldn't text in case Dava was in custody. They could explain a call, but a specific text message would incriminate him. He had no choice but to go to the Royal and wait for David Lorimar to turn up.

Chapter Forty-Two

Kisha

Patrick Lloyd disappeared into his house. Kisha wasn't convinced that he was linked to the murder in any way, but she needed to cross him off the key holder lists. The sooner she investigated the names on the list, the sooner she could join the bulk of the team in the real detective work. She needed to be away from that clown Stevie. He was a creep. The fact that he leered at her was bad enough, but worse still, he was a poor detective. It was procedure for detectives to work a six-month probationary period in plain clothes before they were offered a permanent position. If they weren't up to the job, then the force returned them back to the uniformed division. Kisha doubted Stevie would pass his probation, and she was convinced he would end up walking the beat. If she had to clear the key holder list on her own, then she would. She followed Patrick into the house without hesitation. Her instincts told her to press on and remove Patrick Lloyd from the list.

"Shut the door behind you, please. My central heating system is an antique." Patrick called as he reached the kitchen and turned to see if Kisha was coming in. He was laughing as he spoke. "It's like burning twenty pound notes, keeping this place warm." He smiled as he went out of sight into the living room. Patrick did not have the demeanour of a worried man.

"I know the feeling," Kisha said as she shut the front door. "My boiler is ancient and it burns fuel like a steam train. It sounds like one at times, too!"

"Oh, tell me about it," Patrick said from the other room. "The knocking pipes in here keep me awake some nights. It sounds like someone is banging them with a lump hammer."

Kisha looked around the hallway and up the staircase. She had developed the habit since becoming a police detective. Her brain analysed information as she scanned the decor and furniture, the pictures and photographs, and made lightning fast assumptions about the house owner. It was by no means a science, but gut feeling counted in her job. On the face of things, the place was well kept and decorated with taste. The walls were smooth plaster painted in neutral beige, and the pictures were scenic black and white images of the ocean and seashore somewhere. There was a fragrance plug halfway down the hallway and the smell of fresh pine pervaded the house. Kisha listened and she could hear Patrick opening a drawer in the next room. He whistled a tuneless song as he rummaged.

"I know I have them here somewhere," he chirped. "I'm terrible for keeping things. I can't throw anything away."

She walked down the hallway toward the living room door and peered into the kitchen. It was spotless. The stainless sink was shining and the kitchen worktops gleamed. Patrick kept a tidy house. She looked around the kitchen quickly, noting that he had locked and bolted the back door. Through the window, she could see that his backyard was walled, and that the previous owners had topped the walls with broken glass set into concrete. It had been standard practice in the sixties and seventies to protect your yard with shards of broken bottles and jars. The deserted street would have been full of children playing hopscotch back then, and every house would have housed a family. She could almost hear their ghostly voices echoing from the aging walls. Generations of families had been born and raised in this area. Now it was a crumbling mess.

When she turned toward the living room door, Patrick Lloyd smashed his fist into her nose. Blinding lights flashed in her brain. She tasted blood at the back of her throat, and then darkness closed in on her.

Chapter Forty-Three

Griff Collins

David Lorimar tried to sleep for a few hours, but his mind was racing with ideas of turning into a legitimate member of society. Luke could be his ticket out of this dangerous world he lived in and the chance to move into a safer life. He needed to put his thoughts aside and then move on with the job. The money Jinx would pay him would be enough to invest in the business with Luke and pay his rent for the next few years.

Today he was planning to kill Dean Hines, and he had finally traced him to the Royal Liverpool hospital. He would need to use a disguise today. Dava drove to a lockup a few miles away from his house, changed vehicles and clothes and picked up Griff on the way to the next hit.

"How come you're late?" Griff moaned as he belted up.

"I encountered a few hurdles. Here, put this on," Dava answered irritably as he passed him a freshly laundered green uniform. "Put your clothes in the bag."

"Okay, I know shit happens, and now I have to dress up," Griff grunted. "Who are we after?"

"His name is Dean Hines," Dava answered. Griff had made his way further into the circle of trust on the Jackson job, so there was little point in being secretive. "He proved difficult to find."

"How come?" Griff asked.

"He hasn't been at home." Dava tapped his nose. "Found him in the end though."

They weaved through traffic on the way across the city. It was an uneventful thirty-minute drive to the huge hospital close to the city centre. As they circled the building, Dava said, "He's parked his car outside the Royal, but there's no sign of him yet."

"He must be inside," Griff commented.

"He must be either sick, or visiting someone," Dava nodded. "It's time to sit tight and wait."

David Lorimar parked opposite the hospital away from the CCTV cameras watching the car parks. The hospital was busy, and there were several exits and entrances around the building.

"It will be difficult to monitor them all simultaneously," Griff said as they parked. "There are more exits at the side there, where we can't see. I don't like hanging about."

"I can see Dean's vehicle from this position." David Lorimar smiled. "We can see his car and three of the exits from here." He was an experienced mercenary, and this was second nature to him. "Waiting for our target is all part of the job."

"It's a pain in the arse and a waste of time, in my opinion."

"Shut up," Dava said sourly. "You know the score. In Africa, I waited two weeks one time for a target to surface."

"Two weeks?"

"Two weeks dug into a hole in the jungle with one canteen of water and a bag of beef jerky to live on," Dava recalled. "I was close to giving up when the target arrived."

"Fuck that for a game of soldiers," Griff scoffed. "You should have gone back to base and then gone back after dinner. The bloke would have turned up eventually."

"It was a woman." Dava turned to see his colleague's reaction. Griff looked at him and sneered.

"I like your style," he nodded and looked out of the window, thinking. "How come she was a target?"

"She was a western journalist causing problems with the whale huggers," Dava smiled. "The government wanted her silenced."

"Did it pay well?"

"Yes, it paid."

"Did you ask for a bonus for sitting in a hole for two weeks?"

"It was all part of the job, tracking, waiting and then moving in for the kill," Dava bragged. He was proud of his experiences abroad. "Did you ever work any cleaning jobs?"

"No, never did any hits abroad. It was all close protection work mostly."

"Mostly?" Dava laughed.

"You know the score," Griff smiled. "There were a few people who needed removing from circulation, but it was never a sanctioned hit. It just made life easier."

"Nothing wrong with taking out the bad guys," Dava said as he watched the hospital.

"They were not always bad guys," Griff grunted. "Sometimes our employers didn't want to pay some of the foreign mercenaries. It was cheaper to take them out than to pay them."

"Doesn't sound like cricket to me?" Dava looked at him. Maybe Luke was right about Griff.

"It happens. You know it does."

"I couldn't take out someone I had worked with."

"Everyone has a price."

"I suppose they do," Dava agreed grudgingly, although it didn't feel right. It was a complicated world when fighting for money rather than a belief. He decided to change the subject. "Did you ever work in Africa?"

"No, never did," Griff yawned as he looked around. They were in a quiet spot. "Africa must have been difficult. Murder over there is part of everyday life though. Big difference here is masking the murder."

"Yes, it's different alright."

"Easier over there, I think," Griff scoffed. "In the jungle you could leave your kill dead where they lay, no one would go hunting for you, right?"

"It's never easy." The comment irritated Dava.

"Depends."

"Depends on what?"

"This is not a war zone." Griff pointed out of the window as he spoke. "You can't assassinate in public without recrimination. Murderers are sent to prison for life. It's much harder here. No one gives a shit over there."

"I'm aware of that."

"You have to be careful here."

"I am careful."

"You have to be good here."

"I'm good, too."

"Here you have to kill without being seen," Griff waffled on. "Killing Dean Hines will be simple enough, but the skill is in making him disappear."

"Thanks for the input, but you're getting on my tits now," Dava grumbled. He knew what he was doing. No one would see them take Dean, and no one would find his body. Vanishing people was an art form he had perfected over time. Today he and Griff were dressed in paramedic's uniforms. His estate car was an ambulance fast response unit with a green and yellow-checked pattern.

"Where did you get the car?" Griff asked looking into the rear of the estate car. "I like your style," he added sarcastically.

"I picked it up from an insurance right-off company. Ambulances always come in handy."

"It's a coincidence that the target is at the hospital, but a convenient one," Griff smirked.

"It's not a coincidence. I found out where he was and planned the pickup. Planning works, believe me." Dava didn't look at his associate as he spoke. He was getting on his nerves. "When we're ready to take Dean Hines, we render him unconscious, and it will be simple to put him in the back of an ambulance vehicle unnoticed."

"No one will see him because it's normal, too normal to remember," Griff chuckled. "I like your style."

"Something like that," Dava muttered. He thought Dean would be minced and fed to the prize pigs before the night was out. Dava checked his phone. He had three missed calls from Jinx. Something must have gone wrong. There was no way Jinx should contact him while a job was running. "Shit."

"What's up?" Griff asked.

"Someone is calling for a progress report, no doubt," David replied. He was slightly embarrassed that only one of the three men on the contract was dead. He had stipulated to Jinx that he would take out all three men within thirty-six hours. His reputation was important to him. He decided not to return the calls until he had dealt with Dean. At least then, he would be able to report that Leon was the only target remaining. As he debated the issue, he spotted Dean Hines approaching his vehicle on the hospital car park. David Lorimar started the engine and engaged reverse gear. It was time to go to work. There was a tap on the window, and he jumped in his seat.

"Fucking hell!" Dava hissed. A tall dark figure leaned down to his window and tapped again. He reached for the window winder and then remembered that it didn't work. "What the fuck are you doing here, Jinx?" He exclaimed through the glass. He reached for the door handle.

"I need to talk to you," Jinx said through the glass. He stepped back from the car.

"You shouldn't be here," David Lorimar growled. He was about to open the door when Griff Collins put a sawn-off shot gun against the back of his head and squeezed both triggers. The twelve-gauge blew Dava's head in half as the lead shot ripped through his skull, spraying blood and grey matter all over the windscreen and interior of the car. His left eyeball and three front teeth were stuck to the driver's window and they dribbled down the glass slowly held fast by grey matter.

Chapter Forty-Four

John Tankersley

Tank scrolled through his inbox and checked the information once again. He rubbed his shaven head and thought about the next move. He needed the go-ahead from Major Stanley Timms before he could do anything. His chair squeaked as his huge muscular frame moved. He stood up and walked toward the major's office.

"Major," he nodded as he opened the door. His biceps strained at the sleeve of his shirt, threatening to snap the elastic. "Can I have a word?"

"Come in, John." The major looked perplexed. Something was on his mind. "I was just coming to see you."

"Major?" Tank frowned. His icy blue eyes narrowed slightly.

"I have some interesting information," the major placed his hands under his chin as he looked at his computer screen.

"Jack Howarth?" Tank smiled. It would seem that the major had placed a flag on him, too.

"Exactly." The major didn't seem too surprised that Tank already knew. "I think you should look into it."

"Yes, Major," Tank replied.

"Unofficially, of course," the major added. "You are owed some leave, aren't you?"

"Yes, unofficially, of course," Tank smiled and closed the door behind him. "How much do you know, Major?"

"Just that his name has flagged up in a recent murder," the major raised his eyebrows. "What do you know so far?"

"I put a flag on his DNA when he escaped from the hospital." Tank sat down at the chair facing his superior. "As soon as his name cropped up I checked which force had found it. It turns out it was the boys downstairs, so I contacted Graham Libby as soon as the information came up."

"What did he say?"

"He said the information was brought to light during the investigation into the murder of a young woman. I need to speak to the doctor, but I wanted to let you know what I was doing first."

"Of course you did." The major sat forward and placed his chin on his hands. "What have you found out?"

"I accessed the Major Investigation Team's database to see how far the investigation was progressed. There was no doubt about it. Jack Howarth had left his DNA at a murder scene and he was living here under the guise of one Patrick Lloyd."

"I always wondered how he got out of the country," the major sat back and tapped the desk.

"He didn't go far, Major. He knew every exit was covered, so he did the next best thing."

"So uniform are going after him for murder?"

"More than one, from what I can see," Tank answered with a nod. "There was another murder scene involving his name. The murder of a drug dealer by the name of Benjamin, but by the time the match had been made, Jack Howarth, alias Patrick Lloyd, had been released due to a lack of evidence. Now he's linked to at least four murders."

"Let's not rely on the police to take him out of circulation, John," the major said solemnly. "Howarth slipped through the net last time they crossed swords. I don't want the bastard to get away again."

"Anyone who will cut his own thumb off to slip out of his cuffs is a tough man to hold on to," Tank smiled. "I'll follow it and make sure they take him out. If they don't, I will."

When Jack Howarth had escaped, Tank had left the marker on the system in case he ever raised his head again. It wasn't strictly taskforce protocol to track people traffickers, but the smuggling routes they used were also used to smuggle all sorts of nasty stuff, terrorists and explosives included. Those were taskforce protocol.

Chapter Forty-Five

44 Shankly Way, Kensington

"How are we looking?" Alec asked the uniformed officer next to him.

"Four armed units consisting of six police officers in each are in position around the property. We have two units at the front of the house and two covering the rear."

Alec Ramsay and his team were the second line on this operation until the armed officers assured them that there was no danger to them from an armed suspect. Detective Superintendent Eales raised a megaphone to his lips and called out.

"Patrick Lloyd," he shouted. They would use his alias name for now. "You are surrounded by armed police officers. Come out with your hands held above your head."

"Have we tried the landline at the property?" Alec asked.

"Yes, no answer."

The curtains remained closed and still. They had cordoned the street off at both ends, and despite the fact that the remaining houses were derelict and ready for demolition, crowds were gathering at both ends to watch the drama unfold.

"There is nothing like a few patrol cars to attract a crowd. We have an audience already," Alec said looking at the cordons.

"What do you think?" DS Eales asked Alec.

"I think that if Kisha is in there and he is not responding, then we go in regardless," Alec replied. "The man is a psychopath, let's not hang around."

"What are the chances of the boy being in there too?"

"Slim, to be honest."

"I'll send them in."

"Do it."

"All units go! Go! Go!" Eales said over the radio.

Nate Bradley, once codenamed Gecko, watched from behind a crowd of onlookers as the ARU demolished the front door with a battering ram. He had wanted to silence Patrick Lloyd, but the police had arrived before him. The armed officers moved in unison with practiced ease as they entered the old terraced house. Nate didn't think that they would find Patrick Lloyd in there. He wished he had taken Patrick out himself when he had had the chance at the hotel, but what was done was done. It looked like Patrick was in the wind and the further away he was the better for Nate. He wanted to hit Leon Tanner and his Turkish suppliers where it hurt by stealing his crack shipment and his money. Then he would kill him, if his suppliers didn't kill him first. Patrick Lloyd was out of his reach. There were police everywhere. Locals were milling about the police lines looking for a good vantage point. Press photographers snapped as the action unfolded, but one of the photographers wasn't capturing the action at the house. He was discretely taking pictures of the crowd. He pointed his camera at Gecko just long enough to capture his face. John Tankersley clicked off three frames of the crowd who were watching the police raid because he recognised Nate's face in it. He wasn't sure where he had seen him before, but he knew he had, and he knew that he had been a covert intelligence agent once upon a time.

Chapter Forty-Six

The Child Taker

Jack Howarth felt naked and afraid. He had spent years living as Patrick Lloyd, and now that his cover was blown, he felt like a close friend had died. He had become so deeply wrapped up in being Patrick that he had forgotten where Jack was. He felt that he had woken from a deep sleep and the lights were blinding him. Patrick had been a force field around him, a suit of armour and a cloaking device all in one. Now that he had gone, he felt vulnerable. Jack Howarth was back, and he wasn't happy. In fact, he was furious.

"What was that fucking idiot thinking?" Jack whispered. He was incredulous. "How could he have been so fucking careless?"

"What are you talking about, Paedophile? Don't you blame me, you sick fuck."

"Don't call me that, you fucking imbecile. There are half a dozen bodies behind you, you stupid cunt!" The words spat from his mouth. Spittle sprayed from his mouth as he hissed the words.

"Paedophile, paedophile, paedophile!"

"Stop calling me that! How dare you?" Jack snarled.

"That is what you are, you sicko."

"Careless! Useless! Fucking idiot!" He punched the cold brick wall in front of him. "How could you be so stupid?"

"You loved every minute of it!"

"I always did enjoy it, fuckwit!" Jack snarled. "But I tidied up after myself and never got caught, fucking idiot."

"I could have got rid of them sooner but you wanted me to go back so that you could have some more fun, didn't you, Jack. It was you that wanted me to go back every time."

"I never left bodies everywhere. Fuckwit!"

"You made me go back to them, Jack! You could not let me stop. It was you and your perverted mind that made the mistakes. You have no one to blame but yourself."

"You went too far, you made too many mistakes because you couldn't control yourself," Jack hissed. "I never left clues. You fucking imbecile!"

"You can't talk, you fucking Paedophile," Jack answered himself. "I couldn't control you, Jack. It was you that I couldn't control; you are the sick one. It was your idea to be me, remember?"

"I remember, I slit your throat and watched you bleed to death. I should have left you dead, fucking idiot."

"Exactly, you took my life and my money and I hope you rot in hell," a part of his brain echoed with the voice of Patrick Lloyd. "Rot in hell, Jack Howarth. Can you hear me, Jack? I hope you rot in hell."

"Fuck you!" Jack shouted. He sat up and looked around him. His body was soaked with sweat. It was dark and his eyes took a while to adjust. The sun had gone down hours ago, but Jack couldn't sleep. They made sure he couldn't sleep. Stomp, stomp, stomp, for hours. How long could it take to search a house? One hour? Two hours? Oh no, six hours the bastards had been there already. Stomping up the stairs and down the stairs and up again and down again. At one point, he had nearly given himself up, but that had been Patrick talking. He was dead and gone, the spineless, careless little shit. How could he ever have trusted him? The noises went on and on for hours and hours and the light faded to pitch darkness. Now he could hear them digging in the cellar and pulling up floorboards in the house. They would rip the place apart looking for the evidence that Patrick Lloyd had left behind. The fucking idiot had left evidence everywhere.

The woman had woken up once, but he had put her back out with chloroform and she had stayed quiet. He had tied her up next to the kid. He could only take one of them. One of them would have to stay. The boy was lighter, but the woman would be more fun. She was stronger than the boy was and would last longer. Eventually, he had drifted into a troubled sleep but that bastard Patrick Lloyd was waiting there for him, goading him. The fool had caused the police to find him. It was his fault. He needed to move and escape from the house, but he had to wait for the cover of darkness. They would be thinning out now. Not so many of them around, and the armed officers safely tucked up in bed by now. He would chill for a while and then move. The cordons would be closer to the house now, and that would leave the ends of the terrace unwatched.

Jack listened for any noise on his side of the wall, but it was silent. The house next door was empty for a while, but they came back and he could hear them tearing up floorboards and knocking through walls. It wasn't long before they came down into the cellar. He could hear them talking; they were planning to dig. He reached out into the blackness and touched a plastic bottle. He picked up the water and twisted the top off. The liquid felt cold and refreshing as he swallowed it. It made his senses tingle, and as sleep faded away, he felt very alive, more alive than he had for years, and it felt good. It was like he had been in a dream, and now he was awake with a bang. He had to think things through properly. Patrick Lloyd had left him in deep shit. He would escape this rattrap and then begin again. It was time to reinvent Jack Howarth again. This time, he would make all the decisions, and there would be no mistakes. Jack Howarth needed to get out of the cellar and away from Shankly Way. The police were swarming all over the house, but he was safe for now.

Chapter Forty-Seven

Jinx stepped back from the blood-spattered car, his face frozen in shock. One minute David Lorimar had been talking to him, the next his head had disappeared in a red cloud, his eyes and teeth dribbling down the window. Jinx wiped his face and looked at his hands. There was grey matter clinging to his fingertips. He tried to fathom what had happened. A chunk of the driver's window had been blown away and the visceral matter had been blown out at him in an explosion of sticky spray. The passenger door opened and the shooter climbed out of the car. He broke the sawn off and spilled the spent cartridges onto the floor. He pushed two new shells into the empty barrels and pointed the weapon at Jinx over the roof.

"Are you a hero?" Griff asked. He was smiling, but sweat was running down his forehead.

"I'm no hero." Jinx had no idea who Griff Collins was. They made eye contact and stared at each other for a few long seconds.

"Good answer. I like your style," Griff repeated his favourite saying. The shooter took a clear plastic bottle from inside his overalls and removed the top. He sprinkled the contents over the remains of David Lorimar and the passenger seat and then he smiled at Jinx as he lit a match and threw it into the car. There was a whooshing sound as the petrol ignited and the interior of the car turned into a raging inferno.

"Got to go, that's my lift." A motorbike roared up to the pavement and Griff Collins ran to it. The rider handed him a full-face helmet and he pulled it on as he climbed onto the pillion seat. He took one last look into Jinx's eyes as the bike sped away into the distance.

Chapter Forty-Eight

Tank sat in his Shogun, watching the crowds from a distance. There were fifty or so onlookers at the cordon nearest to him. The armed units were packing up their gear and the forensic teams and detectives were moving into the building. He dialled the major and waited for the call to connect.

"John," the major answered. "How is the holiday?"

"Interesting so far," he replied. "I've uploaded a familiar face to our system. I need to know who he is."

"Let me pull it up." The major looked at his e-mail and opened the attachment. "I've saved the photograph and sent it to the Biometrics Identifications Unit. Who do you think it is?"

"I know his face, Major," Tank explained. "I can't place where I know him from, but I'm sure he was one of us."

"Counter Terrorists Unit?"

"Not an agent, Major, but one of us." Tank just couldn't place him. He banged the steering wheel with his fist.

"Where did you see him?"

"In the crowd at the address Howarth was using. It's a shithole near the edge of town. Most of the houses are empty and waiting to be demolished."

"Have you got any idea who he is?"

"I know he was on our side once, but I can't put my finger on it."

"Did the police have any joy at the address?"

"Nothing so far." Tank scanned the crowd again but the familiar face was gone. The man had disappeared. "The armed units have done their foray into the property and come out empty handed. Howarth is a ghost."

"I've got a name," the major said as the results came back to his computer. "Nate Bradley, he was intelligence core, codenamed Gecko."

"I know him." Tank looked up and down the road but he was nowhere to be seen. "He was an interrogator, right?"

"Right," the major confirmed. "His codename was Gecko. He has quite an illustrious career file here."

"I remember him from some of the rendition flights from the Gulf."

"That's him. It fits with his record."

"What is he doing on a derelict housing estate in Anfield? Why would he be interested in a raid on Jack Howarth's home?" Tank rubbed his shaven head with his palm. "Is he still working for the government?"

"No, definitely not," the major replied. "He was debriefed and pensioned off with a medium security risk marker against his name."

"That makes sense," Tank said. "If he had started writing his memoirs, he would have had to be silenced."

"His file has stayed clear since he left. There has been no cause for concern. Do you think he's connected to Howarth?" The major sounded uncertain.

"I don't know," Tank said thoughtfully. "It just seemed strange that he was there. Maybe he wasn't connected to Howarth. Maybe he was connected to Patrick Lloyd."

"Do you want me to do some digging?" The major asked.

"I'm on it, Major," Tank answered. "I have his civilian file up here on my laptop. It looks like the police have had an issue with him. Leave it with me and I'll keep you posted."

"What does his civilian file read like?"

When the information loaded onto the screen, Tank read over the headlines. "It makes for interesting reading, Major."

"Really?"

Tank wondered how to handle the situation. The news clippings and police reports painted a dark picture of Nate Bradley's civilian life. "There seems to be one family tragedy followed by another. His wife died from a heroin overdose and then his teenage son took an ecstasy tablet on the day of her funeral. He ended up dying in intensive care."

"That's enough to tip a man over the edge."

"Maybe, but what is the connection?"

"Didn't you say that Patrick Lloyd was linked to the murder of a drug dealer?" The Major thought back to their earlier conversation.

"Yes, a man called Benjamin, but there wasn't enough evidence to charge him." Tank dragged up the files. "The dealer was tortured to death."

"That sounds like something Howarth would enjoy."

"It does." Tank was thinking at warp speed. "Bradley would definitely have an axe to grind against a drug dealer."

"There is our connection," the major agreed. "Do the police have Bradley linked to the investigation?" He wondered if the detectives in charge of the Howarth investigation were aware of Nate Bradley.

"There's nothing in the files." Tank considered if the Gecko could be connected to Jack Howarth. "If you ask me, then I think so."

"I think we should throw him their way, John," the major said after a moment of thought. "I'm more interested in taking Howarth out of circulation. If Nate Bradley has lost the plot and turned vigilante, then we should throw him to the wolves."

"I have no problem with him knocking over a few drug dealers, but there seems to be more to it than that." Tank seemed to be mulling over something.

"What do you mean?"

"Looking at the uniformed police reports, when Bradley's son died two of his college friends disappeared. One of them was the same age and allegedly supplied the tablets at the funeral, and the other kid was a year older and had a caution for possession."

"Surely, two missing teenagers flagged up Bradley's name to the police?"

"According to the files CID spoke to him, but he had a cast iron alibi. Both teenagers were active on Facebook after their disappearance."

"So they're missing?"

"Yes, but it stinks, Major." Tank could see through it. "An ex-intelligence operative could make a teenager vanish and make it look like he was alive, no problem."

"Do you think Gecko turned his talents on the dealers?"

"Yes, I do. I don't know how he became involved with Howarth, but the fact that he was linked to the death of a dealer tells me they're connected."

"I agree, but it's not our problem. Give your thoughts to the police and let them tackle Bradley."

"I can do that, Major, but they won't be happy about us sniffing around their investigation."

"I think giving them the link to Bradley might act as a sweetener. If they get hold of Jack Howarth in the mean time, then it's all good. If they don't, we'll deal with it."

"I understand," Tank smiled. "I'll speak to one of the detectives in charge when they leave here. I'll be in touch."

Chapter Forty-Nine

Shankly Way

Alec Ramsay was tired. It had been a long few days and the lack of proper sleep was catching up with him. He had looked at every room in the house, but it appeared that Patrick Lloyd or Jack Howarth had gone. There were blood spots in the hallway. "This is fresh," Alec commented to Will.

"It looks fresh to me."

"Do you think it's Kisha's?"

Will didn't answer the question directly, but the expression on his face confirmed his fears. "There are a few more droplets on the cellar stairs. Looks more like a nose bleed than anything life-threatening, Guv."

"Have they found anything downstairs yet?"

"No, Guv."

"I want to take another look around."

The cellar door was beneath the staircase. As Alec walked down the steps, he could hear the forensic officers chattering as they worked. Large paving stones covered the cellar floor. Two centuries of wear had left the limestone slabs worn smooth and shiny. They had already lifted some of them to expose the clay beneath.

"They look heavy," Alec said as he reached the bottom of the stairs. "Have you found anything so far?"

"No, Guv, but it's early days yet. There's no sign of any recent activity down here apart from a few blood spots on the stairs, which is good news as far as finding Kisha is concerned."

"I'm not sure finding any blood is good news," Alec mumbled.

"I meant we haven't found any bodies, Guv, no offence."

"I suppose so." Alec looked around the cellar. There was a damp smell to it and something else lingered in the air. He walked toward the front of the house, avoiding the areas where the scientists were working. Thick render, cracked and eroded by time, covered the far wall. Time had left the bare bricks exposed, and he studied them, looking for any sign of interference from a human hand. Above him was a skylight, barred with a metal grid. It would have allowed deliveries to drop directly into the cellar in years gone by. Moss and dirt clung to the thick glass, making it impossible for light to penetrate. There were lumps of coal and black dust beneath the skylight, and the dampness made it glisten like new. Alec looked around for a bunker. "Have you found a coal bunker?"

"On the far wall, Guv." One of the officers pointed to the back of the cellar. Alec stepped over a raised flagstone and hugged the wall as he moved through the cellar. Beneath the staircase was a tumble dryer, and next to that was a deep chest freezer. He noticed a double electric plug socket on the wall. Both plugs powered liquid air fresheners. He didn't want to insult the forensic team by asking if they had checked them, but you could not be careful enough in Alec's opinion. He opened the tumble dryer and peered inside. It was empty and smelled damp. Rust crusted the metal drum and mould spotted the rubber seal. No one had used it in years. He closed the door and moved his hair from his face. He rubbed his tired eyes and smiled at Will.

"What are you looking for?" Will smiled back weakly. Their detectives had been through the house in detail. Alec was clutching at straws.

"He has made mistakes all the way along, Will," Alec nodded. "I guess I'm looking for a mistake. Look, you go back to the station and see what the team has come up with, and while I remember, did you get in touch with Salim Oguzhan's grandfather?"

"Yes, Guv." Will pulled out his Blackberry. "I have his number here and when I spoke to him, he was driving north on the M1. He is on the way here."

"Good, as soon as he gets here, I want him in the cells."

"What, arrested?" Will frowned.

"Yes, bring him in." Alec didn't hesitate. "Tell him we need to speak to him about the disappearance of Rose James, and if he gives you any shit, arrest him for possession of drugs with intent to supply. Jessie gave us enough to implicate him."

"Are we jumping the gun, Guv?" Will wasn't sure about the arrest. "All we have is Jessie's statement."

"That's all we need for now. I have no doubt in my mind that the Oguzhan's have her, do you?"

"No, not really," Will shrugged. "I guess I'm seeing it as a distraction. It's easy to prioritise finding Kisha."

"It is, but we can't. They don't mess about, Will." Alec creased his forehead in thought. "If they find out that Jessie has turned informer, she's as good as dead."

"I agree, best to get him in and grill him. If nothing else, we can rattle his cage a bit and see what falls out."

"Yes, arrest him for possession and we can quiz him about the kidnap of Rose James." Alec had decided to meet the gangsters head on. He was tired of their antics surrounding the nightclub. "It will give us twenty-four hours to speak to him."

"He will lawyer up straight away, Guv."

"Good." Alec smiled. "I'm in the mood for a good row."

"Okay. I'll get on it."

"Keep me updated, Will." Alec patted his arm as he headed up the stairs. "I am going to have another scan around and then I'll follow you."

"No problem," Will said as he left. "Catch you later."

"Yes, later," Alec muttered.

Will Naylor took a last look around. He was convinced that there was nothing more to be done until the forensic teams had finished. He took the wooden steps two at a time on his way out of the basement.

"Is he still trying to shag the world?" One of the forensic officers asked sarcastically as Will disappeared up the stairs.

"I will ignore that remark." Alec turned and glared at him. "Have you got nothing more important to do than ask stupid questions about my Detective Inspector?"

"Sorry, Guv," the red-faced officer said sheepishly. "It was just a joke."

"Ha fucking ha," Alec snapped. "If that's the best you can do, then I suggest you keep your mouth shut."

"Yes, Guv."

"We have a job to do here, let's get it done, please." Alec took a deep breath. "Are we clear?"

"Yes, Guv."

"Good, get on with it!" Alec turned his attention back to the appliances in the cellar. "Have you checked all this stuff?"

"Yes." One of the scientists walked over to him. "The chest freezer interested us at first. It could easily contain a human body."

He lifted the lid and a musty smell hit him. "There's no ice, no frozen food and no body." Alec reached for the cable and tugged it. It came away easily. There was no plug fitted to it. He closed the lid and moved on. "Why would you keep air fresheners down here?"

"Beats me, it does whiff a bit of damp though, Guv."

"I can smell something else too, like sewage," Alec wrinkled his nose.

"Maybe there are drains down here somewhere, hence the air fresheners?"

"Maybe, carry on," Alec said. "What else have we got down here?"

"The ceiling slopes down at the rear of the cellar to accommodate a large airspace beneath the kitchen floorboards, Guv," the officer continued to explain their findings to Alec. "The space was utilised to cool perishable foods in Victorian times, a bit like a larder or cold space. Our officers are ripping up the floorboards in the kitchen to ensure there's no one hiding there and no victims stashed in it."

"There is a twin-tub washing machine crammed next to the freezer, and a quick inspection showed us that it too is an unused relic, Guv. It's all scrap metal. The bunker is at the back here."

The back wall was featureless apart from the metal coalbunker, bolted to the bricks by the builders. The bolts were rusted solid and the hinges squealed loudly as Alec lifted the lid. "This could hold enough coal to keep the fires burning in every room for at least a week," Alec thought aloud. "There is coal in the bunker." It bothered him. "Have you checked this bunker?" Alec shouted to the forensic officers who had pointed it out to him. The two men looked at each other and raised their eyes skywards at the question.

"What do you mean?"

"I mean have you checked this bunker?" Alec raised his eyebrows too. "It's a simple question."

"It's empty, Guv, and fixed to the wall."

"It is not empty. There is at least nine inches of coal in that bunker, and unless I'm mistaken, the house is heated by gas central heating."

"Do you think someone is hiding under the coal?"

"Are you taking the piss?" Alec was furious at the flippant remark. He had confronted the same officer earlier. "I am looking for one of my officers, who is missing. The suspect is connected to at least six murders that we know of so far, and you are taking the piss."

"Sorry, Guv, but I'm not sure what you want us to do."

"I want you to stop being an arsehole and look for evidence. Asking me if I think the suspect is hiding under the coal is close to being insubordinate, Sunshine. Now I don't want to fall out with you, but I suggest you dismantle this bunker and look under the coal before you lift any more slabs. Whatever is under there can wait."

"Okay, Guv. You're in charge," the officer coughed into his hand nervously. He picked up his toolbox and headed to where the superintendent was standing. "Are you bothered if we keep it intact?" The officer asked as he looked inside the bunker. "It would be easier to take the sledgehammer to it, if you don't mind."

"Do whatever it takes." Alec calmed down a little. "I don't think that coal should be there."

"Sorry, Guv." The officer sounded genuine. "It really didn't stand out to me if I'm honest. Stand back."

"Is there a shovel down here?" Alec turned to the second officer. "I want this coal moved when he takes the front of it."

"I have one here, Guv." The officer reached down and picked up a shovel. They had been using it to move soil from beneath the paving stones. There was a resounding clang as the sledgehammer hit the bunker. The sides were spot-welded and a long rent appeared down one of the seams.

"It's rotten." The officer swung the hammer again and the metal burst apart beneath the force of the blow. He flattened the front of the bunker against the limestone slabs. "There we go, Guv!" He said cheerfully. "Let's have a look under this bloody coal!" The officer seemed oblivious to how irritating his attitude was. "Pass me the shovel. May I, Guv?"

"Be my guest," Alec nodded. The officer was keen enough. He was just clumsy with his words. The shovel cut through the coal and then scraped loudly across the stone floor. The clang of metal on metal reverberated through the cellar.

"There's something under here, Guv."

"Scrape the coal away and let's have a look, then."

"Here, look." The shovel screeched across the floor. "It's some kind of drain cover."

"Can we get hold of a manhole key from somewhere," Alec asked. "The fire brigade should have some. Is there still a tender outside?"

"I'll take a look, Guv," one of them said and bounded up the stairs.

"No one could have got out through there, Guv."

"I know that nobody escaped through the coal bunker," Alec smiled. "I want to know why it's covered in coal, don't you?"

"I suppose so," the scientist shrugged.

"This guy is a lunatic, but we know he's clever and has killed before." Alec's face wrinkled up as he thought. "There is a reason why we haven't found any more bodies, you see?"

"You think he has hidden victims here in the house?"

"Yes, I do," Alec nodded. "His house is spotless, yet he stores junk in the cellar and has new coal in the bunker."

"By junk you mean the machines, Guv?"

"Well, there are new appliances in the kitchen, yes?" Alec frowned.

"Yes, Guv," the officer agreed. "They may just be broken and stored down here." He pointed toward the rusty appliances.

"Why struggle to carry them down the stairs to put them down here?"

"They're out of the way."

"No, they are in the way and that is the point."

"Got a manhole key here!" The sound of heavy boots on the staircase accompanied the voice. Two firefighters clomped down the stairs into the cellar. One of them chirped, "What do you need opening, boys?"

"This cover here, please, mate," the SOCO replied. "Thanks for your help."

"No problems," the firefighter answered. "We've been bored stupid sat on the engine. Let's get a good look at the lid." The firefighters forced the metal T-bar into the hole and turned it until it caught. "There's usually crap stuck in the edges of these covers. This one is clear." The two firefighters heaved on the metal key. The lid came away immediately. "This has been opened recently." He continued. The cover clanged on the basement floor as they moved it. One of the fire officers recoiled and fell backwards onto the floor. "Jesus Christ!" He retched as the stench of decomposing human flesh hit them.

Chapter Fifty

Dean

Dean checked his watch as he opened the car door. He felt sick to the core. His kids were fighting for their lives and he had to deliver drug money. It all seemed so wrong now. He sighed as he climbed into the vehicle and pulled on his seatbelt. There was a gunshot some distance away. He jumped and twisted in the seat. The belt restricted his movements as he scanned the car park and the roads beyond for the source of the noise.

The roads were raised above the car park; steep grassy banks led up to the pavements. He couldn't see beyond the pavements because of the gradient.

"What the fuck is going on?" He hissed beneath his breath. "That was a shotgun. I know that was a shotgun. What the fuck are you doing here, Deano?"

He kept his head low as he fumbled with the keys. "Come on, come on!" He checked the rear view mirror. Flames flickered and glinted behind him. The keys jangled as he tried to find the ignition. He was starting to panic. "Shit, shit, come on, Deano, keep it together." Black smoke was billowing in the distance behind him. Dean didn't know what was on fire or where the gunshot had come from, but he had an inkling that he was in danger. A sixth sense told him to get the hell out of there fast. The keys fell from his hand and clattered into the foot-well. "Shit!" He unfastened the seatbelt and reached down. As he did, he caught sight of a figure running down the grass bank and across the car park. He was five hundred yards away, but he could make out that the man was tall and well built, and he was black. Dean fumbled about for the car keys, but he couldn't take his eyes off the mirror as the familiar figure weaved through the parked cars at speed. "That is Jinx!" Dean took a deep breath and tried to compose himself. He looked around the foot-well and spotted the car keys under the clutch pedal. He splayed his fingers and stretched them to the limit, as he clawed at the leather fob. He could feel it, but he couldn't clutch it. "Shit, shit, shit," he whispered. Dean leaned back in the chair and checked the mirror again. Jinx was four rows away and sprinting hard across the car park and the fire in the distance was raging. The black smoke was spiralling skyward and orange flames speared the air. Dean raked the floor with his Nike training shoe and tried to drag the keys toward him. He felt them beneath the sole of his trainer and he pressed down with his foot and pulled them. They rattled as they came free of the clutch and he reached forward and grabbed them.

This time, the ignition key slid into the lock and he heard the engine fire up immediately as he turned it. Dean could hear heavy footsteps approaching fast. He checked the rear mirror and saw Jinx flashing out of its corner. He was virtually at the back of the car. Dean looked in the wing mirror and Jinx was upon him. He thought about locking the driver's door, but it was futile. It was too late. Jinx was running towards his car. The fire and the gunshot all added up to trouble. He thought about his children as he closed his eyes and waited. The footsteps sounded louder as they neared, and then they faded just as quickly as they clattered on by. Jinx ran between his car and a Vauxhall parked in the next bay, but he didn't stop. He sprinted by, bobbing and weaving between vehicles, and he didn't glance back once. Dean breathed out a sigh of relief as the big man kept on running. He turned the corner at the far end of the car park and Dean lost sight of him behind a laundry van.

His heart was racing as he put the Ford in gear, and the tyres screeched as he pulled away from the parking bay. He steered the vehicle along the narrow rows between the parked cars and kept his eyes on the smoke in the distance. Sirens were approaching from the direction of the city centre. Dean reached the edge of the car park and stopped at the traffic lights. The exit ramp offered him a better view of the roads around the hospital. To his left he could see a busy roundabout, and across the dual carriageway beyond it, an estate car was burning fiercely. Traffic police were directing cars away from the fire, and the first fire engine arrived as the lights turned to green.

Dean felt relief as he turned the vehicle onto the main road, and he pushed the throttle down hard to put distance between him and the hospital. He had no way of knowing what had happened, but he wanted to get the job done and get back to his kids in one piece. There was no sign of Jinx on the pavements or grass verges as he made his way out of town. It was a short drive to the Crazy Computer shop and it would take him five minutes to retrieve the money from the safe and lock up again. Then he had to travel along Queen's Drive ring road to the drive thru McDonalds there and hand over the money to an associate named Monkey. With that done he could return to his kids. Dean was adamant it was the last job that he was going to do. The Gecko was adamant that it would be his last job, too.

Chapter Fifty-One

Will

Will Naylor walked out of the house his detectives were pulling apart. Jack Howarth was gone and there was no sign of Kisha. The superintendant was harassing the forensic team, so it was time to go back to base and collate what they had so far. There was no point in both of them being there. It was better to let the scientists do their job. He had two important jobs on his to-do list, speak to reporter Lara Bridge at the Echo and track down and arrest Salim's grandfather, Zamir Oguzhan. They couldn't put the kidnap of Rose James on a back burner. She was in dire trouble and had to have the same priority given to her disappearance. He picked his way along the brick-strewn road to the cordon. A group of kids were running riot with a shopping trolley and several officers were trying to take it from them before they mowed someone down with it. A uniformed officer approached him as he neared the dwindling crowd at the barrier.

"Inspector," the officer called. "Can I have a word with you, Sir?"

"What's up, Constable?" Will asked. There were less than twenty people behind the police line. "I see the ghouls are getting bored and going home."

"Yes, Sir," the young officer replied nervously. "There's a guy here asking if I can let you know that he is waiting for you. He says it's urgent, Sir."

"What guy?" Will asked. He looked at the faces along the cordon but didn't recognise anyone. "Is he press?"

"No, Sir," the officer shook his head furiously. "I would have sent them packing. I think he is from the CTU, Sir. He showed me his ID, but I didn't recognise it. Sorry, I'm new."

"No problem, Constable. Where is he?" Will asked. They were expecting the terrorist boys to pop up somewhere, so he wasn't too surprised.

"He's parked in the black Shogun there, Sir." The constable pointed a gloved hand toward a side street. There were a few random cars parked up and two patrol vehicles on one side of the street. Tank had parked the Shogun on the other side.

Will looked at the vehicle. It was a CTU truck. He had seen them around before. The tinted windscreen obscured the view of the driver. He checked his watch before walking through the stragglers to the vehicle, managing to avoid the shopping trolley, which was hurtling around the street powered by a number of scallywag kids laughing hysterically. He opened the passenger door and put his head into the vehicle. "I believe you want to talk to me," Will said abruptly. He wasn't going to be messed about by the government spooks. Will made no attempt to get in.

"Agent Tankersley," Tank replied with equal disrespect. "Get in. I have some information for you."

"We've met, Agent Tankersley." Will said. CTU were police officers, not agents. "Can I see your ID?"

"That's right, Agent, get in." Tank flashed him his badge.

"Are you CTU?"

"No, Terrorist Taskforce." Tank stared at Will. "I have some important information for you, Detective Inspector Naylor. Get in."

"Taskforce?" Will knew that they were a military outfit. "You have information for us?" Will climbed into the passenger seat reluctantly. He was impressed that the agent knew his name. "Now that is a first."

"Is there any sign of Howarth?" Tank opened his laptop and glanced at Will.

"I thought you had information for us," Will said with a straight face. "Not the other way around."

"Do you think Jack Howarth has an accomplice?" Tank ignored his sarcasm and looked out of the windscreen as he spoke. The inspector's attitude was expected. There was little love lost between the conventional law enforcement agencies and the military.

"Why?"

"Don't fuck me about, Inspector." Tank looked at him again. "Your rank means nothing to me, and I haven't got the time to play games. We don't want to interfere in your investigation. If we did, I would have fifty agents swarming all over this and you would be back in your office chasing burglars by now."

"Okay, what do you want to know?" Will bit his tongue. He knew that if they wanted to gatecrash the investigation, there was nothing that he could do about it.

"I'll repeat the question. Do you think Howarth has an accomplice?"

Will thought about it. He was curious to see what the agent really wanted. Helping them was not his first instinct. That was certain. "Yes, we think he has an accomplice."

"Good answer," Tank nodded. He turned his laptop to face Will. "This is Nate Bradley. He's on your police files, and I'm convinced he's the man you're looking for in connection with Jack Howarth. Find him and he will answer some of your questions. I have sent his files to your desk."

"Who is he?" Will was bemused.

"I've just told you. He is Nate Bradley," Tank smiled. "He's your accomplice."

"Just like that?" Will shrugged. "I can't even interview the man on that. You know how it works on our side. We have rules to follow. I need more than just a name."

Tank looked at the detective and rubbed his palm over his shaven scalp. "He's ex-army, intelligence core."

"Ah, one of your lot, then," Will clapped his hands together. "That's how you know about him. What's happened, has he gone off your radar?"

"Look, Detective." Tank snapped the laptop closed. "He was here in the crowd when I arrived. We knew as much as you did an hour ago, but if you read his file, then you will see the connection. His wife overdosed on heroin and his teenage son took a snide ecstasy tablet. They were both killed by drugs."

"Drugs?" Will frowned confused. "This is a murder inquiry."

"Howarth was in the frame for killing a drug dealer a few years back, right?"

"Well, yes."

"It was around the time that Nate Bradley's wife overdosed on heroin. His son died a week or so later, poisoned by a bad ecstasy tablet."

"You think that's his motive to join forces with Patrick Lloyd?"

"It's motive enough to go after a dealer."

"Perhaps," Will nodded slowly. The drugs connected the suspects to the robbery at the nightclub, too. "You saw him in the crowd here and came up with that connection? It's a bit thin, isn't it?"

"Read the files, there's more to it than that."

"Come on, Agent Tankersley." Will held his hands palms up and shrugged. "You made the effort to wait for me, so at least explain what you think is going on, please!"

Tank eyed him for a moment and the muscles in his jaw twitched. Will thought that he looked like he'd been chiselled from bronze. "You have officers watching the crowds at a crime scene like this?"

"Of course we do," Will said. "It's standard procedure."

"I took some pictures of the crowd and recognised his face." Tank opened the laptop again and showed Will. "I couldn't place him, but I knew he was Special Ops."

"Special Ops?" Will wasn't sure what that meant exactly. "You said he was intelligence."

"He was, but he worked for Special Ops. That's all I can say." Tank made a cutting motion with his hand. That was the end of that subject. "I ran a check on him and his name came back as Nate Bradley."

"Okay, I'm with you so far." Will looked the big man in the eye. "How have you made this connection?"

"I read that your Patrick Lloyd was in the frame for topping a dealer and taking his time over it, right?"

"Correct."

"When I read Bradley's civilian file, the death of his wife and son jumped out at me."

"Phew, that's a big jump," Will breathed in sharply and shook his head. He wasn't convinced.

"Look here," Tank pulled up the missing persons' files. "Two of his son's friends are missing. Bradley informed the police that they had supplied his son with the ecstasy. Drug squad investigated the allegations but there was not enough evidence to arrest them. They both disappeared."

"What are you saying?" Will looked at the details.

"Put yourself in his shoes for a minute." Tank scrolled down and the information appeared on the screen. "Let's say your wife overdoses and then your son dies a week later, both deaths caused by taking drugs. Then you find out who supplied them. You pass the information to the police and they can't do anything. What would you do, Detective?"

"Do you know this guy?" Will asked. "I mean could he do this?"

"I don't know the man, but if you're asking me if he is equipped and capable of this, then yes, he is. He was Special Ops."

"I need to look into this, but I can see why you made the connection. We're sure Howarth had an accomplice."

"Do you have any other suspects?"

"No."

"Here is a suspect with the means, the know-how and the motive to torture a drug dealer to death. Why he chose Jack Howarth as the accomplice or what he has to do with your investigation now, I don't know, and I don't care."

"You've sent this to me?" Will asked.

"Yes."

"Thanks," Will frowned again. "Tell me what your interest in this is?"

"We want Jack Howarth out of action, permanently."

"Why would the taskforce be interested in Howarth?"

Tank stayed silent for a few moments. "The long and short of it is that he traffics people and equipment. Some of those people and equipment have been of interest to us."

"What about your intelligence officer?"

"The taskforce has no interest in Nate Bradley. That's why I'm giving him to you."

"We'll sort it, thanks again." Will opened the door and held out his hand. Tank looked out of the front window and ignored the gesture. Will removed his hand and climbed out of the truck. "There's no need for you to get involved in this. We will sort it, you know."

"Good." Tank started the engine and pulled away before Will had chance to close the door properly.

"Fucking spooks!" Will shouted as the Shogun roared away.

Chapter Fifty-Two

Shankly Way

Alec Ramsay covered his nose with the paper mask and peered into the drain. "Give me a torch." He held out his hand and one of the firefighters handed him a Maglight from his utility belt.

"What do you think?" The nearest forensic officer said, peering into the stinking void.

"There is a pile of flesh there." Alec pointed the beam to a pinkish mound. The flesh was rotten and putrid. "I can't tell what it is, but it looks like part of a torso to me. There is more along the drain there." He stepped back away from the manhole.

"What do you want us to do first, Guv?" The SOCO asked.

"These old houses all have a cellar and a large roof space. I want to know if any of them are interconnecting. Pull everything away from the walls, starting in here, and get uniform to search every house left standing in this street." Alec stepped back from the manhole and picked out his phone. He speed-dialled Eales, who answered the call immediately.

"Alec?"

"Have you left any armed officers here?"

"Yes, there's a unit parked outside on standby, why?"

"I need them to go into the adjoining properties." Alec walked toward the stairs. "I'll have the front doors removed and I need your officers to clear the buildings so we can search them."

"Okay," Eales said. "What's up, Alec, have you found something?"

"We've found remains in the drains beneath the cellar. I've a feeling Howarth may have found a way to access the houses next door. If he has, he may still be lying low nearby."

"I'll send another two units immediately," Eales said urgently. "I'll instruct the unit on standby to follow your orders, Alec. I'm on my way too, we'll be twenty minutes. Is there anything else you need?"

"Yes," Alec thought again. "Get the force chopper up. I want their heat-seeking cameras above us. If the bastard sneaks out of one of the buildings, I want to know about it."

"I'll prioritise your crime scene, Alec. It's on the way." The line went dead.

"Right, men," Alec turned to the forensic team. "Put the manhole cover back for now. Howarth didn't leave that way. I want to know if there is another way out of the building. Finding Kisha is my priority. Check behind and underneath everything, no matter how insignificant you think it may be. Leave nothing untouched."

"Yes, Guv," they said in unison.

"If you find any exits, wait until I can get an armed officer with you, are we clear?"

"Yes, Guv."

"Anything we can do, Sir?" The firefighter asked.

Alec thought about the question for a second. "You could get hold of any plans there are available for the sewer system beneath the estate."

"Leave it to us." They charged up the wooden staircase, and dust filled the air in their wake.

"Wait," Alec shouted, "one other thing, too."

"What, Sir?" They ducked through the banister rails to see him.

"I want access to every house on this side of the street. Take the security boarding off every one and force the front doors. Don't go in, just get me access."

"Do we need a warrant or something, Sir?"

"Nah, I can smell smoke coming from one of them, son!" Alec winked. "Can't you?"

"Now you come to mention it, I can. Consider it done, Sir!" They set off up the stairs again and the fire fighter shouted, "Better to be safe than sorry!"

Alec rubbed his hands together and began to climb the wooded stairs up to the house. The rest of the forensic team and his detectives were gathering in the hallway. News of the find in the basement had spread around the team. Alec climbed through the narrow doorway into the hallway and looked at the faces there. Everyone was wearing white paper overalls, gloves and overshoes. It looked like a bizarre slumber party. The armed officers were coming through the front door as the firefighters were going out. There was a buzz of adrenalin in the crowd. The initial disappointment about not finding Kisha was gone. They were eager to hear about the developments in the cellar.

"Okay, everyone," Alec began. "There are human remains in the drains underneath the house." The concern on several faces was obvious. "Don't worry; they're too old to be Kisha or the boy. Howarth went to a lot of trouble to conceal them. Now you have completed the initial sweep, I need you to start thinking outside the box. I need you to look for concealments or exits." He was about to delegate a new plan of action to the relevant officers when a blood curdling scream from the basement resounded through the Victorian terraced house.

Chapter Fifty-Three

Crazy Computers

Dean checked his mobile for messages, but the screen was blank. He was hoping for news from the hospital. He got out of the old Ford and slammed the door. He parked across the road from the Crazy Computers shop and immediately regretted not turning the car around and parking on the opposite side. The road was busy in both directions and he couldn't see a gap in the traffic to cross safely. He checked his watch and swore beneath his breath. His kids were lying in intensive care and he needed to be there. His throat was dry, and sweat began to trickle from his temples. He checked his watch again and decided to make a run for it. The driver of a blue Peugeot braked hard and pounded the horn with his fist. Dean flipped him the finger and sprinted across the road without breaking stride. The door leading to the massage parlour upstairs was ajar. On any other occasion, he would have checked how business was going, but today he couldn't give a toss about it. He wanted to hand over the money and get back to his children as fast as possible. Then that was it, he was out.

Dean opened the metal grill, which protected the door to the bogus computer shop. The padlock came away easily and the hinges creaked as he pulled it open. Mortise locks fastened the shop door top and bottom, and his fingers seemed to have a mind of their own as he fumbled with the keys. His haste was slowing him down, and he whispered to himself as he went through the process of opening the doors. "Get a grip, Dean, keep it cool."

The second lock clicked open. He stepped inside and closed the door behind him. He considered locking them both again whilst he opened the safe, but time was his enemy today. He ran across the dusty shop to the door, which led to the storeroom at the back. He repeated the process with the second security grill and unlocked the storeroom door. The safe was on the far wall, and everything looked as it had when they had left it. He thought about the last time they had been there. Leon had been on one of his Crusades and this time he had wanted Jinx Cotton wasted. The thought of all that money had blinded Jackson, and he had agreed to carry out the hit. He hadn't seen or heard from him since. A shiver ran down his spine as he wondered where Jackson was. There was no way he had just walked away from Leon. Dean had warned him that it was a mistake to go after Jinx, but Leon and Jackson had paid no heed. God knew where Jackson was now. Probably six foot under.

Dean twisted the dial on the safe, first one way, then the next, until the six-digit combination was complete. He inserted the security key. The metal felt cold to touch. He turned the key and pulled the handle at the same time. The heavy door swung open slowly and the stale smell of used notes drifted out. He packed bundles of fifties and twenties into an old holdall and counted aloud as he piled them up. "Two hundred and fifty thousand quid and I am out of here," Dean muttered. He zipped up the bag and slammed the iron door closed. A spin of the safe dial locked it. He sighed deeply as he locked the shop door and padlocked the metal grill into place. If his kids hadn't been critically ill, he might have considered taking the money and running. As he turned to walk out of the door a hooded man walked in, and they met face to face.

Dean froze for a second. His breath felt trapped in his lungs and his heart pounded in his chest. He clutched the holdall in his right hand and his left hand moved onto the Luger Parabellum in his coat pocket. It was an old gun, but it was clean, and it did the job the Germans had designed it to do. The hooded figure put his head down and barged into him.

"Sorry, mate," the man said as he barged past and trotted up the stairs. He was keen to keep his identity secret as he visited the prostitute upstairs.

"Fucking hell, Dean, get your shit together!" Dean took a deep breath and waited for his heart to slow down. He let go of the semi-automatic pistol and peered outside. The pavements were clear and the traffic had thinned out. He checked both ways and sprinted across the road. Dean noticed two men sat in a green Range Rover. They had parked their vehicle next to his Ford and they watched him as he crossed the road. He was sweating as he approached his car, and he glanced at them furtively as he popped the boot and threw the bag into it. The men opened the doors of the Range Rover at the same time and got out. They looked at Dean and then smiled at each other across the bonnet. Dean walked to the driver's door and placed his finger on the trigger of the Luger. "This could be it," he muttered. He watched them from the corner of his eyes, not wanting them to know that he had seen them. Dean was conscious that Jackson had gone missing and that Jinx was still breathing. He could be onto them, and that meant Dean was a target. The other possibility was that the drug squad was onto their deal. One way or the other, this was a dangerous game to be playing when your children were at death's door. He was alone and carrying a substantial amount of cash. There was enough money in the bag to raise questions. They would hold him for intent without having any drugs on him. The two men moved to the front of their vehicle and chatted to each other. Dean waited for them to make a move. He was not going to let them take him in, not today. "Come on if you're coming," he whispered to himself. "I don't have time for this shit."

The men looked at Dean and spoke quietly to each other. They seemed to reach an agreement on something as they nodded their heads and laughed. "Don't bottle it now," one of them said.

"Let's do it," the other one agreed.

Dean tensed and readied for action. The men checked the traffic and ran across the road together. They were laughing nervously as they reached the other side, pushed open the door and ran up the stairs to the brothel.

"Looks like she's going to be busy," Dean sighed. "This is not funny!" Dean put his head on the roof of the car. The cold metal made him feel good for a second. He opened the driver's door and jumped in, starting the engine with one turn of the key. His nerves jangled on a knife-edge. As he indicated and manoeuvred the Ford onto the busy road, he didn't notice that the Gecko was three cars behind him.

Chapter Fifty-Four

Kisha

Kisha was drifting in and out of consciousness. The chloroform numbed her brain and she was fighting for control of her body against the effects of the gases. She knew it was chloroform that gripped her brain and stopped her from functioning, and it would be easy to give into its powers and sleep. Sleeping was an easy way to escape the terror of her real situation. She remembered being in the hallway of the house where a key holder lived. Everything was so fuzzy. His name was Patrick Floyd. She could remember that and she could remember his face. He had seemed harmless enough at the time, but the pain in her nose reminded her that he wasn't harmless at all. She could feel congealed blood running down the back of her throat, and the coppery taste made her feel like gagging. She swallowed, but found it almost impossible. There was something in her mouth. The muscles in her jaw ached painfully, and she bit down hard on the foreign object between her teeth. The drug made her attempt to bite turn into less than a twitch, and her jaw barely moved at all. The overwhelming sensation to retch was uncontrollable. Her eyelids flickered open for a second and her brain tried to make sense of the images it captured before they snapped closed again. There was something attached to her face, a gag of some kind. She was in a dark room with a stone floor, but the rest was a blur.

Kisha drifted up another level out of her drug-induced slumber, and the calm serenity of sleep was turning into a torrid river of fear as the reality of her situation formed in her mind's eye. Her attacker had knocked her out with a hard blow to the face. Now he had gagged her. Had he tied her up? She tried to move her arms but he had bound them tightly behind her back. Suddenly her shoulders began to cramp and ache as her brain started to communicate with her nervous system again. Kisha knew from the pain in her limbs that she had been lying in the same position for a long time. She tried to move her legs, but again it was little more than a twitch. Her eyes flickered open again, this time for a few seconds longer. The room was dark. The floor was cold and made from stone. The stone was smooth and shiny, like the paving stones on her grandmother's street. Did she still live there? Kisha couldn't remember. She could see her face smiling down at her from the front doorstep. Her Nan was no more than five feet tall, so she must have been young then. She remembered strawberry jam with lumps of fruit in it, hot buttered toast and weak tea with sterilised milk. Kisha remembered a funeral and realised her grandmother was dead. She had died years ago. 'The drugs are making you dream, Kisha. Wake up, or you will die.' Her grandmother's voice drifted into her mind.

Her eyes opened again, and she blinked this time. It felt like she had grit under her eyelids. She knew that the whites were bloodshot, and she had the urge to look at them in the mirror. What mirror? She had seen a mirror when she had opened her eyes, hadn't she? Kisha tried to keep her eyes open, but they felt too heavy. Her mind was trying to drag her back down to sleep, but she had to fight it. 'Wake up, or you will die, Kisha,' the voice told her again, but this time it was someone else. She didn't know who the voice belonged to, but she had to listen to it. Her eyes opened again, adjusting to the gloom in the basement. 'How do you know it's a basement?' she thought. 'I saw stairs in the corner and the walls are bare bricks. Was there a mirror?'

She looked ahead into the darkness and saw a dull glow above. 'It wasn't a mirror; it's a skylight above us. Above *us*?' Kisha looked again, but she couldn't keep her eyes open for more than a second at a time. 'What do you mean *us*?' There was a shape near her, a small shape, and she could make out the facial features of a boy. He was a young boy. His features were dark. He was foreign.

Kisha's brain clicked up another notch. There was a young boy tied up next to her. She wasn't sure who he was, but she knew that they were both in incredible danger. Kisha had to think how she had ended up here. She had been interviewing key holders when Patrick Floyd had attacked her, key holders who had access to the unit where someone had butchered Louise Parker. If Patrick Floyd was the murderer, then there were two scenarios. He had tied her and the boy up and absconded, or he had tied them up with the intention of hurting or killing them later. The first option was the preferable one, however, she had to organise her drug haggled brain to focus on the worst scenario possible. If she was to get out of this unhurt and alive, then she had to get her thinking straight. There was a young boy down here, too, and she had to ensure his safety first. She tried to focus her mind on the situation through the fog that the chloroform had caused. It would be so easy to fall back into sleep. So easy to keep her eyes closed and drift back into the safety of nothingness. As her brain wrestled with the choice, she heard footsteps approaching in the darkness.

Chapter Fifty-Five

Jinx

Jinx looked at his reflection in the rear view mirror. He wiped blood and brain matter from his face and tried to catch his breath. His huge pectoral muscles were rising and falling rapidly as his lungs struggled to supply oxygen to his massive frame. He was shocked and frightened by what he had witnessed. The gunman had splattered David Lorimar all over the inside of his car and set his body alight. Jinx had to find out what was happening. There was one man in the city who knew most of what was happening, Gus Rickman. Jinx turned his car stereo off and called him on the hands free system the manufacturers had built into his Mercedes SLK as standard.

"Jinx," the gruff voice answered. "Are you still breathing, then?" The voice had no joviality to it.

"Just about," Jinx tensed his neck muscles and shook his shoulders. He was in no mood for jokes.

"What can I do for you?" Gus growled. "I'm busy just now."

"I want to know what the fuck happened to Dava, Gus." Jinx snapped. He was still shaking from the incident.

"I'm assuming he's dead?" Gus asked in a matter of fact manner.

"Yes, he is dead. Some motherfucker blew his head apart with a sawn-off and then torched him." Jinx tried to keep calm.

"What was he doing, Jinx?" Gus retorted.

"What do you mean?"

"You know what I'm saying," Griff chuckled. "What was he doing when he was blown away?"

"You know that Leon put a hit out on me?" Jinx bounced a question back.

"Yes," Gus replied. "And it sounds to me like you returned the favour."

"What do you expect me to do?"

"Exactly what you did, Jinx," Gus laughed again. "What did you expect Leon to do when he realised you were planning to take out him and his boys first?"

"So it was Leon who whacked Dava?"

"To be honest, I don't know, but if I add up two and two, then I get four."

"Who was the hit man?" Jinx asked. He wasn't sure what he wanted to hear from Gus. In the cold light of day, what had happened had been in retaliation.

"I have no idea what his name is, but I've heard on the grapevine that he was an associate of David's. Sounds to me like he sold out to the highest bidder."

"What happens now?"

"That's between you and Leon. It has nothing to do with me, but I will tell you one thing, Jinx." Gus turned serious.

"What?"

"Where do you think Leon is?"

"He's in the smoke meeting with the Turks, why?" Jinx shifted uncomfortably in his seat.

"Wrong," Gus said. "He knows you're tracking his car. He's back in the city, watch your back."

"How do you know?" The news rattled Jinx.

"I know he travelled north with the old man, Zamir Oguzhan." Gus revelled in how powerful his informer network was. "The old man is coming to sort out funeral arrangements for Salim. You heard they dragged him out of the Mersey?"

"Fucking hell, when?"

"A couple of days ago, it'll be all over the news later on today."

"Why are you telling me that?" Jinx asked. He couldn't trust anyone. If Gus was giving him a tip, then there was a reason.

"You know that Leon is importing meth with the Turks now?"

"I heard he's buying direct from them, but I didn't know he had wormed his way in that far, what about it?" Jinx grabbed something from beneath his seat.

"He has a massive shipment coming in, and when it lands, it will give those slimy bastards control of the city, Jinx. They'll flood the market and slash prices to make sure their dealers clean up." Gus went silent to allow the information to sink in. "We can't allow that to happen. If they corner the market, all hell will break loose, and we'll all struggle. No one will be safe. Things run just fine the way they are, do you know what I mean?"

"If I hear anything about it, I'll let you know. It you're interested, that is."

"I've put the word out that I want to know where and when it's going down. Let me know if you hear anything, Jinx, and I'll owe you one. That shipment would be better off in my hands than theirs, if you know what I mean." Gus cut the call dead.

"Yes, I know what you mean," Jinx said to himself. If Leon was back in the city, then everything had changed. Jinx reached for his satellite-tracking device and checked the details. The map showed that Leon's vehicle was in the Kensington area of London. It was obvious that Leon was on to him and wanted Jinx to think he was out of the city. He must have driven to London, left the car and come back. Jinx changed the programme to check where Dean Hines was. His vehicle was moving along the main ring road around the city. Jinx opened the glove box and took out his gun. He would follow Dean Hines until Leon showed up, and then he would end it.

Chapter Fifty-Six

Shankly Way

The scream echoed from the basement, and the gathering in the hallway was stunned into silence. Alec looked toward the front door, and the armed officers ran toward the basement door instantly. They drew their weapons and headed down the stairs. Alec didn't wait until they called the basement clear. He was right behind them. "We need a paramedic down here!" One of the officers shouted.

"Get me a paramedic!" Alec called from halfway down the staircase. "What happened?" He shouted, leaning over the banister rail.

CRIMINALLY INSANE

"The bastard has booby trapped this stuff," a crime scene officer replied. "The side panels and underneath the appliances are lined with razor blades."

"Ah! Get my fingers!" A SOCO lay screaming on the floor of the basement. It was the annoying officer Alec had had the altercation with earlier. Blood covered his paper suit. He held his hands across his chest and his colleagues held cotton gauze to the stumps of his fingers. "My fucking fingers! Pick up my fingers!"

"Put them in this bag." His colleague opened a specimen bag and they carefully picked up the severed digits from the stone floor. The tips of the rubber gloves still covered the bloodied appendages. "He grabbed the bottom of the freezer and tried to drag it out, Guv. The razors took his fingers off before he realised they were there. The bastard has left us some nasty surprises."

"Keep the pressure on the bleeding and hold his hands up in the air." Alec swallowed hard. He felt a twinge of guilt for giving the order to pull everything out. "The medics are on their way in. Don't touch anything until you've checked it thoroughly, understand?" The officers in the basement nodded in response, but they remained silent.

"Can we get through there?" Two paramedics squeezed past Alec on their way to treat the injured officer. Alec made his way back up the stairs with a knot in his stomach. The officer was a nuisance, but he didn't wish that on him.

"Guv." An armed response officer followed Alec.

"Yes." Alec rubbed his eyes again. He felt drained.

"The boss has told us that you want us to clear the surrounding houses, Guv."

"Yes, please." Alec composed himself. "The fire brigade are going to break down the doors. When they have, I need them clear for my detectives to go in. Keep your eyes open, son. Howarth is a nasty bastard."

"We'll start with the houses either side, and then move outward to the ends of the terrace?"

"Yes." Alec looked thoughtful. "Double-check the attics and cellars."

The armed unit filed through the cellar door with a purpose. Alec went back into the hallway where there was a buzz of alarmed chatter. Superlatives and expletives resounded off the walls. "Right, everyone!" Alec clapped his hands together to get their attention. "Howarth screwed razor blades around the appliances in the basement. He didn't want us to move them, obviously."

"Bastard," Smithy said between his teeth, and the officers around him murmured agreement. "I hope I find him first."

"Let's just concentrate on finding Kisha first, Smithy." Alec splayed his hands in a calming motion as he spoke. "If Howarth has rigged traps around the house, then that is because he wanted to slow pursuers down. I think he planned an exit strategy using the empty houses next to his."

"You think he's still in the vicinity, Guv?" Smithy asked.

"Maybe," Alec nodded. "We know there's a campervan parked in the back alleyway. It isn't registered to him, but no one else lives here, right? If he realised Kisha was a police officer investigating the murder of Louise Parker, then he must have worked out that we wouldn't be far behind her. She had her radio on her, so he could have heard our communications. If he did, then he knew we were on the way with armed backup. He needs somewhere to lay low, and a way of getting past the cordons at the end of the street once the initial incursion is completed. If he is here, find him, but be careful."

"Guv," they replied to the order as a unit.

"Smithy," Alec called to the big ginger detective. "I want you and four of your team to follow the armed units into the neighbouring houses. The rest of you rip this place to pieces and find me the way he took Kisha out of here. If we find that, we find Kisha and the boy."

Chapter Fifty-Seven

Will

The information that John Tankersley had brought to light astounded Will. He wanted to investigate it thoroughly before informing the superintendent. Alec had his hands full with developments at Shankly Way. Will contacted the detective in charge of investigating the death of Nate Bradley's son. She was a detective sergeant with the drug squad.

"Chloe, it's Will Naylor at MIT," he said when she answered her direct line.

"Hi, Will, I got your message, and I'm curious why you're interested in the Bradley case." She sounded a little frosty. A senior officer from a different department picking through the details of your investigation was never welcomed. "How can I help?"

Will leaned back in his chair and loosened his tie. "I need you to confirm some details for me," he began. "What can you tell me about Nate Bradley senior?"

"Why?" She asked. "What has he done?"

"We don't know yet," Will laughed. "I just need to see if he's linked to one of our cases."

"Care to expand?" She toyed with him. They had met at a charity ball once and she recalled that he was a good-looking detective with a reputation for liking the ladies.

"Not at the moment, Chloe," Will kept the conversation formal despite her flirtations. "I need as much information as you can give me, and I need it yesterday."

"Okay, where can I start?" She could sense the urgency in his voice. He wasn't fishing. This was a serious enquiry. "You know that his wife died shortly before his son Nate?"

"Yes," Will replied. "Were there any recriminations from him when his wife overdosed?"

"Plenty," Chloe scoffed. "He called me every day, twice a day sometimes, asking if we had found the dealer who supplied her."

"Did you find the dealer?"

"Are you having a laugh, Will?" It was Chloe's turn to be serious. "She was a grown woman with a serious drug problem. The autopsy showed evidence of drug abuse going back years and she was using a cocktail of drugs. It was heroin that killed her eventually, but it would be quicker to tell you the drugs she didn't use than the ones she did."

"I get that, but did you investigate the dealer?"

"Where would you start, Will?" She laughed. "If we started at Lime Street station at nine o'clock in the morning, I could show you thirty dealers within five hundred yards of the place by half past nine. We couldn't identify the dealer who supplied her if we tried, and if we did, do you think they would cough?"

"Did Nate Bradley think you were investigating the supplier?" Will could see her point, but he didn't think she had considered it from Nate Bradley's side.

"I told him I was making enquiries into her supplier."

"So you fobbed him off," Will said sarcastically.

"I guess so, it was to placate him, that's all," she replied morosely.

"What was his mental state?"

"What is this about, Will?"

"I need to establish how Nate Bradley reacted. Were the dealers involved his main focus?" Will tried another tack.

"Without a doubt," she responded affirmatively, "Especially when his son died."

"Did he make any threats?"

"No, not exactly," she said slowly. "He made a lot of noise and we know that he spoke to some of his son's friends about it. He intimidated them with his questions and the way he asked them. They were genuinely scared and their parents made complaints, but under the circumstances, we didn't pursue it. We spoke to him several times about it."

"Then what?" Will took his tie off. It seemed that John Tankersley was right in his assumptions.

"He came to me with the name of the boy who had *allegedly* given his son the ecstasy. Carl Lewis was in the same year at college," she answered irritably. "Look, Inspector, there wasn't a shred of evidence that the boy had supplied the drugs, and when we interviewed him about it he denied all knowledge of the tablets. What am I supposed to do?"

"I'm not criticising your investigation, Chloe," Will tried to calm her angst. "I need to know the facts."

"Sorry," Chloe sighed. "Am I being sensitive?"

"A little. The boy he thought had supplied the drugs, Carl Lewis, is he still missing?"

"I wondered where this was going," she snapped. "We spoke to Bradley about the boy and he had an alibi. Then Carl made contact made with one of his college friends."

"What type of contact?"

"The kid is on Facebook every few days. He has run away, but from what we can see, he is alive and well. He has a junior savings account which is keeping him going."

"What about the older lad?" Will carried on.

"Same, we think they're together. They posted pictures from a beach in Cornwall a week ago. The local uniform boys are looking for them, but they keep on moving from place to place."

Will was beginning to get a picture of what may have happened. It would not be difficult to make it look as if someone was still alive using the internet, especially if you had extracted their passwords before they died. An interrogator would have no problems finding out that information from teenage boys. "Do you know Nate Bradley's history?" Will asked. He wondered what the military had put on his files.

"Some kind of records clerk in the army," Chloe replied. "Why?"

"He was an intelligence officer and worked in Special Operations," Will dropped the bomb.

"What?" She sounded incredulous. "Bollocks, we checked that ourselves."

"I believe you, but the military are hardly likely to let anyone know that he was a spook, are they?" Will replied calmly. "Trust me, I have it on good authority that Bradley was a spook, and I believe the source. I don't believe those two lads are alive, Chloe."

"Fucking hell, but what about the bank account and the Facebook stuff?" She inhaled air as she spoke.

"Come on, Chloe, how hard would it be to blag that if you had their information?"

"Where are you coming from, Will? What the hell are you looking for?"

Will stood up from the desk and looked out of the window. He could see the big wheel, a new edition at the Albert Docks. It seemed like every city in the UK needed a wheel since the success of the London eye. "I want a reason why Nate Bradley would turn vigilante and set out to take out drug dealers. I think he has a good one, don't you?"

"Oh my god," Chloe moaned. "I'll open the search for the missing boys immediately. I'll have to speak to my governor about making it a homicide investigation."

"Look, Chloe." Will didn't need self-flagellation right now. "The older lad, Paul Grebe, was it?"

"Yes, that's his name, or should I say was his name? Fucking hell, I don't believe this."

"Did you look at him?"

"Of course we did, but there was nothing to charge him with. He had a caution for possession, but that is hardly proof, is it? We had his mother on our watch list and her boyfriend was a real scumbag, but we couldn't find any evidence that he even knew Nate Bradley."

"Who was the boyfriend?" Will asked.

"What?"

"You said the mother had a scumbag boyfriend?"

"Yes, Jackie Benjamin," Chloe said. "You may remember him. He was topped on the Bluebell Estate a while back."

"Thank you, Chloe." Will sounded excited. "You've just given me my link. That is the connection between Nate Bradley and our case."

"You think Bradley topped Benjamin?"

"Yes, I do," Will smiled. "Chloe, can I give you some advice?"

"Yes, please." She was baffled and shocked by the entire conversation.

"Get the technical guys onto your case. Find out where your Facebook posts are coming from and where that savings account is being used, because I don't believe those boys are alive, and thanks again for your help." He hung up before she could respond. He was about to call Alec when the telephone rang as soon as he had put it down.

"DI Naylor," he answered the call irritably. He needed to speak to the superintendent.

"Morning, Will," Chief Carlton said. "I have some news which might impact your case."

"Well, this case is just getting better and better, Chief," Will laughed. "There has been some significant information come to light this morning already."

"Really, what's happened?" The chief sounded surprised. "Have you found Howarth?"

"No, Sir, but we think we have the name of his accomplice."

"Superb, well done, there," the chief chirped. "What have you got?"

"It's early days, Chief, and I'm still checking it out. So if you don't mind, I'll check out my facts and then make a full report to the Super, but we need to talk to a man named Nate Bradley."

"Do you need our help?"

"Yes, Sir," Will made the call to bring him in. "I think we need an APB on Bradley, and we need to call him armed and dangerous, Sir."

"Get his details to me immediately, Will. I'll have the alert and his description distributed this morning at shift changeover. Where has this information come from?"

Will didn't want to end up with egg on his face, so he chose to keep it in the department for now. "Do you mind if I make a few more enquiries before I start speculating, Sir?"

"No problem, I'll wait until you have briefed Alec."

"Thanks, Sir. What have you got for me?"

"Oh, yes, the reason for the call," the chief stuttered. "Two things of interest. Early this morning, we were called to a vehicle fire-up near the Royal. Once the fire boys had extinguished it, witnesses reported hearing a gunshot before the fire started. We recovered the body of a male. He was wearing military dog tags which identify him as David Lorimar."

"He was one of the men at the poker game?" Will wrote the name on his list of things to relay to Alec.

"Correct," the chief confirmed. Dr Libby says that the skull was severely damaged before the fire started, probably a shotgun. There are pellets in the doorframe."

"That's one less to interview, I suppose," Will mumbled. "Any idea what happened?"

"It's all a bit cloudy at the minute. One witness reported seeing a man leaving the scene on the back of a motorbike and others are telling us that a tall black male ran away from the vehicle in the direction of the hospital car park. We're still taking statements now, and we have the CCTV discs from the hospital security room. They should have a decent view of the car park. Once I know anything, I'll let you know."

"Sounds to me like the mobs are kicking off again," Will scribbled on his pad. It hadn't been long ago that they had been killing each other for fun, until the assassination of the Neil brothers had brought things to an uneasy ceasefire. "Do you think it's related to the robbery at Connections?"

"God only knows, Will," the chief sighed. "There is another incident. It won't throw any light onto this at all, however I think it is connected."

"I need another pen," Will joked.

"You and me both," the chief made light of it.

"I feel like Stevie Wonder trying to complete a Rubik's Cube." Will took his jacket off and placed it over his chair as he spoke. Sharon Gould tiptoed up to the desk and placed a note in front of him. She smiled and walked away without speaking, aware that he was talking to the chief constable. Will picked it up and tutted loudly. "Fucking hell, it never rains, it pisses down."

"What?"

"Sorry, Sir, another challenge has just dropped into my lap."

"Don't let the bastards grind you down, Inspector," the chief chuckled. "Listen, I know you have a lot on your plate, but we had a call yesterday to a flat in Toxteth. One of the residents reported that his neighbour's door looked damaged and there was a cleaning company warning sign outside the flat. He thought it looked dodgy. When my officers arrived the flat was empty, but there were signs of a struggle and they found a handgun. Turns out the flat belongs to a chap called Jackson Walker. Do you know him?"

"Yes, we've crossed paths a few times." Will read the note again. Zamir Oguzhan was waiting in the reception area downstairs. "He's one of Leon Tanner's crew."

"That's what I'm being told, although I've never had the pleasure of meeting him."

"I think there was more to the robbery at Connections than we first thought," Will forgot who he was talking to.

"We thoroughly investigated it, Inspector," the Chief's tone changed. "At the time, there was nothing more to do. There was no crime committed."

"I wasn't having a go, Chief." Will stuck two fingers up to the phone. "I meant there is more coming out every day, that's all."

"Yes, quite. Well, keep me posted, Inspector."

Will didn't think the apology had been accepted, but he had more important things to worry about. He decided not to drag the call on any longer and hung up.

Will needed to speak to Alec to see if he wanted him to interview Zamir Oguzhan whilst he dealt with the search at Shankly Way. The third time Alec's phone clicked to voice mail, Will grabbed his jacket and his tie and headed for the lifts. He would tackle the mobster himself.

Chapter Fifty-Eight

The Child Taker

Jack Howarth knelt down between the policewoman and the boy. He smiled in the darkness. As much as he would love to play with the black woman, the boy would fetch a pretty penny on the internet market. Once he was safely away from the police, he would set up business again. It was time to go back to his roots. It was time to become the Child Taker again. The police were scratching about inside number 44, and a muffled scream told him that they were beginning to move things away from the walls. It wouldn't take them long to find his bolt holes, and then the fun would really begin. They would be busy for hours. The time to move was here.

The woman was comatose and the boy was well away, too. He shined his torch into the boy's face. There were dark circles beneath his eyes and his cheeks looked sunken. He was dehydrated. "Poor boy needs a drink," Jack smiled. He reached for a bottle of water and twisted off the top before taking a long swig of the cooling liquid himself. The woman twitched and Jack stopped smiling. He slapped her face with the back of his hand, but she didn't respond. He had bound her hands behind her, and the restraints pushed her breasts outward. He felt her right breast with his hand and squeezed it hard. There was no reaction on her face. The nipple pressed at the material of her wool jumper, and he pinched it between his finger and thumb, turning it forty-five degrees. He leaned over and licked her face, running his tongue across her cheek and her lips. She smelled of designer perfume, but he couldn't tell which one. The woman didn't budge. Jack lost interest and reached for the boy. He pulled his legs toward him and felt for the gag fastened at the back of his skull. Jack pulled the gag down from his face and let it fall loosely around the boy's neck. He lifted the bottle to his lips and allowed the water to dribble into his mouth. It ran down his cheeks onto the floor. The boy moved and coughed as the liquid reached the back of his throat. His eyes flickered and opened.

"Drink this," Jack said. His voice was soft and comforting, as if a father was talking to his thirsty son. "Drink it slowly, because your throat will be dry."

The boy gulped at the liquid and swallowed half the bottle too quickly. He gagged, and the water hurtled back up from his gullet along with thick yellow bile. Jack jumped upwards and backwards at the same time to avoid the stinking vomit. He dropped the torch and scrambled about trying to reclaim it quickly.

"Dirty boy!" He hissed. The boy retched again and began to cry hysterically. He was drugged, frightened and choking. His sobs echoed around the cellar and the retching noise sounded loud in the darkness. "Shut up, you little bastard!" Jack reached for the gag, but warm sticky vomit covered it and he recoiled at the touch. "Dirty boy," Jack hissed again. "Shut the fuck up or I'll choke you myself."

The boy was coming round and his sobs had been getting louder until Jack shouted at him. When he heard the nasty man threatening him, he tried desperately to stop sobbing, but the retching was involuntary, and he felt like he couldn't breathe. The memories of what the man had done to his father and the woman were fresh in his mind. So was the smell of their blood. There had been so much blood, and the sound of their screams replayed in his head. He was terrified, and if the nasty man said shut up, then he had to shut up. Another mouthful of puke gushed from his stomach, and the acid was burning the tender tissue at the back of his nose. His eyes streamed with stinging tears. Mucus dribbled from both nostrils and vomit hung from his chin like a string of melted cheese.

Kisha listened and waited. She opened her eyes but squinted, so that her attacker wouldn't see them move. Patrick Floyd was hopping about with the torch and the boy was sitting up, vomiting from every orifice on his face. He was crying hysterically and every time he sobbed, he sounded like he was going to choke to death. The noise was getting louder. Patrick snarled at the boy, and he tried desperately to stop making a racket, but Kisha didn't want him to stop making a noise, in fact, she needed him to make as much noise as possible, because he was the only one with the gag removed. She had to decide if there was anyone within earshot before making a decision. The simple fact was that she didn't have any choice. She rolled on her back and lifted her feet as high in the air as she could. Patrick Floyd caught the movement out of the corner of his eye, and he turned his attention to Kisha. There was a confused expression on his face as she brought her feet down as hard as she could on the young boy's spindly legs. Her heels connected with the boy's knees and the powerful impact smashed them into the stone floor beneath them. His kneecap splintered into four pieces and his femur snapped above the knee joint. The boy screamed like a banshee. It was the kind of high-pitched scream only a child could make. It was the worst noise that Kisha had ever heard in her life, but it didn't stop her raising her legs again. She swung them upwards as high as her muscles would allow and then smashed her heels into the boy's shattered bones once more. The boy's frantic screams reached a new high before Patrick Floyd jumped on her.

Chapter Fifty-Nine

Leon

Leon squeezed the sesame seed bun together with his fat fingers and Big Mac sauce splurged onto his chubby digits. A tear shaped blob clung to one of the four gold sovereigns he wore. He licked it off, took a huge bite from the sandwich and chewed it with his mouth open. He washed it down with a mouthful of full-fat Coke. "It's warm in here, isn't it?" Leon sprayed coke as he spoke.

"Yes, it's warm," a hoodlum called Gareth agreed. "How did it go down south?"

"It went good." Leon wiped his mouth with a fistful of napkins. "Today is just the start, Gar; I'm telling you now that today is just the start. We are going to cream it in, my friend."

"Nice on, mate, don't forget me when your raking it in," Gareth laughed and took a bite of his quarter pounder. "Don't forget me and Monkey, whatever you do!"

"We're all on this bus together, Gar, all of us." Leon made a circular motion with his fingers. "Has anyone heard anything from Jackson?" Leon's face became serious again. His jowls hung loosely from his chin.

"Nothing, mate, but the Dibble were all over his gaff yesterday. I made out that I was knocking on next door and had a nosey at the flat on the way past. It looks like he's been turned over," Gareth explained. "Do you think he's done a runner or been nicked?"

"I would know if he'd been nicked," Leon frowned, and his fat cheeks wobbled when he shook his head. "And he hasn't got the bottle to do a runner from me. I've always looked after my boys, anyway." He couldn't go into the hit on Jinx. Not with Gareth, because he wasn't far enough up the chain yet. "What time did Deano say he would be here?" He asked. Bread and meat sprayed from his mouth as he spoke. His Ed Hardy watch glistened with diamonds as he checked the time.

"He said eleven," Monkey replied. It came out as 'Hesh shaid elevensh'. A brain injury incurred in an illegal boxing match made his speech slurred. His real name was Mickey, but his pronunciation of it sounded like 'Monkey', and so the name had stuck. He tried to say, "I heard his kids aren't too good." It came out as 'I hearsh his kidsh aren't too goosh.'

"Yes, they are sick, real sick. Get me another Big Mac and fries, Monkey." Leon tossed a twenty-pound note onto the table. "Oh, and a large chocolate milkshake, do you want one?"

Monkey rolled his eyes to the ceiling and frowned. He was used to Leon telling him what to do, but the thought of ordering a milkshake with his speech impediment was daunting. He slid out of the booth and swaggered over to the counter. His black shell suit rustled as he walked. There was a queue at the till, and the lone crewmember was struggling to cope. Monkey noticed that the manager was dealing with a complaint at the drive thru window, and the distraction had caused the front counter service to grind to a halt. Monkey shuffled impatiently from foot to foot, looking down at his sky-blue high-tops nervously. He liked working for Leon, but it always made him nervous, and when he became nervous, his bowels cried out. He could feel his guts cramping and gurgling. His urge to use the toilet was growing stronger by the minute.

Leon had munched his way through his meal, but he was still hungry. "Monkey," he shouted impatiently. "What's happening?"

"Fuck knows." Monkey shrugged. "I need to visit Trevor," he slurred.

"What the fuck are you talking about?" Leon growled. He drained the dregs of the coke noisily from the cup. "Who the fuck is Trevor?"

"I need to visit Trevor, you know what I mean," Monkey said in a hushed slur.

"I haven't got a fucking clue what you're talking about, Monkey." Leon glared at him. "Who is Trevor?"

Gareth laughed aloud and slapped the table with his hand, "Ha, hilarious, fucking hilarious!"

"What's so funny?" Leon was paranoid. Gareth was laughing at him. "Who the fuck is Trevor?"

"His family all say that, mate." Gareth sensed that his boss was edgy. "He wants to have a shit."

"Are you kidding me?" Leon laughed.

"No way, Leon, I was at his one day and his mum said, 'where's Dad?' Monkey said, 'he's gone to see Trevor.' Then she said, 'He spends more time on the shitter than he does with me.' I spat my tea all over the living room!"

"Go and see Trevor, Monkey," Leon laughed. "I don't want you shitting your pants today, mate!" His man boobs shook visibly beneath his Ralph Lauren sweatshirt. The material was stretched to breaking point over his belly. Monkey put the twenty-pound note back on the table and headed toward the toilet corridor, embarrassed into silence. He could hear Leon cursing at him as he opened the door. A miserable-looking woman in her fifties opened the fire door, which led to the restaurant's backups, wedging the door open with a red fire extinguisher so that she could carry an armful of balloons through to the dining area. She smelled of cheap perfume and bleach. The doors to the ladies and gents were on the left. The open fire door was directly in front of him, and the disabled toilet was on the right. Monkey always used the disabled toilets when he went to McDonalds, because there was more room and a little more privacy. He pulled the sliding door open, stepped inside and slid it closed behind him. He twisted the handle ninety degrees and the door locked. Someone had left a copy of the Daily Star on top of the sanitary bin, and he smiled as he undid his belt. He glanced at the front page whilst he unzipped his tracksuit bottoms and he wiggled his podgy hips so that he could pull them down. He sat down and began reading yesterday's news, sighing loudly as the digested ingredients of last night's vindaloo splattered against the porcelain.

As Monkey emptied his lower intestine, Dean Hines parked his Ford in the restaurant's car park and turned the engine off. He could see Leon's massive shape through the window of the store. His blood began to boil as he opened the door and climbed out of the car. "Leon, you fat tosser!" He shouted across the lot toward the store. "You lazy fat fuck. My kids are in hospital and you're feeding your fat fucking face. I don't believe you, you useless fat chuffer!"

His boss was oblivious to the abuse. He was making a call and hadn't noticed Dean arrive. Dean started toward the restaurant in a rage, when the deafening honk of an articulated lorry claxon snapped him back to reality. A McDonald's delivery truck trundled past him and nearly ran over his feet. He jumped back and waited for it to pass.

Nate Bradley watched Monkey head toward the toilets as the articulated vehicle manoeuvred into the delivery bay. Leon Tanner had his huge back leaning against the window and he could see Dean Hines heading into the restaurant. A third gangster whom he didn't recognise was eating a burger opposite his boss. Dean didn't look happy as he opened the dining area door and marched into the restaurant. The back gates of the store opened and two members of staff began dragging empty delivery cages across the drive thru lane toward the lorry. There were a dozen stacks of bun trays stood next to the curb where the wagon stopped. The driver jumped down from the cab and pulled on his safety gloves. He handed the crewmembers the delivery notes and walked to the back of the lorry mumbling something that Nate couldn't hear. As he glanced back into the restaurant, he could see Dean Hines and Leon arguing. Dean was standing next to the booth, pointing his index finger toward Leon in a stabbing motion. Leon was laughing, which seemed to be infuriating Dean further. Nate made a snap decision to even up the numbers whilst they were busy arguing. He checked his pistol. It was a Walther P22 fitted with a polymer silencer. One click released the ten-bullet magazine, and although he had checked it five times that morning, he checked it again before sliding it into the pistol ready for use. He climbed out of the car and headed unnoticed through the open wooden gates at the back of the store.

Chapter Sixty

Shankly Way

The boy's screams were deafening. Kisha felt the air crushed from her lungs as Patrick Floyd jumped on her chest. His knees rammed into her diaphragm, forcing the breath from her body. "You fucking bitch!" He yelled. "Do you think you're clever, do you?" She felt his fist smash into her mouth. The gag forced her lips over her teeth and his knuckles split the tender flesh against them. Her front teeth snapped at the root and the exposed nerves seared white-hot. She felt blood running into her mouth. A second blow slammed into her broken nose. She saw lightning flashing across her mind and blinding bolts of pain stunned her brain. The attack was relentless, and he hammered her face and head with both hands. She could hear him screeching like an animal and as each blow struck, her grip on consciousness waned. A fierce blow split the baggy flesh above her left eye and warm blood ran down her face. Another punch hit the eyeball so hard that she thought it had exploded. The punches stopped for a second as her mind drifted away from the brutal onslaught. She felt that she was going to die. Strong hands grabbed her face and his nails dug deep into the flesh on her cheeks. She felt him leaning over, coming closer to her face. She could smell his putrid breath and feel its warmth on her skin. The boy's screams reached fever pitch and mingled with his as Patrick's teeth closed around her nose. She wasn't sure what was happening until he clamped his teeth together in a powerful bite. He shook his head like a rabid dog attacking a rabbit. She felt her skin and gristle tearing as he bit down hard. His teeth cut through the flesh easily, and he twisted his head violently back and to until her nose was ripped from her face. Blood and mucus trickled into her eyes. The pain was incredible. He spat her mangled nose at her face and she felt it slop against her forehead and then slide off onto the floor.

"How funny is that, Bitch?" He yelled. "Hey, how funny is that?" He punched her bloodied face again and then yanked her head toward him. His forehead connected with the gaping hole in the middle of her face, and the sickening thud echoed across the cellar. Her body couldn't endure anymore, and as he twisted her head to one side and bit into her left ear, her mind shut down completely.

Chapter Sixty-One

Alec

The second phase of the search was underway when muffled screams drifted through the walls.

"Quiet!" a SOCO shouted from the basement. The three-storey house fell silent instantly. The screaming became more urgent and it was painfully obvious that it came from a child.

"Where is it coming from?" Alec shouted downstairs.

"It's coming from my left, Guv," the officer replied. "If you're on the pavement facing the front door, it's the house on the right."

"See if the firemen have taken the door off that house, move it!" Alec ran toward the front door. There were eight sandstone steps leading to the pavement, and he took them two at a time. "Smithy, it's the house on the right!" The ginger detective was emerging from the house on the left with two armed officers and three detectives in tow. The firefighters were in the process of removing corrugated iron sheets from the entrance of the house next door. They heard the commotion coming from number forty-four and saw a stream of officers running toward them.

"What's going on?"

"Get that door open!" Alec shouted. "The boy is in there, we can hear him screaming."

The firefighters tore at the metal with renewed vigour, and the sheets buckled and folded beneath the pressure. When the sheets came away, a third firefighter thrust a battering ram into the lock. The wood was rotten and riddled with worm, and it splintered under the third blow.

"Armed unit first!" Alec shouted, and four officers disappeared into the deserted terrace. The detectives were seconds behind them.

"Armed police!" Their voices boomed through the empty house. "Armed police!" Another warning echoed from the first floor. "Armed police! First floor clear!"

The ceilings in the hallway were hanging down in places. Scrap metal thieves had demolished long sections of the walls in order to get at the electric cable and copper pipes. The building smelled of damp and must.

"Guv!" A voice shouted from the hallway. "Get everyone out, now!" The armed officer shouted an urgent warning. "Bomb!"

CRIMINALLY INSANE

Alec reached the officer and peered into the basement stairwell. On the top of the stairs was an oil drum. Strapped to it was a timing device. "I think there is a motion sensor fitted to the top, Guv," the officer babbled. "When I stepped onto the stairs, the timer activated." The red LCD display was counting down. There were forty seconds left. The child's desperate screams spurred them into action.

"Get everyone out of here now, Guv." The armed officer pushed Alec out of the stairwell. "I'll get the child, do it now!" He slammed the door closed behind him and he left Alec frozen in the hallway.

"We can't let him go down alone, Guv, let us by!" Alec stepped away from the door and the remaining members of the armed response unit hurtled into the basement. Their lack of concern for their own safety was stunning, and Alec swallowed hard. His responsibility was the safety of every detective, scientist and emergency services officer at the scene, and he had to clear the building.

"You heard them!" He hollered, "Everyone out now!"

"Kisha is down there, Guv," Smithy hesitated.

"I hope so, Smithy." Alec shoved him toward the door. "If she is, then they'll bring her back to us, now move!"

They cleared the building with about thirty seconds to go. The firefighters illuminated the interior of the building with the spotlight on the tender, but the beam was lost just yards inside the house. Alec heard frantic shouting from inside. The voices were lost in the building, and they couldn't make out what was being said. A gunshot rang out, and Alec flinched at the noise. They were helpless. A second shot quickly followed the first. A third and then a fourth shot sounded much closer. The cellar door burst open and dark shadows flitted about in the hallway. A figure took on a human shape as it entered the beam of light. He was carrying the body of a woman and butterflies took off in Alec's stomach. "Please let her be alive," he prayed. As the officer reached the steps, the woman cried out in pain. Her attacker had crushed her jaw and the broken bones were jingling together as the officer ran full tilt. It was odd to want to hear a woman scream, but on this occasion, they welcomed the sound. The officer jumped the stone steps in a single bound and he landed in a heap on the pavement. Two of his colleagues followed on his heels. "Get down, get down!" One of them shouted as he jumped for the top step.

"The cellar is full of oil drums!" The third officer added as he joined his comrades in a heap on the tarmac. Firefighters and detectives dragged them away from the building. There was a few seconds of anxious wait as they realised that the fourth armed officer had not returned, and they fell silent as they waited for the incendiary bombs to explode. "Get her to the ambulance!" Smithy shouted. "Paramedic!" He hollered at the top of his voice.

The hallway remained still and silent. There was no sign of the fourth officer or the boy. It was getting dangerously close to the timer reaching the end of its journey. As the seconds ticked by, Alec realised that the Victorian terrace had not turned into a fireball.

Kisha moaned in agony as the paramedics reached her. Alec ran to where she lay and as he approached, he saw the expression of horror on Smithy's face. His mouth hung open and a tear ran from his left eye. He wiped it away with the back of his hand and looked at Alec. Alec looked down at her and his brain tried to comprehend what had happened to her once beautiful face.

"What has happened to her?" Smithy shook his head in disbelief. Her injuries caused her face to swell around the eyes and there was a gaping hole in her face, where her nose used to be. A paramedic cut the gag from her face, and her jaw flopped unnaturally to the side. She moaned and her body began to twitch. Congealed blood poured from the corner of her mouth, and the paramedic put his fingers into her mouth to check if her airway was clear. As her head tipped to the side, Alec could see that her ear was nothing more than a flap of skin and cartilage. A dark red hole was all that was left of it.

"She's been bitten, Guv." The medic glanced up at Alec. "Her breathing is laboured, we need to ventilate, now!"

"You keep her alive," Alec said quietly. "Do you hear me?"

"She's in a bad way." The medic placed a ventilator over her battered face and squeezed air into her lungs.

"Guv!" Alec looked toward the house. The fourth armed officer was stumbling down the steps unharmed. He was panting and puffing like a steam train.

"What happened in there?" Alec ran to where the armed unit was standing.

"The cellar is knocked through to next door, Guv," the lead officer explained breathlessly. "There are ten or more oil drums in the second house and they are all wired up to the device on the stairs."

"It hasn't gone off," Alec looked into the house again.

"It isn't going to, Guv," the officer bent over and put his hands on his knees as he tried to catch his breath. "The timer keeps on resetting when it reaches zero and the oil drums aren't full of petrol. The ones I checked are full of water."

"Are you sure?" Alec raised his eyebrows.

"Positive," the officer nodded his head. "We found your detective in the second room, but there was no sign of the kid. I thought I saw the suspect in the next house and I went through a hole in the wall, which leads into the next one, I think. It's black down there, Guv so I let off four rounds. There was no way I could make it back through the cellar before the timer ran down, so I took cover in the third house. When I realised it wasn't going to explode, I checked out the drums. Definitely water."

"So the cellar in there goes through to the next house?" Alec gestured to the firefighters.

"Yes," the armed officer nodded. "And there are no devices in there."

"Open that front door!" Alec shouted. "Smithy!" The ginger detective was standing over Kisha as the medics worked frantically on her. Alec watched them giving her chest compressions. "Smithy!" The medics picked up her limp body and placed her on a stretcher. Two men carried her whilst a third continued to administer ventilation and heart compressions. They carried her toward the back of a waiting ambulance. Smithy waited until the back doors closed before he turned to face Alec. Tears stained his ruddy face. "I don't think she's going to make it, Guv."

Chapter Sixty-Two

Zamir Oguzhan

Will Naylor peered into the reception area and saw Salim's grandfather waiting there. There was a big man in a black leather jacket stood by the door with his arms folded. "Do you think he's the minder?" Will asked sarcastically. His mood was dark. Sharon Gould smiled. The entire team was on edge.

"Stereotyping again," she laughed sullenly. "He might be his lawyer."

"Do you want to bet twenty quid?"

"Nah," she shook her head. Her mobile buzzed as they waited for the front desk sergeant to open the door. She looked at the screen. "It's the governor."

"Tell him I'm about to interview Oguzhan, will you, and I need to speak to him when he has got half an hour free." Will didn't think a two-minute conversation was going to cut it. The door clicked as the desk sergeant disengaged the electronic lock, which stopped the public from accessing restricted areas. Will opened the door and approached the elderly Turk.

"Mr Oguzhan?"

"Yes." The old man looked up, but he didn't move. His dark brown eyes looked into Will, searching for weakness. Will sensed that this ordinary-looking pensioner was far from ordinary. He kept his silver hair neatly cut, and he wore a dark blue Crombie over a white shirt and blue tie. He looked more like a banker than a mobster. "And you are?"

"Detective Inspector Naylor." Will didn't offer a handshake. "Can we just have two minutes?" Will pointed to a door, which led to a small interview room. Uniformed officers used it to assess exactly what a member of the public needed to discuss, and with whom, rather than for interviewing suspects formally. The proper interview rooms were downstairs next to the cells. Years of misuse by the disgruntled public had left the paintwork on the door scratched and chipped. The old man wrinkled his nose at the thought of walking through it. He looked to his minder and the big man shook his head in the negative.

"I have come to pick up the bodies of my grandson and his family, nothing more," Zamir smiled. It was cold smile, almost a snarl. "If you tell me what I need to do to release their bodies, then we can be on our way." He nodded toward the glass-fronted doors. Will walked to the glass and looked out at the car park. He could smell the minder. The big Turk smelled of Aramis and garlic, more garlic than aftershave. There was a black transit near the front doors. Directly behind them was a second identical van. Inscribed on the sides was the logo of a London funeral parlour. The driver and passenger of the nearest one stared back at Will, expressionless.

"Are they being paid by the hour?" Will nudged the minder with his elbow and laughed. The Turk unfolded his thick arms and glared at Will. "I'm only asking because you have more chance of watching Turkey win the World Cup than you have of taking Salim's body anywhere." The minder moved toward Will and then glanced at the old man. Zamir held up his hand to placate his bodyguard. "You should listen to him," Will patted the minder on the arm patronisingly. The Turk's face flushed red with anger. "You're well off your manor now, my friend, and if you so much as fart in the wrong place, I'll have you banged up before you can blink, understand?"

"Are we going to have a problem, Inspector Naylor?" Zamir asked. He walked to the window and looked out at the funeral van. "You see, in my country we have to bury our dead quickly. It's a religious thing, you know?" His thin smile crossed his lips again.

"Well, my boss wants you arrested. But I think if we have a quick chat, we can sort things out without solicitors and tape recorders." Will pointed to the anteroom again. "I haven't got the time to fuck around, so shall we talk or do you fancy spending the day in the cells? It's your shout." Will shrugged.

"Your manners leave something to be desired." The old man smiled thinly and looked at the river. Dark clouds were rolling in from the Irish Sea and the water looked dark green in the dull light. "How old are you, Inspector?" He asked without looking at Will.

"That really is none of your business," Will smiled and checked his watch. "Make your mind up, Zamir. I don't have time to waste."

"You are thirty-five, Inspector." The old man turned to him. "Your birthday is the twenty-sixth of March, nineteen seventy-seven. You were born in Whiston hospital. Your address is Sixteen Palace Mews, Woolton, and you drive a grey BMW. Do I need to go on?" The minder laughed and folded his arms. He titled his head to the side and grinned at Will.

Will walked to the interview room and opened the door. He looked the old man in the eyes and waved his hand toward the opening. "Nice party trick, Zamir, last chance." The desk sergeant buzzed the electronic lock and Sharon Gould walked into the reception area. She looked shocked and grey with pallor. Her conversation with Alec had been a disturbing one. "My colleague here will either get your pet thug a cup of tea while we chat, or she can summon two officers to arrest you and show you to the cells, which one is it to be?"

"Call our lawyer," Zamir said to his minder. "He takes two sugars, and you have five minutes, Inspector." He brushed past Will and walked into the small room.

"I'll be five minutes." Will turned to Sharon.

"What are you doing, Will?" Sharon hissed and raised her eyebrows in surprise.

"Trust me," Will smiled. "Is everything okay with the governor?"

"No, it isn't, far from it!" She shook her head. What he was about to do was completely irregular.

"You can fill me in later. This won't take long," Will said briskly. He looked at the minder and smirked. The Turkish minder bent his knees and farted loudly. He smiled at Will and farted again. "You should probably check your underwear. That sounded moist," Will returned the smile and closed the interview room door.

The old man leaned against the radiator and warmed his hands on it. He looked at the bleak walls and frowned. "Police stations are real shitholes, aren't they?" His thin smile appeared briefly and then disappeared.

"Most of the people we deal with belong down a toilet." Will indicated that they should sit down. "Would you prefer to stand?"

"What do I need to do to release my grandson and his family's bodies, Inspector?" The old man said, ignoring Will's question. "It is imperative that we take them home."

"Simple." Will sat down on a metal framed chair. "Release Rose James unharmed, and we will talk to you about their bodies. Until then, they stay in the morgue."

Zamir's face darkened and he sighed. He rubbed his hands together and then placed them back onto the radiator. Will noticed the liver spots on them and the thin dark blue veins crisscrossing his wrists. "Rose who? I have no idea what you are talking about, Inspector. I want my family's bodies today."

"I want a Ferrari and a night out with Cheryl Cole, but it's not happening. You can make one phone call before I slap the cuffs on you, Zamir. I don't know why people pussyfoot around you, to be honest. Release Rose James and we'll ask the coroner when their bodies will be released, but be sure of one thing, we will not be speeding anything up for you."

"Salim is my only grandchild, you know?" Zamir wagged his index finger at Will. "His children are my only great grand children, and I am too old to be gifted with any more. My family have been murdered and I'm grieving, Inspector. When we lose a family member, the grieving cannot properly begin until we have washed the body. It is our religion, you see, an important tradition. You are insulting my family in our time of grief, and everything has a price."

Will put his hand to his forehead and frowned as if he was in deep thought. "Are you threatening me?" He laughed. "We have a few important traditions ourselves. One is that we don't kidnap women because all our heroin has been nicked, and another one, which is my particular favourite, is that we lock up scumbag gangsters and drug dealers and we throw away the keys. That's a good one, eh?"

"I don't think you have any idea who you are dealing with, Inspector Will Naylor, none at all," Zamir shook his head. He put his hands into his pockets and looked at Will. "You have no respect."

"Yes, I do," Will smiled. "I am dealing with a tired old mobster who lives in the past. Your mob is on the way down, Zamir. Look around you. The Tottenham Boys, the Kurdish Bulldogs, the Bombacilliers and at least three Albanian gangs are crawling up your arse. Personally, I would put the lot of you on a boat and send you back to Turkey. I can't do that, but I can promise you that I will block the release of Salim's body and link it to every investigation we have for the next two years. If you don't play ball, Salim will be nothing more than a puddle before you get him home. Make a call and we will talk to the coroner."

"You are pushing me, Inspector," Zamir said. "And there is a price to pay for that."

"Whatever. Make the call or we'll go downstairs and do this formally." Will pressed the panic bar, which ran around the walls of the room and then opened the door. He looked Zamir in the eyes before he closed it and locked it from the outside. On hearing the alarm, three uniformed officers and Sharon Gould ran into the reception area. The minder grabbed the handle of the interview room door and rattled it anxiously. "You fucking pig, you are as good as dead!" He turned on Will. "Open this door."

"Arrest him for breach of the peace and making threats to kill," Will ordered. The officers struggled with the big Turk, but soon had him face down and cuffed on the floor. The air was blue with his protestations. "Give the old man ten minutes, and then arrest him on suspicion of possession with intent to supply. Let me know when his lawyer arrives," Will said.

"Are you sure about this?" Sharon asked.

"Just do it." Will straightened his tie and made his way back into the station.

CRIMINALLY INSANE

Chapter Sixty-Three

The Gecko

Nate Bradley stepped into the backyard of the restaurant and headed for the rear door. An empty gas canister that had once held CO2 held it open. The back corridor was deserted and the door leading to the public area was still open. The red fire extinguisher, put there minutes before by the lobby hostess, held it ajar. Nate zipped up his black raincoat and pulled the hood over his head. At the end of the corridor, he turned right and pushed open the door to the gents' toilets. The single stall was unoccupied and the door was wide open. No one was at the urinals either. Nate looked through the reinforced fire glass into the restaurant's dining area, and he could see Dean Hines still rowing with Leon. The third gangster was standing at the back of the queue, waiting for a crewmember to serve him. There were six people in front of him, and it looked like he would be waiting a while before it was his turn. He tapped on the disabled toilet door with his left hand. "Fuck off, someone's in here!" He heard.

Nate took a fifty-pence coin from his pocket and slid into the centre of the handle. The design was like a huge screw head so that employees could open the lock from the outside in the case of an emergency. The coin was the perfect thickness and he twisted it easily between his finger and thumb. "Oh!" A startled shout came from inside. "Fuck off, Gar, is that you?"

He slid the door open, stepped inside and shut the door behind him in a matter of seconds. He pointed the Walther at Monkey. "You wanker, Gar, is that you messing about? I'm having a shit!" Monkey's smile faded when he realised that the man with the hood and gun was white. He dropped the newspaper and held his hands above his head. He wanted to shout for help, but fear constricted his throat. Nate pulled the trigger three times, tap, tap, tap. Two rounds into his chest and one to the forehead. The 22 calibre bullets were perfect for a close range execution because they weren't powerful enough to exit the body. They bounced about inside his chest, ripping and tearing the vital organs to shreds. The head shot rattled around inside his skull like a marble inside a jam jar, liquidising the brain matter on its way. Monkey slumped sideways and fell onto the toilet floor twitching. There was one less enemy to cope with at the drug deal.

Chapter Sixty-Four

Shankly Way

The front doors were systematically bashed open by the firefighters, and the Armed Response Unit was ready to clear the first building. "The helicopter's here, Guv!" Smithy shouted as the sound of helicopter rotor blades neared.

"Good, I just hope it's not too late," Alec said, looking up. "I want those people moved back from the end of the street." As he spoke, two more armed response units screeched to a halt. Uniformed officers lifted the orange tapes, allowing the vehicles to drive into Shankly Way. He called one of the firefighters over to him. "Listen, if Howarth has built a rat run through the houses, then he may be heading for the end of the terrace. Start at the end house and let the ARU clear the buildings from that end. We'll work this way toward them."

The ARU officers acknowledged the orders and sprinted after the firefighters. "Smithy," Alec said, "I want you to coordinate everything from up here. I need to see what's going on down there."

"Guv," Smithy said sullenly. He wanted the chance to catch Jack Howarth. Just a minute alone with the animal would do. "The bomb squad are on their way."

Alec walked toward the police cordon at the end of the street and watched as the firefighters smashed open the door. Eight armed officers waited impatiently to enter. "Split up," Alec ordered. "One unit in this one and the other unit next door."

"Armed police!" They bellowed as they disappeared into the end terrace. "Kitchen clear!"

"Ground floor clear!"

"First floor clear!"

Alec could hear similar shouts coming from further down the street. He walked down the hallway, which mirrored the others they had seen already. The officers opened the basement door and filed down the stairs in formation. "Armed police!" Alec followed them and used the Maglight to guide him in the darkness. Moss covered the wooden stairs and water ran down the exposed walls. A strong musty odour pervaded the basement. "Armed police!" echoed off the bricks. Alec reached the bottom of the stairs and shined the torch around. "It's clear, Guv, and there's no way in or out of here."

"Are you sure?" Alec blinked as torchlight shone in his eyes. "Yes, the walls are all intact, and there is no access to the drains down here."

"Okay, let's check out the house next door but one." He had one last look around. "We can alternate with the other team."

"Guv." The armed officers took off up the stairs. Their heavy boots left deep tread marks in the moss.

"No one has been in here for years," Alec muttered to himself. "Where were you going when you scurried through the walls, you bastard?" Alec thought about the injuries to Kisha's face, and his stomach twisted. He stepped into the hallway and shined the beam at the ceiling. Fungus grew along the Victorian architrave. Alec illuminated the wide staircase, which led up to the bedrooms. Dust swirled in the torch beam. "Where are you, Jack? You are so close, I can smell you." Silence answered his question. He turned on his heels and followed the ARU out of the house and along the street. The helicopter whirled above them, and the bomb squad pulled their transporter outside number forty-four. There were muffled shouts coming from inside the terraced houses, but Alec heard something else. The pitch was too high for it to be coming from an adult. "Wait!" He called. He turned his head to pinpoint where the sound was coming from. Alec ran back into the house they had just left. He mounted the stone steps at speed and stopped when he reached the bottom of the wooden stairs. Heavy footsteps resounded as officers followed him into the building. "What is it, Guv?"

"Shush a minute!" Alec listened intently. He shined the Maglight up the stairs, and the dust swirls were thicker this time. A dull thud came from the floor above somewhere. A shrill scream followed it. "Upstairs!" It took all his willpower not to bolt up the staircase first. He stepped aside and allowed the ARU to lead the way. "Armed police!" Their cries seemed to resonate from the damp walls. Alec followed them to the top of the stairs and waited until they emerged from the bedrooms. Torch beams cut through the darkness casting long shadows. "It's clear, Guv."

Another thud came from above them, and this time the screams that followed did not subside. "It's coming from the attic." Alec looked for an access hatch in the ceiling.

"It's in the bathroom, Guv."

"Get me a ladder in here!" Alec shouted down the stairs. "Tell Smithy to send the other armed units into the attic spaces." He walked into the bathroom. Two armed officers formed a step with their hands joined between them. Their colleague placed his foot on it and they lifted him toward the hatch. He moved the wooden lid over to one side and grabbed the rafters inside. When the lid moved, the screaming from the attic became unbearably loud. "Wait for the ladder," Alec ordered. The officer couldn't hold his torch and pull himself up at the same time. He holstered his gun and reached up.

"Let me use your shoulders," the officer said. "If I use your shoulders to stand on, I can climb in. I'm sorry, but I can't listen to that, Guv."

Alec leaned out of the bathroom and looked down the stairs. "Where is that ladder?" He shouted.

"Coming, Guv!" A voice answered.

Alec wanted the screaming stopped just as much as they did. He turned to stop the officer, but his head and shoulders were already through the hatch, and his colleagues were pushing him up. There was a loud creaking noise from above, which reminded Alec of a tree trunk bending in the wind. A creaking groan joined a whooshing noise. It sounded like a whip before it cracks. "What's that?" Alec took a deep breath. The officer's torch fell from his hand and clattered onto the rotten floorboards. His body went limp and his knees buckled. He released his grip on the rafters suddenly and without warning. "Mike?" One of the officers shouted. "What's wrong Mike?"

His body seemed to fold onto itself like a piece of string dropped vertically onto the floor. The officers grabbed at his legs in an effort to keep him upright. Blood sprayed onto their faces in a torrent. It poured into their eyes and sprayed into their open mouths as they tried to comprehend what was happening. One of them let go of the body in panic. He spat the foreign blood from his mouth and stepped back. He tripped over a raised floorboard and fell onto his rump with a thud. His colleague cried out in pain as an object hit him square in the face. It was heavy and soggy. It bounced off his face and landed on the floor at Alec's feet. The body crashed down on top of the sprawling police officers, and they kicked it away as if it was chasing them. They pushed themselves back against the wall and pointed their weapons at the hatch above. Nothing came through it except the sound of the boy crying uncontrollably. Alec shined his torch onto the object at his feet and stared at the severed head in disbelief.

Chapter Sixty-Five

Dean

"I cannot believe that you've made me leave my kids in intensive care when you could have grabbed the cash yourself, Leon." Dean sat down opposite his boss. "The cash is in my car, take it, buy your drugs and then shove them up your fat arse!"

His boss looked angry, but Dean was beyond caring. Leon felt in his pocket for his tin. He expertly opened the lid and pinched some of the powder between his fingers. He snorted it and tilted his head back. "Keep your voice down, Deano." Leon glanced around at the other diners. Their raised voices were attracting attention.

"I won't keep my voice down." Dean leaned over the table and glared at Leon. "Listen to me and listen well. I am out."

Gareth approached the booth with a brown plastic tray in his hands. "What's up?" He asked, oblivious to why they were arguing. He put the tray down and Leon reached for the Big Mac. Dean swiped at the box with the back of his hand and the messy sandwich exploded from the cardboard. A meat patty covered in sauce slapped a postal worker in the face and then settled on his shoulder. He brushed it off and turned angrily, but when he saw the three huge black men glaring at each other, he decided to say nothing. He picked up his tray of food and moved to another table.

"Fuck off, Gareth," Dean said without taking his eyes from his boss, "this is between me and Leon."

"What's your problem?" Gareth looked offended.

"This fat fuck is my problem." Dean stabbed a finger toward Leon. "Now do yourself a favour and fuck off!"

Gareth looked at Leon for instructions. "Go and find Monkey." Leon sat back and smiled. "I wasn't hungry anyway." He shrugged his huge shoulders. "I can see you're stressed out, Deano. Go and be with your kids. Call me and let me know how they are. I'll send Gar to get the money from your car. We'll have to get off now, anyway. Remember, we're going to hit the jackpot today. Don't throw it all away."

"I don't think you heard me, Leon." Dean was shaking with anger. "I left my missus in bits at the hospital because you said nobody else could get the cash. My kids are lying there with tubes coming out of every fucking orifice while you stuff your fat face with Laurel and Hardy. I am out, Leon. Finished, understand?"

"Don't push it, Deano," Leon warned. He kept his voice low. "I've always looked after you. I know you're pissed off. I don't want Jinx to know that I'm back in town, that's why I asked you to go and get the cash. He has put a hit out on us."

"Fucking hell! That's all I need right now." Dean laughed sourly. "I told you not to fuck about with Jinx. And what do you mean he put a hit on *us*?"

"I heard that he put a hit on me, you and Jackson." Leon leaned forward and whispered. "Jackson has disappeared, so I think he's toast. I did a bit of digging and came up with the name of a mercenary who has links to a couple of Jinx's associates."

"How did Jinx find out that you wanted him whacked?"

"I put some feelers out to see who would back us up when it kicks off." Leon shrugged. "Someone must have blabbed."

"I warned you," Dean sighed. "Jackson is toast, are you sure?"

"Pretty much," Leon nodded. "Look, I paid this mercenary off, and he guaranteed me that he would take out the hit man. As far as I know, we're in the clear for now."

"Brilliant," Dean laughed. "Fucking brilliant, I am so out of this shit."

"Do you think Jinx is going to let you walk away?"

"Fuck Jinx, and fuck you, too. I am gone." Dean stood up and looked toward his car. "Send one of the retards out for the money. I'm going back to the hospital."

"Leon!" Gareth shouted from the toilet corridor. "Leon, get here now!" He panicked.

"Alright, alright!" Leon frowned at Dean and they walked toward the toilets. "What's the panic?"

Gareth slid open the disabled toilet and they saw Monkey lying in a pool of blood next to the toilet with his pants around his ankles. "Yes, I see what you mean, Leon," Dean shook his head. "I think we're in the clear, too."

"What's going on?" The dining area hostess walked by. She peered into the toilet and then screamed. She ran through the door and headed for the counter in a panic. Concerned onlookers walked toward the three men.

"Let's get out of here now," Leon growled. "Call the police and an ambulance," he said to the nearest bystander to detract attention from them. Dean put his head down and headed for the door. Leon and Gareth followed closely behind him. "Whoever shot Monkey can't be far away," Leon muttered as they exited the restaurant. A stream of other customers filed out. They didn't want to be around when the police arrived asking for statements.

The car park was busy, as was the drive thru lane. It was impossible to identify the assassin. "Come and get the money, Leon, before I fuck off with it." Dean ran to his car.

Leon waddled behind him like a huge black duck. By the time he reached the car, he was sweating and breathless. "You can't do one now, Deano," Leon looked around the car park nervously. "You could be next. Look how easily they hit Monkey right under our noses."

"They shot him under your nose, Leon. Bollocks to it." Dean opened the boot and thrust the holdall into Leon's chest. He grabbed it, his top lip curling up into a snarl. "I'll take my chances alone, Leon."

"You are making a big mistake." Leon walked away. "Nobody walks away from me."

"Watch me, Leon." Dean looked at him in the eye. "You've got enough problems without me on your case as well. Just leave it." Dean opened the door and ducked inside. He started the engine and the wheels spinned as he accelerated across the tarmac to the main road. He indicated right and drove in the direction he had come from. Leon raised his middle finger as a final salute, and then stormed off to his Lexus. "He'll be back with his tail between his legs when he is skint. Just you see if he isn't," he grumbled. As he did so, he waved to Gareth. "Get in. We need to get out of here."

Nate Bradley collected a cheeseburger from the drive thru window, keeping his eye on Leon. There was a commotion going on in the dining area, and he assumed that they had discovered the dead gangster. He followed the Lexus from the car park as it pulled onto the ring road. It headed toward the docks, which were less than five miles away. Jinx Cotton saw Dean heading back toward the hospital, and he waited for Leon to get into his car before pulling into the traffic. The Lexus cut across three lanes erratically and then turned right at a set of traffic lights. He floored the Mercedes to keep Leon in sight and then changed his mind as the lights changed. He pulled a sharp u-turn, taking the Mercedes in the opposite direction to follow Dean Hines.

Chapter Sixty-Six

Jack

Jack crawled along the rafters on his hands and knees. That bitch police officer had caused this mess. He could taste her blood in his mouth. It would have been nice to hurt her some more, but there just hadn't been time. He needed to get back to his own house without being shot or arrested. That was easier said than done. It was a good job that he was always well prepared. The police had chased him across four continents for decades, but he had avoided capture so far. He could hear them running around, shouting and bawling at each other. They would comb the cellars and the attic space. He was counting on that. There were some nasty surprises lurking in the dark places. Jack had found some wonderful websites, demonstrating how to make lethal booby-traps using flexible carbon fibre poles and cheese-wire. It was amazing what you could find on the internet. If only he could hang around and see how effective they were. He knew what cheese-wire could do to skin and bone because he often used it to hurt his guests. Attaching it to something that could generate force made it more dangerous, and much more fun; after all, that was all that mattered.

Jack heard footsteps approaching, and he dropped his body to the rafters. He slowed his breathing down and waited for the boots to pass overhead. Muffled shouts drifted to him. The heavy boots were above him somewhere. Dust and grit tumbled through the gaps in the boards. They were close, very close indeed, but they wouldn't find him. Jack had lived in the house for three years and he had spent hours knocking through the cellar walls to explore the empty buildings around his. He had made thousands of pounds cashing the metal piping and copper wiring in to scrap yards. It was also perfect for entertaining his guests when he had the urge. He occasionally kept the odd person in the cellars before transporting them to their buyers, but that was rare. It was whilst exploring the houses one day that he had noticed that the bedroom ceilings on the upper floors were lower than on the other floors. Victorian buildings had high ceilings and were difficult to heat, especially the upper floors. Jack assumed that the council or housing association who had converted coal fires into gas central heating had lowered the ceilings to insulate them. Whatever the reason, the void space had become his refuge.

He waited for the footsteps to fade away before making his way back towards his own house. He didn't think it would be long before the bomb squad arrived. They were probably there already. He hoped so, because the sooner they arrived, the sooner he could get out of there.

Chapter Sixty-Seven

Shankly Way

The scene at Shankly Way was bedlam. Paramedics were carrying the decapitated body of an ARU officer into a waiting ambulance. The two colleagues who had witnessed his gruesome demise were sitting on the pavement, covered in his blood. Their superior officer, DS Eales, squatted next to them, offering support to his officers. Alec watched as two armed units entered the adjoining buildings at the end of the terrace, carrying ladders to access the attics.

"Is the boy still crying, Guv?" Smithy approached. News of the beheading had forced them to evacuate the houses and wait until they deemed them as safe. Bomb squad officers and the heavily armoured Tactical Support Group now backed up the armed units. Identifying potential booby traps was paramount to keeping their officers safe.

"Yes, he was before we evacuated." Alec pushed his hair from his forehead. Dried blood smeared his fingers. "They'll get him out of there this time."

"He must have spent weeks building that stuff in there." Smithy was in shock. Seeing Kisha's injuries had rocked him. "I'll tell you what I don't understand, Guv."

"Go on." Alec didn't think there was much to understand, really. Howarth was a psychopath, full stop.

"Why build a fake bomb?" The ginger detective looked baffled.

"Who knows what that bastard is thinking?" It had puzzled Alec too, but the priority was finding Kisha and the boy.

Raised voices inside the end terrace disturbed their conversation. "Paramedic!" An ambulance crew ran to the steps and waited. Alec feared the worst. He wondered if another of Howarth's traps had injured or maimed an officer. Two ARU officers emerged from the house. Between them, they carried the fragile figure of a child. "We've got him, Guv. He's alive, but I think his legs are broken."

"Any sign of Howarth?" Smithy shouted.

"No sign of him."

The paramedics took the boy and placed him on their stretcher. After a quick assessment of his injuries, they applied a foam brace to each limb to restrict their movement. For the third time that day, they watched an ambulance drive through the police cordon. "Did he say anything?" Alec asked.

"No, Guv. He's in shock."

"Who is in charge here?" Alec turned to see an officer from the bomb squad approaching. He had that stride military personnel had. He had tucked his camouflage trousers into black boots, which had a mirror finish to their polish.

"That will be me." Alec walked toward him. "Detective Superintendent Ramsay."

"I'm Captain Riley, bomb squad." The captain pointed to the property where the device was. "We have a big problem, Superintendent."

"Great, what is it?" Alec looked at the grey skies and blew out a deep breath.

"Those drums in number 44 are not full of water." Riley called over one of his team. "Have you got the info?"

"What do you mean?" Alec asked surprised.

"We've inspected it, and the litmus test is telling us that it isn't water. It is clear and odourless, which is why your men assumed that it was, but it isn't."

"Sir," said the soldier jogging over to them. "A swab test is showing that the drums are full of Chlordane. I think the timer is a decoy. We're guessing the real detonator is somewhere inside the drums. Here's what we've got on the stuff. I printed it off in the transporter, Sir." He handed the captain two sheets of information about the chemical.

"What is that? I've never heard of it," Alec asked.

"It's a liquid used in insecticide production, and it is highly flammable. I've never come across it, but I know it's been used to make incendiaries before."

"Can you make it safe?" Alec frowned, and the creases in his face deepened with concern. "We have a dangerous suspect in there somewhere, and we need to find him."

"Until we find the detonator you will have to call your people out of there and pull them back, Superintendent."

"For fuck's sake." Alec turned to Smithy. It was obvious now why Howarth had built the device. "How far back and for how long?"

The captain thought for a moment. "According to this data, a tanker load of this stuff went up somewhere in Chechnya, and it flattened everything within a half mile radius. I need your people back a thousand yards at least."

Chapter Sixty-Eight

Jinx

Jinx accelerated down the dual carriageway until he was directly behind Dean's Ford. He flashed his headlights, signalling him to pull over. He could see Dean's eyes in his mirror looking uncertain. The Ford carried on at the same speed for a few hundred yards before it indicated and turned off the main road onto a Tesco supermarket. Dean drove his car to the front of the store where there were plenty of people milling about before pulling into a parking bay. He took out his mobile phone and jumped out of the Ford. Pointing it at the silver Mercedes, he captured images of the number plate and the driver. "What do you want, Jinx?" Dean shouted at the top of his voice. Passersby looked toward the noise. Dean didn't think that Jinx was going to shoot him in public, but he wasn't going to take any chances. "His name is Jinx Cotton. Remember that!" Some people laughed, thinking it was horseplay, but others put their heads down and scurried off.

Jinx smiled and turned his vehicle into the next bay. He lowered the driver's window. "Funny, Dean!" He shook his head. "Everyone will think you're a nutcase."

"Better than everyone thinking I'm a dead nutcase, eh, Jinx?" Dean didn't share the humour of the situation. "What is this about?"

"I want you to know that I am not coming for you, Dean," Jinx lowered his voice. "Get in, let's talk."

"No, thanks." Dean kept his distance. "I was never coming for you. I said No, so say what you have to say and fuck off."

Jinx eyed Dean coolly. "If your kids weren't sick, you would already be dead. I saw you arguing with Leon. If you want a way out of this, we need to talk."

"What, like the chat you had with Jackson and Monkey?" Dean bent down to make eye contact. "I don't think so, do you?"

"Monkey?" Jinx frowned. "Who the fuck is Monkey?"

"Someone whacked him in the bogs at Mac's on Queens Drive, but then I think you know all about that." Dean looked for a reaction from Jinx but none came. He looked genuinely confused.

"I don't know the guy," Jinx shrugged.

"Bollocks, I don't have time to chitchat," Dean tutted. "What do you want?" A fat woman with a trolley full of shopping walked between them. Her black leggings were so tight that her cellulite looked like dimples in the material. She hurled a string of four letter words at her three fat children, oblivious to the conversation she was interrupting. They waited patiently for the tirade to subside as she carried on her way. "I need to get off, Jinx."

"Okay, I'll give it to you straight." Jinx looked around to make sure that no one was in earshot. "Leon is too close to the Turks. Let's just say that certain parties want him out of business. Tell me where his shipment is coming in, and I will guarantee you are left alone."

Dean looked confused and spat on the floor. He had been loyal to Leon for years, but he needed to leave this life behind. "You guarantee it?" Dean's biggest fear was the safety of his family. If they recovered from their illness, the chances were that they would need months of aftercare, and that meant he had to stay in the city. "How do I know that I can trust you, Jinx?"

"You don't know me well, Dean but you know of me. I helped your sister out once, didn't I?"

"Yes." Dean wanted a passport to another life. This was it.

"I have no beef with you, Dean," Jinx said. "There's a tracking device under your rear wheel arch, left hand side."

Dean hesitated for a moment and then walked to the back of his car. He knelt down and looked underneath the wheel arch. "Fuck me!" Dean hissed. "How long has that been there?"

"Long enough," Jinx winked.

Dean swallowed hard and checked his watch. He had a decision to make, and he needed to make it quickly. "The shipment is coming into Bootle docks today. It's a Dutch cargo ship. He has the port security in his pocket, so the parcel will leave the docks without any bother. They meet at the old Dockers' Clock, do you know it?"

"The transport café?" Jinx looked surprised.

"Yes, that's it. It'll be a simple exchange, nothing heavy."

"Take it easy, Dean," Jinx nodded and put the window up as he pulled the Mercedes away. "I hope your kids make it," he called through the window as he drove away. He grabbed for his mobile and redialled the number for Gus Rickman.

Chapter Sixty-Nine

Shankly Way

Jack heard the police leaving the house in a rush. Loud shouts accompanied the sound of heavy boots stomping across the aging floorboards. It sounded like everything was going according to plan. The bomb had done what he had designed it to do, which would give him the time he needed to get away. He waited half an hour to make sure that it wasn't a ploy to lure him out of hiding, and then he dropped through a hatch onto the attic floorboards and moved quickly through the attic spaces until he reached the house next door to his. He listened intently. The building was silent apart from the odd creak or groan from the ancient roof trusses. He lifted the hatch in the bathroom ceiling and then dropped down into the house. He had a ladder hidden there, which he had used to drag the boy up into the loft, but he chose not to use it now. Time was against him. The bomb squad must have cleared the area when they realised what they were dealing with. Jack had the idea from Nate Bradley. He had planned to rig an incendiary device to his lockup, so that in the event of his capture, he could destroy the evidence of drugs and money remotely. Jack had liked the idea and built a much bigger device over a period of months. It wasn't rocket science, although the detonator was yet to be tested. He was confident that it would explode if he dialled the correct number with his mobile. Jack used another mobile phone to provide the spark required to ignite one of the drums. If one drum went up, it would be a matter of seconds before the others ignited.

He made his way down the stairs to the ground floor cautiously. The police had smashed the front door in, and he could see out onto the empty street. There was no sign of them outside. He crept as close to the door as he dared and peered out into the grey daylight. A radio buzzed with garbled messages somewhere out of his field of vision. He could see the shadow of the bomb squad transporter, but he couldn't see the vehicle. It was too far down the road. He placed his back against the damp wall and moved away from the door into the darkness. The floorboards in the long hallway creaked loudly as he crept to the cellar door. He was less than twenty-five yards from an open manhole cover. It led into the Victorian sewers, which carried human waste and rainwater under the city to the river. A drum full of Chlordane covered his escape route. He knew that the bomb squad wouldn't risk more than one officer at a time, and they would be occupied disconnecting the decoy-timing device. Jack had rigged it with four separate power sources and connected it to the main electricity supply. He guessed that they would disconnect the electricity supply first and then concentrate on the others before confirming their suspicions that the timer was a decoy. By that time, he would be safely in the sewer system, miles away. He was so close that he could smell freedom. He could taste it. Patrick Lloyd was dead and gone, and Jack Howarth was back in business. The cellar door creaked as he opened it. In the silence of the empty house, it sounded deafening. He stepped onto the staircase and closed the door behind himself. The steps were slippery, and he took each one carefully. It was impossible to put weight on the rotting wood without it making a noise. He listened intently for any sound from the cellar next door, but he couldn't hear anything. If there was a bomb technician working there, then he couldn't hear them. He could hear his own breathing as he crept down the stairs. His heart beat quickly, and he could feel the blood rushing through the veins in his temples as he reached the drums. He stepped between them until he reached the furthest one away, and then he knelt down and used them as cover whilst he pressed his shoulder against it. The drum shuddered, and he could hear the liquid inside sloshing around as it moved slightly. There was a squeal as metal scraped on metal, and he froze in the darkness. There shouldn't be any metal there. He had removed the manhole cover months before. He felt down with his hand, but felt only stone. Using a torch here was out of the question. Any flicker of light would give away his presence. There was a waterproof flashlight stashed in the sewer along with a wetsuit and a loaded Glock. He waited a few long seconds and then heaved the drum again. It stuck fast and then slid slowly across the floor.

He reached for the open manhole but touched cold metal. His breathe stuck in his throat and his heart missed several beats. Someone had put the lid back in place.

Lights blinded him, and their suddenness made him catch his breath. He cried out like a wounded animal caught in a trap. "Are you looking for a way out, you piece of shit?" Alec Ramsay said from the stairs. "Armed police, show me your hands!" DS Eales shouted at the top of his voice as he came through the hole in the wall, followed by two of his unit. "Do it now, show me your hands, or I will shoot."

Jack Howarth looked like a rabbit caught in the headlights of a car. His eyes were wide open and glassy and there was no comprehension of what was happening in them. He put his hands above his head but didn't move. "Stand up, do it now!" A second armed officer screamed. Jack flinched visibly and stood up on shaky legs. His knees wouldn't lock out, and he felt like they were pipe cleaners that couldn't hold his weight.

"Jack Howarth, I am arresting you for the murder of Louise Parker. That will do for a start. You do not have to say anything, but whatever you do say may be given in evidence." Alec stepped aside as the armed officers dragged him from between the drums. DS Eales grabbed his arm and twisted it behind his back painfully. He slammed his face into the wall, splitting his lip and cracking a tooth. Jack gave a muffled shout, but a powerful blow to the kidneys silenced him. They frisk-searched him and then slapped solid handcuffs onto his wrists. "Get the bastard out of my sight," Alec sighed. He reached for his radio. "Captain Riley?"

"Yes, Superintendent," the radio crackled.

"Send your men in; we have the suspect in custody." Alec walked up the cellar stairs and ignored the fact that his suspect's head seemed to be thumping into each one individually. Jack cried like a baby, and it sounded good. "Smithy," Alec clicked the transmit button again.

"Yes, Guv." Smithy sounded hyper. "You got the bastard!" Alec cringed at the use of profanity over the police band, but he didn't think anyone would mind this time around.

"We did." Alec felt flat despite the result. "Has the cordon been moved back?"

"All done and dusted, Guv," Smithy replied. It had taken over an hour to move the police lines back and evacuate an area a thousand yards square.

"Good. I want everyone back at the station in an hour," Alec ordered. "Hand the scene over to uniform until the bomb squad is finished. This isn't over yet."

Chapter Seventy

CRIMINALLY INSANE

Bootle Docks

Leon drove the Lexus down the dock road away from the city. Prestige car showrooms had replaced derelict warehouses which had stood empty for decades, and a new passenger terminal gobbled up acres of the old port. Liverpool was now on the cruise ship tourist map, and liners from all over the world docked directly beneath the iconic Liver Buildings. Few reminders of Liverpool's dark history as the centre of the world's slave trade remained on the riverbank. Fashionable restaurants now occupied the waterfront where galleys had once docked, and a huge cargo and container port operated closer to the Irish Sea near the northern suburb of Bootle. "Are we doing this on our own?" Gareth asked nervously. "I can't believe they shot Monkey, Leon. What am I going to tell his family?"

"We'll tell them what we know, which is fuck all, Gar," Leon growled. He reached for his silver tobacco tin and opened the lid with his left hand. He placed it on his knee and spooned some of the white powder onto the back of his hand. He sniffed it and then repeated the process. "Monkey had a lot of enemies, mate. You know that."

"I suppose so, but I've known his family all my life. Are you sure it's nothing to do with today?"

"I don't know for sure, but I'll find out." Leon looked at him to reinforce his words. "We'll get whoever did that, I swear down that we will, motherfuckers!"

Gareth looked in the wing mirror and then turned around to look out of the back window. "That fucker has been following us for miles." He pointed out of the window.

"The guys on the motorbike?"

"Yes." Gareth looked concerned.

"I know, Gar." Leon smiled. "They're our backup, mate. They're hardcore mercenaries."

"You could've told me," Gareth grumbled and turned back toward the front. "I almost shit my pants then after seeing Monkey shot dead."

Leon chortled and punched his associate in the arm. Gareth laughed it off, but the heavy blow would bruise later. A high security fence stretched for miles to their left hand side, and containers of every shade and colour were stacked high as far as the eye could see. Cranes worked tirelessly, lifting cargo from container ships from all over the globe. The port was enjoying a new lease of life, and the increased number of international ships docking brought opportunities for the criminal fraternity, too. Checking every crate and pallet was physically impossible. HM Customs worked flat out to police imported goods, which meant they tendered out the port's boundary security to private security companies. They were at the mercy of the integrity of their employees.

"We're here," Leon said smiling. He indicated and turned the Lexus off the dock road, away from the container terminal. A plot of land designated for development was utilised as a temporary car park, servicing a busy Sunday market nearby. It was desolate wasteland pitted with potholes full of rainwater. Bricks poked out of the compacted earth, causing havoc to tyre treads and wheel balance. There were a few parked cars on it and a scattering of vans dotted about. The only building remaining was an old pub called the Dockers' Clock, which the owners had converted into a truckers' cafe. It flourished by offering greasy breakfasts twenty-four hours a day to hungry heavy goods drivers. "Our suppliers should be in there stuffing their faces with bacon and eggs."

"I haven't been down here for donkey's years," Gareth said, looking around. "I used to get all my snide gear from that market when I was a kid."

"Me too, Gar," Leon laughed. "No more snide gear for you after today, mate. You can go to town and buy as much Armani as you want."

They watched the motorbike slowing on the road behind them, but it didn't pull onto the waste ground. It stayed on the road and drove nearer to the cafe entrance. The pillion rider dismounted and removed his helmet. Griff Collins glanced at Leon, waiting for a signal. Leon put a thumb up. Griff lit a cigarette and walked toward the cafe. The driver stayed on the bike and waited. "Grab the bag from the boot, Gar," Leon ordered.

Leon pressed the release switch and Gareth climbed out of the car. He walked around the back of the vehicle to open the boot lid. Leon kept his eyes on the pillion rider as he stubbed out his smoke and entered the cafe. The boot lid opened, and he felt Gareth reaching in to remove the bag. He could hear him muttering something, but he couldn't understand it. The car rocked as he clumsily fished around in the boot. He heard Gareth swearing under his breath and wondered how difficult getting a holdall could be. Leon's mobile buzzed and he fumbled around in his pocket for it. "I'm here," the voice said. "Do you want a brew?"

"Yes, I'll be two minutes." Leon ended the call. The pillion rider confirmed that the suppliers were in the cafe waiting for them. "We're on, Gar!" He laughed as he opened his door and struggled to lift his huge frame out of the vehicle. "Gareth, move it!" He locked the doors and looked at the boot. The lid was up, blocking his view. "Gareth?" Leon took three steps to the rear of the car and the colour drained from his face.

Chapter Seventy-One

MIT

Alec was sitting at his desk opposite Will and Chief Carlton. The coffee jug on the desk was half-full, or half-empty, depending on how you looked at things. Today it was definitely half-full. He rubbed his tired eyes and tried to digest everything they had uncovered in the last few days. "So you're convinced that this guy, Nate Bradley, is Howarth's accomplice?" He asked, taking a sip of the strong black brew.

"Yes, it makes sense from what we know so far." Will slurped coffee and nodded his head.

"And CTU gave you this information?" The chief raised his eyebrows.

"No, the Taskforce," Will corrected him. "Look at Bradley's profile and what happened to his family. It all adds up."

"Maybe it does," Alec mused, "but what evidence do we actually have that connects him to anything?"

"Nothing yet, but if we arrest him and search his property, we may be able to connect him to the missing college kids through his laptop." Will was racing ahead with his theory. "If we can connect him to the missing lads, we may be able to connect him to the Benjamin murder?"

"Not a chance, Will." Alec shook his head vehemently. "It's all circumstantial evidence. I can see how it fits, but we have no hard evidence on him."

"What about these two killings?" Will picked up an update that the chief had brought with him from the uniformed division. "David Lorimar, shot and set alight outside the hospital, and then Mickey Grieves shot three times in McDonalds?" He put the update in front of Alec. "Come on, Guv. Someone is systematically assassinating drug dealers. He's moving up the chain."

"I don't agree." Alec was adamant. "We have no information to connect Lorimar to drug dealing. We know he's associated with Jinx Cotton, but he's a moneylender, not a drug dealer. Uniform arrested him in a firearms case, but the judge threw it out of court. As for Grieves, I've never heard of him, do we know he's a dealer?"

"The drug squad says he's linked loosely to Leon Tanner, but he was a small time dealer at best," the chief added. "We'll find him and bring him in. Don't we need to concentrate on the case against Howarth for now?"

"We do, but until the doctors have assessed his mental state, we can't go near him. I think he'll be transferred straight to Ashworth Secure Unit or the Cat-A nit in Manchester tomorrow morning. When we get around to interviewing him, I think it will be at Ashworth." Alec drank some more coffee and topped up his cup from the jug.

"He'll be in good company there," Will scoffed. "Is Brady still in there?"

"Ian Brady, one of the infamous Moor's Murderers. Now that is a blast from the past. I had just joined the force when they caught them," the chief reminisced. "He spent most of his life in there. He's being force-fed through a tube now. It's less than, what, six miles as the crow flies from here, Alec?"

"I think so," Alec nodded. "Wherever Howarth ends up, he won't be getting out until he's in a box, that's for sure."

"Sooner the better for me," Will added.

"We still have to focus on his accomplice. If Will is correct in his assumption, then Nate Bradley is out there, knocking over drug dealers and their associates until one of them kills him or we stop him," Alec shrugged. "Either way, we need to make his arrest a priority. I think we should use the press coverage of the Howarth arrest to find Bradley."

"I agree the tabloids will be all over the arrest of the 'Child Taker.' It will be front-page news for a week! If we tell them we're hunting an accomplice, we may get lucky. In the meantime, his picture has been distributed to every officer in the city," the chief said proudly. "If he is out there, we'll find him."

Alec's desk phone rang, interrupting their debate. He took a drink of dark liquid before answering it. "Smithy?" Alec said. He listened for a while. The conversation from the other end was a mystery to the others in the room. "What time?" Alec squeezed the bridge of his nose between his finger and thumb and closed his eyes. "Okay, let everyone know, please." He hung up the receiver and looked at Will. His face was ashen. "Kisha didn't make it." Alec stood up from the desk and walked to the window. The sun was fading fast, and the river looked like liquid metal in the dusk. "The doctors said she had massive internal injuries. She never regained consciousness."

"I am so sorry, Alec." The chief stood up and held out his hand. "That's two damned good officers we have lost to that bastard. We can carry this on when you have told your people. I'll speak to the press. Give me a call when you're ready." He patted Will on the shoulder and let himself out of the room without another word.

"I didn't realise she was hurt that badly. Was she a mess?" Will asked his boss. "I mean did she look like she wouldn't make it?" He couldn't believe that she was dead. Will opened his collar and the button below it.

Alec kept his face to the window. "Yes, he made a mess of her. The bastard bit her face off."

"The team will be rocked, Guv." Will indicated to the officers they could see through the glass. "She was a good copper."

"She was." Alec turned around and his face was like thunder. "She should never have been there alone. Stevie Neil is out of this department as of now, and if I find out he was talking to the press, I want him locked up for reckless endangerment, understand?"

"Yes, Guv," Will agreed. "Lara Bridge won't take my calls at the moment, but when I get hold of her, she'll tell me who the leak is."

"Make sure she does." Alec didn't care how he did it. "Bang her up in the cells if you need to. I want to know how she got hold of that information."

"I'll call her again. If I offer her the full story, she may spill the beans on her source." Will took another swig of coffee. "Now the chief has gone, what happened with Howarth, Guv?" He asked. "Smithy called in saying that the army were pulling everyone out of there, and the next thing we heard, you had Howarth in a van?"

"The bomb squad captain has a twenty-five-year-old daughter." Alec sat down at the desk. "I told him what Howarth did to Louise Parker and the Oguzhan family. He was wavering when one of his men came over and told us he'd seen a manhole cover leaning against the cellar wall in the second house, but he couldn't see the drain anywhere. He moved a couple of drums and found the open manhole. I knew Howarth was planning to use it as his escape route. I asked him to let me wait for one hour and we took the gamble. It paid off this time."

"Phew, big gamble, Guv," Will gasped. "What if it had gone up?"

"The technician was positive that the timer was a decoy. It just made me even more convinced that the bomb wasn't built to go off, it was his way out of there. He wanted us to evacuate the area so he could slip away unhindered. He would be miles away by now if we hadn't taken the chance."

"I can't believe he's in the cells, can you?" Will laughed, but it was a nervous laugh. "Do you think they'll section him?"

"Probably," Alec nodded. "It's difficult to believe anything that animal has done," Alec agreed. "He's in the cells, and that is all that counts. Anyway, I believe we have a few more problems to deal with in the cells?" Alec pointed his finger at Will.

"Yes, Guv." Will blushed red. "I took a gamble of my own, but it hasn't worked quite as well as yours did. Oguzhan and his minder have been in the cells about four hours now. His lawyer is kicking off big time. He cooled off a little bit when I told him that we had Salim's killer in custody."

"What have you said to him?" Alec asked. The creases around his eyes deepened.

"Just that we had made an arrest in connection with the murders, Guv, like you said, it will be all over the news tonight. I told his lawyer we're briefing the drug squad and they will be dealing with him. I said it could take a while." Will seemed unperturbed by the matter. "As soon as they heard about the arrest, they started jabbering in Turkish. The old man was frothing at the mouth."

"Have you briefed anyone from the drug squad?"

"No, Guv." Will smiled. "I can't see them making anything stick, can you?"

"No," Alec agreed. "He owns the property and that's all we have. He'll be out in an hour or so."

"Well, it's early days yet, I suppose," Will smiled thinly. "We'll see if he wants to play ball."

The desk phone rang again. The two detectives looked at it with concerned expressions on their faces. The way things were panning out, it was probably bad news. Alec paused before answering it. "Smithy?" Alec sighed into the receiver, anticipating the worst. He listened for a minute and asked exactly the same question he had earlier. "What time?" He paused again. "Let everyone know, will you." He hung up and looked at Will across the desk.

"It must be your lucky day," Alec smiled. "Rose James walked into a police station in Shrewsbury half an hour ago."

CRIMINALLY INSANE

Chapter Seventy-Two

Leon stopped dead and put his hands on his head. "What the fuck?" He muttered as he looked at the dead body of Gareth Bates. There was a single bullet hole in the centre of his forehead, a trickle of blood running from it into his left eye. The skin around the wound was charred black. His eyes were wide open and his face was fixed in a sneer, showing his yellowed teeth. Gareth was lying on his back in a puddle of dirty rainwater. Leon looked around, but there wasn't a soul in sight. It dawned on him that Gareth was recovering the holdall from the boot, but he couldn't see it. He leaned over to find it, but the boot was empty. "Shit! Motherfucker!" He looked again, but it was nowhere in sight. Leon struggled to kneel down to check under the Lexus. He gasped for breath as he strained his fat neck, but the holdall was gone. Leon stood up and leaned against the back of the car. The nearest vehicle was fifty yards to his left. It was an unoccupied green Vauxhall Omega. Seventy yards to the right was a beaten-up Iveco Daily. It was post office red and had the Parcel Force logo printed along the panels. Leon reckoned it was too old to be in service. It was the only vehicle parked close enough to the Lexus for the thief to reach unseen. He had been distracted for just a few moments whilst Gareth had gone to the back of the car. The van was the only possible place that the killer could have gone. He jumped when his mobile buzzed in his pocket.

"Is there a problem?" Griff was sitting in the window of the cafe waiting for Leon. "Your coffee is going cold here, if you know what I mean." Griff could see that the suppliers were getting tetchy. They were grumbling and checking their watches every few minutes. They were nervous, and the deal could go sour if Leon delayed it any further.

"I'll be there in a few minutes." Leon looked at the cafe. Sweat ran down his head onto his neck. "Are you in the window?"

"Yes, why?"

"Did you see anybody near my car?" Leon reached inside the boot and lifted the spare wheel with his free hand. He held the phone under his chin and lifted a 7.75mm Scorpion machinegun from the tyre well. The Scorpion was small enough to slip into his jacket pocket. Only the magazine protruded.

"What are you talking about?" Griff sounded irritated. He wanted the handover completed without complications. Babysitting Leon was easy money as long as nothing went wrong. "Is there a problem?"

"Answer the question; did you notice anyone near my car?" Leon repeated, with more urgency this time. He didn't want to let the mercenary know that the money had gone.

"No." Griff hissed. "I'm here to watch what is going on in here. You said you had outside covered."

"Yes, it's covered alright." Leon took out his tobacco tin and fumbled with the lid. He spooned the white powder onto the lid with shaky hands and then cut it with his gold MasterCard. He snorted three lines in succession before slipping the tin back into his pocket. Closing the boot, he rushed back to the driver's door and climbed into the car. The motorcycle rider watched as the Lexus engine roared into life, and the wheels sprayed a fountain of mud and grit into the air as they tried to find purchase. The vehicle lurched forward, and Leon snatched the wheel hard left. The vehicle swerved toward the red parcel van at speed. "The deal's gone bad. They're ripping me off!" Leon shouted into the phone as his car neared the van.

He lowered the passenger window and took out the Scorpion. As he pulled to a halt in front of the vehicle, he unleashed the entire magazine into the front windscreen. Glass and metal ricocheted into the air as the van disintegrated beneath the maelstrom of bullets. The gun clicked empty before he took his finger from the trigger. He removed the empty magazine and snapped in a full one. "Jinx!" He screamed at the van. "Is that you in there, you fucking prick?" He opened the door and struggled to climb out. Holding the Scorpion at arm's length, he approached the ruined vehicle with trepidation. "Where is my money, Jinx, you arsehole?" The front seats were empty and the bulkhead prevented him from seeing into the back. He ran to the sliding door, which gave access to the rear and leaned against the van to gather his wits. The cocaine was coursing through his bloodstream, and anger replaced caution. The fact that his money was gone sent him into a blind panic. This was the deal of a lifetime. It would lift him into the premier league of international drug dealers, and he wanted that desperately.

The diners in the cafe heard the gunfire, and several of them ran outside to watch the action. Griff kept his eyes on the suppliers. The gunshots had startled them, and after looking out of the window, one of them grabbed their vehicle keys off the table and they looked around the old pub for a way out. They were searching for a rear exit. The old pub still had the same floor plan it had had when it was full of dockers drinking pints of mild and smoking Woodbines. A corridor led from the main seating area to the toilets at the rear of the pub. The suppliers headed down the corridor. Griff knew that there was a fire exit situated there which would lead them onto the road at the back of the building. He waited a few seconds and then followed them. They looked uncertain as to where they were going. Griff jogged down the corridor toward them. "There's a fire exit here, mate," he feigned concern. "Fuck knows what's going on out there, but it's best to go out the back here."

"Thanks, we'll follow you," a Turkish-looking man answered warily. His English was broken. The two men weren't carrying anything with them. Griff assumed that the drugs were in a vehicle outside, and he knew into which pocket the Turk had put the keys.

Leon took three deep breaths and then reached for the door handle. He yanked it with his left hand and aimed the Scorpion with his right. "Fucking bastard, Jinx," he yelled as he pulled the door, but it didn't budge. The owner had locked the door. He ran around to the back doors as fast as his huge frame would allow him, and he grabbed the handle and twisted it. "Bastard!" He roared, his cheeks wobbling. Spittle flew from his lips as he cursed the locked van. The doors held fast. "I know it's you, Jinx, I know you're in there." Leon stepped back and pulled the trigger. The machine pistol bucked in his hand as the bullets drilled into the rear doors. The magazine emptied in seconds, and the gun clicked as the last bullet fired. Leon threw the gun at the van and it clanged off the bumper and clattered onto the dirt. He bent over and put his hands on his knees, breathless.

Griff pressed the push bar and the fire exit burst open. He let the Turks run past him, but as they did, he knocked into one of them. Several other diners had had the same idea and they barged past Griff in their hurry to escape. The suppliers ran to the left of the building and peered around the corner. They knew that their contact was a fat black man, and a man fitting that description was waving a machinegun around on the car park. They exchanged words, which Griff didn't understand and then ran toward a white Transit compact. The other diners were scattering in all directions, and at least four engines started at the same time. He could hear wheels spinning in the dirt as frightened onlookers fled the scene. Griff ran to the front of the pub and waved to the man on the motorbike. His associate started the engine and drove the machine along the road to the front of the cafe. Sirens wailed in the distance. There wasn't much time, and it seemed that Leon had lost the plot. Griff watched him hurl a machinegun at a red van, and then he picked it up and began hammering the vehicle with the weapon like a man demented. The Turks reached their compact and began searching their pockets for the missing keys. They exchanged angry words, but they were never going to find them because Griff had them in his hand.

Leon heard the police sirens, and his sense of self-preservation tried to take hold of his cocaine clouded brain. He threw the gun underneath the van and then immediately regretted it. His prints were all over it. "Fuck! Fuck!" He kicked the van, and tears of frustration ran down his face. "Jinx, you fucking bastard!" He sobbed as he kneeled down to recover the weapon. It was closer to the other side, out of his reach. The siren was coming closer; others had joined it. Leon scrambled up, using the van to support his massive bulk. He stumbled around to the opposite side. His chest heaved and perspiration drenched his skin, making his clothes stick to him uncomfortably. Vehicles whizzed past him, their engines at full throttle as innocent bystanders tried to escape the scene. A green Omega started at speed toward the exit. If Leon had paid attention, he would have noticed the driver climb out of the back seat. Leon didn't notice them, it was all a blur. He had to retrieve the gun and get away from there before the police arrived. Jinx had his money. Leon was convinced that he was his Nemesis. There was a huge puddle at the other side of the parcel van, and Leon cursed at the top of his voice as he knelt in the icy water to reach the gun. Wheels screeched by and engines roared as he stretched his podgy fingers toward the Scorpion. His face was inches away from the puddle. "Fucking bastard!" He cried. Snot ran from his nose and dribble hung from his lips as he tried desperately to reach the gun. His fingers brushed it, and he felt the cold metal. He pinched it between his index finger and thumb and inched it backwards toward him. Strong hands grabbed the back of his head and a crushing weight pinned him to the floor. The water saturated his clothes; he struggled to get up, but the combination of his own weight and the weight on his back forced him further into it. He gasped as his attacker drove his face into the deep puddle. His body twitched and wriggled, and bubbles flowed to the surface of the dirty water. He desperately tried to hold his breath. He knew he would drown, but his lungs were burning from the exertion. The hands pushed him deeper still as his strength faded. Leon opened his mouth and sucked in rainwater, which rushed into his lungs. He felt darkness creeping into the corner of his mind as the oxygen ran out and his brain began to shut down. "Say hello to my wife and my son Nate, you fat fucker," Gecko whispered into his ear as his body stopped moving.

When the huge dealer was dead, Nate Bradley jogged over to the green Vauxhall Omega and climbed into the driver's seat. Leon's money was in the holdall on the backseat. As the sirens neared, Nate decided it was time to cut and run. He headed for the exit, dropping the car over the kerbstone and onto the dock road.

As Leon choked, Griff climbed onto the pillion seat and pointed to the Transit. The driver nodded, twisting the throttle. The motorbike lurched toward the white vehicle and the Turkish suppliers. They were flapping about and arguing over who had held the keys last. One of them pointed toward the old pub and ran in the direction of the fire exit at the rear, thinking that they may have left them on the table. As he ran past them, the bike reached the compact and Griff pulled the sawn-off from his coat and aimed it at the remaining Turk's face. "Are you looking for these?" Griff said. He waved the keys and then climbed off the motorbike. "Don't be a hero. Are you a hero?" Griff ran to the back of the vehicle. The Turk took the opportunity to run, following his colleague toward the old pub. "I like your style," Griff laughed as the supplier ran. He whistled at the number of packages that the suppliers had wrapped onto a single pallet. "We'll have to take the van." Griff ran to driver's door and inserted the keys into the ignition. He tried to imagine how much the drugs were worth. Leon had screwed up the deal, but if he could commandeer the cargo of drugs, then there would be some kind of salvage money owing. He intended to claim that salvage. The ignition key turned, but the engine didn't fire. There was a two-second delay before he turned it again. Again, it stayed silent and failed to fire up. Griff engaged reverse gear and checked the mirrors before turning the key again. A huge green refuse crusher trundled into his field of vision from behind. The doors opened and he saw men dropping out of it. The motorcycle rider revved the engine and sped away. Griff called after him, but then he realised why the rider had left him behind. He counted six dark skinned men around the compact. They had dismounted from the crew-cab of the bin lorry, and an array of weaponry pointed at him. "I thought there would be more than two of you." He put his head in his hands and laughed. "I like your style!" Griff said as he opened the door of the transit and rolled out onto his back. As he came upright, he pulled both triggers on the sawn-off. A nine-millimetre bullet hit him in the cheek. It rocked his head backwards sharply, snapping his spine at the neck before travelling through his body turning brain cells into pink mush. It exited his head just above his right ear, ripping a chunk of bone the size of a man's hand from his skull. Bullets, blood and bone splinters tore through the material of his jacket, and a barrage of nine millimetre rounds to the chest blew him off his feet. He was dead before he hit the floor. The Turkish gang left him bleeding in the dirt, and when the police cars arrived, the bin wagon and the compact were long gone.

Jinx watched Griff Collins fall, and he recognised him as the hit man who had looked him in the eyes after killing David Lorimar. The motorcycle was the same machine he had used to escape the scene. The Turks were there in numbers, but they remained well hidden until their shipment was threatened. If Gus Rickman had intended to hijack the deal, then he probably realised that his men were outgunned and retreated gracefully. The motorcycle raced past him, and Jinx put his foot down in the Mercedes to keep pace with it.

CRIMINALLY INSANE

The rider accelerated to nearly ninety miles an hour along an arterial route, which ran parallel to the dock road. Jinx kept him in sight, but he was a dozen vehicles behind him as they approached a set of traffic lights. The motorcycle weaved through stationary traffic and then indicated to turn off the main drag onto a slip road, which accessed the Wallasey tunnel.

The tunnel under the Mersey linked the city to the Wirral peninsula. Jinx pressed the accelerator down and followed the motorcycle onto the tunnel approach. A bank of tollbooths slowed the traffic again, but Jinx headed for the express lane, which allowed regular users to drive straight into the tunnel. A camera used vehicle registration recognition to identify vehicles with a prepaid pass, and as Jinx approached, the barrier raised automatically. The motorcycle joined the queue for the pay booths and had to wait his turn in line. As Jinx headed down the tunnel, the motor cycle raced alongside him, unaware who was driving the car next to him. Jinx took the inside lane, forcing the bike into the outside line. A row of reflectors buried into the tarmac was all that separated it from the oncoming traffic. The lanes were narrow and overtaking forbidden, even for a motorcycle. There was a coach in front of the motorbike, keeping it level with the Mercedes as they drove further under the river. The coach and Jinx's Mercedes hemmed the powerful machine in. As the tunnel began to climb, Jinx saw an eighteen-wheeler coming the opposite way. All four lanes were crammed with vehicles, and the air was thick with exhaust fumes and engine noise echoing from the curved walls. As the articulated lorry approached, Jinx swerved toward the motorbike. The rider glanced at him and swerved away to avoid a collision, but the Mercedes clipped the rear wheel, and the machine hurtled across the reflectors into the path of the oncoming truck. "That's for you, Dava," Jinx said. The motorbike shattered as it hit the lorry, and the force catapulted the rider underneath the front wheels. In his rear view mirror, Jinx could see the traffic grinding to a stop. A blue and white crash helmet bounced off the road and as it hit the tunnel wall, blood splattered the paintwork. The rider's head sprung out of the helmet and smashed through the windscreen of a Nissan Micra.

Chapter Seventy-Three

MIT

Alec opened the front door of his house and stepped inside. He had hoped that the lights and central heating would be burning and the smell of cooking would greet him, but it didn't. The house was dark and cold and his heart sank. Gail hadn't relented. He hadn't thought that she would, but hope had kept him positive. All those years of marriage had to count for something. Alec switched on the light and kicked the door closed with the heel of his foot. "Hi, honey, I'm home," he said to the empty hallway. "What's for tea, oh, is it quorn sausages, my favourite?" He wasted his sarcasm on the hall carpet. "I miss you, but not the quorn sausage surprise," he chuckled dryly. "What is the surprise anyway? Surprise! It's not a sausage at all, it's quorn!" He joked to himself, but if he had had the chance to sit down and eat his tea with his wife opposite him, he would have. Alec felt a terrible emptiness inside. He missed her already. The house felt alien to him without her there, but he thought about how much time she had spent there alone. Alone and waiting for her husband to come from work. Alone, wondering if he would take his days off this week. She had spent her married life alone. Alec realised it now. Now she had gone, it was obvious.

He was tired and needed to sleep. The adrenalin from the investigation had worn off, and his mind felt numb. Arresting Jack Howarth had felt like an anticlimax. He walked into the kitchen and flicked on the light. The kettle was full, so he switched it on and grabbed his favourite mug from the cupboard. He caught his reflection in the window, and the man he saw there was much older than he had expected. The job was aging him rapidly, but he couldn't see the day that he would retire coming anytime soon. It was no wonder that Gail had left him. He lived for the job. Apart from a few stolen hours a day, she had lived her life alone, constantly waiting for him to come home.

His mobile rang, and he tutted as he took it from his coat. "Tell them you've only just arrived home, Alec," he mimicked his estranged wife. "You haven't even had a cup of tea yet and they are ringing you. Can't they make any decisions themselves? Are you the only detective in Liverpool?"

"Hi, Will," he answered the call just before it clicked over to answer service. "What's up?"

"You okay, Guv?" Will sounded concerned. "You seemed a bit down when we left."

"I'm just tired, nothing a good night's sleep won't fix." Alec put coffee into the mug and then added another spoonful for good measure. Gail wouldn't have approved, but then she wasn't here to complain. "I thought you'd be in the pub with the troops."

"I was going to, but I can't face putting on a smile and acting like nothing has happened. Smithy has gone with them, but he's just putting on a brave face. He was close to Kisha."

"A few pints with the team will do him good." Alec wasn't so sure it would, but it sounded like the right thing to say. "It will hit him sometime sooner or later. Anyway, what's up? You're not calling just for a chat, are you?" Alec opened the fridge, swearing under his breath when he saw that there was no milk.

"No, I thought you'd want to know that they have sectioned Howarth."

"No big surprise there," Alec said. He was relieved in a way. "The man is a raving lunatic."

"The medical staff said that he was behaving normally one minute, and the next he was like a rabid animal," Will explained. "He bit the solicitor we appointed to defend him."

"Bloody hell!" Alec laughed. "Who was it?"

"Wilkins," Will laughed with him. It wasn't funny, but sometimes they had to make light of the darkness that surrounded them. "It took six coppers to hold him down, and after they restrained him, he began to plead that he didn't know why he had been arrested!"

"Poor old Wilkins." Alec poured boiling water into the mug. "I never liked the man anyway."

"They're transferring him to the cat-A in Manchester tomorrow morning," Will added.

"A bullet through the back of his head would do it for me, but that's the way it goes." Alec stared at his reflection in the window. He considered using an anti-wrinkle cream, but decided that it was probably too late. "Have you heard anymore about what happened at the docks?"

"It's all a bit sketchy at the moment," Will sighed. "Leon Tanner has been positively identified as one of the victims, and one of his boys, Gareth Bates, took a bullet through the head, but the other guy is still John Doe. Dr Libby reckons he was shot at least thirteen times, but he can't say for definite how Tanner died until he completes the autopsy. He thinks that he drowned."

"Drowned?" Alec was shocked.

"Well he was found face down in a puddle so they assumed he'd been shot and he'd fallen down into it, but when they moved the body, there were no other injuries," Will explained.

"How did they move his body, with a forklift truck? Tanner is a big man," Alec commented. "Holding him down would be difficult. Could he have been knocked unconscious?"

"Guess we'll find out when the doctor cuts him open. They found a Scorpion machinegun next to the body."

"Sounds like a drug deal gone bad?" Alec asked, although he had a sneaking suspicion that it was linked to their investigation somehow.

"Sounds like Nate Bradley to me, Guv," Will spoke his mind. "I think the guy is on a mission. The drug squad has been after Leon Tanner for as long as I can remember, and they reckon he supplied our dead friend Jackie Benjamin. If Bradley had a hand in killing Benjamin, then it makes sense that he's moved up the chain."

"Any sign of him yet?" Alec sipped the black coffee and winced. It was strong and bitter.

"Nothing yet," Will scoffed. "He isn't likely to go home, is he?"

"I wouldn't be surprised, Will," Alec said. "If he is behind all this, then is he likely to have anything incriminating at his house? I doubt it."

"You might be right, Guv."

"Have we got a warrant to search the place yet?"

"First thing in the morning, Guv."

"Good." Alec had a thought. "What happened to Oguzhan?"

"Drug squad swerved it and released him, Guv."

"How come?"

"They reckon that some big noise in the Met told them to back off. There is an undercover investigation going on, and they didn't want it compromised."

"That makes sense," Alec said. "Did Libby release any of the bodies?"

"No, Guv. When Oguzhan found out the little fella was still alive, he broke down in tears. Apparently, he went straight to the Royal to see him. His solicitor is filing a formal request for the early release of the bodies in light of the Howarth arrest. Oguzhan wasn't happy with me, but fuck him!"

"We can't please everybody all the time, Detective," Alec said sourly. He turned off the kitchen light and walked into the living room. Everything was neat and tidy. Gail must have tidied up before she had packed her bags and left him. "What time are you going in tomorrow?"

"I'm thinking about seven, Guv, if that's alright with you?"

"Let's make it nine, eh?" Alec said. "We both need some sleep, and the courts won't process the search warrant until gone ten."

"Nice one," Will agreed. "See you in the morning. Say hello to the missus for me, Guv."

"Yes, will do." Alec hung up and sat down. "Will says hello," he said to the empty room.

Chapter Seventy-Four

Jack

Jack woke up with a banging headache, and it took him several seconds to remember where he was. 'Locked up, stitched and fucked up, all because of Patrick Lloyd,' Jack thought. He tried to move his arms, but thick straps fastened them to a restraint belt around his waist. It was early, half-light filtered through thickened security glass high above his urine-stained bunk, and it hurt his eyes. His right eye was swollen and bruised as a result of his arrest. Apart from the restraint, he was wearing white pants made from paper. The cell door rattled as the custody sergeant inserted the key to open it. Jack closed his eyes and clenched his bowels. He grunted and defecated. "You can clean this up later," Jack laughed hysterically and grunted again as he emptied his rectum. "Poo! That stinks, doesn't it?"

"Dirty bastard," the sergeant grumbled. "He's all yours, get him out of here." The sergeant wrinkled his nose at the foul smell and retreated from the cell. Three uniformed officers entered the cell. They wore full protective helmets and body armour more suited to a full-scale riot than transporting a single prisoner. "Put the face bar on him first," the sergeant ordered. "He's a biter." The officers threaded a leather strap behind Jack's head and forced the bar over his face before fastening the buckles. "That'll stop you biting, arsehole!"

One of the officers said as he fixed the straps painfully tight. Once they had attached the face shield, they untied the straps, which held Jack to the bed.

"What are you doing?" Jack's face suddenly changed. His words were barely audible. "Can I go home now?"

"You won't be going home at all, you sick bastard." The officers pulled him to his feet and dragged him across the cell. "You're going to a nice new cell in the nuthouse. Put the hobble straps on him." They fastened leather shackles around his ankles, avoiding the faeces dribbling down his thighs.

"Why are you doing this to me?" Jack asked innocently. "Can I see the doctor? Because I don't feel well."

"Shut up," one of the officers snarled. They marched him down the corridor and the custody sergeant opened the metal gates as they went. A thick steel door led them out to an underground car park where a prison van waited. The van was white with two blacked-out windows on the side. They bundled Jack up the steps and pushed him into a holding cage, where they secured him to a mesh seat.

"We're all going on a summer holiday, a summer holiday, me and you, where the sky is blue," Jack sung tunelessly as they closed the door and locked him in.

"He's a fucking fruitcake," an officer said. He cleared phlegm from the back of his throat with a guttural sound and spat through the mesh. The sticky blob trickled down Jack's cheek.

"Are we there yet?" Jack looked around and ignored the globule that was tickling his skin. "Stop the bus, I want a wee wee, stop the bus, I want a wee wee, stop the bus, I want a wee, and the driver wants a poo!" He rocked his head back and laughed. The officers muttered and cursed him as they closed the rear doors. "Do they think we are mad?" Jack stopped laughing and asked himself the question. "I think we might be, you know," he answered. Jack closed his eyes and went to the dark place in his mind where he often sought sanctuary in times of trouble. It was the place he had found when he had been a young boy. The place he had hidden when the priest at the care home had buggered him. He felt no pain there, no humiliation or embarrassment. As a boy, he had spent many hours there whilst the men tasked with his wellbeing had abused him.

He heard security guards climbing into the front of the vehicle, and he felt the vibration as the engine started. The seat was hard and uncomfortable, and his arms were aching in the restraints. He drifted away from the pain and discomfort, and the gentle rocking motion of the van made him doze. It was a quiet place where he went, peaceful and serene. Jack wasn't sure how long they had been travelling when a violent shudder woke him. The cellular van tilted and then tipped over. He felt the world spin upside down, and the judder smashed him into the side of the cage with force. Blood rushed to his head as he dangled upside down from the seat. The thick straps held his bodyweight to the chair despite gravity trying to pull him down. He could hear yelling coming from the guards, and then it stopped suddenly. They were silent for a moment, and then there were other voices. Loud voices shouting things that he couldn't understand. He could hardly breathe. The straps cut into his skin and the material dug into his neck as he hung upside down in the cage. The face shield cut into his mouth, and it was impossible to swallow. It occurred to him that the prison van had been in a collision, upended by another vehicle maybe. He felt his blood pounding in his head, and the fragile vessels in his face strained under the pressure. There was a scratching sound at the back of the van, and he heard keys rattling in the locks. Jack couldn't breathe because his bodyweight forced him down against the restraints around his chest. His eyes bulged from his head as the blood pressure increased. He thought about Louise Parker hanging upside down, and her screams echoed around his mind as unconsciousness descended on him.

Chapter Seventy-Five

Will

Developers had built number 16 Palace Mews at the end of a leafy lane in a suburb of Liverpool called Woolton. The predominantly Jewish community was secular and quiet, which suited Will. He wasn't one for making friends out of neighbours, and the job devoured most of his waking hours, leaving his social time at a minimum. When he did socialise, it was usually with other law enforcement officers. He found talking to people outside of the job about how his day was going almost impossible, and his previous relationships hadn't lasted long because of that. Katie Osborne was the only woman he had ever wanted to marry, but she was already married to another man. The affair had blown up in his face, damaged his career and broken his heart. When Katie's husband had found out about them, he had said he would forgive her if she resigned from her job, and they had moved away from the city to begin again. Will had begged her to stay with him, but when the chips had been down, she had jilted him for her husband. All the promises she had made had been lies, all the plans they had made to be together had been nothing more than romantic dreams, shattered on the harsh rocks of reality. Katie's husband was a senior executive with Shell Oil and the heir to a large family fortune. Her love for Will hadn't been powerful enough for her to lose her life of privilege. She had resigned from work by telephone, and he had never heard from her again. When he had rung her mobile, the number had been out of service, and after five days of torment, he had driven to her house to find the building totally empty and a for sale sign outside. The loss had devastated him. Will would have walked over razor blades for Katie, and she had promised him that her marriage was a sham and that their future was together. Her husband's money and the security it offered her had meant more than she had thought in the end.

Since then, Will concentrated on work. He still had an eye for a pretty woman, but his heart was somewhere else. It was months before he met a woman he was interested in, and in true Will Naylor style, it was the wrong woman, a married woman. She was older than he was, but still very attractive. They met at a charity function and hit it off immediately. He was vulnerable since Katie had jilted him, and she was in a sexless marriage with a man she didn't love anymore. They went to a wine bar after the function and opened their hearts to each other. The sex they had was exactly what they both wanted and needed. They both knew the relationship was destined to go nowhere, but they enjoyed their time together whenever they could. She had called earlier that day and arranged to come to his house when he eventually finished work. He needed her touch and the warmth of her body to take his mind from the case. She was a generous lover, making up for all the intimate experiences she had lacked for years.

The Howarth case had taken its toll, and he was exhausted. After speaking to Alec, Will opened a bottle of Pinot. He poured a generous measure into a glass tumbler and swallowed it in one gulp. The doorbell rang and he switched off the television, grabbed the bottle and headed for the front door.

"Hello, Detective," she cooed. He could smell her perfume, and the scent made him heady.

"Come here." He pulled her inside and pushed her body against the wall. "You smell good enough to eat," he whispered as he kissed her lips. She opened her mouth and welcomed his tongue into her mouth, tickling it with hers.

"Good, because I like it when you eat me," she gasped into his ear. "Are we going to stand here all night or are you going to take me to bed and show me how hungry you are?"

Will picked her up in his arms, and they giggled as he carried her upstairs. Their lovemaking was frantic, almost desperate, and when they were spent, she slept soundly in his arms. Will reached for the wine. The liquid burned his throat, but it helped his mind to rest and allowed him to sleep soundly. He thought about replacing the top on the bottle, but decided to empty the remainder into the glass. Will downed the wine, and it made his eyes water. Two minutes later, he closed his eyes and turned on his side next to her. The wine numbed his senses. Sleep claimed him quickly, but his dreams were dark and haunted by the murder victims he had seen through his career. His mind kept asking him questions about the case whilst his body cried for rest. It took a long time before his breathing settled and he fell into a deep sleep, but when he did, the days of working constantly caught up with him.

Downstairs the front letterbox opened, and a length of green hosepipe poked through it. The pipe grew longer as a man dressed in black fed it through the gap, and it was four yards along the carpet when petrol began to pour from it. The fuel seeped into the thick carpet and soaked from the hallway into the lounge. Petrol saturated the area from the front door to the narrow staircase, and fumes filled the air. At the back of the house, another man dressed in similar fashion sprayed petrol from a pressure tank used for applying weed killer. He soaked the back door in the liquid and sprayed it through the keyhole into the kitchen. Fuel covered the linoleum floor before the man threw the tank into the bushes. As Will drifted deeper into an exhausted sleep, a single match turned the ground floor of 16 Palace Mews into a vision of hell.

CRIMINALLY INSANE

Chapter Seventy-Six

Alec

Alec heard the telephone ringing in his dream. He was wearing a coat, which was much too tight, and the boat he was on was sinking fast. Someone was behind him calling for help, but every time he turned around, they were gone. His dream made no sense, and it faded rapidly. The telephone rang again. He opened his eyes. They felt gritty and sleep held them together. He rubbed them with the back of his hands and looked at his watch. It was eight o'clock in the morning, and he was still on the couch. The television was on, but the movie he had been watching had finished six hours ago. The ringing continued, and he rubbed his hands across his chin, feeling the stubble there. He reached for his mobile and looked at the screen. "Morning, Alec," the chief spoke first. "Are you okay?"

"Morning," Alec yawned. "I feel like I was out on the piss until four o'clock. Another night on the sofa, what's up?"

"Look, Alec, I'm sending an Armed Response Unit to your house. They should be with you in five minutes," Chief Carlton babbled. "I don't want you to panic, but pack some things, just enough for a few days..."

"Woah!" Alec interrupted. "I have just opened my eyes, I feel like shit, and you are rattling on about armed units!" Alec stood up and stretched. "Slow down and tell me what the hell is going on." He walked to the curtains and looked outside. Daylight was creeping up behind the grey clouds, but the streetlights still glowed. The shadows in the park looked dark and foreboding.

"There have been some developments, Alec, and I think you may be in danger." The chief took a moment before he tried to explain. "We transferred Howarth to the Cat-A unit in Manchester as a precaution. The cellular van was involved in an RTA en-route."

"You are fucking kidding me!" Alec put his hands through his hair. "Don't tell me that bastard is on the loose."

"We don't know what's happened yet, Alec." Carlton cleared his throat. "Traffic responded to an alarm call, found the van upended and there are fatalities at the scene. Look, there is much more to this, Alec. I need you to listen to me."

"What fatalities?" Alec asked angrily. The chief was dancing around something. He was too tired to play guessing games. "Just cut the bullshit and tell me straight!"

"Howarth is not at the scene, Alec," Carlton explained, sounding embarrassed. "The vehicle's alarm was activated by the driver an hour ago, but when traffic arrived on the scene, they reported the guards shot, one fatality, and the prisoner missing. Look, this isn't the reason for the call."

"Did it crash or was it ambushed?" Alec didn't feel like he was getting a straight answer. The fact that the guards had been shot was lost on his sleepy brain. The Category-A unit in Manchester held the most dangerous criminals. Gangsters and terrorists were always an escape risk whilst in transit. "Was Howarth the only prisoner on board, I mean who shot them, for Christ's sake?"

"It looks like an ambush, but we don't know who did the shooting. Howarth was the only prisoner," the chief admitted. "Look, Alec, there is more."

Alec heard the sound of sirens approaching. They weren't far away. "What the fuck is happening, Chief?"

"There's been a fire, Alec."

"A fire?" Alec was baffled, tired and irritated. "What are you talking about?"

"The fire brigade were called to an address in Woolton in the early hours of this morning," the chief sighed. "One of my officers attended the scene and recognised the address as Will Naylor's house." Alec stayed silent. He felt the hairs on the back of his neck tingling.

"Fucking hell, Chief, isn't this a bit over the top?" Alec had a bad feeling. The sirens seemed much closer now. If Gail were home, he probably would have her pack some things.

"Did you hear what I said?" Carlton asked. "Are you there, Alec?"

"Yes, I'm here." Alec watched an armed response unit turning into the street. The lights flashed and rotated in the half-light. "What has happened?"

"They think someone started the fire deliberately near the front door. There are signs of accelerant. They found the bodies of a man and woman on the stairs. It looks like they tried to escape, but the smoke overcame them on the stairs."

"They?" Alec repeated. His voice was emotionless. "Who are they?"

"I'm sorry, Alec, there really is no easy way to say this," the chief stalled again. His voice was thick with emotion.

"Say what?" Alec was becoming agitated. "Is Will okay?"

"Will is dead," the chief said. There was no of saying it without sounding blunt. "I'm afraid he died from smoke inhalation."

"Jesus wept," Alec whispered. "Are they positive?"

"It is Will. That is definite." Chief Carlton coughed nervously. "Look, Alec, about the woman."

"What woman, who was she?" Alec was confused.

"Her car was on the driveway, and they found her driving license in her handbag." Carlton paused again.

"What are you trying to tell me, Chief?" Alec's throat choked and his eyes watered.

"The woman is Gail, Alec, I'm afraid she's dead."

Alec felt the wind knocked out of him as sure as if he had been punched in the guts. His knees trembled, and he felt bile rising in his throat. "Gail is dead?" He croaked. "How the fuck could she be at Will Naylor's house?"

"We don't know, Alec." The chief coughed nervously again. "I am worried about your safety, Alec, hence the armed unit. They could target you next."

"Someone set fire to his house? Yes, I can see why you were worried now," Alec muttered. "You're sure it's Will and Gail? Have they got the right address?"

"Yes, there's no doubt about it." The chief was adamant. "I don't know what to say to you, Alec, I know you and Will were tight, but Gail?"

"There isn't much to say really." Alec was choked. "It hasn't sunk in yet. Were they fully clothed or naked?"

"I'm not sure," Carlton lied.

"Don't insult my intelligence," Alec growled. "Were they naked?"

"Yes, Alec, but it might not be how it looks," the chief said too quickly. "I think it's linked to Jack Howarth," he added. "It must be."

"No, Chief, Will wasn't involved in the arrest." Alec sat down on the couch as if a huge weight had knocked him over. He covered his eyes with his free hand, and hot stinging tears filled them. They spilled over his lids and trickled down his cheeks. He had to control a sob by biting his lip. All the angst of the case, the brutality of the murders, added to Gail leaving, had left his nerves raw and exposed. It had all built up over the last few weeks, and the news of this betrayal brought it all crashing down on him. The two most important people in his life had been cheating on him, sleeping together, having sex with each other, and then behaving perfectly normally to his face. Gail hadn't left because she was lonely; she'd fallen in love with another man. A man who had given her all the things that he hadn't. A man who had given her sex, probably the best sex she had ever had. He couldn't remember the last time they had had sex. His hands began to shake uncontrollably, and tears streamed from his eyes. He couldn't stop them running down his cheeks.

"Alec, I know this is shocking news, but I need to make sure that you are safe."

The chief was making sense, but then he would. He hadn't just discovered that his wife and his best friend had been lovers and had died in an arson attack. He waited until he had control of his voice again before speaking. Thinking about work was all he could do to soften the pain. "If Howarth planned that escape, then I'm Houdini. It was public knowledge that we had Howarth in custody, wasn't it?"

"It was all over the late editions and the evening news," the Chief agreed. "It's not important right now. Why does that matter?"

"Once he was arrested, it was obvious that he would be moved to a Cat-A unit," Alec thought aloud. There was a loud knock at the door, and Alec could see armed officers walking up the path. He was conscious that his eyes were red and full of tears. "Zamir Oguzhan threatened Will at the station. If he knows that Howarth killed his grandson and his family, and he blames Will for keeping their bodies in the morgue, then this could be retaliation. It would take a well-armed team to knock over a cellular van with an armed guard on board. Oguzhan's organisation could carry out a job like that." The officers banged on the front door, but their knocking was louder this time. "I'll be there in fifteen minutes. Does any of the team know about Will and Gail?"

"Yes, rumours are flying around the station. We can't keep a lid on something like that, I'm afraid, Alec."

"No, I realise that, I'll see you shortly." Alec ended the call. He couldn't decide whether he hated them or not. Half an hour ago, he had loved them both. Now he knew the truth, but it didn't make any sense, or did it? He could understand why Gail had been unhappy, but of all the men to fall into bed with, why him? Why Will?

"Poor Will," Alec wiped tears from his face, "you're the talk of the town in life and death, my young friend, and your choice of women was shite. You always picked the wrong ones." Alec ignored the pounding at the door and picked up a photograph of their wedding. Gail looked beautiful, but she always had. He touched her face with his fingertips. He put his back to the wall and slid down onto the floor. His legs buckled and the tears flowed down his face. His body trembled and shook as he looked at her picture, and the thoughts of their life together tumbled around his head. "When I find out who did this to you, they will pay. I promise you that. I did nothing for you while you were alive, but I promise you this one thing. They will pay."

Chapter Seventy-Seven

Jack

Jack felt a hard slap to his face, and his teeth cut the lining of his cheek. He tasted blood in his mouth. "Open your eyes," a foreign voice ordered. Another stinging blow hit him, and he opened his eyes and looked around. He didn't like what he saw. He closed them again, trying to drift off to his special place. A bottle of smelling salts cleared his senses and dragged the clouds of unconsciousness away from his mind. "Open your eyes," the voice bellowed. Another slap rocked his head to the side. Jack tried to speak, but the face guard hindered him. "Are you Jack Howarth?" a different voice asked.

Jack turned to the voice and looked into the cold watery eyes of an old man. He looked foreign. He looked like Salim Oguzhan, but much older. "Oh, fuck," Jack tried to say. The old man was smartly dressed. A heavy slap sent a bolt of light through Jack's brain. He looked at the man who had hit him. He was a man-mountain with hands the size of shovels. Jack tried to move, but they had tied his hands above his head. The straps and restraints fixed by the police were still there, but his new captors had repositioned them. His paper pants were gone. They had hung him from the ceiling and stripped him naked. The sensation of travelling and engine noise told him that he was in some kind of lorry. The size of the space around him made him think that he was in a large container, probably an articulated vehicle. There were several large crates built from new wood. The scent of resin drifted in the air. The big man punched him hard in the stomach, and the blow forced the air from his lungs. He rocked backwards like a human punch bag. Jack gasped for oxygen, choking on the face guard.

"Answer the question." The big man grabbed his cheeks and squeezed them hard. The face bar dug into his lips, and Jack felt his lungs wheezing for breath. "Are you Jack Howarth?"

"Take that thing off his face." The old man waved a hand. "I don't want him to choke to death."

Clumsy fingers fumbled with the straps at the back of his head, and the mouth guard fell away onto the floor. The relief was welcome; he sucked in air greedily. "Who are you?" Jack spluttered. "Why am I here?"

"Are you Jack Howarth?" The old man asked calmly. "Answer me, or Sami will hurt you."

Jack thought about giving a smart answer but thought again. "Yes, I am Jack Howarth." He spat congealed blood onto the floor.

"Do you know who I am?" The old man raised his eyebrows.

"No, I haven't got a clue." Jack tried to smile, but it turned into a sneer. "I'm figuring you're not my parole officers."

The old man smiled and nodded his head. "Funny," he pointed at Jack with his index finger, "very funny indeed." His smile faded quickly. "My name is Zamir Oguzhan."

Jack swallowed hard and kept eye contact with Zamir. "Am I supposed to know who you are?" He sounded confused but a flicker in his eyes gave his lie away.

"You murdered my grandson, his wife and my great-grandchildren, Mr Howarth." Zamir pointed his finger again and wagged it from side to side. "Family is everything to me, and you slaughtered them."

"I don't know what you're talking about." Jack looked surprised at the accusation. "I was arrested for murder, yes, but I killed my partner in a fight. I don't know anything about your family."

"Oh dear," Zamir frowned. He looked at his minder and shook his head. "Until we know that you killed Salim for sure, we can't exact our revenge, Mr Howarth. An eye for an eye, a tooth for a tooth, you know what I mean, don't you?"

"Not really," Jack said shakily. "I don't know your family."

"The police are convinced that you are their murderer," Zamir shrugged his shoulders. "Am I supposed to think they got it all wrong?"

"They get it wrong all the time," Jack insisted. "Honestly, I killed my business partner because he was ripping me off." Jack nodded his head and looked both men in the eyes. His eyes flicked from one to the other. "You've got it all wrong."

"I've been reading all about you, Mr Howarth." Zamir walked past Jack. He was out of view, but Jack heard the rustling noise of paper moving. "You're famous, look!" Zamir held up three different newspapers, all leading with the story about the capture of the 'Child Taker'. A dated photograph of him appeared on the front pages. "I'll read this to you, shall I? It may jog your memory. 'Jack Howarth, people trafficker, known paedophile, was arrested on suspicion of the murder of Louise Parker. Police sources are indicating that they will further charge him with the murders of Salim Oguzhan, his wife and two children.' It goes on. Shall I read on?"

"They're stitching me up!" Jack's eyes filled up with tears. He knew he was in terrible trouble. The anticipation of the pain that was coming made his stomach cramp. Sheer terror gripped him. He knew they were going to hurt him. The memory of Father Thomas pulling him along the corridor by the scruff of his neck crept into his brain. The priest who had dragged him night after night into his stinking office seemed almost real, as if he was next to him. Jack could smell his sweat, he could feel his fetid breath on his neck, and he could taste his semen at the back of his throat. He remembered the anticipation of the pain he was about to endure, and it occurred to him that those memories drove him to do the things he did. They frightened him so much that he relived them by hurting others. It was role reversal. He was the predator in a bizarre fantasy world where he lived and breathed his own pain and the sweet pain of others. It was all about helplessness and suffering. It was about knowing that no one was coming to help. "It wasn't me who killed your family, it was Patrick Lloyd," Jack began to whimper.

"Patrick Lloyd, Patrick Lloyd, let me see, because that name rings a bell." Zamir scanned one of the newspapers. "Ah yes, here it is. Patrick Lloyd. 'It is alleged that Howarth lived for several years under the guise of an ex-soldier, Patrick Lloyd.'"

"They made it up!" Jack's lip quivered. He looked at the Turks, pleading with his eyes. "It was the other bloke, what's his name?"

"I've heard enough, make him admit it," Zamir said to his minder. The big Turk dragged a wooden crate over to Jack and picked up a claw hammer. "The sooner you admit what you have done, the sooner you can say sorry and begin to pay for it. Everything has a price, you see?"

"That would make a nice coffee table." Jack nodded toward the crate. He spoke as if they were friends chatting in Ikea. "It's not my cup of tea, but a bit of dark wood stain would do it." He removed his thoughts from the painful reality he faced. Something came into his head, and he looked like he had had an idea. "Nate something, the guy's name was!"

The Turks ignored his jabbering. Sami bent down and grabbed Jack's ankles. He lifted his feet from the floor as if they were straws and dropped them roughly onto the crate. His body bent at the waist as if he were sitting in mid air. Jack heard a nail ping onto the floor.

"Clumsy muffin," Jack laughed, but it was the laugh of a nervous frightened boy. It was the laugh of a boy who knew that he was about to spend the next few hours at the mercy of a drunken priest. "You'd better pick that up, or it will ruin the Hoover when you tidy up."

"I know you killed my family, and we will kill you in return, that's obvious, isn't it?" The old man smiled. "What people are telling me is that you killed Salim because you wanted to know where he kept my drugs, it that right?"

"No," Jack shook his head. "I didn't kill him, but I know who took your drugs, and I know where they are. Let me go and I'll take you there."

"You are going to die, Mr Howarth," Zamir said seriously. "Have no doubt in your mind about that. All that concerns you is how long it will take for you to die. You can tell me what I need to know, or we can make you tell us the hard way."

"There's not much incentive for me in that package, really, is there?" Jack chuckled. "If you let me go, we could discuss a cash bonus for the return of your drugs, maybe?"

"You are a funny man, Mr Howarth." Zamir didn't smile. His eyes looked into Jack's soul. "Make sure he can't move them."

Sami took a four-inch nail and pinned it through the leather ankle restraints. He hammered it into the crate and then pulled the straps. "He's going nowhere, left or right first, funny man?" The big man sneered. His accent was much thicker than Zamir's.

"Left for love, right for spite," Jack whispered. "Nate something, what was his name? Where did he put all the drugs? I can't remember!"

Sami held his left ankle and pressed his foot flat against the wood. He smiled at Jack as he aimed the claw hammer. Jack closed his eyes and waited for the pain. The hammer came down and splattered his little toe across the crate. The nail clung to the hammerhead along with a lump of pink skin. Bone turned to pulp beneath the force of the blow.

"Nate Bradley did it!" Jack screamed in a high-pitched whine. His body twitched and convulsed with the pain. The anticipation had been as bad as he had expected, but the pain was far worse. "Please don't hurt me. His name is Nate Bradley!"

"Do all of that foot." Zamir was losing patience.

"No, no, no, please!" Jack screamed. He heard Louise Parker's screams in his head. She had used the same words he had. "Please don't hurt me again!" The cries rebounded in his brain "Please, no!" The voices of Salim Oguzhan and his children joined his own screams, and their faces twisted in agony flashed through his mind. The screaming reached earth-shattering volumes as the cacophony of their voices deafened him. Their suffering mingled with his own. The hammer fell again and again, smashing nails and splintering bones against the wood. Each blow sent a violent jolt through his body, and he felt as if his joints would rip apart. Blood and flesh splattered the big Turk's face, but he carried on hammering Jack's toes until they were nothing but a bloody mush with no recognisable shape remaining. The screams that Jack could hear were his own. Tears streamed from his eyes and snot dribbled from his nose. The tendons in his neck looked like they would snap at any second. Saliva hung from his chin and he babbled incoherently even after the hammering had stopped. His body shivered visibly and blood flowed across the crate, soaking into the wood.

"Is that funny, Mr Howarth?" Zamir tilted his head and smiled properly for the first time. "Can you see the funny side of that? Maybe your coffee table idea wasn't such a good one, what do you think. This is very messy." Zamir pointed to the bloody mush that had once been Jack's foot. "Have we got anything to clean up this mess, Sami?"

Sami laughed and walked past Jack. He heard the big man chuckling and the sound of wood creaking. Jack opened his eyes and looked at the old man. "Kill me, please?" How many times had he heard that? How many times had Louise Parker begged him for death, how many? The names and faces of his victims flashed onto the big screen in his mind. How many were there? He remembered telling the bishop that he wanted to die because Father Thomas had repeatedly abused him. When he had finally plucked up the courage to tell someone about his ordeals at the hands of the priest, he had chosen the bishop. The bishop had listened intently and pretended that the story concerned him, but instead of offering words of sympathy and helping him, he had scolded him and called the priest immediately. They had explained that the priest was teaching him humility and punishing him for his evil behaviour. They had warned Jack that if he repeated his wicked allegations to anyone, the police would throw him into an asylum for the remainder of his life. After caning his bare backside, the men of the cloth had then taken it in turns to bugger him over the desk. Jack had never mentioned his abuse again, what was the point? It just made things worse. He must be evil because the bishop had told him he was and punished him for it. As the years went by, the lack of humanity shown by the men who had educated him had rubbed off on him. Brutality made the strong stronger, and the weak weaker. Jack had become the abuser, not wanting to be the abused ever again. "Just kill me," he wailed. Had he he shouted that here in the present, or was it a scream from his past life? He didn't know.

Sami returned with a bottle. "This will clean up the mess, and then we can see how your coffee table looks, eh, funny man?" He poured the sulphuric acid over the ruined foot, and the liquid hissed and bubbled frantically as it dissolved flesh and bones. "We use this stuff especially for cleaning, funny man." The Turk stood back and put his hand over his nose as the noxious fumes hit him.

Jack's screams reached a new pitch, which he had not known was possible. He could not have imagined that such pain was physically possible to endure without the body switching off. His head felt like it was going to explode. He wondered if any of his victims had screamed as loud or as long. His mind tried desperately to reach that place where he went to avoid pain and strife, but he couldn't find it. It was gone. The door was closed and the key thrown away. The agony in his foot seemed to be spreading through his entire body. His muscles began to twitch involuntarily.

"Was that funny, Mr Howarth?"

Jack shook his head from side to side, dribbling spittle from his chin onto his chest. "No more, please!" He whimpered. "The drugs are in a lockup at the back of Smithdown Road. It's the one with the brown door. Just kill me, please."

"We haven't started yet," Zamir laughed. "When you admit that you killed my grandson and his family, then we can begin, simple."

"I didn't kill them," Jack whined. He sobbed like a baby. "Please believe me."

"Do the other foot," Zamir shrugged to Sami. Sami picked up the hammer.

"No, no, no, please, no!" Jack wailed. The hammer crashed down onto the remaining toes repeatedly. Blood and bone sprayed into the air like a pink mist rising. Sami seemed to enjoy the torture as much as Jack once had. He could see that glimmer in his eyes. Only his big toe remained intact when Jack broke. "Okay, okay, I did it!" His words were barely audible. "Please stop, please stop it!"

"What a shame to stop now!" Sami laughed. "Fuck it! I'm not leaving just one toe. That is just sloppy." He slammed the claw hammer down five times more until the big toe was goo. Jack's screams became a howl of anguish and saliva globules shot high into the air. He thought his heart would explode through his chest.

"Good," Zamir said, shaking his head. "Now we can begin. Did you rape my grandson's wife?"

Jack was barely lucid. The pain was warping his mind. He was shaking and gibbering. He couldn't take it anymore, and he nodded in the affirmative, indicating that he had raped the woman. He didn't remember much of it because he had been in a rage when he had killed her, but he usually raped them before he killed them, didn't he? Yes, his mind answered, of course you did. He listened to his brain and muttered, "Yes."

"You did?" Zamir took the hammer and grabbed Jack's knees. He forced his trembling legs apart and handed the hammer to Sami. "Nail his bollocks to the wood." Jack's eyes widened as this new terror threatened. He kicked against the restraints and tried to twist his body away from the danger, but the straps held him fast.

"No, don't do that, no please don't do that, I beg you, please!" Jack bucked and writhed, but he couldn't escape their grip. He gritted his teeth, and the veins in his arms swelled to bursting.

Sami laughed as he picked up a nail. He pressed the point against the wrinkly scrotum and then hammered the nail through the skin into the wood. Blood and plasma splattered over Sami's fingers. Jack wailed in agony, his body thrashing in the air. "Another one," Zamir ordered. Sami put a nail between his teeth for safekeeping and knocked a second nail through Jacks right testicle. Jack thrust his pelvis forward so hard that his scrotum ripped away from his body. Sami hammered the third nail through the purple head of his flaccid penis, stapling it to the crate. Jack couldn't believe that he was still alive. The pain from his broken feet seemed to dissipate as this new agony erupted from his groin. His breath was nothing more than short gasps and his eyes rolled back into his head as his body convulsed in agony. He felt his skin blistering and popping as the acid burnt through each layer with increasing intensity. Zamir snatched the bottle of acid from the floor and tipped the burning liquid over Jack's genitals. The skin began to blister and liquefy immediately. Jack's head rocked back and his mouth lolled open, a dreadful screaming rasp echoing around the lorry. Zamir tipped the sulphuric acid into his open mouth, and the scream turned into a gurgle as his tongue melted and dissolved. The acid blistered his windpipe and burnt his larynx. His oesophagus ruptured, and the old Turk held his head back, pouring the contents of the bottle into his mouth and then into his eyes. Jack's body writhed, convulsions racking him. The Child Taker twitched for at least three minutes before his heart finally gave up the struggle. Zamir watched him die with a sense of justice for his slaughtered family. *An eye for an eye, a tooth for a tooth* was the code he lived by.

Chapter Seventy-Eight

CRIMINALLY INSANE

Two Weeks Later

"Ashes to ashes, dust to dust." The vicar scattered freshly dug soil into the grave. Six feet below him lay the body of Detective Inspector William Naylor. Police uniforms filled the graveyard as far as the eye could see. Alec threw a handful of soil from the vicar's box onto his friend's coffin, and then he turned and walked away without speaking to anyone. His emotions were spinning. Will had been his friend and colleague for years, yet he had betrayed him in the worst way possible. He had taken his wife. There didn't seem to be any sense or reason to it. He was angry and terribly sad at the same time. He didn't want to get involved in any chitchat until he was sure that his eyes wouldn't give away the pain that he felt inside. He felt the eyes of fellow officers on him, and he could see the whispers on their lips as he neared them. The news that they had found his wife dead next Will Naylor had fuelled the gossip merchants for hours. Alec was struggling to cope with Gail's death, but the manner in which she had died was inconceivable to him. It all seemed like a surreal nightmare.

"Funerals, eh?" Chief Carlton appeared on his shoulder. "They don't get any easier, do they?" He added. Alec didn't reply. He just smiled weakly. "Are you going to the Griffin for the wake?"

"No," Alec shook his head. "If I have a drink now, I'll never stop. I want to get back to the station. I'm better off keeping my mind occupied."

"The commissioner wants you to oversee the case, Alec. I think it's best that you are seen to be removed from leading the investigation, without actually being so," the chief gave a knowing wink.

"I understand." Alec knew the fact that his wife was now a victim meant that he couldn't be seen to be investigating her murder. The senior hierarchy followed protocol but left him some room to be involved indirectly. "I spoke to him last week. He thinks the Bradley side of the case is far enough removed not to break protocol. It's keeping me busy."

"I know, I'm snowed under, too," Carlton frowned. "This case has created a shit storm that is unprecedented in my lifetime. I'm chasing my arse around in circles with the press."

"I know the feeling, you and me both," Alec sighed. He took his mobile from his inside pocket and switched it off silent mode. "Do you know which idiot left his phone on in the church?"

"Not yet, but when I do find out, I will kick him up the back entry for you!" The chief took his phone out and checked the screen. "Graham Libby has called me and left a voicemail." He frowned. "He never has any good news lately."

"He's called me, too." Alec raised his eyebrows and showed the chief the screen. "Will you call him, or shall I?"

"You do it, Alec, let me know if it's important." The chief veered away toward his car. "If it is, tell me tomorrow. If it isn't, tell me tomorrow!"

Alec waved and jogged through a gap in the low wall which encircled the graveyard. The roads would be gridlocked with mourners if he didn't beat people to his car. He pulled his coat tightly around him to stop the cutting wind from reaching inside, but it had little effect. His fingers felt numb from the cold. A row of sycamore trees bent dangerously in the wind, and a Primark bag floated past him at speed. Alec remembered waiting for nearly an hour while Gail had shopped at the Primark on Lord Street. A semicircle of husbands and boyfriends had waited impatiently on the pedestrianised road outside while their partners hunted for bargains. Alec had gone inside the massive store once, but once was enough. It had reminded him of pigs feeding at a trough, pushing and shoving each other out of the way to get to the rails. Everywhere he had looked, garments had lain on the floor. The bag bounced off a Mini and took off high into the air. Alec watched it, part of him wishing he could float away from his shattered life. Maybe it was time to retire and take his pension. He could live cheaply in the sun somewhere and lick his wounds. His phone rang as he reached his car. Alec unlocked it and answered the call as he climbed into the driver's seat.

"Alec?" Dr Libby wasn't sure if it was him or his voicemail. "Is that you or that bloody machine?"

"It's me." Alec tucked the phone under his chin and pulled the seat belt around him.

"How are you?"

"Fine," Alec replied. He was far from feeling fine. What was he supposed to say when people asked? Gail's death had turned his world inside out. How did you cope with such a shock to your system and still feel fine? "I was about to call you."

"I didn't know if you were working yet, so I left a message. Have you had some time off?"

"No." Alec was finding it hard to indulge in small talk. Everyone talked to him differently now, as if he would shatter into a thousand pieces if they said the wrong thing. "What did you want to talk to me about?"

"Well, it's good news, I think, depends on how you look at it," the doctor began.

"Well, if you tell me what it is, I can make my own mind up." Alec started the engine and drove slowly toward the exit. The car park was filling up with mourners returning for their vehicles. He waved at a group of detectives from the robbery squad. He hadn't seen them at the graveside. "Look, I'm driving, so if you could get to the point, I'd appreciate it."

"Yes, sorry." Dr Libby sounded irritated. "I've had a call from our guys in London, Hammersmith, to be precise. They found human remains in bin bags last week. The body was dismembered and there was no head or hands to get dental records or prints from, but their DNA tests have come back with a hit on the system."

Alec waited as the pregnant pause dragged on. "Do I have to ask who it is, or are you going to tell me?"

"It's Jack Howarth," the doctor said flatly. He was disappointed that Alec wasn't as enthusiastic as he had expected him to be. "I thought you would want to know straight away."

"I'll let the chief know, thanks for that." Alec cut the call off and pulled the car onto the main road. The traffic was light as he drove away from the churchyard. Jack Howarth was dead. The world would be a safer place without him, but Alec felt nothing. There was no elation, no relief, just numbness. He turned on the wipers as a deluge of rain fell. The wind rocked the car as he drove through a tree-lined stretch of road. He thought about calling the chief but decided to wait. His hands were shaking and his bottom lip began to quiver. Hot tears ran from his eyes, and he wiped them away with the back of his hand. "Zamir Oguzhan did that," he muttered to himself. "He killed Jack Howarth and he murdered my wife." Alec had a feeling in his guts that he hadn't felt for a while. There was a fire burning there and it felt good. Clarity returned to his thoughts. Zamir Oguzhan had killed Gail.

Chapter Seventy-Nine

The Gecko

Nate Bradley held a Glock 17 in his left hand. He caressed the barrel lovingly with his right. The gun felt cold to touch, yet it was familiar and comforting to hold. He knew the police were outside watching, but he didn't care. There didn't seem to be any answers to his questions or any finishing line ahead. He had tracked and killed the dealers directly responsible for supplying the drugs, which had killed his son and destroyed his wife. His partnership with Patrick Lloyd had been madness, but then the world was mad. The newspapers told him that Patrick Lloyd was Jack Howarth. A notorious paedophile wanted for murder and kidnap. How had he not seen through his lies until it had been too late?

Nate had seen the evil that man could inflict upon man at close quarters. He had designed and carried out some of the most horrific torture techniques known to man, but it had been a means to an end. What Patrick Lloyd had done had been evil for the sake of being evil. Nate had caused suffering in order to extract information. It was his profession, his job, his legacy. Intelligence officers across the planet used his techniques. Human suffering had meant nothing to him back then, but suddenly that had changed. He had thought that killing the dealers responsible for his loss would somehow stop the pain, but it hadn't. It was still there. Pain and guilt oozed from every pore. Nate wasn't sure which was worse, the pain of losing his family or the guilt for the years he had neglected them. Had he caused them to take the path they had chosen, or would it have happened anyway? He couldn't answer the questions.

He pressed the barrel of the gun to his temple and squeezed his eyes closed. His finger wrapped around the trigger, and he felt the sensitive mechanism budge slightly. A few millimetres more and his pain would stop, he could be with his family and the agony would end. There would be no more hatred, no more questions and no more guilt, just peace. He longed for peace, an end to the gut-twisting grief he felt night and day. His hand was steady, but his finger refused to move the final distance. He just couldn't end it now. He wasn't scared of death, when it came he would embrace it, but now wasn't the time. He would know when the time was right. He didn't know how he would know, but he would. He was convinced that he would.

Nate put the gun into a polystyrene box moulded to house it and then placed the box back under the floorboards where it couldn't be found. He slid the carpet back into place and walked to the window. His living room was neat and tidy. It was over a week ago that he had returned home and an army of police had descended on him. They had searched his house, confiscated his computer and telephone and questioned him at the station for twenty-four hours. Nate could hardly remember any of the questions they had asked. Despite all their theories, they had nothing to hold him on. His home was clean, and they had returned his computer and telephone to him. The superintendent in charge of the case knew he was lying, but there simply wasn't any proof. They had put him under surveillance, but Nate went about his business as if they weren't there. He hadn't moved the drugs from the lockup after killing Leon Tanner because no one would stumble across them. Nate had taken the money from the lockup and along with the holdall full of cash, which he had snatched at the docks, he had parcelled it up and posted it to the headquarters of the charity Help for Heroes. He wasn't sure how much there was, but he reckoned it was close to four hundred thousand pounds.

He moved the curtain slightly and peeked through the blinds. Two detectives were watching his house from a black Nissan. They were less than a hundred yards up the road. He wasn't sure who had taught them their surveillance skills, but he was sure that they needed more training. He closed the curtain and headed into the kitchen. A radio stood next to a silver microwave, and a boy band that he couldn't recognise crooned an irritating ballad. He switched it off and opened a cupboard above the microwave. He took a glass tumbler out and then reached for a half-empty bottle of Bells whisky. It had been full an hour ago. He twisted the top off and poured the amber liquid into the glass. It helped to silence the questions in his head. As he took a sip, he heard a tapping on the kitchen window. His heart beat faster as he turned toward it. The light reflected off it and at first, all he could see was his own reflection. He thought about running for the Glock, but it was too far away. A fraction of a man's face appeared at the window and he tapped again. Nate thought he recognised the man, but the shock stopped him from moving. The man pointed to the back door, indicating that he should open it. Nate sipped the whisky again and thought about his next move. The man knocked again, but this time it was louder.

Chapter Eighty

Smithdown Road

"There it is," Sami pointed to a row of shops. "The North Pole?" He sneered. "I don't get it. Why call a shop that?" A joke shop stood between a charity shop and a newsagent. A taxi office and a kebab shop flanked them. The shop fronts were decayed and scruffy looking, a mishmash of coloured signs and peeling paint caged behind metal security grills. "The garages are behind the shops." He pointed to his telephone screen and an aerial photograph of the area zoomed in on the alleyway at the rear of the joke shop. "Google earth says so," he laughed. "You want the one with the brown door."

"What if there's anyone around?" A young Turk leaned between the front seats of the black Audi to get a better look at the screen. "Can you see anyone on there?" He said, looking at the picture.

"Are you fucking stupid, Murat?" Sami laughed. "Take that bag and go get the boss's drugs." Murat looked offended as he grabbed a dark blue rucksack off the back seat. "Go with him," Sami instructed a third man. "Make sure he doesn't get scared on his own."

"Fuck you, Sami," Murat laughed as he climbed out of the car. "Why don't you make yourself useful and get us a kebab. This won't take long."

"Why not, I'm starving," Sami grunted and shuffled his huge frame out of the vehicle. "Don't fuck it up, any problems, call me."

"Blah blah," Murat moaned as he crossed the road. It was late, and there were a few cars on the road. "Have you got the bar, Raba?" He asked his colleague. Raba opened his long coat to reveal a steel wrecking bar. The men walked by the taxi office, which was manned by a single radio operator. She glanced up as the Turks walked by but didn't pay any notice to them. The smell of stale urine hit them as they turned into the alleyway. The yellow glow from the streetlights on the main road couldn't penetrate the darkness at the back of the shops, and it took a while for their eyes to adjust. "I didn't hear him calling me stupid when we torched that pig's house, did you?"

"No, we did a good job there," Raba chuckled. "No one was getting out of there, went up like a firework, boom!"

"I can't see fuck all," Raba muttered.

"Look for the one with the brown door." Murat took a narrow torch from the bag and shined it along the garages. One of the garage doors was missing. Another was hanging off at an odd angle, a single bolt suspending it. There were wheelie bins dotted about and rubbish overflowed from the lids. The smell of garlic drifted from the extractor fans at the back of the kebab shop. "Smells good, eh?" Murat sniffed the air.

"All I can smell is piss," Raba moaned. "There's a brown one." He pointed along the alleyway, two shops down. Graffiti covered the panels. The artist had wanted to tell the world that Carol G sucked cocks so much that he had sprayed it four times. The Turks approached the lockup and checked the alleyway for people. Apart from the bins and the rats, it was empty. Murat pulled the handle and the metal door rattled loudly. It sounded louder in the quiet of the alley. "It's locked," Murat said.

"What, they locked it?" Raba shook his head, "Sami is right about you, you are fucking stupid."

"Get the bar under there and less of your shit," Murat snapped angrily. He hated it when Sami called him stupid, but to be fair to Sami, he knew he was less intelligent than those around him. What he lacked in sense, he made up for in brawn. Murat was a big man packed with muscle. Related to the Oguzhan family, he was fiercely loyal. Raba forced the bar under the door and pushed down as hard as he could. The metal shook noisily but didn't budge.

"Let me try." Murat nudged him out of the way. He slid the bar further under and pulled the opposite way to Raba. The metal vibrated, the hinges creaking. There was a screeching noise and the lock snapped. He pushed the door up and over the opening. Plastic drums cluttered the garage. There was a grey filing cabinet against the left hand wall. Murat pointed the torch at the cabinet. He stepped inside the garage and picked his way between the drums. "Check that side," he ordered Raba. Raba walked toward the darkness at the back of the lockup.

"There's a clock or something here," he mumbled as he noticed a red glow from the corner. Murat looked over at it. They looked at each other with concerned expressions as the first drum of chlordane exploded. By the time the fourth drum ignited, Murat and Raba were cinders.

Chapter Eighty-One

The Gecko

CRIMINALLY INSANE

Nate Bradley swallowed a mouthful of whisky and felt the alcohol burning his throat on the way down. He watched the man walk by the window for a second more, and then he walked to the back door. He unlocked the mortise and twisted the handle. When he opened the door, he caught sight of the figure of a man stepping through the back gate. It creaked closed and the figure was gone. Nate looked around the garden, but there was no one there. He looked down and saw a brown envelope wedged into the doorframe. Taking one last look around, he picked up the envelope and closed the door, locking it immediately. Nate switched the kitchen light off and picked up the whisky glass and the bottle. He walked into the living room and put the glass and the bottle down on the coffee table.

Nate peered out of the curtains again. The two detectives were still sitting in their vehicle. They could not have made it back to the car so quickly if they had left the envelope. Nate was convinced that he had recognised the man, but it seemed so bizarre that he doubted his memory. He had only caught a glimpse, so he could be mistaken. It didn't add up. He put the curtain back and opened a door on the sideboard. Removing a pair of rubber gloves, he slipped them over his fingers and opened the envelope. Inside was the police file and photograph of Zamir Oguzhan. Nate took the file and sat down on the settee to study it. It made for interesting reading. The police suspected the Turk and his organisation were responsible for importing the bulk of the heroin and cocaine that came into the country. Nate twisted the top off the whisky bottle and filled up his glass. He took a mouthful and swallowed hard before filling it up again. Nate read on and learned that Zamir ran his business from London but had interests across the country. He knew that Salim was dealing from Connections nightclub, and he knew that Leon Tanner had been associated with him, but he had not known who was at the top of the tree until now. There were newspaper clippings in the envelope. He tipped them onto the table. The police accused Jack Howarth of murdering Salim and his family, which troubled Nate, but it seemed that one of the children had survived and was recovering at the Alderhey Children's' Hospital. Zamir Oguzhan was responsible for importing the drugs which had poisoned his wife, and he was still in the city, waiting for the doctors to transfer his great-grandchild to a hospital in London.

Nate emptied the whisky glass and refilled it. He gulped it down. Someone wanted Nate to kill Zamir Oguzhan. Why else would they give him the information? Whoever had left the envelope believed he had killed the other dealers, despite the lack of evidence. Either they wanted Oguzhan dead or they were setting Nate up, or the third possibility was they wanted both. The man at the window was using Nate as an assassin, and Nate was almost certain that the deliveryman had been the officer who had arrested him the week before. He was a ginger man called Detective Smith. He swigged the remainder of the whisky and felt the alcohol numbing his senses. His thoughts were swirling around in his mind as he took another bottle from the sideboard. He decided to have a few more drinks before making his mind up. It was late, and nothing would happen tonight.

Chapter Eighty-Two

Zamir

"It's freezing cold," Zamir shivered. "I'm too old to live in this climate, maybe it's time to go home." The wind from the Irish Sea penetrated his Crombie and tickled his skin with its icy fingers. A ferryboat sounded its foghorn as it docked a mile away on the Pier head. It was just before dawn, but the darkness hadn't faded yet and the only light came from ornate wrought iron lampposts, which lined the river from the Pier head to Otterspool promenade. "It doesn't matter how long I live here, I still miss the sun."

"You can afford to go home now, can't you?" Gus Rickman shuffled his Rockport boots from side to side to keep the blood flowing to his feet. He rubbed his black leather gloves together as he spoke. "We can look after things here for you, no problem," he laughed.

"Can you, though?" Zamir frowned and shook his head. "This is one mess after another." He leaned against the thick metal railings, which ran for miles along the promenade. There was a twenty-foot drop to the muddy flats below them. Rusty mooring rings protruded from the sea walls at regular intervals. "I have had nothing but trouble since we set foot in this godforsaken city."

"What did you expect?" Gus snorted. "If you had come to me in the beginning, none of this could have happened. I wouldn't have allowed it to." He took out a slim cigar and his minder lit it without saying a word. Gus puffed the blue smoke out and the wind took it away. "Leon Tanner was a cokehead, and with all due respect, Salim was a lightweight. I control this city, always have and always will."

Gus pulled the lapels of his thick black leather jacket together and stared the old man in the eyes. Zamir smiled thinly and held out a gloved hand. "If you can guarantee the safety of my shipments, then we have a deal in principle."

Gus ignored the outstretched hand and spat over the railings into the murky water. The fast flowing river whisked the phlegm away in seconds. Sami looked annoyed at the action, and the big Turk stepped forward, but Zamir held up his hand to placate him. Gus laughed. In comparison, Gus's build dwarfed Sami, and his minder was bigger still. "If you fancy an early swim, kiddo, let me know," Gus smirked and pointed to the dark water below them. He laughed dryly, "You wouldn't be the first one we've dumped in there, so have a word with yourself before you get hurt."

He stopped laughing as he spoke and his face turned into a snarl. "If you want to sell your gear in this city, fine, but let me explain how it works." Gus maintained eye contact with Sami although he was speaking to his boss. "Your shipments come through me, if I hear it's coming in elsewhere, the deal is off." He pointed to Zamir's chest with his index finger. "I'll pay you the wholesale price of the drugs plus ten percent; if I think you are taking the piss, the deal is off. My network distributes the gear to my dealers and dealers sanctioned by me; if I hear you are selling outside of my network, the deal is off." Gus looked from one Turk to the other. "If you move any further north, the same deal applies, or the deal is off; take it or leave it."

"Tell him to get fucked, Boss," Sami growled. "We don't do business like that!"

"It's the best offer you're going to get," Gus smiled at the minder. "You've lost five kilos plus so far this week, I promise you that you will lose a lot more if you try to move into my city. Nothing moves here unless I know about it." He turned his attention to the old man. "Ten percent and you don't have to worry about a thing. You ship the stuff into the docks. I'll pay you for it, job done. It's a good business proposition."

"Maybe it is." Zamir looked away across the river. A tanker drifted in the distance, headed out to who knew where. The wind blew stronger and he shivered. A black cab appeared from the direction of the Albert docks, its diesel engine rumbling as it ambled past. The driver glanced at the four men and looked away when they returned his glance. Whatever the men were doing at this time in the morning, it wasn't something he wanted to witness. He accelerated toward the city to pick up nightclub stragglers who needed a ride home. Across the road was a coach park, which serviced tourists, visiting the Beatles museum at the docks. The coaches were long gone and none would return until much later in the day. It was deathly quiet as they watched the taxi trundle away. Zamir looked thoughtful. "Fifteen percent on top of the wholesale price and five percent of the final retail figure. If just one of my shipments goes astray, the deal is off as you say." Zamir held out his hand again. "If I think you are taking the piss, the deal is off." Zamir tilted his head questioningly. "Take it or leave it!" He smiled.

"You have a deal." Gus gripped his frail hand and shook it firmly. "I think we can work well together."

A nine-millimetre bullet punched through the back of Gus's leather jacket, and he looked down at the gaping hole the flattened slug had made as it exited his chest. Blood spurted across Zamir's face, and broken rib bones protruded. Gus's eyes widened in shock, and his hands reached up for Zamir's throat. He thought the old Turk had set him up, until a split second later the old man's left eye exploded in a shower of vitreous jelly. The back of his skull burst and the contents of his head sprayed over the railing and into the dirty water. As his knees buckled, Gus saw Sami blown backwards by a maelstrom of hot metal. He hit the railings and tumbled head first over them, falling face down in the water with a huge splash. Four more bullets slammed into Gus, smashing bones and ripping his internal organs to shreds. His spine shattered and his body seemed to fold backwards on itself. Two bullets to the face dropped Gus's minder, the first shattering his cheekbone and ripping the top of his skull off, and the second tearing his lower jaw apart, leaving his tongue dangling from what was left of his face. In a matter of a few seconds, a full clip from a Mach-10 had ended four lives.

Chapter Eighty-Three

Alec

Alec awoke from a shallow sleep. He looked at his watch through bleary eyes and cursed the ringing phone. "What, what, what," he muttered. "Ramsay," his voice sounded rough and thick with sleep.

"Sorry to call you so early, Guv," Smithy apologised. "There's been a shooting on the river."

"What time is it?" Alec fumbled for his wristwatch.

"It's six." The detective sounded nervous. "I thought you'd want to know straightaway."

"Don't worry, if it's important." Alec sat up and switched on the light. The other side of the bed was unruffled. He still slept on his side of the bed, as if Gail was snoozing next to him. His mouth was like sandpaper. He rubbed his eyes as he spoke. "What's happened?"

"There's been a shooting on the prom, Guv," Smithy explained. "Get this, Zamir Oguzhan, his minder Sami Ahmed, Gus Rickman and a meathead called Darren Howes were blown away about forty minutes ago."

"Where?" Alec swung his legs out of bed and scratched his testicles with his free hand. He caught his reflection in the mirror. It reminded him of a chimpanzee at the zoo. It was no wonder Gail had fallen into the arms of a younger man. He suddenly felt very old and lonely. Fifty-two wasn't ancient these days, but he felt older, much older. His reflection backed up his feelings.

"On the promenade near the coach park, uniform found their cars a few hundred yards away parked up near the kerbs."

"Can we tell what happened, have they shot each other?" Alec thought aloud.

"Doesn't look that way, Guv." Smithy sounded certain. "It looks like they've been sprayed with at least one machinegun from across the road. They found the bodies in a group next to the railings. Ahmed was in the mud over the wall. Rickman was armed, but his gun was still holstered, Guv."

"Sounds like someone caught them with their pants down?"

"Definitely." Smithy sounded nervous again.

"Well, my money is on Nate Bradley, have you spoken to his observation team?" Alec stood up and climbed into a pair of worn black underpants. His legs looked pale in the mirror. His potbelly protruded over the elastic. He sucked it in and turned sideways. Alec felt the anticipation of closing a case inside his stomach. He wanted Smithy to tell him that they had caught Bradley red-handed with the smoking gun in his hand.

"As soon as we identified the victims, we sent them in to Bradley's house, Guv." Smithy paused. "Bradley was unconscious in the armchair with two empty bottles of whisky next to him. They're adamant he hasn't moved all night, Guv."

"Are they positive?" Alec was amazed and disappointed at the same time. "Could he be faking it?"

"They're sure, but they thought the same and breathalysed him just in case. He's five times over the limit, Guv," Smithy stuttered a little nervously. "They found a copy of Oguzhan's police file on the coffee table, too."

"What?" Alec frowned. "How the bloody hell has he got a copy of that?" Alec opened the wardrobe and fumbled for a clean shirt. His dirty ones were building up into a pile on the floor waiting for the tidy fairy to arrive. They would be waiting a long time. She was dead. "I don't think we can charge him with that. That man is either incredibly good or incredibly lucky."

"Maybe a bit of both, Guv," Smithy said ironically. "At least that bastard Oguzhan is dead. That's payback time."

"Yes, I suppose it is, Smithy," Alec said quietly. He looked at a photograph of Gail he kept next to his bed. She was smiling and happy. "I guess what goes around comes around, eh?" Alec thought that he should feel a sense of satisfaction, but he didn't. Gail was gone and he missed her terribly.

Chapter Eighty-Four

Epilogue

"Hey Deano, great news about the kids." The sun was shining and the view across the river was breathtaking. The view from the balcony was the reason he had bought the flat. It overlooked the water and a yacht marina, and on a sunny day, it was a little piece of paradise on the edge of the big bad city.

"Yes, they pulled through, man." Dean Hines sounded tired. "I've never prayed so hard in my life."

"I am made up for you."

"Okay, thanks." Dean sounded cautious. "That's all the bullshit out of the way, what do you want?"

"I'm letting you know that when your kids are better, there is a job with me for you. Leon got greedy, Dean, and teaming up with the Turks would have ended up in a bloodbath eventually."

"Leon was an arsehole," Dean grunted. "I heard the Turks got whacked with Gus Rickman."

"Yes, I heard that too. Rumours are that Gus was going to jump into bed with the Turks. He was a two-faced bastard, no one trusted him. If he'd done a deal with them, the other gangs would have turned on him and each other, fighting over the scraps."

"He would have been massive with the Turks behind him," Dean said. "Now that would have ended with tears."

"Blood and tears, Deano, greed always ends that way. That's why you should work for me."

"Why would I want to work for you?"

"What are you going to do, Deano? How are you going to feed your kids and pay the mortgage?"

"I need to get away from all that shit, man." Dean wasn't convinced.

"You know me. I have fuck all to do with drugs, Dean. I know the kids want to get high, that's fine, but I didn't like the way Leon was force-feeding the weak ones who couldn't pay for it, you know what I mean?"

"Yes, I know. Let me think about it." Dean sounded keen. "I've got your number. I'll call you."

"Make sure you do." The line went dead. A yacht drifted silently below the balcony, hoisting its mainsail as it headed out to the river. The water was calm today. Jinx Cotton reached down and picked up a bundle of rags from the decking. He tossed the bundle over the balcony into the river. There was a dull splash and the concentric ripples appeared to move with the fast moving water. The tide had turned, allowing the fresh water to flow at speed into the Irish Sea. The rags sunk quickly, weighed down by the Mach-10 machinegun hidden inside them. "Greed kills them all eventually." Jinx raised his face to the sun and let its warmth soak through him. Today was the start of new era, and he felt good inside.

ABOUT THE AUTHOR

If you could take two minutes to review this book, it would help the author very much.

HTTP://WWW.AMAZON.CO.UK/CRIMINALLY-INSANE-DETECTIVE-MYSTERY-SUSPENSE-EBOOK/DP/B00GY8VBXC

Thank you for reading my book. If you enjoyed this book, it is in the Detective Alec Ramsay Series. The others http://www.amazon.co.uk/s/ref=nb_sb_noss?url=search-alias%3Ddigital-text&field-keywords=detective+alec+ramsay+series+conrad+jones&rh=n%3A341677031%2Ck%3Adetective+alec+ramsay+series+conrad+jones

And the sixth novel, which features 'Tank' in the Soft Target series.
http://www.amazon.co.uk/s/ref=nb_sb_noss?url=search-alias%3Ddigital-text&field-keywords=soft%20target%20series%20conrad%20jones

If you would like a free book, email Conrad at; jonesconrad5@aol.com

Facebook page; https://www.facebook.com/conrad.jones.397

Twitter; https://twitter.com/ConradJones

Don't forget to read, Slow Burn, Frozen Betrayal, Desolate Sands and Concrete Evidence.

MORE HORROR FROM CONRAD JONES

http://www.amazon.com/Hunting-Angels-Diaries-ebook/dp/B00GZ0TH7G/ref=la_B002BOBGRE_1_5?s=books&ie=UTF8&qid=1402581462&sr=1-5

Review from Amazon Vine Voice; From the very first chapter there's a real old school feeling about this novel. Think of the great horror writers of latter part of the last century (Masterton, Saul, Herbert) and Jones' style would feel at home. From the first few pages there a great sense of wrongness, which later allows Jones to grow the menace so sought after by the better writers in the genre.

http://www.amazon.com/Child-Devil-Hunting-Angels-Diaries-ebook/dp/B009OIVDZK/ref=la_B002BOBGRE_1_11?s=books&ie=UTF8&qid=1402581692&sr=1-11

THE BOOK OF ABOMINATIONS

http://www.amazon.com/Book-Abominations-horror-collection-ebook/dp/B00K1GBP2U/ref=sr_1_2?s=books&ie=UTF8&qid=1402581917&sr=1-2&keywords=THE+BOOK+OF+ABOMINATIONS